Nichole Severn writes explo[...] strong heroines, heroes wh[...] hell of a lot of guns. She resides with her [...] and patient husband, as well as her demon spawn, in Utah. When she's not writing, she's constantly injuring herself running, rock climbing, practising yoga and snowboarding. She loves hearing from readers through her website, nicholesevern.com, and on Facebook at nicholesevern

Danica Winters is a multiple-award-winning, bestselling author who writes books that grip readers with their ability to drive emotion through suspense and occasionally a touch of magic. When she's not working, she can be found in the wilds of Montana, testing her patience while she tries to hone her skills at various crafts—quilting, pottery and painting are not her areas of expertise. She believes the cup is neither half-full nor half-empty, but it better be filled with wine. Visit her website at danicawinters.net

K-9 DETECTION

NICHOLE SEVERN

SWIFTWATER ENEMIES

DANICA WINTERS

MILLS & BOON

First Published in Great Britain 2024
by Mills & Boon, an imprint of HarperCollins*Publishers* Ltd
1 London Bridge Street, London, SE1 9GF

www.harpercollins.co.uk

HarperCollins*Publishers*
Macken House, 39/40 Mayor Street Upper,
Dublin 1, D01 C9W8, Ireland

K-9 Detection © 2024 Natascha Jaffa
Swiftwater Enemies © 2024 Danica Winters

ISBN: 978-0-263-32217-0

0224

This book contains FSC™ certified paper and other controlled sources to ensure responsible forest management.

For more information visit: www.harpercollins.co.uk/green

Printed and Bound in the UK using 100% Renewable Electricity at CPI Group (UK) Ltd, Croydon, CR0 4YY

K-9 DETECTION

NICHOLE SEVERN

For you.

Chapter One

She was making the world a better place one cookie at a time.

And there was nothing that said *I'm sorry that your deputy ended up being a traitorous bastard working for the cartel* than her cranberry-lemon cookies.

Jocelyn Carville parked her SUV outside of Alpine Valley's police station. If you could even call it that. In truth, it was nothing more than two double-wide trailers shoved together to look like one long building. The defining boundary between the two sections cut right down the middle with a set of stairs on each side. One half for the courts, and the other for Alpine Valley's finest.

A low groan registered from the back seat, and she glanced at her German shepherd, Maverick, in the rearview mirror. "Don't give me that pitiful look. I saw you steal four cookies off the counter before I wrapped them. You're not getting any more."

Collecting the plate of perfectly wrapped sweets, Jocelyn shouldered out of the vehicle. Maverick pawed at the side door. Anywhere these cookies went, he was sure to follow. Though sometimes she could convince him they were actually friends. He was prickly at best and standoffish at worst. Good thing she knew how to handle both. His nails ticked at the pavement as he jumped free of the SUV.

"Jocelyn Carville." The low register in that voice added an extra twist in her stomach. Chief of Police Baker Halsey had come out of nowhere. Speaking of *prickly*. The man pulled his keys from his uniform slacks, hugging the material tight to his thigh. And what a thigh it was. Never mind the rest of him with his dark hair, deep brown eyes or the slight dent at the bridge of his nose telling her he'd broken it in the past. Nope. She'd take just his thigh if he were offering. "Here I was thinking my day had started off pretty good. What's Socorro want this time?"

A tendril of resentment wormed through her, but she shut it down fast. There wasn't any room to let feelings like that through. Jocelyn readjusted her hold on the plastic-wrapped plate, keeping her head high. "I'm here for you."

Maverick pressed one side of his head against her calf and took a seat. His heat added to the sweat already breaking out beneath her bra. She was former military. It was her job to call on resources to aid in whatever situation had broken out and stay calm while doing it. To look at pain and suffering logically and offer the most beneficial solution possible. She was a damn good logistics coordinator. Most recently in the Pentagon's war on the Sangre por Sangre cartel. Delivering cookies shouldn't spike her adrenaline like this.

Baker pulled up short of the ancient wood stairs leading up to the front door of the station's trailer. "For *me*?"

"I brought you some cookies." Offering him the plate, she pasted on a smile—practically mastered over the years. Just like her cookies. "They're cranberry-lemon with a hint of drizzle. I remember you liked my lemon bread at the town Christmas bake sale last year. I thought you might like these, too."

"Cookies." He stared down at the plate. One second. Two. Her arms could only take the weight for so long. Lucky for her, she didn't have to wait more than a minute. Because the chief walked right up those stairs without another word.

Maybe *prickly* wasn't the right word. A couple more descriptors came to mind, but her mama would wash her mouth out with soap if she ever heard Jocelyn say them out loud. Well, if her mama made an effort to talk to her at all.

She didn't bother calling Maverick as she hiked up the three rickety steps to the station's glass door and ripped it open. Her K-9 partner was always in hot pursuit of any chance of cookies.

This place looked the same as always. Faux wood paneling on the walls, an entire bank of filing cabinets with files that had yet to be digitized, with the evidence room shoved into the back right corner. Though it looked like someone had gotten the blood out of the industrial carpet recently. Courteously put there by said deputy who'd turned out to be working for the cartel. Jocelyn tracked the chief around one of two desks and moved to set the plate on the end. "Have you had any luck finding a replacement deputy yet?"

Frustration tightened the fine lines etched around those incredibly dark eyes. "What do you want, Ms. Carville? Why are you really here?"

"I told you—I brought you cookies." She latched on to Maverick's collar as he tried to rush forward toward the treats.

"Nobody just brings cookies." Baker locked his sidearm

in a drawer at the opposite end of the desk. "Not without wanting something in return, and certainly not when that someone is attached to one of the most dangerous and un-restricted security companies in the world."

And there it was. Him lumping her in with her employer. Seemed every time she managed to get a word in edgewise, Baker couldn't separate her from what she did for a living.

"I don't want anything in return." She motioned to the cookies she'd stayed up all night to bake. For him. Maverick was pawing at the carpet now, trying to get free. "I just thought you could use a little pick-me-up after everything that went down a couple weeks ago. I wanted to say—"

"A pick-me-up?" His dismissal hit harder than she'd expected. Baker faced her fully—a pure mountain of muscle built on secrets and defensiveness. He was a protector at heart, though. Someone who cared deeply about the people of this town. A man who believed in justice and right-ing wrongs. He had to be to do this kind of job day in and day out. "Let me make one thing clear, Ms. Carville. I'm not your friend. I don't want to pet your dog. I don't want you to bring me cookies or make arrangements for you to check on me to make sure I'm doing okay. You and I and that company you work for aren't allies. We won't be partnering on cases or braiding each other's hair. Police solve crimes. All you mercenaries do is make things worse in my town."

Mercenaries. Her heart threatened to shove straight up into her throat. That…that wasn't what she was at all. She helped people. She was the one who'd gotten Fire and Res-cue in from surrounding towns when Sangre por Sangre had ambushed Alpine Valley and burned nearly a half dozen homes out of spite. She didn't hurt people for money, but no amount of explanation would change the chief's mind. He'd already created his own definition of her, and any fantasy she'd had that the two of them could work together or even become acquaintances instantly vanished.

Jocelyn's mouth dried as her courage to articulate any of that faltered. She almost reached for the cookies but thought better of it. "For your information, Maverick doesn't let anyone pet him. Not even me."

She dragged the K-9 with her and headed for the door, but Maverick ripped free of her hold. He sprinted toward the chief's desk. Embarrassment heated through her. Really? Of everything she could've left as her last words, it had to be about the fact her K-9 wasn't the cuddly type? And now Maverick was going to make her chase him. Great. No wonder she'd never won any argument about the importance of bonding as a team back at headquarters. She let herself be railroaded in the smallest conversations. No. She squared her shoulders. She wasn't going to let one tiff get the best of her. She was better than that, had overcome more than that.

But Maverick didn't go for the cookies.

Instead, he raced toward a door at the back and started sniffing at the carpet. The evidence room. Crap on a cracker. She didn't need this right now.

"You forgot your dog." The dismissiveness in Baker's tone told her he hadn't even bothered to look up to watch her leave.

"Thank you for your astute observation, Chief." Jocelyn dropped her hold on the front door. She'd almost made it out of there with her dignity in one piece. But it seemed that wasn't going to happen. At least not today. "You wouldn't happen to have any bomb tech in your evidence room, would you?"

Maverick's abilities to sniff out specific combinations of chemicals in explosives was unrivaled in his work as tactical-explosive-detection dog for the Department of Defense. And here in New Mexico. As cartels had battled over territory and attempted to upend law enforcement and local government, organizations like Sangre por Sangre had started planting devices where no one would find them—until it was too late. Soccer balls at parks, in a woman's purse at a restaurant in Albuquerque, a resident's home here in Alpine Valley. No one was safe. And so Socorro Security had recruited K-9s like Maverick onto the team in the name of strategy—find the threat before the threat found them. They were good at it, too. Protecting those who couldn't protect themselves. Ready to assist police and the DEA at a moment's notice. Founded by a former FBI investigator, Socorro had become the premier security company in the country by recruiting the best of the best. Former military operatives, strategists, combat specialists. They went above and beyond to take on this fight with the cartels. And they were winning.

Frustration and perhaps a hint of disbelief had Baker setting down his clipboard and pen on the desk. Closing the distance between them, the chief pulled his keys from his slacks once again. "Not that I know of. I can't account for every case, but most of what we keep here is from within the past five years. Unregistered arms, a few kilos. Maybe Fido smells the cheese I left in the rat trap last week."

Moving past her, Baker unlocked the door, shoving it open.

"He's a bomb-sniffing dog, Chief, and his name isn't Fido." She barely caught Maverick by the collar as he attempted to rush inside the small, overpacked room. The fluorescent tube light overhead flickered to life and highlighted rows and rows of labeled boxes in uniform shape and size.

A low beeping reached her ears.

Pivoting, Jocelyn set sights on the station's alarm panel near the front door—though it'd been disarmed when Baker had come inside a few minutes ago. "Do you hear that?"

Maverick pressed his face between two boxes on the lowest shelf and yipped. Her skin tightened in alarm.

"We have to get out of the building." Jocelyn unpocketed her cell from her cargo pants and whistled low for Maverick to follow her out. The K-9 growled low to argue, but he'd obey. He *always* obeyed when it counted. She hit Ivy Bardot's contact information and raised the phone to her ear. Someone had planted a device in the police station. She needed full response.

"What?" Baker asked. "I can't just leave, Carville. In case you weren't aware, I'm the only officer on shift today."

They didn't have time for bickering. She grabbed on to his uniform collar and rushed to the front of the station with the chief in tow. "We have to go!"

Fire and sharp debris exploded across her back.

Jocelyn slammed into the nearest wall.

The world went dark.

HE SHOULD'VE GOTTEN out of the damn trailer.

Baker tried to get his legs underneath him, but the blast had ripped some crucial muscle he hadn't known had existed. Oh, hell. The wood paneling he'd surrounded himself day in and day out warbled in his vision. That wasn't good.

The explosion… It'd been a bomb. She'd tried to warn him. *Jocelyn.* Jocelyn Carville.

He shoved onto all fours. "Talk to me, Carville."

No answer.

Heat licked at his right shoulder as he tried to get himself oriented, but there was nothing for his brain to latch on to. The trailer didn't look the same as it had a few minutes ago. Nothing was where it was supposed to be, and now daylight was prodding inside from the corner where the evidence room used to be. Flames climbed the walls, eating up all that faux wood paneling and industrial carpet inch by inch. A weak alarm rang low in his ears. Maybe from next door?

They had to get out of here. "Jocelyn."

A whine pierced through the crackle of flames. He could just make out a distant siren through the opening that hadn't been there before the explosion. Fire and Rescue was on the way. But that wasn't the sound he'd heard. No, it'd been something sullen and hurt.

"Come on." His personalized pep talk wasn't doing any good. Baker shoved to stand, though not as balanced as he'd hoped. His hand nearly went through the trailer wall as he grasped for support. Smoke collected at the back of his throat. He stumbled forward. "Where the hell are you?"

Another whine punctured through the ringing in his head, and he waved off a good amount of black smoke to make out the outline ahead. The dog. Baker couldn't remember his name. The German shepherd was circling something on the floor. "Damn it."

He lunged for Jocelyn. She wasn't responding. Possibly

injured. Moving her might make matters worse, but the walls were literally closing in on them. He'd have to drag her out. The shepherd had bitten on to the shoulder of her Kevlar vest and was attempting to pull his handler to safety. Baker reached out.

The K-9 turned all that desperation onto Baker with a warning and bared teeth. His ears darted straight up, and suddenly he wasn't the bomb-sniffing dog who'd tried to warn them of danger. He was in protective mode. And he'd do anything to keep Baker from hurting Jocelyn.

"Knock it off, Cujo. I'm trying to help." Baker raised his hands, palms out, but no amount of deep breathing was going to bring his heart rate down. His mind went straight to the drawer where he'd locked away his gun. He didn't want to have to put the dog down, but if it came to getting Jocelyn out of here alive or fighting off her pet, he'd have no other choice. Though where the desk had gone, he couldn't even begin to guess in this mess.

He leaned forward, moving slower than he wanted. The fire was drawing closer. Every minute he wasted trying to appease some guard dog was another minute Jocelyn might not have. Baker latched on to her vest at both shoulders and pulled, waiting for the shepherd to strike. "I'm here to help. Okay?"

The K-9 seemed to realize Baker wasn't going to hurt its handler and softened around the mouth and eyes.

"Good boy. Now let's get the hell out of here." He hauled Jocelyn through a maze of debris and broken glass out what used to be the front door. His body ached to hell and back, but adrenaline was quickly drowning out the pain. Hugging her around the middle, he got her down the stairs with the German shepherd on her heels.

High-pitched sirens peeled through the empty park across the cul-de-sac and echoed off the surrounding cliffs protecting Alpine Valley. A lot of good they'd done these past few weeks. First a raid in which the cartel had burned down half a dozen homes. Now this.

Baker laid the woman in his arms across the old broken asphalt, shaded by her SUV. Ash darkened the distinct angles of her face, but it was the blood coming from her hairline that claimed the attention of every cell in his body. "Come on, Carville. Open your eyes."

Apparently she only took orders from her employer.

But she was breathing. That had to be enough for now—because there were still a whole lot of people in the trailer next door.

Baker set his sights on Fido. Bomb-sniffing dogs took commands, but he didn't have a clue how to order this one around. He pointed down at the K-9. "Uh, guard?"

Carville's sidekick licked his lips, cocking his head to one side.

"Stay." That had to be one. Baker swallowed the charred taste in his throat as he took in the remains of the station. Loss threatened to consume him as the past rushed to meet the present. No. He had to stay focused, get everyone out.

Fire and Rescue rounded the engine in front of what used to be the station as court staff escaped into the parking lot. Baker rushed to the other half of the trailer. A woman doubled over, nearly coughing up a lung.

He ran straight for her. "Is anyone still in there?"

She turned in a wild search. "Jason, our clerk! I don't see him!"

Baker hauled himself up the stairs, feeling the impact of the explosion with every step. Smoke consumed him once inside. It tendriled in random patterns as he waved one hand in front of his face but refused to disperse. Damn it. He couldn't see anything in here. "Hello! Jason? Are you still in here?"

Movement registered from his left. He tried to navigate through the cloud, fighting for his next breath, and hit the corner of a desk. The smoke must've been feeding in through the HVAC system, and without a giant hole in the ceiling it had nowhere to go. Smoke drove into his lungs. Burned. Baker tried to cough it up, but every breath was like inhaling fire. "Jason, can you hear me?"

He dared another few steps and hit something soft. Not another desk—too low. Sweat beaded down the back of his neck as a tile dropped from the ceiling. It shattered on the corner of another desk a couple feet away.

This place wasn't going to hold much longer. It was falling apart at the seams.

Reaching down, Baker felt a suit jacket with an arm inside and clamped onto it. "Sorry about the rug burn, man, but we gotta go."

Morning sunlight streaming through the glass door at the front of the trailer was the only map he had, but as soon as his brain had homed in on that small glimpse of hope, it was gone. The smoke closed in, suffocating him with every gasp for oxygen. Pinpricks started in his fingers and toes. His body was starved for air. Soon he'd pass out altogether.

A flood of dizziness gripped tight, and he sidestepped to keep himself upright. "Not yet, damn it."

He wasn't going to pass out. Not now.

Baker forced himself forward. One step. Then another. His lungs spasmed for clean air, but there was no way to see if he was heading in the right direction. He just had to do the one thing that never ended well. He had to trust himself.

Seconds distorted into full minutes…into an hour…as he tried to navigate through the smoke. He was losing his grip on the court clerk. His legs finally gave into the percussion of the explosion. He dropped harder than a bag of rocks. The trailer floor shook beneath him. Black webs encroached on his vision. This was it. This was when the past finally claimed him.

Baker clawed toward where he thought the front door might be. Out of air. Out of fight. Hell, maybe he should've had one of those cranberry-lemon cookies as a last meal.

"Jocelyn."

He had no reason to settle on her name. They weren't friends. They weren't even acquaintances. If anything, they were on two separate sides of the war taking over this town. But over the past couple of months, caught in his darkest moments, she'd somehow provided a light when he'd needed it the most. With baked goods and smiles as bright as noon day sun.

The smoke cleared ahead.

A flood of sunlight cut through the blackness swallowing him whole.

"Chief Halsey!" Her voice cut through the haze eating up the cells in his brain, though it was more distorted than he was used to. Her outline solidified in front of him. Soft hands stretched an oxygen mask over his mouth and nose. "Don't worry. We're going to get you out of here."

A steady stream of fresh air fought back the sickness in his lungs, and he realized it wasn't Jocelyn's voice that time. It was deeper. Distinctly male. Another outline maneuvered past him and took to prying his grip from the court clerk. Baker let them. He clawed up the firefighter's frame and dragged himself outside with minimal help. It was amazing what oxygen could do to a starving body.

The sun pierced his vision and laid out a group of onlookers behind the century-old wood fence blocking off the station from the parking lot. A series of growls triggered his flight instinct, but Baker pushed away from the firefighter, keeping him on his feet. The dog. He'd ordered him to guard his handler.

Baker caught sight of the German shepherd from the back of Alpine Valley's only Animal Control truck. Fido was trying to chew his way through the thin grate keeping him from his partner. Baker's instincts shot into high alert as he homed in on the unconscious woman on the ground, surrounded on either side by two EMS techs. He took a step forward. "Jocelyn?"

They'd stripped her free of her Kevlar vest to administer chest compressions—and exposed a bloodred stain spreading right in front of his eyes. He didn't understand. She'd been breathing when he'd left her.

Baker took a step forward. "What's happening? What's wrong with her?"

"Chief, we need you to keep your distance," one of the techs said. Though he couldn't be sure which one. "She's not responding. We need to get her in the bus. Now."

Strong hands forced him out of the way, but all he had attention for was Jocelyn, a mercenary he hadn't wanted anything to do with but who had insisted on sabotaging his life. Baker tried to follow, but the firefighter at his back was strong-arming him to stay at the scene. Helplessness surged as potent as that day he'd watched everything he'd built burn to the ground, and he wanted to fix it. To fix *this*. "Tell me what's happening."

But there was no time to answer.

The EMTs loaded Jocelyn onto a stretcher and raced for the ambulance. "Let's go! We're losing her!"

Chapter Two

Okay. Maybe cookies didn't make everything better.

Though she'd kill for one right now.

Jocelyn swallowed through the bitterness collecting at the back of her tongue, like she'd eaten something burned beyond recognition. And a grating rhythm wouldn't let up from one side. Ugh. She'd always hated that sound. As helpful as heart monitors were to let physicians and nurses know the patient was still alive, they could've set the damn sound on something far more pleasant.

That wasn't really what she was mad about, but it helped her focus. She curled her fingers into her palms. Her skin felt too tight. Dry. One look at the backs of her hands confirmed the blisters there. The monitor followed the spike in her heart rate, but the pain never came. That was the beauty of painkillers. They masked the hurt inside. But only temporarily. Sooner or later, she'd have to face it. Though, based on the slow drip into her IV, she still had some time.

"Here I thought a visit from Socorro would be the worst part of my day." Recognition flared hot and uncomfortable as Chief Baker Halsey leaned forward in the chair set beside her bed. A few scratches marred that otherwise flawless face she'd memorized over the past six months. It was easy, really. To catch herself watching him. To lose herself in that quiet intensity he exuded. "Sorry to tell you I couldn't save the cookies."

"Good thing I made extra." She tried to sit up in the bed, but the mattress was too soft. It threatened to swallow her whole if she wasn't careful. Glaring white tile and cream-washed walls closed in around her. Right back where she didn't want to be. Her attention shifted to the chart at the end of her bed. Her medical history would be in there. Clear for all physicians and nurses to see. What she could and couldn't have in moments like this. A wave of self-consciousness flared behind her rib cage. Would the hospital keep it confidential during the investigation into the bombing? Or did Baker already know? "You got me out?"

"You wanted me to leave you there?" He was distracting himself again, looking anywhere but at her. "It was nothing. If it hadn't been for that small moose you order around, I would've gotten you out quicker. Maybe realized you'd taken a piece of shrapnel sooner."

Maverick. Her nerves went under attack. If he'd been hurt in the blast... Fractured memories of the seconds leading up to the explosion frayed the harder she tried to latch on to them. The monitor on the other side of the bed went wild. "Where is he?"

"Animal Control got hold of him at the scene. He was trying to fight off the EMTs, but that might've been my fault." Baker spread his hands in a wide gesture, highlighting the scraps and bruising along his forearms. "I told him to guard you before I nearly died trying to get a clerk out of the other side of the trailer. Apparently Fido took me seriously."

She didn't have the energy to fight back about Maverick's name. "But he's okay? He's not hurt?"

"Yeah. He's fine." Confusion, tainted with a hint of concern, etched deep into Baker's expression. "Gotta tell you, Carville. I figured you'd be more worried about the chunk of metal they had to take out of you than your sidekick."

"Maverick saved our lives." It was all she was willing to offer right then. "If it wasn't for him picking up that bomb, neither of us would've made it out of that trailer."

"You're right. I'm sorry." Baker scrubbed one busted up hand down his face, and suddenly it was as though he'd aged at least three years. He looked heavy and exhausted and beaten. Same as when he'd discovered one of his own deputies had secretly been working for the cartel.

Her chest constricted at witnessing the pain he carried, but she couldn't focus on that right now. They had more important things to contend with. Like the fact that Alpine Valley's police department was under attack. "Any leads?"

"Nothing yet. Albuquerque's bomb squad is en route. As of right now, all I've got is theories." Baker leaned back in his seat. "Alpine Valley hasn't seen any bombings like this before. Most of what we respond to is domestic calls and overdoses."

Until recently. He didn't have to say the words—the implication was already there. A fraction of residents in Alpine Valley had rallied against a military contractor setting up their headquarters so close to town. They'd believed having the federal government so close would aggravate relations between Sangre por Sangre and the towns at their mercy. So far, they'd been right.

"Socorro employs a combat controller," Jocelyn said.

"Jones Driscoll has investigated IEDs overseas. I'm sure he'd be able to help until the bomb squad can get here."

"You want me to bring in a mercenary to investigate the bombing." It wasn't a question.

She wasn't sure if it was the pain medication, his determination to call her K-9 by the wrong name or his insistence that she was part of a group of people who killed targets for money. None of it was sitting very well with the explosive memories fighting for release and the blisters along the backs of her hands. Her determination to hang on to the silver lining was slipping, threatening to put her right back into the hole she'd spent months crawling out of. "Is that all you think of me when you see me in town? When I handed you that piece of lemon bread or brought you those cookies earlier today? Do you really look at me and see a killer?"

He didn't answer.

"Either you just don't get it or you don't want to—I don't know which, and frankly, I don't really care—but you and I are on the same team. We want the same thing. To keep Sangre por Sangre from claiming Alpine Valley and all those other towns just like it." She didn't like this. Being the one to tell the hard truths. Dipping her toes in that inky-black pool of who she used to be. "Socorro has federal resources you'll never be able to get your hands on, and shutting us out will be the worst thing you can do for the people you claim to be protecting. So use us. Use *me*."

Tension flexed the muscles running from his neck and along his shoulders as he straightened in the chair. Such a minor movement, but one that spoke volumes. The small fluctuations in that guarded expression released. "Does the dog have to come with the deal?"

The knot in her stomach relaxed a bit. Not entirely, but enough she could take a full breath. After months of pushing back, Baker was entertaining the thought of trusting someone outside of his small circle of officers. It was a step in the right direction. "Yeah. He does."

"All right, but I'm not going to blindly trust a bunch of mercs—*soldiers*—without getting the lay of the land first. I want to meet your team." A defensiveness she'd always wanted to work beyond encapsulated him back into chief mode, where no one could get through. "This is still my investigation. I make the calls. Everything pertaining to this case comes through me. I want background checks, service records, financials, right down to what you're all allergic to—the whole enchilada. Understand?"

Mmm. Enchiladas. Okay. Maybe a half a roll of cookie dough for breakfast wasn't the best idea she'd had today.

"I think that can be arranged." Jocelyn felt the inner warmth coming back, the darkness retreating. This was how it was supposed to be. Her and Baker working together for a common goal in the name of justice. Not on opposite sides of the table. Still, as hard as she might try to keep sunshine and unicorns throughout her days, she wasn't going to roll over to the chief's every whim. "But I have a condition of my own. You have to call Maverick by his real name."

A small break in that composure sent victory charging through the aching places in her body. "Why does that matter? It's not like he's going to take orders from me. I already tried that. Look how it turned out—he almost took my hand off."

"Maverick is very protective when he needs to be, but

he deserves your respect after saving your life back at the station," she said.

"All right, then. Maverick. Easy to remember. He's not going to growl at me every time I'm around, is he?" Baker looked around the room as though expecting her K-9 partner to appear out of thin air.

"He just needs a couple minutes to get to know you. Maybe take in a good crotch sniffing." She tried to keep her smile under control, but the outright terror contorting Baker's face was too much. *This.* She'd missed this. The bickering, the smiles and private jokes. She hadn't gotten to experience it in a long time. Not since before her last tour. "I'm kidding."

Baker's exhale outclassed a category-one tornado. The tightness around his eyes smoothed after a few seconds. Wow. The man acted as though he'd never heard a joke before. This was going to be fun. "Oh. Good. In that case, I'm not really sure what we're supposed to do now."

"I think this is the part where you hike down to the cafeteria and get me one of those enchiladas you were just talking about. You know, seeing as how I'm injured and you're…" She motioned to the entire length of him. "Just sitting there with barely a scratch."

"You haven't seen the inside of my lungs."

A mere crack of his smile twisted her stomach into knots. Well, look at that. It did exist.

Baker pushed to stand, in all his glory. "I thought all you Socorro types ran on nuclear power. Never stopped or slowed down for anything when you took on an assignment. You're like that weird pink bunny with the drum."

"You're thinking of Cash Meyers, our forward scout,

when he took on the cartel a few weeks ago." Made a hell of a mess in the process. Destroying Sangre por Sangre headquarters in an effort to recover a woman who'd become the obsession of a cartel lieutenant. His personal mission had been a success, too. Cash had brought the entire organization to its knees for the woman he loved.

A flare of pain bit into her heart at the memory of what that felt like. Of not being able to save the people you cared about the most.

Nervous energy shot through her. She couldn't just sit here. That gave the bad feelings permission to claw out of the box she'd shoved them into at the back of her mind.

Jocelyn threw off the covers, only acutely aware of the open-backed gown she'd been forced into upon admittance. She grabbed for her singed pants and slid them on with as much dignity as she could muster. Which wasn't much given she was still attached to the damn monitors. "I happen to run on powdered sugar, a whole lot of butter and melted cheese."

Baker handed off her jacket as she pulled the nodes from her skin. Such a simple gesture. But one that wasn't coated in sarcasm or negativity. Progress. "Not sure anyone has ever told you this, but your idea of an enchilada sounds disgusting."

WHAT THE HELL had he been thinking agreeing to this?

Baker notched his head back to take in the height of the building as Jocelyn pulled into the underground parking garage. Sleek, modern angles, black reflective windows—the place was like something out of an old spy movie. Half-built into the canyon wall behind it, Socorro Security headquarters swallowed them whole. He was in the belly of the beast now. Who knew if he'd ever make it out.

Jocelyn navigated through the garage as though she'd done it a thousand times before. Which made sense. As far as he could tell, she, like the rest of her team lived, worked, ate and slept out of this building. No visitors as far as he'd been able to discern in his spurts of surveillance. If the operators employed here had personal lives, he hadn't seen a lick of it, and Baker couldn't help but wonder about the woman in the driver's seat as she shoved the SUV into Park.

She took out what looked like a black credit card. Heavy, too. Aluminum, if he had to guess. Maybe an access card. The bandages wrapping the blisters along the backs of her hands and wrists brightened under limited lighting coming through the windshield.

"I get one of those?" he asked.

She shook her head. "I didn't think accessing the elevators was high on your priority list of things to do today. Otherwise I would've had one made in your honor."

"What? No access to the secret vault?" He watched her pocket the card.

"Sorry. That's reserved for VIP members." Her laugh burned through him with surprising force as she climbed out of the vehicle. The flimsy fabric the hospital staff claimed was an actual piece of clothing was gone. She'd somehow managed to get herself dressed without much distress. Guess that was the upside of painkillers after getting stitched up.

While the EMTs had been forced to remove her Kevlar vest to get access to her wound, it seemed she carried an extra. As though she expected an ambush at any moment. In fact, Baker couldn't think of a time when she didn't have that added layer of protection. Even at the Christmas bake sale.

"You'll have to pay extra for that tour," she said.

He followed close on her heels, absorbing everything about the parking lot he could with barely visible lighting and cement walls. Most likely designed that way to confuse anyone stupid enough to try to breach this place. Though Jocelyn seemed to know exactly where she was going. Still, collecting as much information on these people as he could get would only prove his theory about military contractors' lack of interest in protecting towns like Alpine Valley.

"You been with Socorro long?"

She pressed the key card to a smooth section of wall off to her left and stepped back. "Six months. Signed on a little after my last tour."

Elevator doors parted to reveal a silver car.

Jocelyn stepped inside, holding the door open for him as he boarded.

His limited knowledge of gender representation in the military filtered through the catalogue he was building on her in his head. "Air Force?"

"Army." The small muscles in her jaw flexed under pressure. "Logistics coordinator. Same job I do for Socorro."

Baker filed that away for future reference. Logistics coordinators weren't just responsible for keeping track of military assets. They procured rare resources in times of panic, stayed on top of maintenance operations and covered transportation of any materials, facilities and personnel. People in her position were essential to strategy and planning in the middle of war zones and conflicts. Without operatives like her, the entire military would grind to a halt.

He noted which pocket she slid her key card into despite the admiration cutting through him. "Deployed overseas?"

"Afghanistan. Two tours. Then a third in Africa." There was something missing in that statement. It took him longer than it should have to recognize it, but no one else in his life had the ridiculous positivity Jocelyn seemed to emanate with every word out of her mouth. She didn't like talking about her service in the military. Interesting.

"Wow. Right in the middle of the action." He'd known a couple of deputies from surrounding towns who'd served in the Middle East over the past decade. None of them had held a candle to Jocelyn's level of optimism after what they'd seen. Question was: Was it just for show or a genuine part of her personality? Hard to tell.

The doors parted, dropping them off in the middle of the freaking Death Star. Gleaming black walls with matching tile. The artwork nearly blended in with the walls, only distinguished by outline of the frames. Blinding fluorescent lights reflected off the floors like a crazy hall of mirrors as Jocelyn led them through what he thought might be a hallway.

"Everybody's waiting for us in the conference room," she said.

He tried to map out a mental route through the maze, but there was just too much to index. Everything looked the same. How the hell did anyone navigate this place? "You have many visitors come through here?"

"No. Just you." She wrenched open a glass double door and held it open for him. Not an ounce of pain from her wound reflected in her expression. Hell, just thinking about his body slamming into the trailer wall made him want to cry. How did she do that? Jocelyn motioned him inside. "Welcome to the inner circle."

A wall-to-ceiling window—bulletproof, if he had to guess—stretched along the backside of the conference room. The oversized table led to two Socorro representatives waiting for their arrival. One he recognized. Driscoll. Jones Driscoll. He was the company's head of combat operations, according to Jocelyn. Someone who could help them with the investigation into the bombing. Made sense he'd be here. But the other... Baker didn't know her.

"Chief Halsey, thank you for joining us. I'm Ivy Bardot." The redhead stood from her seat at the head of the table, smoothing invisible wrinkles from her black slacks.

This was the founder of Socorro Security. Jocelyn's boss. Taller than he'd expected, thin and pale, with a few freckles dotted across the bridge of her nose. He hadn't been able to gather much intel on her other than a minuscule peek at her federal record. Former FBI. Highest number of cases closed in Bureau history, which meant she had to be damn good at her job. But clearly...unfulfilled. Why else would she have started Socorro and dragged a team out into the middle of the desert? Emerald-green eyes assessed him as easily as he'd assessed her, but Baker wasn't going to let her get into his head.

Ivy extended her hand. "I'm glad we finally have a chance to meet."

He took her hand out of social obligation as he tracked Jocelyn around the table before she took her seat down by Driscoll. "Yeah, well. Keep the enemy close and all that."

"Is that what we are?" Ivy withdrew her hand, careful not to let those perfectly manicured eyebrows move a millimeter. She was good. Maybe as good as he was at keeping other people in the dark. No, probably better.

In truth, he didn't know what they were at the moment. Not partners, that was for damn sure. Because the minute he trusted these people, they'd leave him and Alpine Valley for dead. They were a temporary solution. One at the mercy of the feds with no real attachment to his town.

"I've got a bombing investigation to get back to, so let's skip the small talk and get this over with," he said.

"A man after my own heart. Please, sit." Ivy headed back to her seat at the head of the table—a position of power she obviously cared about. "This is Jones Driscoll, head of our combat unit. He's our expert in all explosive ordinance and IEDs."

Baker nodded a greeting at the bearded, tattooed mountain man who looked like he belonged in the middle of a logging site rather than in a sleek conference room. Then took a seat beside Jocelyn. He interlocked his hands together over the surface of the table, right beside hers. "Albuquerque bomb squad got to the scene a couple hours ago. They're still trying to put the device back together, but from what little I saw of it before the explosion, we're most likely looking at homemade. Given your experience, I'm not sure why you'd want to attach yourself to a random bombing case."

"Because I don't believe this is random, Chief." Driscoll cut his attention to the company's founder, who nodded in turn. The combat head pried open a folder Baker hadn't noticed until then. "I took the liberty of getting in touch with Albuquerque's squad. They forwarded photos taken of what's left of the station."

"You went over my head." He barely had a second to give in to the annoyance clawing through him.

Driscoll templed his fingers over one of the photos from the stack and spun it around to share with the others. "The device that exploded in your station this morning? I've seen it before. In a car bombing outside of Ponderosa three months ago. The truck belonged to the chief of police there. Andrew Trevino."

Ponderosa. Baker sat a bit straighter under the weight of Jocelyn's gaze as he tried to come to terms with this new information. None of this made sense. He reached for the photos. "I haven't heard about any car bombing."

"You wouldn't have. Socorro was called to the scene. Ponderosa PD kept as much as they could from the media out of respect for their chief," Ivy said.

"What the hell does that mean?" He locked his gaze on each of the operators in turn, but none of them were giving him an answer.

"It's not uncommon for the cartel to target law enforcement officers it believes might intercept their plans or to make an example out of them in front of the towns they want to move in on." Driscoll tapped his index finger onto the photo positioned between them. "It shows control. Power. Manipulation. Call it your friendly cartel calling card."

"You're saying this was a targeted attack." Baker sifted through the possible scenarios in a matter of seconds. He'd taken this job to keep what had happened to him from happening to anyone else, but most of the cases he'd tackled since being elected to chief hadn't invited this type of attack. Who the hell would want to kill him? "The bomb was left for me."

Chapter Three

She could be miserable before she had a cookie and miserable after she had a cookie, but she could never be miserable while she was eating one. Or the dough.

Jocelyn dug out another spoonful from the Tupperware container in which she'd saved the last bit of cranberry-lemon dough. Whoever had said raw cookie dough would make her sick was a liar. Some of the best memories she had were between her and a bowl of homemade dough. Though some kinds whisked away the pain better than others. Gauging the mental list of ingredients she'd need, she calculated how fast she could whip up some chocolate chip dough while Baker was floating every other theory past Jones other than the most obvious.

Someone had planted a bomb in his station. Timed it well enough to ensure Baker would be in the trailer. And then detonated it with him inside. Well, they couldn't actually be sure of that last theory until the Albuquerque bomb squad recovered all the bits and pieces of the device. But how many other options were there?

Heavy footsteps registered, breaking her out of her thoughts. One of the most dangerous places to be. Cash

Meyers—Socorro's forward observer—angled into the kitchen, dusted with red dirt. He'd been in town again, helping rebuild the homes Sangre por Sangre had destroyed in their last raid. She could see it in the bits of sawdust on his shoulder.

He nodded at her in the way most of the men on the team did, his chin hiking slightly upward. "Heard you saw some fireworks this morning."

"Quite the show, for sure." Her phone vibrated from the inside of her cargo pants, but she wasn't ready to leave the protective walls of the kitchen. To acknowledge there was an entire world out there. This was where she thrived. Where nothing existed past the buzz of her stand mixer, the radiant heat of the oven and timers beeping in her ears. Jocelyn stuck the end of her spoon through the softening combination of butter, flour, sugar and cranberries. "Got a souvenir, too. Unfortunately, they made me hand it over to the bomb squad. Otherwise I'd put it on my bookshelf."

"You're sick, Carville." Cash wrenched the refrigerator open and grabbed a bottle of water. In less than thirty seconds, he downed the entire thing. Then he tossed the bottle into the recycling bin—her initiative—and leveled that remarkably open gaze on her. It was the little changes like that Jocelyn had noted over the past couple of months. Ever since Cash had taken up with his client. Elena. She'd done something to him. Made him as soft as this cookie dough to the point that he wasn't entirely annoying to be around. "You good?"

"I'm good." What other answer could she possibly give? That the pain in her side was the only thing keeping her from running back into the numbness she'd relied on before she'd come to Socorro? That the mere notion of painkillers threatened to drop her back into a vicious cycle that absolutely terrified her? Cash Meyers wasn't the person nor the solution she needed right then. Nobody on her team fit the bill. After loading her spoon into the dishwasher, she topped off the Tupperware and set it back in the fridge. "Tell Elena I'll drop off a batch tomorrow. I know she and Daniel really like my peanut butter cookies."

She moved past Cash and into the hallway. Air pressurized in her chest. It was always like this. Like she was preparing for war. Only in her case, the metaphor fit better than anything else. The onslaught of pain and suffering and death outside these bulletproof walls had the ability to crush her. It was a constant fight not to retreat, to hide, to fail those she'd sworn she would help. Even a grumpy chief of police.

"Jocelyn." Cash's use of her first name stopped her cold. The men and women of Socorro worked together as a team. They relied on one another to get them through their assignments and to keep each other alive. They were acquaintances with the same goal: dismantling the cartel. While most military units bonded through down time, inside jokes and pranks, the people she worked beside always managed to keep a bit of physical and emotional distance. Especially when addressing one another. The fact that Cash had resorted to verbally using her name meant only one thing. Her cover was slipping. "You sure you're all right?"

She pasted on that smile—the one honed over months of practice—and turned to face him. In an instant, the heaviness of the day drained from her overly tense muscles, and she was right back where she needed to be. "Never better. Stop worrying so much. You'll get crow's feet."

Jocelyn navigated along the black-on-black halls and faced off with the conference room door. Baker was still there, immobile in front of the window stretching from floor to ceiling as the sun dipped behind the mountains to the west. One arm crossed over his chest, the other scrubbing along his jawline. She catalogued every movement as though the slightest shift in his demeanor actually mattered. It didn't, but convincing her brain otherwise was a lost cause.

Stretching one hand out, she wrapped her fingers around the door handle. She could still feel the heat flaring up her hands as she'd tried to take the brunt of the explosion for him. It'd been reactive. Part of her job. Nothing more. At least, that was what she kept telling herself. The bandages across the backs of her hands started itching as she shoved through the door. "You're still here. Figured you and Jones would already be meeting up with the bomb squad back in town."

Turning toward her, Baker dropped his hands to his sides. Desert sunlight cut through the corner of the window at his back and cast him in blinding light. It highlighted the bruises along one side of his face. A small cut at his temple, too. "Guess he had something else to take care of. Said I could wait for you here."

"Right. Makes sense you would need a ride back into town." She tried not to take it personally. Of all the operators Socorro employed, her skill set didn't do much good in a bombing investigation.

"Well, yes. And no." Nervous energy replaced the mask Baker usually wore. "He told me you were the first one who responded to that car bombing in Ponderosa. Thought maybe you could walk me through it, see if anything lines up with what happened at the station."

"You mean other than the fact that the bomb that went off this morning wasn't attached to the undercarriage of your car?" she asked.

"Right." His low-key laugh did something funny to her insides.

As though she'd subconsciously been holding her breath just to hear it. Which was ridiculous. He didn't want to be here. Baker didn't want her help. He wanted to solve the case. She was only a means to an end. Tendrils of hollowness spread through her chest. Exhaustion was winning out after surviving the impact of the explosion. Her hand went to her side for Maverick but met nothing but empty air. Right. Animal Control.

"You know you won't be able to go back to your place," she said. "At least not until we have a better idea behind the bomber's motive. Too risky."

"I've been crashing on the couch at the station for a while." Baker rounded the head of the conference table, closing the distance between them. A lungful of smoke burned the back of her throat. Still dressed in his uniform, he was walking around smelling as though he'd just stepped out of one of those joints that smoked their meat instead of barbecuing it. Her stomach rumbled at the sensory overload. "Does that make me homeless?"

"Well, it certainly doesn't make you stable." Her instinct to take on the problems of the people around her—a distraction she'd come to rely on through the hard times—flared hot, but Baker wasn't the kind to share. Let alone trust a mercenary with personal information. She could help, though. Maybe that would ease the tightness in her stomach.

Jocelyn headed for the conference room door. "Come on. I'm sure one of the guys has something you can wear. You can borrow my shower while I find us something to eat."

"Why are you doing this?" His voice barely carried to her position at the door, but every cell in her body amplified it as though he'd spoken into a megaphone. "Why are you helping me?"

"Because despite what you might think of Socorro, Chief, helping people is what we do." She didn't want to think about the ones she hadn't been able to save. The ones who took up so much space in her heart. "It's why we all enlisted. Whether it be military or law enforcement. It's what keeps us going. It might not seem like much, but even the slightest deviation from a recipe can alter the taste of a dessert. It makes a difference."

"Damn it. I was hoping you were going to say something like money or authority or to take credit for dismantling the cartel." His expression softened. "And now I'm hungry."

"Sorry to disappoint you." The bruising along one shoulder barked as she hauled the heavy glass door inward, but she'd live. Thanks to him. "We've got some prepackaged meals in the kitchen. I'll grab you one while you clean up."

"Baker," he said from behind.

She hadn't made it more than two steps before the significance of his name settled at the base of her spine. "What?"

"We survived a bombing together, and you and your employer are going out of their way to help me find who did it." He slipped busted knuckles into his uniform slack pockets, taking the intensity out of his body language. "You can call me Baker."

The chief was asking her to call him by his first name. Giving her permission to step beyond the professional boundaries he'd kept between them since the moment they'd met. It shouldn't have held so much weight, but in her line of work, the gravity hit as hard as that explosion.

"Baker." She could practically taste his name on her tongue. Mostly sour with a hint of sweetness. Like a lemon tart packed with sweet cream.

Or maybe she just needed to brush her teeth.

"THIS DOESN'T TASTE like an MRE." Baker stabbed his fork into another helping of turkey, mashed potatoes and green beans and took a bite. It was enough to thaw the past few hours of adrenaline loss and brought his blood sugar back in line.

"It's not." Sitting straight across the table from him, Jocelyn scooped up a forkful of what looked like chicken with some kind of green vegetable and brought it to her mouth. As she chewed, her hair slid over her one shoulder, brushing the surface of the table. Unremarkably mesmerizing. "I put together about six dozen meals every week to make sure we're not living off carbs and protein shakes."

He wasn't sure if it was the blast or finally getting something other than microwave noodles in his stomach, but Baker had only just noted the way the light reflected off the black waves of hair she usually kept in tight rein. A hint of sepia colored her skin from long days out in the desert, but there wasn't a single piece of evidence of sun damage. Jocelyn Carville fit the exact opposite of everything he'd expected of a soldier, yet there was no denying the part she played in helping him with this investigation. "You made this? Hell, maybe I need to come out here more often."

Jocelyn pressed the back of her hand to her mouth to keep her food in place. "I'd drop some off at the station, but as of this morning, I'm not really sure where I would take it. Have you heard anything from the Albuquerque bomb squad?"

Right. The station he'd taken to holing up in had become a crime scene. He'd almost forgotten about that, sitting here as though the world had stopped and nothing existed outside of this place. They'd taken their seats at an oversized dining table set just on the other side of the kitchen that didn't look as though it got much use. Though from what he knew of Socorro, the contractors had been here for over a year. Maybe they just didn't use the table due to the onslaught of assignments. "Not yet. It may be a few days, but once they have something solid, it's only a matter of time before we find the bomber."

All he needed was proof the bombing was tied to the cartel, and ATF would get involved. Then he could finally take down Sangre por Sangre. For good.

Baker forced himself to focus on his next bite and not the way Jocelyn's eyes practically lit up as she savored her meal. The woman liked food—that much he could tell. Lemon bread, cranberry cookies, full-sized meals packaged in to-go containers. Her physical training had to be hell to stay as lean as she did. Then again, he wasn't entirely sure what was under all that gear she insisted on carrying throughout the day. Even indoors. Then again, what the hell was he doing noticing anything about her when they had a case to work?

"Tell me what you remember of the bombing outside Ponderosa," he said.

"Sure." She hiked one knee into her chest. Playful. Relaxed. At home. The feeling almost bled across the table and seeped into his aching joints with its easiness. Almost. "Ponderosa PD called it in. They hadn't been able to get a hold of their chief that morning, even though he was scheduled for the first shift. The sergeant sent out two patrols. One of them came across the scene about a mile outside of town in one of the canyons nearby. Too far away for anyone to notice."

She took a sip of water. "It was a pickup truck matching the description of Chief Andrew Trevino's vehicle. They initially believed it'd been a fire. That maybe Trevino had forgotten to clean up some oil from under the hood or had a gas leak. He was a smoker. His deputies wanted to believe it'd been an accident."

"But you determined otherwise." Her combat teammate—Jones Driscoll—had said as much, and Baker couldn't help but wonder what an optimistic, high-spirited woman like Jocelyn had seen in her life to make that assessment.

Her gaze detached, as though she were seeing it all play out right in front of her. "The front half of the vehicle was missing. Not even a gasoline fire would instigate that kind of damage. I went through what was left behind, but the resulting fire had burned away most of the evidence. Except a police badge. The edges had melted slightly, but it was clear who was in the vehicle when the bomb discharged."

It was easy to picture. Her crouched in the dirt, studying a replica of the badge currently pinned to his chest. Would she have done the same thing had he been killed in today's bombing? Acid surged up his throat at the notion.

"Maverick recovered a piece of the device. It wasn't sophisticated in the least, but it got the job done. Jones was the one who determined nitroglycerin had been used as the explosive. He could smell it. Anyone with an internet connection can build a bomb, but there was one distinct piece of evidence we couldn't ignore that helped us determine it was planted by the cartel." Jocelyn twisted her fork into the center of her dish but didn't take another bite. "The pager used to trigger the device was registered to a shell company owned by one of Sangre por Sangre's lieutenants. Benito Ramon. Has a history of arson and a mass of other charges, growing up in the cartel."

Confirmation that his leads weren't dead after all sparked anticipation through his veins, but he ate another forkful of dinner to settle his nerves.

"I read about him." Baker wouldn't tell her why. "Sixteen bombings all over the state, each suspected of linking back to Sangre por Sangre, but there was never any evidence to prove he was the bomber. From what I understand the man is a ghost, a legend the cartel uses to keep towns like Alpine Valley in line. Like the boogie man."

Tingling pooled at the base of his spine. He'd never been able to find evidence Benito Ramon existed. All he'd uncovered was a trail of death and destruction when he'd assumed the mantle of chief of police. Crime scene photos, witness accounts, evidence logs—none of it had led to the man who'd taken everything Baker cared about. Until now.

"Ghosts—real or otherwise—can still do a lot of damage," she said.

He could almost read a hint of suspicion in her voice—as though he'd somehow become attuned to the slightest inflection since they'd survived the explosion together. "You think something else was going on. That's why Jones wants you involved in this investigation."

Her mouth parted. Jocelyn didn't answer for a series of seconds. Considering how much to tell him? Then again, he guessed that was the problem with military contractors. Always working their own agenda.

"You said it yourself," she said. "There was never any evidence Benito Ramon was responsible for those sixteen bombings. So why would he make the mistake of using a pager registered to one of his shell companies to trigger the bomb that killed Chief Trevino?"

Good question. Hell, one he should've had the sense to ask himself. "You think someone was trying to pin the chief's murder on Benito Ramon?"

"It's just a theory." Jocelyn collected her meal, snapped the storage lid on top and shoved to her feet. She set the food back in the refrigerator with far more grace than he'd expected out of a five-foot-five woman carrying at least thirty pounds of gear. There was a hidden strength in the way she moved. Practiced.

A theory. He could work with a theory. Baker gathered up his own dinner and set about disposing of what he couldn't finish. "This place is a lot quieter than I figured it'd be."

"Socorro is on call 24/7. It's hard to get everyone together when we're all working different shifts, but we try." An inner glow that hadn't been there a few minutes ago seeped into her expression. "Birthday parties, movie nights, Thanksgiving and Christmas. It's rare, but being together helps us bond better as a team, you know? Takes the harshness out of the work we do."

Baker watched the transformation right in front of him. Where a heaviness had tensed the muscles along her neck and shoulders, exhilaration took its place as she talked about her team. He'd never seen anything like it before. "You like this kind of stuff. Cooking, baking for people, movie nights…"

There was a hitch in Jocelyn's step that she tried to cover up as she moved from one side of the kitchen to the next. She'd taken a mixing bowl out of the refrigerator and peeled the plastic wrap free. Cookie dough, from the look of it. Did the woman ever just sit still? She dragged a cookie scoop out of one of the drawers and started rolling the dough into perfect golf ball–sized pieces onto a baking sheet. "Of course. Keeps me busy."

"Aren't you already busy responding to things like car bombings and coordinating resources from surrounding towns?" He couldn't help but watch her roll one section of dough before moving onto the next. It was a highly coordinated dance that seemed to have no end and drove his nervous system into a frenzy. He wanted to reach out, to force her hands to stop working, but Baker had the distinct impression she'd bite him if he interrupted. Like her dog almost had back at the station.

"Well, yeah, but this ends in cookies. And who doesn't like cookies?" Her smile split a small cut at one corner of her mouth. A sliver of blood peeked through.

His discipline failed him right then. Baker closed the short distance between them, swiping the blood from her mouth. One touch catapulted his heart rate into overdrive. A sizzle of heat burned across his skin faster than the flames created by the bomb this morning.

Instant paralysis seemed to flood through her. She stopped rolling dough into bite-sized balls, her hands buried deep in something that smelled a lot like peanut butter. Three seconds passed. Four. Her exhale brushed against the underside of his jaw.

Jocelyn took as big of a step back as she could with her palms full of dough. "What are you doing?"

"I'm sorry." He knew better than to touch her without permission. Cold infused his veins as he brushed his thumb against his slacks. They were already spotted with blood. A few more drops wouldn't hurt. "You just…had a bit of blood on you."

"Don't. Just…don't." Lean muscle running the length of her arms flexed and receded as she peeled layers of dough off her hands and tossed it back into the bowl.

Right before she sprinted from the kitchen.

Chapter Four

No amount of cookie dough was going to fix this.

Jocelyn scrubbed her hands as hard as she could beneath the scalding water. She could still feel his touch at the corner of her mouth. Baker's touch. It'd been calloused and soft at the same time, depending on which feeling she wanted to focus on. Only problem was she didn't actually want to focus on any of it.

Her skin protested each swipe of the loofa. To the point it'd turned a bright red. The blisters she'd earned this morning were bleeding again, but it wasn't enough to make her stop. The dough just wouldn't come off. She could still feel it. Still feel Baker's thumb pressed against her skin.

"Jocelyn?" Movement registered in the mirror behind her. Baker centered himself over her shoulder though ensured to keep his distance. Dark circles embedded beneath his eyes, taking the defiance and intensity she was used to right out of him.

She ordered one hand to turn off the water, but she just kept scrubbing, trying to replace one feeling with another. It was working. Slowly. The tightness in her chest was letting go. "How did you get in here?"

"That guy Cash told me where your room was. I knocked, but there was no answer. I just wanted to make sure you were okay." His voice didn't hold the same authority it had while he'd been asking her about the bombing in Ponderosa.

"So you thought you would just let yourself in?" The conversation was helping, somehow easing her heart rate back into normal limits.

"I knocked for fifteen minutes," he said. "Listen… I'm sorry about before. I shouldn't have touched you. I was out of line, and it won't happen again. I give you my word."

Her hands were burning, and the last few pieces of agitation slipped free. She finally had enough control to turn off the water. All was right with the world. Jocelyn reached for the pretty hand towel to her left and took a solid full breath for the first time in minutes. "I'm not crazy."

Three distinguished lines between his eyebrows deepened as she caught his reflection in the mirror. "That didn't even cross my mind. A lot of soldiers have trouble differentiating the past trauma from the present. I've seen it in one of my deputies. There's no shame—"

"I'm not suffering from PTSD, Baker." She rearranged the hand towel back on its round metal hardware. No one understood. Because what she'd done—what she lived with every day—was hers alone. But what she wouldn't give to let someone else take the weight for a while.

Jocelyn turned to face him, the bathroom doorframe putting them on opposite sides of the divide. Here and outside these walls. "You want to know why I bake so many cookies and breads and cakes and pies? Why I feel safer with a glob of dough in my hands than with my sidearm? Because it makes me happy. It helps me forget."

"Forget what?" He moved toward her then, resurrecting that hint of smoke in his uniform.

Discomfort alienated the pleasure she'd found with her hands in that peanut butter dough. She'd already let her control slip once today. Did she really want to take a full dive into trusting a man who couldn't even stand to be in the same room as her? "My husband."

"Oh." His expression went smooth as he leaned against the doorjamb. "I didn't realize you're married."

"Was. I was married." She'd never said the words before, never wanted to admit there was this gaping hole inside of her where Miles used to be. Because that would be when the sadness got to be too much. When the world tore straight out from under her and past comforts reared their ugly little heads. "He passed away about a year ago."

"I'm sorry." Folding his arms over his chest, Baker looked as though he belonged. Not just here in headquarters but in this moment. "I didn't… I didn't know."

"Nobody knows. No one but you." She let her words fill the space between them, but the weight didn't get lighter. If anything, her legs threatened to collapse in the too-small bathroom attached to her room.

Eyes to the floor, Baker scrubbed a hand down his face. "So when I touched you—"

"It wasn't your fault." She crossed her feet in front of her, her weight leveraged against the vanity. Of all the places she'd imagined having this conversation, in a bathroom with the Alpine Valley's chief of police hadn't even made the list. "The most affection I get now days is from Maverick, and he's not as cuddly as he looks. You just…took me by surprise is all."

"As cuddly as he looks? Your dog nearly took my hand off when I was trying to get you out of the station."

His attempt to lighten the mood worked to a degree. But there was still a matter of this…wedge between them. One she wasn't sure she could fix with cookies and a positive attitude. "A spouse isn't usually someone you want to forget."

"It's not him I want to forget, really." She tried to put her smile back in place, feeling it fail. Her fingers bit into the underside of the vanity counter, needing something—anything—to keep her from slipping back into an empty headspace she didn't want to visit. "He died of cancer. While I was on my last tour. I tried to make it home—to be there for him, you know—but communications on assignment were spotty at best and arranging transport is hard when the enemy is shooting down anything they come across."

Tears broke through. The pain was cresting, sucking her under little by little, and she had nothing and no one to hold on to.

He took another step forward. "Jocelyn—"

"I know. Not exactly how you imagined your day would play out, right?" Years of practice had to be worth something. She swiped at her face, but getting rid of the physical evidence of her hurt wasn't enough. It'd never been enough. Turning to the mirror, she plastered that smile on her face. There. That was better. She could just make him out through the last layer of tears in her eyes. "First a bombing at your station, then a mercenary crying in front of you over her dead husband. Maybe next you'll get food poisoning from the dinner I put together. Wouldn't that be the icing on the cake?"

She had to get moving. Jocelyn grabbed for the first aid

kit under the sink and started wrapping the blisters she'd broken open. Staying put gave the bad thoughts a chance to sneak in. They should've heard from Albuquerque's bomb squad by now. She had to finish those cookies for Elena and Cash, too. She should—

"Jocelyn, look at me." Baker's voice brought the downward cycle of to-do lists to a halt. He said her name as though it were the most beautiful word in his world, as though right then he saw who she really was. Not a mercenary. Not Carville. Just Jocelyn. Something behind her rib cage convinced her that he could fix everything with that single shift between them, but that wasn't how the world worked. How *grief* worked. No amount of pity was going to change the past.

But she still found herself locking her gaze on his.

Baker offered her his hand, palm up. Inviting. "I want to show you something."

He was giving her a choice to be touched, and appreciation nearly outpaced a rush of possibilities that crashed through her. She'd spent every day since getting the news that Miles hadn't survived his disease learning new languages, recipes, combat techniques and dozens of other experiences, but she couldn't imagine what a small-town police chief would want to show her.

She slipped her hand into his. His skin was bruised, cut, scabbing, harsher than she'd expected. But real. Baker dragged her free of the bathroom and toward the wall-to-ceiling window on the other side of her room. From here she could just make out Alpine Valley with the west end of the town peeking out from the canyon guarding it on both sides. An oasis in the middle of the New Mexican desert.

"You see that collection of buildings out there?" Radiant heat bled through the tinted panes of glass, but it was nothing compared to the warmth spreading through her hand. "Just outside of the canyon mouth?"

She focused everything she had on finding what he wanted her to see. Her heart pounded double-time in expectation of a full-blown breakdown as sadness worked through her, but the fear that usually rode on its coattails never came. As though their physical connection was holding her steady. "I see a barn, maybe a house. Though I'm not sure who lives there."

"I do." The window tint wasn't enough to block the sunset from highlighting all the small changes in his expression. "The barn, the house, the land. Three acres."

"So you're not as homeless as you led me to believe earlier?" She tried to make out the property lines to mentally gauge Baker's private kingdom, but there didn't seem to be anything but dirt and emptiness surrounding the structures. Dread pooled in her gut. "Why have you been crashing at the station for the past few months?"

"My sister and I had big plans to move out west and buy up land here in New Mexico. We were going to raise horses and start a bed and breakfast." He stared out at the land, not really here with her. "Took us a lot longer than it should have, but neither of us had built anything in our lives. We had to learn as we went. And buying up horses?" A scoff released the pressure of the moment. "Man, we were suckered into paying more than we should have, but we didn't care. We just wanted a place that was our own. Away from the chaos of the city. Somewhere we could hear ourselves think."

Why was he telling her this? "The two of you must be close."

"We were. Spent every second of our days together. Well, almost. There were times we got on each other's nerves because we were overheated, sunburned and hungry from working the land all day, but we'd still sit down to dinner every night as though nothing had happened." His grip tightened around her hand. "The last time I saw her was during one of those stupid arguments. I don't even remember what I was so mad about. Guess it doesn't matter now, though."

Her mouth dried. "The last time you saw her?"

"About two weeks into getting the place off the ground, the cartel came calling. Talking some BS about how they owned the land we built on." Baker shifted his weight between both feet, his attention still out the window. She recognized the agitation for what it was: an attempt to distract himself. "Come to find out they'd set up one of their delivery routes straight through the property and weren't too keen on the idea someone had moved in on their territory. But we weren't just going to get up and leave."

"What happened?" In truth, she already knew the answer. Knew this story—like her own—didn't have a happy ending. How could it?

Baker locked that penetrating gaze on hers. "They burned everything we built to the ground. And took my sister right along with it."

HE HADN'T TOLD anyone about Linley before.

Not even his own deputies, but he didn't trust them anyway. Not after discovering one of his own had been working for the very people Baker despised. Of course, there'd been rumors. Questions as to why an outsider like him would want to suddenly apply for the position of chief of police. They hadn't trusted him. Still didn't. Not really. But he'd live up to his promise to protect the people of Alpine Valley. Especially from cartels like the one that had destroyed his life.

Baker memorized the rise and fall of the landscape as they shot across the desert inside Jocelyn's SUV. Surrounded by miles of desert, Alpine Valley had provided life to an entire nature preserve. Trees over a hundred feet tall crowded in around the borders and protected the natural hot springs and centuries-old pueblos tucked into the canyons. It was beautiful. Not in the same way he'd loved the leaves in the fall back east or watched snow pile up outside in his parents' backyard. There was honestly nothing but cracked earth, weeds and cacti as far as the eye could see.

But it was home now.

What had Linley called it? An oasis to forget their problems. If only that had been true.

"We need a plan." Baker turned his attention back to the file on his lap—the bombing outside of Ponderosa. Jocelyn had gone the extra mile to call in a favor from their department there, giving them full access to the case. They could dance around the present all they wanted with dark personal confessions and frank observations, but it wasn't going to change the fact that a bomb—most likely linked to the cartel—had been left in his station. Just as one had been left for the Ponderosa chief to find. "Albuquerque's bomb squad isn't going to like us just showing up on scene. There are protocols to follow so we don't disturb the evidence."

"It's all taken care of." Her hand—ringless, he couldn't help but notice—kept a light grip on the steering wheel as she maneuvered them along the familiar street lined with flat-roofed homes, rock landscaping and a few porch lights.

"What do you mean?" he asked.

Jocelyn didn't answer as she pulled into the parking lot that used to hold a much larger police station than what was left behind. Crime scene tape cut off access to approaching vehicles, but his cruiser was still parked outside the make-shift perimeter. She pulled the SUV beside it.

He'd reached out to his deputies to give them the rundown of what'd happened. It didn't matter that their station was sporting a sunroof nobody had wanted. Alpine Valley PD didn't get to take a vacation from answering calls. Though now his remaining two deputies would be answering and responding to calls for the foreseeable future from the town rec center. Good a place as any.

"Looks like the courts are barred from working out of their half of the building," he said.

"Standard procedure. Fire and Rescue doesn't want to run the risk of evidence contamination, even from people who know how important that evidence is in a case." Jocelyn put the vehicle into Park. "The fire marshal is waiting for us."

"You called Gary?" Baker shoved out of the SUV, a little worse for wear. Hell, his whole body hurt from this morning's events. How did Jocelyn do it—moving as though she hadn't been impaled by a piece of debris as she pulled something from the back seat?

Gravel crunched under his boots as he followed the short path from the asphalt to the base of the station stairs. "I can't even get him to return my calls. Seems he doesn't agree with my choice in baseball teams. Though I'm not sure why he would take that so personally."

"You just have to know how to make him talk." She produced a plate of plastic-wrapped goods and grabbed her phone. With the swipe of her thumb, she raised the phone to her ear and rasped in a thick, Russian accent, "I have what you asked for."

She hung up. Waiting.

"Are we in the middle of delivering a ransom payment I don't know about?" Movement registered from the corner of the station to Baker's right. Instant alert had him reaching for his sidearm. Then recognition tendriled through him as Alpine Valley's fire marshal hauled his oversized frame closer. He relaxed a fraction. "Gary."

"Chief." Not Baker. Seemed grudges died hard with this one. Gary cut his gaze to Jocelyn, and the marshal's overall demeanor lost its bite. Yeah, she had the tendency to do that—ease into a person's subconscious and replace any darkness with rainbows and silver linings. "I believe you have something for me."

She handed off the plate as though embroiled in an illegal trade. "Fresh batch of oatmeal. No raisins. They're all yours."

"You got ten minutes before Albuquerque wants me to check in." Gary had suddenly lost the ability to make eye contact, his entire focus honed in on the disposable plate in his hand.

"Thanks. We won't be long," Baker said.

The marshal didn't bother answering as he headed for his pickup across the street.

Baker motioned her ahead of him. "Seems you have your fingers in all the pies around here."

"Like I said, you just have to know how to get people

to talk." Jocelyn took the lead up the stairs and produced a blade from one of her many cargo-pant pockets. The woman was better prepared than an Eagle Scout.

Cutting through the sticker warning trespassers of what waited for them if they were caught breaking into a crime scene, she braced her foot against one corner of the door to let him by. "With Gary, it's straight through his stomach. He kept coming back for my oatmeal cookies at the fund-raiser last year. Later, I found a pile of discarded raisins in the parking lot."

"Here I thought the best way to a man's heart was through his third and fourth ribs." He unholstered his flashlight from his duty belt, then maneuvered past her, though he couldn't help but brush against her as he did. The physical contact eased the unsettled part of him that knew he was breaking a dozen different laws crossing into this crime scene, which he'd have to answer for, but the clock was ticking. The bomb squad's investigation could last days, maybe weeks. Possibly even months, if Chief Andrew Trevino's murder was anything to go by. They didn't have that kind of time—this was the first lead he'd had on Sangre por Sangre in months. He couldn't let it die.

Once inside, Baker punched the end of the flashlight, and a beam cut across the charred, debris-coated carpeting. "You always been able to read people like that?"

"I have a good sense for it." Jocelyn followed along the path through the building that the bomb squad had cleared for techs. She walked past what used to be the small kitchenette the former dispatcher had set up opposite the evidence room. "I see you more as a home-cooked-meal kind of guy."

"What gives you that impression?" The bitter scent of

fire lodged in the back of his throat. Caustic. Suffocating. Baker felt his heart rate tick up a notch. He blinked to focus on the scene in front of him, but there were too many similarities. Sweat broke out across his forehead.

"You turned down my cranberry-lemon cookies this morning." Jocelyn's voice warbled there at the end. "And considering you've been crashing in a police station trailer armed with nothing but a microwave, I'd bet that dinner we had earlier hit the spot."

Baker couldn't move, couldn't speak. Every cell in his body put its energy into studying a half-destroyed coffee stirrer, and he lost any ability to get his lungs to work.

"Baker?" His name sounded distant. Out of reach.

Gravity held him hostage in that one spot despite the left side of his brain trying to catch up to the right. The flavor of smoke changed, contorting into something more acidic and nauseating. He took a step forward, though the layout of the station had vanished. He was walking toward the barn. What was left of it, at least. Intense heat still clung to the charred remains, flicking its tongue across his skin. "Linley?"

His shallow breathing triggered a wave of dizziness. She wasn't here. She couldn't be here. Because if the cartel had done this… No. He couldn't think like that. Baker took another step, his boots sinking deep into mud. The barn door nearly fell off its hinges as he wrenched it to one side. The entire building was about to crash down around him. All of this damage couldn't be from the result of a random fire. This was something far more explosive.

"Baker."

He knew that voice. Well enough to pull him up short. It

whispered on the ash-tainted air around him. Like he could reach out and grab onto it. Jocelyn?

"Can you hear me?"

The fragment of memory jumped forward. To him standing in front of the body positioned in the center of the barn. Nothing about the remains resembled his sister, but he knew the cartel had done this. That they'd kept their word to burn his entire world to the ground if he didn't comply with their demands. And he'd let it happen. All because he'd gone into town for more hay.

Fury and shame and grief clawed through him as he sank to his knees. "I'll find them. Every single one of them. I give you my word... I'll make them pay."

"Baker!" Strong chocolate-brown eyes centered in his vision, replacing the horrors. Jocelyn fisted both hands into his uniform collar and crushed her mouth to his.

The past dissolved from right in front of him, replaced by physical connection tethered to reality. Her mouth was soft—hesitant—on his. The horrors clinging to the edges of his memory were displaced by the mint taste of her toothpaste and the slight aroma of oatmeal cookies. Baker lost himself in the feel of her mouth against his. On the slight catch of the split in her lip.

It was absolutely the most inappropriate thing to do in the middle of a crime scene, but his heart rate was coming back down. He had sensation back in his hands, and he latched on to Jocelyn as though he'd lose this grasp in the present if he didn't. The helplessness consuming him from the inside crawled back into the dark void he'd walled away. Until there was nothing left but her.

She settled back onto her heels, a direct mirror of his

position on the floor. Her exhale brushed the underside of his jaw, and that simple rush to his senses was all it took. Jocelyn's eyes bounced between both of his, concern and fear and something like affection spiraling in the depths. "You with me?"

"Yeah." Baker tightened his hold on her vest. Because she was the only real thing he had. "I'm with you."

Chapter Five

Well, wasn't that just the milk to her cookies?

Jocelyn pried her grip from Baker's uniform collar and put a bit of distance between them. She'd kissed him, and in the moment, it'd been all she could think of to snap him out of whatever he'd been reliving. But now… Now there was a pressure in her chest reminding her that everything she touched died. House plants. Friendships. Her husband.

Shame burned through her as she tried to smooth the imprints of her hold from the fabric of his uniform. "I'm sorry. I…didn't know what else to do. You weren't answering, and I thought—"

"It's okay." Baker seemed to come back to himself then, but she couldn't help but wonder if his mind would pull him back into that terrifying void with the slightest reminder of what he'd been through.

She'd always known people who'd survived trauma—in war, in their own homes, as children or adults—could be caught in the suffocating spiral of PTSD, but the chief of police had never crossed her mind. And now his assumption that she suffered from post-traumatic stress made sense. It wasn't one of his deputies he'd been talking about who experienced nerve-wracking flashbacks. It was *him*. And she'd dragged him straight into a similar scene to what he'd witnessed.

"I shouldn't have brought you back here," she said.

He was still holding on to the shoulders of her vest. Gauging his surroundings, Baker finally let go. Yet he struggled to stay on his feet. Stable but weak. As though the past had taken everything he had left for itself. "I'm fine. It hasn't happened in a while. It just caught me off guard."

She reached out, resting her hand on his arm. She'd seen physical contact work in the field before. "If you need to wait in the car, I can go through—"

"I'm not leaving." There was a violence in his voice she hadn't heard until then. Just as she'd responded to him after he'd touched her mouth. It was reflected in his eyes as he seemed to memorize the scene around them. "I can do this."

Shame, guilt, helplessness—it all echoed through her just as it did him, and Jocelyn backed off. His response made sense. Fellow soldiers who'd lived through what could only be described as the worst days of their lives on tour kept going back, comforted by the very horrors that had scarred and disconnected them. Baker wouldn't admit defeat to the ambushing sights, sounds and smells in his head. No matter how unhealthy or unexpected. Because without them, he had nothing.

They were similar in that respect, and her heart wanted to fix it. To make everything better. But she couldn't even help herself. How was she supposed to help him?

"Okay." Jocelyn swiped clammy hands down her pants. It'd been jarring and terrifying to see a man as confident and driven as Baker shut down right in front of her, but deep down she knew he wouldn't let it affect this investigation. The marshal had given them ten minutes inside the scene. She wasn't sure how much time they had left. They had to keep moving. "I'll see what I can find around the evidence closet."

She didn't wait for an answer. The hollow floor threatened to collapse from her added weight, but she kept to the path that the bomb squad had charted.

"Jocelyn, hold on." His hand encircled her arm, and she turned into him, though not out of some fight-or-flight instinct she didn't have control over. Because she wanted to. The flashlight beam cut across the floor from where he'd dropped it a few minutes ago, casting his expression in a white-washed glow. "I…"

Words seemed to fail him then. This man who fought for everyone in this town but himself. He didn't have to say the words. Despite the distance they'd kept lodged between themselves and the rest of the world, invisible connections were forged through survival. That was what they'd done today. Survived. And in that single act, she found herself more in line with Baker than she'd thought possible.

"I know. It's okay." She tried to put that smile back in place. The one that could save the world, according to her husband. No matter what had been going on in their lives or how bad the pain had gotten from treatment, all he'd needed was that smile. And in the end, it was all he'd asked for, according to his nurses. But she hadn't been there.

The muscles around her mouth wavered. "We're all just trying to navigate the same road to healing," she said. "Every once in a while, we take a wrong turn or end up going in reverse. But that's why I'm glad you're here with me, in the passenger seat. Helping me navigate."

She slipped free of his hold, almost desperate to prove she could be his navigator in turn. That she could find something—anything—in this mess to give him some sense of peace. Squaring her shoulders, Jocelyn kept to the perimeter of where the blast had originated.

The bomb squad most assuredly had been through all of this. They would've spent hours trying to piece the device back together to identify its creator through a signature or fingerprint. But everything else would've had to wait. She took in the outline of the hole blasted through the far wall and low corner of what used to be a closet. The moments leading up to the blast played out as clearly as if they'd happened mere minutes ago, rather than hours.

Maverick had sniffed out the bomb's components in a box stacked at the back of a bottom shelf. It'd been a clever hiding place. But why there? "The evidence room."

"What did you say?" Baker kept his footsteps light as he carved a path through the makeshift kitchenette.

"Ponderosa's chief of police—Trevino—was killed with a bomb strapped to the underside of his pickup truck. There was no doubt that whoever set the device had targeted him. His wife had her own vehicle, and their kids were raised and grown. Moved out of state to start their own families." Her mouth couldn't keep up with her theory—as it did sometimes when her mind raced ahead in a recipe she'd memorized but her hands didn't work that fast. "The device from this morning was planted here. In the station. Where anyone could walk in."

He closed the distance between them, his arm making

contact with the back of her vest. Just the slightest pressure, but enough to elicit a response. "You and Jones were convinced the bombing was meant for me. Now you're saying it wasn't?"

"Did you see the device this morning?" she asked.

Baker stilled, his gaze narrowing as she practically watched him replay the events of the day. There was still a hint of sweat at his temple. Evidence the tin man was all too human. "No. Maverick was in the way. He was sniffing around...an evidence box."

"It was on the bottom shelf. You remember?" She tried coming up with the case numbers marked on the outside, but there were still gaps in her memory from when her head had been lodged at the far wall. "Albuquerque's bomb squad is working off our assumption the device was meant for you. They'll put everything into putting what they can find of the bomb back together, but what if it was actually planted to destroy whatever was in that box? To stop a case from moving forward?" Her voice hitched with excitement. "Think about it. There are countless other places they could've set that bomb to get to you. Why would they purposely choose a box stashed on the bottom shelf of the evidence room unless they wanted to make sure no one could put the pieces back together?"

"Makes sense." Baker stared at the space where the floor should've been. "Question is, which case would they have wanted to destroy?"

"Did you have any active cases running on the cartel? Maybe one of their soldiers or an incident that occurred within Alpine Valley town borders?"

"Son of a bitch." Baker took a step back, scrubbing a hand down his face. "I should've seen it before now."

"You had a case," she said. "What was it?"

"Cartel lieutenant. Guy named Marc De Leon. We arrested him about three months ago. He'd taken to strapping a bomb to a woman's chest after torturing her for a couple hours. Best we could get from him, she was a random target. Unfortunately, she didn't survive, and the extent of her injuries kept us from identifying her. We've searched missing persons reports and interrogated the bastard any chance we could, but it's gotten us nowhere. Everyone just calls her Jane Doe." Sorrow dipped his voice into a whisper. "We could prove he was at the scene. Dead to rights. Found his fingerprints on the weapon he left behind. I picked him up on foot just outside of town covered in blood within a couple hours. It was easy to connect him back to the cartel through his priors. The lawyers are going at it right now, trying to claim some insanity defense, but it's not working. He knew exactly what he was doing when he killed her."

She'd heard about the raid. Known the town had nearly burned to the ground the night that another lieutenant had ordered his men to bring Elena Navarro and her eight-year-old brother, Daniel, to him. They'd torn apart families, destroyed homes and shops and set Alpine Valley right back under their control. By fear and intimidation. But now Baker was adding murder to the list. Why hadn't she known about this before tonight?

"The case wasn't going away. What better way to get your man off the hook than to send in your resident bomber to destroy all the evidence?" she said.

"Yeah, well. They got what they wanted, didn't they? We

had the knife. We had his fingerprints, witness statements, GPS from his phone that put him in that house at the time of the raid." Baker kicked at a half-cremated box that hadn't gotten caught in the blast. "All destroyed. The prosecutor won't be able to do a damn thing about it, and that woman's family gets nothing. No sense of closure. No justice."

Her heart hurt at the idea of the victim's family knowing what'd happened to her but never being able to move on. Because Baker was there, too. Haunted by what'd happened to his sister, never finding peace. Never being able to move on from the past. Jocelyn wanted that for him. A chance to heal, to live his own life apart from the horrible trauma that'd taken away everything he'd loved.

And there was only one way to do it.

She stepped to his side, staring down at the singed hole where the evidence room used to be. It wasn't just Marc De Leon's case that'd been destroyed but all of them. Dozens of victims who'd never see the resolution they deserved. "Lieutenants like De Leon are indispensable. It takes years of loyalty and trust to rise up the ranks. It's what he knows about the cartel's operation that they'd go out on a limb to save, but that doesn't make men like him untouchable."

"You sure about that?" he asked.

"Yeah." Jocelyn breathed in smoke-heavy air, mentally preparing for the war they were about to start. "I am."

HE WAS BACK at square one.

The promise of a new lead in his sister's murder was wearing thin. Pain radiated up his side as the SUV's shocks failed to navigate the uneven landscape. He'd once believed Alpine Valley was where he belonged, that his future rested here in miles of desert, star-streaked skies and protective canyons. Somewhere he could build a future.

He didn't have a future anymore.

Not until Sangre por Sangre paid for what they'd done. To him, to the residents of his town. To the hundreds of future victims they would discard in a power struggle to gain control. It wasn't just about what'd happened to Linley or that lieutenant trying to squeeze himself out of a murder charge. It was *all* of it. The constant threat and the repercussions of a cartel's choices determined who would live at the end of the day and who wouldn't. And Baker couldn't accept that. These people deserved better, and he wasn't going to stop. Not until every last man and woman connected to the cartel was behind bars or six feet under.

The rush of adrenaline he'd suffered at the smallest inkling of a threat refused to let go. It was tensing his hands until he found it nearly impossible to release. His body had yet to get the signals there wasn't any actual danger right in front of him, and there was only one way to force it back into submission.

"I need you to do me a favor." His voice failed on the last word. Exhaustion had gotten the best of him long before now, but he was somehow still holding it together. They were coming up on the road that would either take them back to Socorro or to the edge of town. "Turn right up here at the T."

Jocelyn's mouth parted in the dim light given off by the SUV's controls behind the steering wheel. The slightest change in facial expression spoke volumes. She knew exactly what he was asking, and she was the only one who could help. "Are you sure?"

"I just need…" He didn't know what he needed. Something familiar? Baker didn't have the capacity to explain right then. The gnawing hollowness in his chest wouldn't let him. "I'm sure."

She navigated north.

He'd driven this way so many times, he could practically feel his breath coming easier as he anticipated every bump in the dirt road. But it wasn't enough. A war between getting relief and putting himself at risk raged as the rough outline of the structures separated from the surrounding darkness up ahead.

"You can stop here," he said.

Momentum kept his upper body moving forward as Jocelyn brought the SUV to a full stop outside the cattle gate, but the pain stayed at a low simmer. "I'll just be a few minutes."

"You don't have to go in there alone." Her hand shot out as he shouldered the passenger side door open, clamping on to the top of his thigh. The contact should've set him on high alert, but there was something about Jocelyn Carville that put him at ease. "I could come with you."

His automatic answer rushed to the front of his mind. He should shut her down, take the time he needed to get his head back in the game. But the logical part of him understood she'd already seen him at his worst, that walking into that house without support could break him.

Baker let his hand slip from the door. "Yeah. Okay."

The vehicle's headlights guided them to the gate. A chill ran through the air. A storm was on its way in, the first few drops collecting along the top of the gate. Baker grabbed for the padlock securing the gate to the frame and took out his key, twisting it in the lock. The chain hit the dirt, and he swung the gate open. "Welcome to my humble abode."

Gravel crunched under their feet as they hiked the empty driveway. The barn sat in the distance, more than half of the structure gone from the explosion. Its rugged outline stood stark against the backdrop of the last bit of blue behind the mountains. But the house was still intact. The single story was exactly as he'd left it. Tan stucco practically glowed in the beaming moonlight and highlighted the black window casings, two-car garage and front door. Mid-century metal floral details held up one corner of the porch, matching the color of the exterior of the house. It was a weird, old addition on a brand-new build, but Linley had insisted. Now he couldn't imagine taking it out.

Baker hauled himself up the front steps and gripped the front door handle with one hand. The oversized picture window stared back at him from his left, and he couldn't help but let his senses try to penetrate through the glass. As though his sister would be waiting for him to come home on the other side as she had so many times before.

Jocelyn followed his hesitant footsteps. "We can still turn back…"

No. As much as he wanted to pretend the past didn't affect the present, his body kept score.

Baker slid the key into the deadbolt. "Don't you know by now, Carville? There is no going back. Not for people like us."

Hinges protested as he pushed inside. A wall of stale air drove down his throat. The breeze cut through the opening in the front door and ruffled the plastic coating the furniture, and an instant hit of warmth flooded through him. He tugged the key from the deadbolt and moved aside to let Jocelyn over the threshold, flipping on the entryway light.

"It's much bigger than it looks from the outside." She carved a path ahead of him. Her bootsteps echoed off the hardwood floors and tall ceilings. Taking in the stretch of the great room and the fireplace mantel he and his sister had crafted by hand, Jocelyn moved as though she'd been here before. "You built all this?"

Baker shut out the cold, letting the entire space seep into his bones. "Me and my sister. I did most of the heavy lifting. She picked out all the extras. The color of the floors, paint on the walls. A time or two I'd needed her help framing out the closet or installing the toilets. She really could do it all."

"What was her name?" Jocelyn carefully ran her hand the length of the mantel, as though she knew that was the final piece he'd installed in this house.

"Linley." It'd been so long since he'd let himself speak her name, it tasted foreign on his tongue. Though not as bitter as he'd expected. "She had a talent for stuff like this. I always told her she could be a designer, but she loved horses more."

Jocelyn intercepted the single framed photo and lifted it off the mantel. One taken of him and Linley, each holding hammers in a ridiculous power pose in front of their finished project. "Is this her?"

"Yeah." He maneuvered around the sectional, his thigh brushing over plastic, and took the frame from her. "This was the day we officially finished the house. We were trying to pose like those brothers on the renovation show, but we couldn't stop laughing because every time we set my phone up to take the picture on top of this bag of concrete, it fell off. I ended up cracking my screen, but we somehow managed to make it work."

Heat seared through him as Jocelyn's arm settled against his side. The need for something familiar didn't seem to have as great a hold on him. Not with her here. "She looks like you. Same eyes. Same smile. She's stunning."

"Does that mean you think I'm stunning, then, too?" Where the hell had that come from? And what did he care what she thought of him?

"I wouldn't call you ugly." Jocelyn backed off, hands on her hips, and he swore a flush rushed up her neck. "Unless you piss me off."

Baker pressed his thumb into the corner of the framed photo. "Well, I wouldn't want that. Who else is going to feed me something other than prepackaged ramen noodles?"

Her smile did more to light up the room than the light-fan combination above them. "Oh, is that all I'm good for? You got what you wanted out of me, and now I'm back to being the mercenary who bakes?"

"Nah. Once you survive a bombing together, you can never go back to being acquaintances." Baker set the photo back on the mantel. He liked this. The back and forth they'd shared since this morning. It came with a weird sensation of…lightness. Like he'd been cutting himself off from everything that made him happy as some kind of penance. "You heard from Animal Control?"

"Yeah. Socorro's vet picked Maverick up a little while ago," she said. "He's got a slight limp, but for the most part he's fine. Should be back to normal in a couple days. Just needs a bit of rest."

"He's not the only one." He prodded at the lump behind

his left ear. It'd kept itself in check for most of the day, but after coming here, his nerves had reached their end. "If the hospital hadn't told me otherwise, I would've sworn I cracked my head open."

"Your head hurts?" She moved in close. Close enough he caught a hint of color in her eyes before she raised her hands to him. Angling the side of his head toward her, she framed his jaw with one hand while sliding her fingertips against his scalp. "I don't see any changes in the bruise patterns since we left the hospital. We've been running on fumes most of the day. I'm sure your body is just trying to get you to slow down. I can keep watch if you want to grab a couple hours of sleep."

His scalp tightened at the physical contact. At the way she kept her touch light. It shouldn't have meant anything, but for a man starved of the smallest comforts and pleasures since he'd lost everything, it hit harder than he'd expected. And he liked it—her touching him. "You noticed my bruise patterns?"

"Isn't that what partners are for?" Jocelyn moved to retreat, only he wasn't ready for the withdrawal. "To notice each other's wounds and then poke and prod at them?"

Baker caught her wrist, tracing the edge of gauze across the back of her hand. Warning speared through him. Because just as he'd found himself reliving the worst seconds of his life back at the station, Jocelyn had her own regrets. Of not being there for her husband when he'd died. One touch was all it'd taken to send her running, and he didn't want that. For the first time in ages, he couldn't stand the thought of being alone. "I'm pretty sure if I prod your wound, you're going to bleed out."

Her breath hitched. "That's possibly the most romantic thing anyone has ever said to me."

A laugh took him by surprise, and he released her. A frenzy of feeling rushed into his hands, as though his body had been craving the feel of her skin.

"I'm glad you brought me here." She threaded an escaped strand of hair back behind her ear. Such a soft thing to do in light of all the weapons and armor she wore. A welcome contradiction to everything he thought he'd known about her. "I can tell how much you love this home."

"Home." The word tunneled through the drift-like haze clouding his overtired brain, but he forced himself to focus on the present. "Back at the station you said it takes years for lieutenants like Marc De Leon to rise up Sangre por Sangre's ranks, that the organization tends to protect them because of what they know. The cartel provides their lieutenants security, income, even compounds. But that they aren't untouchable."

"Yeah," she said. "There have been times when the lieutenants let the power and ego go to their heads. They take on their own agenda and use cartel resources as their own personal arsenal. I've seen it before. The soldiers—no matter how far they are up the ladder—are usually punished by upper management."

"You mean executed." He latched on to her arms as the burn of anticipation sparked beneath his skin. "If our theory about who planted that bomb at the station is right, that means the cartel ordered Benito Ramon to destroy evidence De Leon killed that woman. They know he stepped out of line, but they haven't put him down. Why?"

Jocelyn shifted her weight, the first real sign that the day was getting to her as much as it had to him. "I don't know. It makes sense they'd want to tie up that loose end before it unraveled their operation. Unless…he actually was ordered to kill her."

"We need De Leon to give us the name of the bomber." Releasing his hold on her, he tried to put everything he understood about the cartel into play. "And I think I just figured out a way to get Sangre por Sangre to stop protecting him."

Chapter Six

Life was starting to feel like a box of cookies.

Some she couldn't wait to bite into. Peanut butter. A really soft chocolate chip. Maybe a homemade Oreo. Others she'd always leave in the bottom of the tin. Peppermint. Orange. Even worse, orange peppermint. And this plan had an aftertaste that left a horrible bitterness in her mouth.

Jocelyn shoved the SUV into Park about a quarter mile from the house and cut the lights. It wasn't difficult to uncover Marc De Leon's home address, especially for Alpine Valley's chief of police. But being here—without backup—in the middle of the night pooled tightness at the base of her spine. She'd gone up against the cartel before. Using one of their lieutenants to flip on a bomber they believed to be the Ghost wasn't going to end the way Baker hoped.

"I don't see any movement or lights on in the compound," she said.

"Doesn't mean he's not there." A battle-ready tension she'd noted during the flashback that'd ambushed him at the station bled through his hands.

This was a bad idea. "Baker, I know you think you have

to do this to find whoever blew up your station, but Socorro has ways of getting that information without—"

"Without what? Getting their hands dirty?" The muscles in his jaw ticked in the glow of the vehicle's control panel. "Not sure you know this, but most police work isn't done from a distance with unlimited resources and military equipment. Most of my job is climbing into the sandbox and uncovering the next lead myself. Marc De Leon is our best chance of confirming Benito Ramon is the Ghost, and I'm not leaving until he does."

Baker didn't wait for her response and ducked out of the SUV.

Damn it. He was going to charge in there with or without her. Maybe even get himself shot. Or worse. Jocelyn followed his silhouette to the front of the hood, then moved out of the vehicle. Taking on the cartel—no matter the angle— had only ever ended in blood. She wasn't going to let him walk in there unprepared. "Then you're going to need some of those resources."

Rounding to the cargo area, she punched the button to release the door. She flipped the heavy black tarp back to expose the full range of artillery at her disposal.

"You've been driving around with this back here the whole time?" His low whistle preceded Baker's hand reaching for the nearest weapon—an M4 automatic rifle. "I could have you arrested for some of these. You know how to use all this?"

Nothing like witnessing shock and awe when confronted with the fact the woman driving you around could do more than bake cookies. "It's all legal. Socorro operatives are licensed and trained with a variety of weapons. There isn't anything in this trunk I don't know how to handle." She gestured to the M4. "You'll want to be careful with that one. The trigger is sensitive. Extra magazines are closer to the back seat."

He collected what he could carry. "Why do I get the sense you've been holding out on me?"

"Funny coming from a man who's referred to me as a mercenary on more than one occasion." She armed herself with an extra magazine for the pistol holstered on her hip. More wasn't always better. Despite all of the resources and gear available, Jocelyn trusted herself over a gun in any situation. Because that was all she could count on at the end of the day.

"Yeah, well, I might have changed my mind over the past few hours." Baker threaded one arm through the gun's strap and centered the weapon over his sternum, barrel down like the good officer he was supposed to be.

She hauled the tailgate closed and locked the vehicle. Couldn't take the chances of someone else getting their hands on her gear. "You mean after I kissed you?"

"That helped." He seemed to be trying to steady himself with a few deep breaths. "You ready?"

"You really believe the only way to get to the Ghost is through De Leon?" Because the moment they crossed that property line, Sangre por Sangre would consider their visit an act of war. He had to know that.

He nodded. "Yeah. I do."

Her gut trusted his answer. It'd have to be good enough for her. She handed off a backup vest. "Then I'm ready."

They moved as one, keeping low and moving fast along the worn asphalt road. According to satellite imaging, the cartel lieutenant's property sat on the edge of a cliff looking down into Alpine Valley, though she could only see the front of the compound from here. Thin, modern cuts of rock, pristinely stacked on top of each other, created a seven-foot barrier between them and the main house. Hopping over the fence at one of the distant corners was the smartest strategy, but Jocelyn couldn't dislodge the warning in her gut. Like they'd be walking right into an ambush.

They each pulled back at the gate and scanned the interior of the compound. Heart in her throat, she stilled. No floodlights. Or any movement from a guard rotation. No signs of life as far as she could tell. Not inside the house, either. This didn't make sense. The cartel wouldn't leave their lieutenant unprotected. "There's no one here."

She set her palms against the gate and shoved. Metal hinges protested as the heavy structure swung inward. Something wasn't right. No security-conscious cartel operative would leave the gate unlocked. Jocelyn caught sight of a security camera mounted above her left shoulder, but the LED light wasn't working. Was the power out?

Baker paused before crossing over the threshold. "Guess that makes our job easy, then."

She didn't trust *easy*, but they didn't have a whole lot of choice here, either. She crossed beyond the gate. Every cell in her body ratcheted into high alert. Waiting for…something.

Thick fruit trees branched out from their line along the driveway and clawed at her exposed skin and hair as she headed for the front door. Pavers and old-world exposed beams created a feeling found nowhere else other than New Mexico. Drying chilis hung from beside columns built of the same stone as the wall they'd bypassed. Black sconces—unlit—stood as sentinels on either side of a wood double door. Marc De Leon was out on bail, but this place was a ghost town as far as she could tell.

"I don't like this," she said.

"I'm starting to understand what you mean." Baker nudged the toe of his shoe against the front door. It swung inward without much effort. "Ladies first?"

Once they stepped into the house, there was no going back. No reason she could give to Ivy and the rest of the team for explaining why she'd breached a cartel lieutenant's home without authorization.

Jocelyn centered the man at her side in her line of vision, but the shadows were too thick here. All she could see was that look on his face as he'd stood helpless in the middle of the station, caught up in the horrors his mind craved to process. It spoke of how little he'd let himself feel since losing his sister. His life had stopped moving forward that day the cartel had come calling. She could see it in the way he pushed everyone away, including her, in the way he committed himself to finding any angle, any strategy to catch Sangre por Sangre in the smallest infraction.

"You believe the Ghost is responsible for Linley's death." She wasn't sure where the thought had come from, but it explained a lot. Why he wanted to keep their little operation off the books, why he was so determined to get to De Leon.

Baker didn't answer, and he didn't need to. She already knew.

"Stay behind me." She unholstered her weapon and took that step over the threshold. For Baker. There was no end to the war raging in her head, but she could help him win the one in his. "Whatever happens, I want you to get yourself out alive. Socorro will help."

He didn't bother arguing. Of the two of them, she was by far the most trained, and they both knew it. Jocelyn tried to force her senses to catch up to the darkness, but all she could make out was a window detail cut into the entryway wall ahead of her. They were dead center in a long hallway, cut off from seeing the spaces straight ahead. This would be the perfect angle for an ambush—unprotected on either side. But nobody jumped out from the shadows.

Moonlight punctured through the windows to her left, and she found herself stepping across dark-colored tiles in that direction for a better layout of the house. The entryway hall ended abruptly, revealing an oversized living room on the other side. This place was massive. Well over twenty thousand square feet. There was no way they'd be able to search it quickly. She memorized the configuration of individual sitting chairs and sofas. Untouched. Everything in its place.

"Where is everyone?" Jocelyn slowed her path through the living room to the kitchen visible through another window cut out at the end of the room. Her heart threatened to beat straight out of her chest as her reflection cast back at her from the large mirror angled over a stone fireplace spanning the entire wall.

A significant part of her work in the military and Socorro was based off being able to predict and anticipate the needs of those around her, and she'd jumped at the opportunity to take on Baker's personal demons instead of facing off with her own. But something wasn't right here. "We need to get out of here."

"Not yet." He made a move for the second entry into the living room, weapon raised. "He's here. He has to be here."

Baker was going off script. They were supposed to stick together. They didn't know what waited inside the house. They could be walking into a trap. Her brain grabbed for frantic imagines of her husband as Baker disappeared down the hall. Of Miles's head supported by that silky white pillow in the casket. Of the wrinkle she couldn't get out of his suit no matter how many times she'd tried. Of Baker's face replacing that of her husband's.

Jocelyn tried to suck in enough air to wash them out. It worked, but the pressure in her chest refused to let up. Holding her back. "Baker, wait."

The sound of shuffling cut through the darkness somewhere out of reach of her current position. She squeezed her sidearm between both hands. At the ready. Clearing the dining room, she moved into the kitchen. Another sitting room was attached to this space with a second set of furniture and a fireplace. She scanned every inch, but Baker wasn't here. "Damn it."

A breeze tickled the hairs on the back of her neck. She turned to face an open patio door.

And the silhouette waiting in the dark.

"Oh, good. You found the place."

A gunshot exploded.

Just before the pain took hold.

THERE WEREN'T ANY gunshots in his nightmares.

A groan worked through his chest. Baker eased onto his side. Cold floor bit into his skull and shoulders. Hell, his head hurt. A waft of smoke dove into his lungs and threatened to send him right back where he didn't want to be. Standing in the middle of his barn, taking in the aftermath of what the cartel had done.

He pressed one palm into the floor—no, this didn't feel like ceramic—trying to get his bearings. He rolled onto his back. And met nothing but a starry sky. Dirt infiltrated his clothing and worked under his fingernails. He was outside. The smoke was coming from his uniform. He blinked to try to get his brain rewired. The last thing he remembered was being inside the compound. How the hell...

"Jocelyn?"

"Is that her name?" an unfamiliar voice asked. "Sorry to say I didn't ask before I pulled the trigger."

Baker's instincts had him reaching for the weapon strapped against his chest. Only it wasn't there. He went for his service weapon. Empty. He rolled onto one shoulder, unable to get his hands under him. He'd been bound. Zip ties. The vest he'd borrowed from Jocelyn was suddenly much heavier than he'd estimated. His belt was gone, too.

Using his weight to his advantage, he got to his feet. Agony ripped through his head, and he doubled over before stumbling a couple feet and hitting what felt like a cactus with one hand. The sting spread faster than he was expecting.

"You're going to want to take it easy. Can't imagine two concussions in twenty-four hours will be a walk in the park." Movement registered from his right. Or was it his left? Hard to tell with his brain in a blender. An outline solidified as a vehicle's headlights cut through the night. "I'd apologize for the theatrics, but your showing up here left me with little choice."

Baker shielded his eyes against the onslaught, dead center in the headlight's path. His head pounded in rhythm to his heartbeat. The logical part of his brain attempted to catalogue distinguishable features of the man in front of him, but the added light only made it more difficult. "Who the hell are you?"

"That's not what you really want to ask me, Chief." The outline set himself against the front of the hood of what looked like a pickup truck. Similar to Baker's.

The headache was easing. Not entirely, but enough to recall he'd been ambushed the second he'd stepped into the hallway of Marc De Leon's compound. His fingers curled into the center of his palms to counter the heat flaring up his spine, but he couldn't keep the growl out of his voice. "Where is Jocelyn?"

"Inside." A slight shift of weight was all Baker managed to take in with the amount of space between them. "I'm not sure if she's still alive, but in all honesty, I needed her out of the way. To get to you."

Still alive? Panic and a heavy dose of rage combined into a vicious cocktail that had Baker closing the distance between them. "You better pray she's alive."

Something vibrated against his chest.

He froze, grabbing for whatever was lodged against his rib cage.

"That's close enough, Chief." The figure ahead took his own step forward. An LED light lit up the man's hand, and another vibration went through Baker. "You know what this is?"

Son of a bitch.

"I'm going to guess it's not a box of chocolates." Baker

was forced to back off. He was still wearing the vest Jocelyn had lent him, but it'd been altered. Turned into a weapon rather than a protection, and he was instantly reminded of the woman Marc De Leon had tortured and killed. With a vest just like this. Packed with explosives. A touch of a button—that was all it would take for the bomber to finish what he'd started.

"Let me guess," he said. "You set the bomb in my station."

The man raised his hands in surrender, all the while pinching that little detonator between his thumb and palm. "To be fair, I didn't expect you to make it out of there. Otherwise I wouldn't have had to go to all these lengths."

"You're the Ghost. Sangre por Sangre's go-to bomber. Sixteen—well, now seventeen—incidents over the span of two years. All this time, we've been thinking a man named Benito Ramon was responsible, but that was just another alias, wasn't it? Marc De Leon." The bomber he'd been looking for. Who'd set the device that'd brought down his future and killed his sister. Undeniable grief and rage flashed through every fiber of his being. He dared another step forward. The vibrating intensified in warning. "You took everything from me."

"I never liked that name. The Ghost. Always gave too much credit where none had been earned." De Leon straightened, matching Baker in height. The lack of accent was telling. Baker had always found it out of place during their interrogations. Not born and bred from within Sangre por Sangre, but an outsider. A hired gun. A true mercenary who killed on orders and walked away with his pockets all the heavier. "But since we're getting to know each other, here's what's going to happen. You're going to get in the truck, and when I push this button, you're going to be blown to pieces and lefts for Albuquerque's bomb squad to put back together, and we can all live happily ever after."

Not a chance. "If this was your pitch to Ponderosa's chief of police, I gotta tell you, it needs some work."

"Let me ask you something, Chief." De Leon inched closer, within reach, though the headlights made it impossible to decipher the bomber's features out here in the pitch black. "When you found your sister's body, what was the first thing you did? Scream? Cry? Or did you just stand there staring at her, trying to find some semblance of the woman she'd been beneath all that burnt skin?"

A tightness in his throat threatened to wrench away his control. Baker pressed his wrists against the zip ties until the edges cut into his skin. "Shut your damn mouth."

"You think you're the only one who's lost someone to Sangre por Sangre?" De Leon lost a bit of aggression in his voice. "My friend, you don't know what pain is. They might've taken your sister, but you didn't have to watch her suffer. You didn't have to hear her screams while they held you down and made you watch as she begged for you to help her. You got off lucky."

"Lucky. Right. You know what? I do feel lucky." The fire that'd been driving him since finding Linley bound with a flaming tire around her neck threatened to extinguish itself. No. The man in front of him was not an ally, and Baker sure as hell didn't trust a single word out of his mouth. "You've obviously been keeping tabs on me. Knew I'd be here, looking for the man who could give up the Ghost. You might have even connected the dots. My sister was killed by the cartel with a device just like the one the bomb squad recovered. Stood to reason this incident might be connected to hers. Hell, you even called me by my first name. Like we're friends."

De Leon didn't answer, as though sensing the rising flood churning inside of Baker.

Baker took a step forward, ignoring the vibration from the device pressed against his midsection. "You probably think you know me pretty well. My habits, my motives. Who I've talked to, how I spend my free time. But do you know why I took the job as Alpine Valley's chief of police?"

"Wasn't hard to fill in the blanks," Deo Leon said. "Anyone with half a brain can see you'd want to use your authority to get to the cartel."

"See, now that's where you're wrong." Baker strained against the zip ties. "I took the job because I was afraid of what I'd do to the man who killed my sister and burned down my barn with her horses inside when I found him."

He took another step forward. "So you're right. I am lucky. I didn't have to wait my entire life hunting for you." Baker pressed his knuckles together and snapped the zip ties in one clean break. "You were stupid enough to come after me yourself."

De Leon's laugh penetrated through the low ringing in Baker's ears. "That's quite the speech, Chief. I like the theater with snapping the zip ties, too, but you're forgetting one thing." He raised the detonator between them.

"You think that little black box scares me?" Adrenaline dumped into Baker's veins. Out here in cartel territory there were no rules, but time didn't bow down to anyone. Jocelyn was injured, possibly bleeding out, and the longer he faced off with the ghosts of his past, the higher the chance she didn't make it out of this alive. He grabbed on to the bastard's collar and dragged him close. "As long as you and I are together, you won't pull that trigger. You'll just end up killing yourself in the process."

Baker cocked his arm back and rocketed his fist forward.

De Leon dodged the attempt, then again as he threw a left. "You don't want to do this, Chief. It's not going to end the way you think."

The momentum thrust Baker into the hood of the truck.

"You know what? I think I really do." He spun back, ready for an attack, but it never came. Frustration and an overwhelming sense of desperation to make this right burned through him faster than the flames had singed his skin at the station. Shoving off the truck, he aimed his shoulder into De Leon's midsection and hauled the son of a bitch off his feet.

They hit the dirt as one.

And an explosion lit up the desert.

The compound was engulfed in a dome of bright flames, black smoke and hurling debris less than a quarter mile away.

"No." De Leon pried himself out from Baker's grip and shot to his feet. "I was talking about your partner."

A fist slammed into Baker's face. Once. Twice.

Lightning struck behind his eyes as a burst of heat expanded out from the blast site, paralyzing him at the realization that someone he cared about had been lost to the cartel all over again.

Chapter Seven

Raisin cookies that looked like chocolate chips was one of the main reasons she had trust issues.

Jocelyn hurled herself through the open patio door.

Barely conscious, she let herself get sucked beneath the surface of the outdoor pool as a wave of flames splintered out from the house.

The explosion punctured deep under the water and pressurized the air in her lungs and ears. Bubbles raced upward from all the nooks and crannies of her gear and tickled her skin along the way. Chlorinated water drove up her nose and into the back of her throat, but she wouldn't inhale. No matter how much her body wanted to.

A submersive shift reverberated through her as debris rained down from above. Covering her head as best she could, Jocelyn tried to wait it out, but she hadn't caught a full breath before going in.

Something heavy hit the water.

She forced her head up just before a section of the compound's protective wall sank directly over her. She kicked as hard as she could against the pool's bottom to get out of the way, but her gear held her down. The wall landed on her right ankle. Her muted scream echoed in her own ears as the wall's weight crushed down on the bones between her foot and calf.

Wrapping both hands around her thigh, she pulled as hard as the bullet wound in her shoulder allowed. Flames lit up the surface of the water and highlighted strings of blood floating out of the wound. She'd been hit. Now she was pinned beneath the pool's surface and running out of air. An entire pool of water battled for domination as she pulled at her leg again. The pain spiraled down into her toes and suctioned a larger percentage of air.

The harder she fought, the sooner she'd drown. Debris settled in the bottom of the pool, and she grabbed for something—anything—she could use to wedge beneath the stone wall. Dirt and rock dodged her attempts to placate her survival instincts. Fire flickered above her as the remnants of the house settled.

Her heart thudded too hard at the base of her neck. Each pulse beat stronger than the one before it until she was sure her chest might explode from the effort. Jocelyn pressed her hands to her vest, searching her own gear. The pain in her chest was spreading. Panic sucked up oxygen in the process. Black tendrils encroached on her vision as her fingers hit something heavy in her belt. Her baton. It was all she could think of.

Frantic to make the agony stop, she ripped the tactical baton free. With too much force. The steel slipped from her grip and disappeared into the inky darkness beneath her. Pinching her eyes closed, she tried to feel for it but met nothing but the coarse coating used to protect pools from cracking. It scraped against her knuckles and lit up her dying nerves.

Her toes had lost feeling. The sensation was spreading up into her ankle and taking hold, but she couldn't let herself pass out. The moment she gave up, her body's automatic functions would kick her lungs to inhale. She'd drown within seconds. No. She had to find that baton.

Seconds slipped through her fingers as she stretched her wounded arm. Her fingertips hit something cylindrical and heavy in the initial pass, but it slipped out of reach. The bullet had torn straight through her shoulder. If she could just extend a bit more—

Unimaginable pain ricocheted through her arm and into her neck. She lost the last reserves of air in a silent scream, sinking deeper. She tried to leverage her free foot beneath her, but the angle was all wrong. She had no strength here. Groping for the baton a second time, she couldn't ignore the crushing weight pressing against her chest.

She was out of time. Out of options.

Jocelyn fought against the drugging pull of heaviness and kicked at the section of wall on her foot. It wouldn't budge. This couldn't be it. This couldn't be how she was going to die. Because she hadn't really given herself a chance to live.

The days, weeks and months after Miles's death had been spent in pure survival. She'd shut down the part of herself that could connect with others on a cellular level while outwardly portraying a woman who was trying to pull her team together. Truth was she'd gone numb inside a long time ago. But the past twenty-four hours had given her a purpose. Something—no, someone—to focus on. A puzzle to solve. One she wasn't ready to give up on yet.

Jocelyn leveraged her free foot into the bottom of the pool and shoved off with everything she had left. It would have to be enough. The last few air bubbles shook free of her clothing and escaped to the surface as she forced her arm against the torn muscles.

Her fingers brushed over the top of the baton.

She wrapped her grip around the solid metal and extended it to its full length. There was a chance the steel would crumple under the weight of the wall, but she had to try. She wedged the tip alongside her trapped ankle and, using both hands, forced her upper body to do something impossible.

The wall shifted upward.

Feeling rushed back into her foot, and Jocelyn dragged her leg free. Relief didn't have a hold on her as the weight of her vest and weapons countered her one-handed strokes. Her insides were eating at themselves, the lack of oxygen shutting down organ after organ in an attempt to save energy for her heart, brain and lungs.

The very same armor she'd donned to protect herself would be what killed her in the end. Jocelyn tore at the shoulder of her Kevlar vest and loosened its hold. Its familiar weight was lost to the darkness creeping along the bottom of the pool. She couldn't think, couldn't remember what she had to do next. Her boots felt too tight. They had to go. She let go of the baton and pulled her backup magazines and weapons from her pockets.

In a last attempt at survival, she kicked at the bottom of the pool. The momentum carried her upward with the help of one hand grabbing onto what felt like a thin ladder.

She broke through the surface. And gasped.

Her chest ached under the influx in oxygen. Jocelyn clung to the side of the pool. Exposed skin was instantly assaulted by heat from all sides, but she couldn't convince her body to move. Someone had shot her and left her for dead. It was only when she'd regained consciousness on the floor of the kitchen that she'd noted the thin wires strung throughout the exposed rafters of the house. The ones connected to a similar device Albuquerque's bomb squad was currently trying to piece back together.

Only much larger and a whole lot more complicated.

If she hadn't woken when she had…

Jocelyn clawed her upper body over the edge of the pool and collapsed—face down—onto debris-ridden cement. Chunks of stone and what used to make up Marc De Leon's compound bit into her face. Hell, she hurt, but she couldn't stop now. "Baker."

He'd been in the house with her. But had he made it out alive?

Dragging one knee beneath her, she pressed herself up. The compound was burning right in front of her eyes. Embers raced toward the sky with thick clouds of smoke.

A rumble vibrated underneath her, and thin cracks split the cement beneath her hands. "Oh, no." The compound sat on the edge of a cliffside looking over Alpine Valley. If the explosion had been strong enough…

Jocelyn shoved to her feet. Her balance failed, and she stumbled into a low wall that'd somehow managed to survive the blast.

This whole area was on the verge of collapse.

They had to get out of here.

"Baker!" She forced one busted foot in front of the other.

Making out the remnants of what was left of the kitchen, she maneuvered around a turned-over hood vent and crossed into a house on its last legs. An exposed beam crashed off to her left and decimated the fireplace from the sitting room off the kitchen. Old tile flooring threatened to trip her up as she tried to re-create the layout of the house in her head. She'd lost Baker somewhere between the main living space and the bedrooms on the other side of the house.

"Baker…can you hear me?"

No answer.

Her heart stuttered at the thought of finding him in this mess. The house groaned under its attempt to stay standing, but another rumble threw her into a half-failing wall between the kitchen and dining room.

"Baker, we have to get out of here!"

Smoke chased down her throat and silenced her voice. No amount of coughing dislodged the strangling feeling of nearly drowning in a cartel lieutenant's pool. Glass and rock cut into the bottoms of her bare feet as she launched herself down what used to be the hallway.

He had to be here.

"Where are you?" Covering her mouth and nose with her soaked T-shirt, she stumbled through the house's remains, but there was no sign of him.

Except… She pulled up short of the hallway leading to the bedrooms. He must've turned left out of the living room when she'd gone right. Because there, in the middle of a section of broken tile, flames were in the process of melting something shiny and gold. Something familiar.

Her breath left her all at once, as though she were back beneath the surface of the pool. Trapped. Deprived. In agony. She grabbed for a piece of charred wood and knocked the police badge out of the flames. But no amount of staring at it changed the dread pooled in her gut. Jocelyn searched the surrounding hallway as another groan escaped from the home's bones. "No. No, no, no."

There was no point in denying it.

The chief had been inside the compound when the bomb detonated.

A POINT WAS coming where his head wouldn't be able to take much more.

Baker pulled his chin away from his chest. Pain arced down his spine as he dragged his head back. His skull hit something soft. Cushioning. Prying his eyes open, he stared out over his truck's dashboard. A hint of gasoline added to the burn of smoke in his lungs from earlier. Must've spilled some the last time he'd gassed up.

Pins and needles pricked at his fingers and forearms, and he moved to adjust. But couldn't. Two sets of cuffs slid along the curve of the steering wheel. "What the hell?"

It took a few seconds to kick his senses into gear. This was his truck, but he hadn't driven out to the middle of the desert… Jocelyn had.

Fractures of fire, an explosion and the hole in his chest tearing wider jerked him into action. Baker wrenched against the cuffs, digging the metal into the skin along his wrists. He always carried a set of handcuff keys on him. He went for his slacks, but the chains linking the cuffs refused to give. Just short of reaching his pocket. Pressing his heels into the floor, he tried to lift his hips to his hands, but it was no use. The seat had been moved farther up than he'd set it at.

A warm glow flickered through the pickup's back window, and Baker centered himself in the rearview mirror. Flames breached outward from what used to be Marc De Leon's compound. The structure was caving in on itself, lit up by dying fires. "Jocelyn!"

She'd been in the house. She might be hurt, suffering. He wedged one hand against the other and tried to slide the opposite cuff free, but it wouldn't budge. The son of a bitch who'd knocked him out had known exactly what he'd been doing. Baker thrust his upper body forward and licked the skin around the cuff on his right hand. Anything to get the damn thing off.

The Kevlar vest he'd borrowed from Jocelyn hit the steering wheel.

A muted beep issued from somewhere inside the fabric.

Baker's heart threatened to stop.

He pinched his elbows together, trying to get a view down the front of the vest, but it was too dark inside the cabin of the truck. He was still wearing the device. He hadn't gone through a whole lot of bomb training, but he knew any movement on his part—any shift in his weight—could set it off. Giving the bastard who'd ambushed him exactly what he wanted—Baker dead.

A flare burst from the scene behind him, and a thousand tons of grief and rage and loss knotted in the spot where his heart used to reside. He hadn't been there for his sister when she'd needed him the most. He wasn't going to sit here and lose Jocelyn, too.

Baker knew every inch of this truck. The Ghost had most

likely stripped out the weapons and obviously had gotten hold of his keys, but the bastard wouldn't have been able to search every hiding place. Baker just had to figure out a way to get to them.

He tried to bring one foot up to leverage against the dashboard, but there was no room between him and the seat. Tugging one hand toward the center console, he jerked his wrist as hard as he dared. But the cuff wouldn't break. There was only one way out of here, and it would come with a lot of pain.

"You can do this." He had to. For Jocelyn. He'd sworn that day in the barn that he would see this through to the end, but he couldn't do that without his partner. No matter how incredibly frustrating her positivity and enthusiasm and outlook on life was, Jocelyn had somehow buried beneath his armor and taken over. They'd survived together. That meant more to him than anything else he'd known with his own deputies. Baker threaded one hand into the smallest opening on the steering wheel, grabbed hold of it with the other and set his head against the faux leather. "You can do this."

Taking a bracing breath, he pulled his wrist against the steering wheel frame with everything he had. The crunch of bone drilled straight through him just before the pain struck. His scream filled the cabin and triggered a high-pitched ringing in his ears. Every muscle in his body tensed to take the pressure off, but it didn't do a bit of good. Baker threw his head back against the headrest. "Damn it!"

The cuff slipped over his hand. Lightning and tears struck behind his eyelids as he drove his broken hand between the driver's side door and seat. The panel came away easily, and he pulled a backup set of truck keys from the hidden space. Along with a handcuff key. Exhaustion and pain closed in fast, demanding he shut down, but Baker wasn't going to stop.

Not until he knew Jocelyn was safe.

He made quick work of the second cuff and shoved the truck key into the ignition. The speedometer wavered in his vision, and he felt himself lean forward as the metric dashboard lit up. He paused just before the engine caught. What were the chances De Leon hadn't rigged the vehicle to blow as a backup plan?

Baker released his hold on the keys and stumbled from the truck. He couldn't risk it. Cacti and several acres of dry, cracked earth were all that stood between him and his partner. He took that first step. The device packed into his vest registered a beep. Then again as he took another step. Every foot he added between him and the truck seemed to anger whatever was packed against his ribs.

He clawed at the Velcro securing him inside the heavy material, but the damn thing wouldn't release. Warning shot through him. His entire nervous system focused on getting out of the too-tight armor while valuable seconds ticked away.

The house was crumbling a mere eighth of a mile away, and he couldn't hear any kind of emergency response echoing through the canyon below. He was all Jocelyn had. His own life be damned.

Baker pumped his legs as fast as they'd allow. His wrist was swelling twice its normal size, but he couldn't think about that. "I'm coming, Joce. Just hang on."

The flames were the only source of light a thousand feet above Alpine Valley. It would be impossible to miss them.

Backup was coming. He had to believe that. He shoved through the front gate barely hanging by its hinges and up the now rippled paved path to where the front door used to sit. Jocelyn had been right from the beginning. They'd walked straight into a trap at his insistence, and now she was going to pay the price.

Just as his sister had.

The beeping coming from his vest kept in rhythm with his racing heart rate. Any second now, it would stop, but he'd do whatever it took to find Jocelyn before then.

The floor shook beneath him as the house fought to stay in one piece. Smoke fled up through the new hole in the ceiling, leaving nothing but an emptiness Baker couldn't shake. "Jocelyn!"

He forced himself to slow enough to pick out a response through the crackling flames licking up walls still standing, but he got nothing. He shouldn't have left her. They'd agreed to stick together because they hadn't known what they were walking into, but uncovering the link between Marc De Leon and the Ghost was the first real lead he'd had in months. It'd consumed him and wouldn't let go.

Now he knew the truth. He'd had the man who'd killed Linley within reach all this time.

Baker lunged back as a beam swung free from the ceiling and crashed into its supporting wall two feet ahead. Embers exploded from the impact and sizzled against his skin.

This place was falling apart at the seams, and unless they got out of here right now, they were going down with it. He shook his head to keep himself in the present. "Come on, woman. Where *are* you? Jocelyn!"

Another tremor rolled through the house.

Only this time, it didn't feel like it was from the walls coming down on themselves. Baker backed up a step, staring at the floor. A myriad of cracks spidered across the tiles. Most likely from the impact of the bomb, but his gut said that last quake was from something else. Something far more dangerous.

His vest hadn't given up screaming at him to get back to the truck, but the incessant beeping had become background noise to everything else going on around him. He took another step backward toward where he'd come in, watching one crack spread wider at his feet. The compound sat at the edge of a cliff overlooking Alpine Valley. This place wasn't just coming down on itself…

It was about to slide right into the canyon.

Panic welded to each of his nerve endings. He searched the rubble within arm's reach, then shot forward to clear as many rooms as he could. The living room, dining room, kitchen, patio—

He caught sight of the pool outside, nearly falling in as desperation to find something—anything—that told him Jocelyn was still alive took hold. That he hadn't condemned her to the same fate as his sister. But it was too dark, and the device's beeping had reached an alarming rate. He couldn't do a damn thing for Jocelyn if he suddenly became spaghetti. "The water."

The devices used in the Chief Trevino's murder and at the station had been triggered by pagers. If he could disrupt the signal, he might have a chance. Baker took a deep breath and launched himself into the pool feet first. The Kevlar dragged him straight to the bottom, and it took everything he had to claw back to the surface.

The beeping had stopped. Relief flooded through him. Whatever receiver De Leon had utilized to trigger the device had failed. Latching on to the side of the pool, he hauled himself to the lip. A footprint gleamed from a few feet away. Bare. No more than a size seven or eight. Jocelyn's?

A crack splintered through the cement in front of him.

A resulting groan registered from the ground. The split shot beneath the water, and a frenzy of bubbles escaped to the surface. Every cell in his body ordered him to move. What'd started as a hairline fracture widened until Baker had to swim to keep from getting sucked down into the cyclone forming in the middle of the pool.

Water drained within seconds, and he stabbed his toes into the wall for leverage. Only he wasn't fast enough to get out. Pain splintered through his broken wrist as he tried holding on to the edge with both hands to avoid getting sucked into the black cavern nine feet below. "Jocelyn!"

His fingers weren't strong enough to hold his weight.

And he slipped.

Chapter Eight

She could give up cookies, but she was no quitter.

Jocelyn pumped her legs as hard as she could. Cacti and scrub brush tore at her soaked pants and threatened to bring her down, but she had to get the SUV.

It was the only way to warn Socorro of what was about to happen.

Tremors radiated out from where Marc De Leon's compound used to stand. The entire cliffside was about to slide into the canyon and wipe out Alpine Valley with it. They had to evacuate. She clamped a hand over the wound in her shoulder to distract herself from the pain, but it was no use. The bullet had torn through muscle and tissue and left her with nothing but a craving to numb out. She couldn't. Not now. Not again.

The SUV came into sight as she charged full force along the dirt road that'd once lead to the compound. Her head pounded in rhythm with her shallow breathing. She was almost there. She was going to make it. Jocelyn might not have been able to save her husband from the suffering and agony, but she could save those people down there.

Hitting the lock release on her keys, she slowed as the

headlights failed to light up. She'd gone into the water. The mechanism had most likely shorted out. She pushed herself harder. Every second it took to get word back to Socorro was another possible life lost when the cliff crumbled.

"Jocelyn!" Her name tendriled through the focused haze. That voice. She knew that voice. It was enough to stop her short of the SUV and turn back to the flaming remains of the house.

"Baker?" A war raged behind her breastbone. He was alive! Within reach if she retraced her steps, but that need to bury the pain of not being there for her husband at his last moments held her incapacitated. Seconds distorted into frozen minutes as the ground crumbled beneath her feet. The cliff was failing. And it would take Baker with it if she didn't do something. Jocelyn cut her gaze to her SUV. It was right there.

But she didn't have time to warn the people of Alpine Valley and get to Baker, too.

"I'll make the choice easy for you." A fist rocketed into the side of her face. "You don't get to save either."

She hit the ground. The wind was knocked out of her as rock and dirt infiltrated the hole in her shoulder. She tensed against the kick headed for her rib cage. Her attacker's boot ricocheted off her kneecap and sent her body into overdrive. Jocelyn shoved upright with one hand. Hugging her injured arm close, she swung with the other. But missed.

"You're a fighter, aren't you?" The back of the bastard's hand swiped across her face. "Can't even be put down by a bullet. I'm impressed but in a bit of a hurry."

Momentum spun her to one side. Blood bloomed inside her mouth where her teeth cut into the soft tissues of her cheek. It took longer than it should have to recover, but she'd already been running on fumes. Adrenaline would only take her so far.

"Who the hell are you?" She stuggled to keep her balance.

"I've gone by a lot of names. Your chief of police called me a ghost." The dark silhouette with his back to the flames advanced. "But to my friends, I'm simply a craftsman."

The Ghost. The same bomber who'd killed Baker's sister?

"Your friends." She'd trained her body not to shut down in the face of danger, but the numbness was already starting to kick in. It cascaded from her fingers into her chest and blocked her ability to stay in the moment. And without that, she was nothing. "Sangre por Sangre."

"I'm curious. What made you think you'd be enough to take on an organization who pays back any strike tenfold in blood, Jocelyn?" he asked.

He knew her name. Had most likely researched her and her team. Read about her past. "Is that what this is? Payback for a Socorro operative destroying the cartel's headquarters?"

"That's a little above your pay grade." He turned his back on her, heading toward the compound. To finish what he'd started with Baker? "For now, walk away while you still can."

"The cliffside is about to collapse. Hundreds of people are going to die if we don't warn them to evacuate." Piercing pain burned through her side. The stitches. She must've torn them sometime in the last few minutes. Something warm and wet battled with the chill of pool water in her waistband.

"Blood for blood, Jocelyn." The bomber barely angled his head over his shoulder as he strode away from her. "The warning is right there in the name. Go home. You're going to need your strength before I'm finished."

Jocelyn dug her thumb into the bullet wound. Her nerves took care of the rest, sending feeling and another shot of adrenaline through her. She couldn't let any more innocent lives pay for her mistakes. Couldn't let Baker die. The weight would crush her.

"No."

She lunged. Grabbing for the bomber's shoulder, she dropped to both knees as he swung to face her and slammed her good elbow into his gut. He took the impact better than she'd expected. Right before arcing his fist into her face.

The world turned upside down as she landed on her chest. Her ribs couldn't take much more before they snapped. Jocelyn stared up at figure standing above her, and the first real tendril of fear snaked into her brain. She was supposed to be stronger than this.

"You really should've quit while you were ahead." He reached for her. "Oh, well. I guess I could use you to my advantage after all."

Jocelyn rocketed her bare foot into his ankle with everything she had. His legs swept out from under him, and she rolled to avoid getting pinned beneath his body. His rough exhale was the only evidence she'd delivered any kind of damage, but she didn't have time for victory to take hold. Spinning on her hip, she secured the bastard's head between both thighs, then locked her ankles together. And squeezed. "I think you've done enough damage for one day."

He dug his fingertips into the soft skin of her legs to get free, but it was no use. His strangled sounds barely reached her ears. She was no longer ashamed of the thunder thighs other girls had teased her about in high school. Soon, they would be what saved Alpine Valley.

"You...need me." The bomber tried to pry her knees apart. Then lost consciousness.

Jocelyn unlocked her ankles from around each other and shoved back. He lay motionless on the ground, but the rise and fall of his back said she hadn't killed him. She thrust herself to her feet and ran for the SUV. Stabbing the key into the door lock, she twisted and ripped the door back on its hinges to get to the radio inside. "Socorro, this is Carville. Do you read? Over."

Static infiltrated the sound of her heart thudding hard behind her ears. She pinched the push-to-talk button again. "Socorro, this is Carville. Please respond."

"Jocelyn, what the hell is going on out there?" Jones's voice ratcheted her blood pressure higher. "There was an explosion at the top of the cliff. We need you to run logistics. Fire and Rescue can't get there in time. Where are you?"

She pinched the radio. "I'm already here. Listen, I don't have time to explain. It was a bomb, and the cliff is going to give out any second. We need to get everybody out of Alpine Valley. Now!"

Jocelyn didn't wait for an answer. She'd done what she could to raise the alarm. But Baker was still inside the compound. Tossing the radio, she pulled a set of cuffs from the middle console. The bomber was still there, lying face down in the dirt.

She centered her knee in his lower back and hiked each hand into the cuffs. "You're not going anywhere."

A burst of flame shot up from one side of the compound. She raced across dry desert as her body threatened to fail. Blood seeped down her leg from the wound in her side, but she wasn't going to stop. Not until she got Baker out of here. Intense heat licked at her exposed skin as she wound through the front gate and back into the collapsing structure.

It was harder to breathe in here. "Baker!"

"Jocelyn?" His voice grew more frantic. Louder. Stronger. "I'm here! In the pool!"

She tried to keep her clothes and hands from brushing against the walls—afraid she'd take down what was left of the structure from contact alone—and cut through what used to be the kitchen.

She froze at the destroyed patio door.

A wide chasm split through where the pool should've been. The water was gone. The chunk of wall that'd pinned her to the bottom of the pool balanced precariously over a mini canyon before falling straight into the darkness. Her mouth dried. Had she been too late? "Baker!"

"Over here!" His voice cut through the panic setting up residence inside her and led her to the edge of the gap splitting the earth in two.

"Just hold on. I'm coming!" The chasm had widened to at least three feet and was growing every second she stood there, but she could make it. She had to. Jocelyn shuffled backward a handful of steps, then launched herself over the unending blackness. Glass and rock cut into the bottoms of her feet as she landed on the other side, but it wasn't enough to slow her down. Reaching the edge of the pool, she thrust her hand down. "Grab onto me!"

Baker's calloused palm grated against hers before it slipped free. He was at the bottom of the pool. Nine feet below her. He had to jump to reach. "You're too high!"

But there was nowhere else for him to go. The shallower the pool, the closer he'd get to the chasm tearing away from the canyon wall. She got down onto her chest, wedging her injured shoulder against the cement. "Come on. You can do it! Try again."

He jumped, securing his hand around hers.

Just as the cliffside gave way.

THE GROUND DISAPPEARED out from under him.

Baker leveraged his toes into the side of the pool, but it was no use. The rough coating merely flecked beneath his weight. He dropped another inch, threatening to take Jocelyn down with him. The pool was gone. Nothing in its place as the earth split in two.

"Hang on!" Her voice barely registered over the ear-deafening sound of destruction as rock, metal and cement gave into gravity. She clamped another hand around his and tried to haul him higher. "I need your other hand!"

He swung his broken wrist toward her, and she latched on. Agonizing pain radiated through his hand and arm. But his scream didn't compare to the compound slipping into the protective canyon around Alpine Valley.

Jocelyn somehow managed to drag him upward, high enough for him to get one foot over the edge of the pool. "Almost there."

Gravel and glass pressed into his temple as he collapsed face-first. Dust drove into his lungs. He fought for breath, but it was useless against the overwhelming tide of grief swallowing him whole. Staring out at the new ridge overlooking the town he loved, he willed the people below to survive. Though didn't know how they would.

"We were too late," he said.

Another tremor rumbled beneath them, and Marc De Leon's compound sank another foot into the ground. The entire structure leaned at an impossible angle, hiking Baker's nervous system into overdrive.

"We have to get out of here." Jocelyn shoved back from the edge of the pool with her hands and feet. No trace of enthusiasm or lightness in her expression, and he needed that slice of inner light. Just a fraction to counter the ramifications of Alpine Valley being crushed by thousands of tons of rock.

Dust kicked up and threatened to choke them both as they launched over the half wall blocking off the backyard from the house itself. Quakes seemed to follow their every step as they maneuvered around the perimeter of the compound. A gut-wrenching tremor divided the front of the house away from the back. The ground lurched beneath them, and Jocelyn fell into him.

"I've got you." He kept her upright as best he could while trying to stay on his own two feet. The chasm that'd split the pool in half had grown. There was no way to jump it, but they still had a way out. "We have to go over the wall. I'll give you a boost."

She didn't wait for an explanation as he bent down to clasp her foot. Blood stained his hand as he hiked her against the wall. Jocelyn turned back for him from the top, offering one hand. "Watch out!"

The ground shifted, knocking him off his feet. The cavity cutting through the backyard was inching toward him.

They were out of time.

Baker fought against the weight of the Kevlar vest packed

with explosive and lurched upward. He caught Jocelyn's forearm, and together, they hauled his weight over the wall. But they couldn't celebrate yet. The crack in the earth was spreading. Darting right toward them.

They rolled off the top of the wall as one. Only Jocelyn didn't land on her feet. The thud of her body registered harder than it should have.

"Come on, Carville. We've got to move. This place is coming apart at the seams."

"I think I broke something." Her voice tried to hide the pain she must've been feeling, but he didn't miss it. Something was seriously wrong. Hell, she'd already survived two explosions. How much more could he possibly ask of her?

"Hang on to me." Out of breath, Baker threaded his broken wrist beneath her knees and dragged her away from the barrier crumbling two feet away. Meant to be a protective guard between the compound and the outside world, every stone was swallowed as the cliff broke away from the canyon wall.

The last remnants of the compound slipped over the edge as Baker collapsed with Jocelyn in his arms. The bomb had destroyed more than a single home. There had to be hundreds buried under rubble and dirt below. His heart strained to rip out of his chest as he considered the loss of life of the very people he'd sworn to protect. "It's gone. All of it…is gone."

"I'm sorry. I tried to warn them." Jocelyn framed one hand against his face. Cold and rough. Nothing like when she'd kissed him. Her voice wavered. "I…radioed my team…"

Her hand fell away, and every muscle in her body went slack.

"Joce?" He scanned her face in the bright moonlight. Then realized she was no longer wearing her vest. And noticed the blood. Wet, glimmering against her clothing. Oh, hell. The echo of a gunshot in his head rendered him frozen for a series of breaths.

Baker laid her across the desert floor, ripping at her T-shirt. There was a hole in her shoulder. She'd taken a bullet but somehow still managed to get him out of the compound in one piece. How was that *possible*? And where the hell was Maverick when Baker needed him? "Talk to me, Goose."

He couldn't think about all those lives down there in Alpine Valley with Jocelyn needing him right now. Struggling to his feet, he hauled her against his chest and started walking toward the SUV. Her added weight wiped his strength from him, and Baker collapsed to one knee.

Two bombs. Losing a fight to a cartel bomber. A device strapped to his chest. And now an apocalyptic event that'd destroyed everything he had left. All within twenty-four hours. He wasn't sure he could take much more, but he wouldn't leave Jocelyn out here to fend for herself. She'd saved his life. The least he could do was return the favor.

Baker bit back a groan when pain singed through his nerve endings as he regained his footing. A hundred feet. That was all he had left before they reached the SUV. They were going to make it. They had to. Because they'd survived too damn much to give up now. "We've got this."

But every step seemed to put them farther away from the vehicle. Or maybe his mind had finally started shutting down from all the explosions going on around them. His clothing suctioned to him with Jocelyn's body heat furnaced against him. "Just a little farther."

He stepped on something that didn't belong. Metallic and light. Too far from the blast area. Maneuvering his partner out of the way, Baker made out a pair of cuffs lying there in the dirt. Open. Warning triggered at the base of his spine, as though he were being watched. Marc De Leon had left Baker for dead inside his own truck, but even though the son of a bitch's plan failed, that didn't mean this was over.

He set sights on Jocelyn's SUV. He couldn't trust his own instincts right then, but something was telling him getting in that vehicle would be the end of them both. Emergency crews would have their hands tied trying to dig residents out of the landslide. The SUV was the only way to get Jocelyn help in time. Baker took another step toward the SUV.

The explosion lit up the sky.

Heat licked over his skin and knocked him back on his ass. His head snapped back and hit the ground harder than he expected. Blinding pain became his entire world right then, and Jocelyn slipped out of his hold. It took too long for his senses to get back in the game despite his desperation to keep moving.

The threat wasn't over. He had to get up. Had to keep fighting.

Baker risked prying his eyelids open. The crackle of flames was too bright, too loud. His brain was having a hard time processing each individual sound, mixing it up with the pop and crack of those that'd burned down his life.

Jocelyn's hand moved to touch his between them, a simple brush of skin-to-skin. The past threatened to consume him from the inside. He felt as though he were about to leave his body, but the grounding feel of her kept him in one place.

Light reflected off her dark pupils as she set sights on him. The smile he'd once resented tugged at her mouth. "I've…got you. Always."

Adrenaline drained from his veins and brought down his heart rate as black webs spidered in his peripheral vision. Baker secured his hand around hers, and the constant readiness and vibrations running through him quieted for the first time in years. Because of her. "I've got you, too, partner."

Bouncing bright lights registered from over Jocelyn's shoulder. Flashlights? Baker couldn't be sure as he tried to force his body to move, but none of his brain's commands were being carried out. He'd given his fight-or-flight response permission to take a break, and now it would take a miracle to come back online. He gripped Jocelyn's hand harder. Then again, he was starting to believe in miracles. "I want an entire tray of cookies after this."

"Done." Her smile weakened as she slipped back into unconsciousness.

Heavy footsteps pounded against the desert floor. Closing in fast. Baker rolled to one side, ready to protect the woman who'd nearly given her life for him. It took every ounce of strength he possessed to get to his feet. Then he raised his fists. He'd take on the entire cartel if it meant getting Jocelyn out of this alive. The bouncing flashlights merged into one. His brain was playing tricks on him, but he wasn't going to back down.

"Chief, is that you?" Jones Driscoll slowed his approach, a flashlight in one hand and a weapon in the other. Utter disbelief contorted the man's expression. Hell, Baker must've looked a lot worse than he'd thought.

The combat controller holstered his weapon and pressed his hand between Jocelyn's shoulder blades. "She's still breathing. Damn. You two sure know how to throw a party. What happened out here?"

"You mean apart from the fact a Sangre por Sangre bomber just destroyed an entire town in a landslide?" Baker stumbled back as the fight left him in a rush. His knees bit into the ground beside Jocelyn. "She saved my life."

Chapter Nine

Today would be a cookie dough day.

Because the beeping was back. The sound she hated more than Maverick's howls in the middle of the night. She was back in a hospital. Jocelyn lifted one hand, though something kept her from extending her fingers completely. She fought the grogginess of whatever pain medication the staff had put her on. Her breathing came easier when she couldn't feel, but it wasn't permanent. It couldn't be.

A low growl vibrated through her leg. Then something familiar. A metallic ping of ID tags. She turned her hand upward, fisting a handful of fur. "Maverick."

He was here. And pinning her to the bed with his massive weight. The German shepherd licked at her wrist before laying his head back down, and Jocelyn summoned the courage to force her eyes open. Only this time there were no bright fluorescent lights or bleached white tile to blind her.

She wasn't in a hospital.

Instead, black flooring with matching black cabinets encircled the private room. Socorro's medical wing. The overhead lights had been dimmed, and the beeping, she just realized, was definitely not as loud as it could've been.

"Thought you could use some time together after what happened." Baker's voice pulled her attention from her K-9 partner to the man at her left. Dark bruising rorschached beneath one eye and across his temple. There were other markers too—cuts and scrapes that evidenced what they'd been through. Though the splint around his wrist was the most telling of them all.

Jocelyn didn't have the will or the energy to try to sit up. "How long have you been sitting there watching me sleep?"

"About six hours." Baker got up from his chair positioned a couple feet from the side of the bed. "Dr. Piel—is that her name?—patched me up nicely, and hey, no waiting to get looked at. I think I might switch providers. Do you know if she takes my insurance?"

"I'm afraid she only sees private patients." Her laugh lodged halfway up her throat, stuck in the dryness brought on by aerosolized dirt and debris and ash. But there wasn't any pain—which, now that she thought about it, shouldn't have been possible.

Not as long as she'd been given the right painkiller.

Jocelyn followed the IV line from the back of her hand to the clear baggy bulging with liquid above her. Morphine. Dr. Piel wouldn't have known. Nobody in this building knew. She moved to disconnect the line from the catheter, but the moment she pulled it free, the pain would come back.

Maverick lifted his head, watching her every move. Not unlike Baker. He was intelligent, focused and observational. No one in their right mind would choose to go through unending waves of pain after what they'd been through rather than numb out with painkiller. Weaning herself off the meds now would only raise suspicion. And she couldn't deal with that right now.

"You okay?" Concern etched deep into the corners of Baker's mouth. "Do you need me to get the doctor?"

"I'm…fine." She tried recalling the events leading up to her arrival back at headquarters, but there were too many missing fragments. "Tell me what happened."

"Well, your warning worked." He moved to the side of the bed, sliding one hand over her wrapped ankle. The thin gauze around the joint said she hadn't broken it as she believed. More likely a hard sprain. "Socorro was able to evacuate nearly everyone who might be impacted by the landslide. Though that didn't stop the canyon wall from caving in. You saved a lot of lives, Joce. Without you, Alpine Valley would be in rough shape. Well, rougher shape."

Joce. He hadn't called her that before. It made her want to believe they were more than two people thrust together in the aftermath of a bombing, but her heart hurt at the idea. Of tying herself to someone else. Because when that tie broke—as they inevitably did—she would be right back in the dark hole she'd spent so long trying to climb out of. Just like she'd done after Miles's death. Her stomach twisted into one overextended knot. "Were there any casualties?"

"Not a single one." He shook his head, a hint of wonder in his voice. "You and your team, as much as I hate to admit it, really saved our bacon. Thank you, Jocelyn. For everything. If I hadn't rushed to find Marc De Leon, maybe none of this would've happened, and I'm so sorry for that."

"He killed your sister, didn't he?" she asked.

"Yeah. He did." Baker scrubbed a hand down his face, a habit he'd picked up on whenever he wanted to avoid a tough topic. It was a defense mechanism. Avoid the question to avoid the feelings that came with it, but it didn't make the hard things go away. At least, not in her experience. "I thought we would find De Leon and get him to identify the Ghost, but the explosive he packed into my Kevlar vest turned out to be the same blueprint for those used to kill Jane Doe three months ago. I had him, Jocelyn. All this time. I just didn't connect the dots."

Jocelyn bit back the urge to remind him of her warning before they'd gone into that house. A Sangre por Sangre lieutenant's compound had been attacked. The cartel would only take the event as an act of war. Sooner or later, they'd learn Alpine Valley's chief of police and a Socorro operative had been there, and then... The crap would really hit the fan. It was only a matter of time. "But?"

"I was so sure of myself, going in there." He shook his head again, much more aggressively as though to dislodge the theory altogether. "But something is off. The man we fought... He told me I didn't have to watch my sister die right in front of me, that I was spared that horror as she burned. Made it seem like he'd gone through all that himself. That he'd lost someone, too."

"Cartels like Sangre por Sangre experience infighting all the time. Hostile takeovers, executions for not following orders. Dozens of people have died in their attempts to claw to the top of the ladder." Her heart hurt. Which didn't make sense because the morphine was supposed to numb her from her scalp to her toes.

Jocelyn fisted her hand back into Maverick's fur. She needed to get out of here. To not be forced to stay still. To get her hands in some dough. "Or maybe, after everything you've been through, you want what he said to be true. Maybe, after all this time, you've been looking for someone who's been through the same thing you have."

"You could be right. Maybe everything he said out there was just another way to mess with my head. Unfortunately, Marc De Leon is in the wind. Nobody, not even his attorney, has been able to get a hold of him. The prosecutor is trying to go through the cartel, but it's looking like we've hit a dead end." He blew out a frustrated breath. "So far, he's managed to detonate three bombs without leaving much of a trace. From what I can tell, he was planning on blowing me up just like he blew up Ponderosa's chief of police."

Baker took up position at the side of the bed, the mattress dipping beneath his weight and triggering a low growl from Maverick. "Cool it, Cujo. I got you out of your crate."

She scratched behind Maverick's ear. As much as it'd annoyed her in the minutes leading up to the explosion at the station, she found Baker's nicknames for the German shepherd the exact kick to get her out of the spiral closing in. "One of these days, he's going to make you wish you'd called him by his real name."

"One of these days?" Surprise glimmered in Baker's dark eyes and tendriled through the numbness circulating through her body. Hard to imagine a man like Baker being surprised by anything, but she'd somehow managed. "Does that mean you're not tapping out of this investigation?"

Jocelyn pressed her shoulders into the pillow to distract herself from the unpleasant thoughts waiting for a clear path through her mind. She'd fought them off this long. She could do it a while longer. She just had to concentrate and paste another smile on her face. "Hey, that guy blew me up, too, remember? I have as much a personal stake in this as you do."

"How do you do it, Jocelyn?" His voice dipped into a near whisper. "How can you stay so positive after everything that's happened?"

It was his turn to walk straight past the barriers she housed herself inside. Pinching the hem of the thin white sheet beneath her thumbnail, she sifted through a thousand answers in search of the one that would change the subject as quickly as possible. But her threshold for pain, for loss, for defensiveness had been reached long before they'd walked into Marc De Leon's compound. "It takes a lot of effort. A lot of forcing myself to look for silver linings on stormy days."

"Then why do it?" he asked.

"Because if I don't, I'm afraid of who I'll become." She'd been on the morphine too long. It was inhibiting her internal filter. "I'll go back to who I used to be. Hollow. Terrified of feeling anything real. I'll shut down, and without the sarcasm and baked goods, movie nights, Christmas parties and trying to bring the team together, I'm afraid they're going to realize I don't have anything to offer. No reason to keep me around, and I want to stay, Baker. I need to be part of the team. Socorro's team. Otherwise, I'll go back to…"

No. She couldn't. She couldn't give up that piece of herself. Not to him. Not to any of them. Nothing good had come of it before.

"Back to what?" Yet even as he spoke the words, he seemed to accept she wasn't going to answer that question. Baker interlaced his fingers with hers. A vicious scrape had scabbed over between his thumb and forefinger, arousing the nerves in her hand. "You run logistics for your entire team. You made sure soldiers got what they needed overseas. You fight for towns like Alpine Valley to get the resources they need in a crisis. I've seen it. You're vital to this operation." He swallowed hard. "If it wasn't for you, I'd be dead right now and half the people of this town would be buried under a landslide. Whatever you're afraid of, you're stronger than you think you are."

She wanted to believe him, with every ounce of her being, she wanted what he said to be true. But that alone didn't make it reality. Jocelyn watched as another drop of pain medication infiltrated her IV line. "That was before."

His thumb skimmed over the top of her hand. "Before what?"

Closing her eyes, she lost the battle raging inside and let her eyes slip closed. "Before all I cared about was being numb."

JOCELYN HAD BEEN cleared to recover in her room.

Mid-morning sunlight infiltrated through the floor-to-ceiling window at his back and cast his shadow across Socorro's dining room table. Baker wasn't sure how long he'd stared at his own outline, willing his brain to produce something—anything—that would give him a clue as to where Marc De Leon had gone. And his motive for wanting him dead.

He replayed the bastard's words in his head too many times to count, until he wasn't sure which thoughts had been his own and which had belonged to the bomber. Baker leafed through Albuquerque's scene report from the initial bombing at the station. Nitroglycerin packed into a pipe bomb. De Leon obviously didn't care about the impact of his chemicals on the environment, but Baker couldn't actually name a cartel soldier who did. Newspaper dated over the past two weeks had been used as filler, but pulling fingerprints had been impossible.

The bomber had been careful. Most likely worn gloves. A brand-new car battery had been used to spark the initial charge, and the device had been triggered by a pager. In line with the other sixteen incidents accredited to the Ghost, including the bombing on Baker's property. Though he was looking at another dead end there. The company who'd manufactured this one had gone out of business years ago. A relic. No way to trace the purchase, and the number of the damn thing was registered to an unending list of dummy corporations. "Why trust an old piece of technology when you could get your hands on something guaranteed to go off?"

Why take the risk? Baker had been asking himself the same question for over two hours in front of a dozen crime scene photos scattered all over the dining room table. He'd helped himself to one of the prepared meals Jocelyn was known for—this one lasagna and a heavy helping of garlic bread and a citrus salad he hadn't touched yet. But no matter how much food he packed into his stomach or how many minutes he sat there with his eyes closed, the answer refused to surface.

The trill of dog tags cut through the headache building at the base of his skull. He was running on fumes, and he knew it. Awake for more than twenty-four hours. Hell, he shouldn't have been able to walk, but this was important. Cutting his attention to the German shepherd perched to one side, Baker bit back his annoyance. Maverick had followed him from Jocelyn's room. Though he couldn't think of a reason other than Baker had access to her food. "Are you allowed to eat from the table?"

Maverick cocked his head to one side and licked his lips. The K-9 really was something now that Baker got a look at him. Lean, healthy, warm brown eyes. It was any wonder Jocelyn had fallen in love with him, but how they'd ended up together was as big a mystery as why Marc De Leon had blown up his own compound.

Jocelyn worked logistics for the military. No reason for her to come in contact with explosive ordinance on tour. Which made Baker think they'd met through some other means.

"You protect her, though. That's why you nearly bit my hand off at the station."

Maverick pawed at the floor.

"You want to bite my hand off right now, don't you?" Baker collected his fork and took a stab at a section of lasagna, then offered it to the dog.

The shepherd licked the entire fork clean. Overhead lighting caught on the mutt's ID tags, and Baker got his first real look at them. "Those aren't military tags."

Maneuvering his legs out from under the table, he stretched his hand out. A warning signaled in Maverick's chest, and Baker stilled. No show of teeth, though. That was something.

"I'm not going to hurt you. Just want to look at your tags," he said. "I promise to stop calling you Cujo if you promise not to bite me while I do that. Deal?"

He inched forward again, slower this time. His fingers

brushed against course black and brown fur at Maverick's neck, and the shepherd closed his eyes in exhilaration. The dog's tongue made an appearance as Baker targeted the area he'd noticed Jocelyn scratching in the med unit. "There. See? We're friends. You like that?"

He kept up the scratching with one hand and brought the other to the tags to read the stamped lettering: "Maverick. Federal Protective Service. Miles Carville."

An invisible sucker punch emptied the air out of his chest. More effective than any bomb he'd survived thus far. "Your mama wasn't the only one who lost someone, was she?"

Maverick's whine almost convinced Baker the dog had understood him. It made sense now. Jocelyn's husband had worked for the Department of Homeland Security, and when he'd died, Maverick would've been forced to retire, too. The relationship between handler and K-9 took years to cultivate, from the time the German shepherd would've been a puppy. Maverick wouldn't have responded to anyone else and ultimately would've become useless for the team once Miles Carville had died. But Jocelyn had kept him, literally kept a piece of her husband that followed her into the field and slept in her room at night. That protected her when it counted. "Damn, dog. I think I might be jealous of you."

"That's possibly the weirdest sentence I've ever heard in my life." Jocelyn leaned against the wide entryway into the kitchen, and hell, she was a sight for sore eyes. A few visible cuts here and there, but nothing that could take away that inner brightness that'd gotten him through the past day and a half.

His gut clenched at how much pain she must've been in. "You're supposed to be resting."

"Girl's gotta eat, doesn't she?" She limped into the dining room and dragged the chair beside his out from beneath the table with her good arm, then took a seat. "Besides, it's hard to sleep when you know the bomber you arrested in the middle of the desert got away. You find anything in Albuquerque's report that might give us an idea of where De Leon might've gone?"

Maverick moved in to be at Jocelyn's side, marking his territory. Funny—Baker felt inclined to do the same. To erase all the times he'd been such an ass to her over the past few months and give her a reason to feel again.

"Not a single clue." They were back at square one. "Bomb was pretty simple. Nitroglycerin explosive, a fresh car battery to initiate the spark, but there's one thing that doesn't make sense."

She reached over the crime scene photos and grabbed for what was left of Baker's dinner. "What's that?"

"The receiver was an old pager," he said.

Three distinct lines deepened between her brows as she sat a bit straighter. Warm brown eyes, almost the same color as Maverick's caramel irises, scanned the photos he'd set across the table. Setting down the fork, she picked up one image in particular. A photo of a motherboard. No transmitter on the once leprechaun-green chip. Just a receiver.

"You're right, but it fits with the Ghost's preferences," she said. "Harder to trace, maybe? Was the bomb squad able to recover a registered number?"

"Not yet." It was easy to look at her and see the wheels turning. To know she was taking that incredible amount of knowledge she'd gleaned throughout her life to try to figure out why De Leon wanted him dead. Why after all this time, the Ghost had come back to haunt him.

Baker couldn't help but smile as she silently read something to herself. Despite her claim to have as much at stake in this game as he did, that simply wasn't true. She was here for him, and thank heaven for that. Otherwise he'd be at the bottom of that landslide or burned to the driver's seat of his truck. "They're still working through—"

"Let me guess. Dozens of shell companies." Leaning back in her seat, she took a bite of lasagna. Hints of exhaustion still clung beneath her eyes and in her slowed movements. Every shift in her body seemed to aggravate the corners of her mouth, but she wouldn't admit it. She'd never want him to know she was in pain, but not just that. There was something else she wasn't telling him, something she'd held back in the medical suite. Because she still didn't trust him. "I'm starting to feel like I've been here before."

"Chief Trevino's murder." Baker lost the air in his lungs. "Yeah. I had the same thought. By the way, Maverick licked that fork."

Jocelyn let the silverware hit the table. The metallic ping put a dent where it'd landed on the pristine wood, and understanding hit. There were no other dings in the table because nobody used it. All this time, he'd assumed Jocelyn's efforts to bond the team over Christmas breakfasts, birthday parties and family dinners had succeeded.

But the table said otherwise. She'd said she needed to be part of the team. Socorro's team. That she was afraid they'd have no use for her. Because nobody cared as much as she did. No one else made the effort like she did. She needed her team. Needed friends. A physical connection to this world.

"In that case, enjoy the rest of your food." She pressed away from the table, her long, ebony hair sliding against her back. "I'm going to get something from the fridge."

He'd never seen her like this before. The sight was surreal, as though he was witnessing the real her. Not what she wanted everyone to see. Not the logistics coordinator or the former solider. Just Jocelyn. Or, hell, maybe he'd hit his head a lot harder than he'd thought.

Baker tracked her into the kitchen, keeping his feet moving to close the distance between them.

"Don't say anything about how a dog's mouth is cleaner than mine." She wrenched open the refrigerator door between them and pulled a large metal bowl covered in plastic wrap, identical to the one he noted earlier, from inside. Discarding the wrap, she set the bowl on the counter and threw open a drawer to her left. She drove a spoon straight into what looked like a giant bowl of cookie dough. "I don't lick my own butt or chew on my feet."

"Good to know," he said.

She shoved an entire spoonful into her mouth and seemed to sink back against the counter, completely at ease and absolutely beautiful.

Baker shut the refrigerator door and took the spoon from her hand.

Just before he crushed his mouth to hers.

Chapter Ten

A balanced diet consisted of a cookie in each hand. Or in her case a spoonful of dough.

But having Baker pressed against her was pretty damn fulfilling, too.

Her chest felt like it might burst open, and Jocelyn did the only thing she could think to do. She gave up her hold on the spoon. Sugar, butter, flour and a hint of peppermint spread across her tongue, but this wasn't the gross kind of peppermint. It was Baker. Kissing her. Deep and hard.

And she kissed him back. With every ounce of herself she had left. Because she felt something. As though she could breathe easier, like there was a life outside of her trying to force friendships and combating danger, secrets and grief. Despite all his sharp edges and barbed words, Baker's mouth was soft and determined and capable of washing the violence and fear out of her, leaving her utterly and completely defenseless against the past.

His hand found her waist, just shy of the wound in her side. He was being careful with her, didn't want to cause her any pain, but life never guaranteed there wouldn't be pain. Just that it had to be worth living.

Baker eased his mouth from hers, rolling his lips between his teeth. "Is that the cranberry-lemon dough you've been trying to get me to try?"

"Yeah." Her breath shuddered out of her. Uncontrollable and freeing. She'd only kissed one other man in her life. She and Miles had been high school sweethearts, marrying straight out of basic training before he'd gone to work for the Department of Homeland Security. He had always been able to knock her for a loop, but this… This was something she hadn't expected. Easy. And she desperately wanted easy. Free of fear and grief and expectation.

"It's really good," Baker said.

Jocelyn worked to swallow the taste of him, to make him part of her. The effect cleansed her from the inside, burning through her and sweeping the last claws of the past from her heart. She'd loved her husband. Deeply. And she should've been there at his last moments. But punishing herself day after day didn't honor him. That wasn't the kind of legacy he deserved. "It's even better when it's baked."

"Not sure it could get much better." Baker pressed his mouth to hers a second time, resurrecting sensations she'd forgotten existed. His hands threaded into her hair as though they both might fall apart right there in the middle of the kitchen if he didn't.

A profound shift triggered inside of her, reminding her she was more than a grieving widow, more than an operator for the world's best military contractor. More than her mistakes and flaws. Baker Halsey reminded her she was a woman. One who still had a lot of living to do. Here. In Alpine Valley. "You have no idea what I'm capable of."

A laugh rumbled through his chest and set her squarely

back in the present. They'd just made out in Socorro's kitchen, in plain view of anyone who might've walked by. Jocelyn pressed her fingertips to her mouth to keep the smile off her face, but the effort proved in vain.

"Are you going to run away again?" Baker added a few inches of distance between them. "You know, like after I touched you."

"What? No." Her brain scrambled for the words to describe what she'd felt when he'd kissed her, but she was still wrapped up in the heat sliding through her. "This… Things are different between us now than they were then. And that kiss…" Jocelyn scanned the hallway just outside the dual-entrance kitchen. "It was not unpleasant, sir."

"Oh, good. 'Cause I'm a little out of practice. Other than when you kissed me back at the station." The tension in his shoulders drained, and right then she couldn't help but think another invisible scale of his armor was shedding before her eyes. "I didn't hurt you, did I?"

The reminder shot awareness into the wounds and threatened to break whatever this spell was between them, but she didn't feel any pain. There was still a hint of morphine left in her body that would take a few hours to burn off. Blissful numbness that only Baker seemed to penetrate.

The thought pulled her up short. She'd lost her ability to feel because of the loss of one man and had sworn never to go back to that shell of a life. What would happen if she lost another?

Jocelyn forced herself to step back to give her brain a chance to catch up. It was the painkiller throwing the promises she'd made herself out the window. It'd stripped her of her internal fight, but she couldn't lose herself now. Not with a bomber on the loose. "Has Albuquerque PD recovered anything from the landslide?"

They'd been so caught up in trying to locate Marc De Leon, she'd let her focus be pulled in a thousand different directions. The cartel lieutenant had been charged with murder by Alpine Valley PD. The bomb planted in the station had destroyed any evidence the prosecutor could leverage against him. Though it was starting to look like De Leon was working his own agenda, they couldn't overlook a direct tie to Sangre por Sangre.

"Not yet. I've got my deputies trying to help when they can, but that's hard when they're stuck working out of the rec center. Seems those volleyball players aren't as nice as they look when it comes to sharing the building." Baker slid his hands into his jeans, and it was only then she realized he'd changed out of his uniform. So this was what he looked like outside of his job.

A laugh escaped. But this time it wasn't forced. It took her a few seconds to comprehend that unremarkable detail. Everything about her had been forced over the past two years…everything but this. "I guess it's a good thing you're stuck here with me, then."

The humor drained from his expression. "I'm not stuck, Jocelyn. I'm choosing to be here. With you. Because you're a good partner, and you deserve to have a team that supports you. Not out of obligation, but because they want to."

"What makes you think I wouldn't get that from Socorro?" If she had a tell, it would be all over her face right then. Uncomfortable pressure lit up inside her chest to the point she wasn't sure if her next breath would come without physical orders.

"The dining table." Three words that didn't make sense on their own but drilled through her harder and faster than the pain she'd run from. Baker reached for her, and an engrained shift had her accepting that touch. Needing it more than she'd needed anything ever before. "You talk about brunches and birthday parties. Thanksgiving and dinners together. Movie nights and all those types of things. But there isn't a single scratch or ding in that table except the one you just put there a few minutes ago."

Her mind raced for memories of Cash, Jones, Scarlett, Granger, even Ivy, having her back. "We're military. We watch after each other. No matter what."

"But which one of them would talk to you about your husband, Jocelyn? Which one of them would jump into the fray with you if the bullets weren't flying?" he asked.

And she didn't have an answer.

"I know you're hurting more than you let on. I know what lengths you have to go to to find the silver lining in all of this, but did you ever consider all you're doing is constantly escaping?" His words punctuated with experience she didn't want to recognize. They weren't the same. They hadn't been through the same experiences, but there was a line of connectedness she felt with him. A shared loss that linked them more than she'd ever expected. "Sooner or later, your positivity isn't going to be enough. Your mind and your body are going to force you to process everything you're running from, and you're going to need someone to be there for you."

Truth hit her center mass. He was right. She knew it, and maybe her desperation to bring the team together had been out of some kind of preparation for what waited on the horizon, but it wouldn't be today. Today they had a bomber to find.

Jocelyn straightened a bump in his T-shirt collar with her uninjured hand. "And here I thought you were nothing but a grumpy cop who'd rather save the world alone rather than trust anyone again."

His smile cracked through the intensity of the moment. "Yeah. Well, I guess you surprised me, too."

"Thank you. For having my back out there." She slid her palm over his heart. "And in here."

"You got it, Goose." His gaze locked onto her, and it took her a few moments to remember what it felt like to be fully grounded in the moment. To feel Baker's pulse beneath her hand, his warmth and strength. It was almost enough to bury the shame of the past. Almost.

"Not sure if you know this," she said, "but most women don't like nicknames that relate to overly loud pests of the sky."

"You can't expect Maverick to fly without his wingman." He motioned to the shepherd currently serving himself the rest of Baker's lasagna on his hind legs.

She was going to regret letting him have cheese. "Isn't Goose the one who dies?"

"Yeah, well. Eventually." He was trying to backtrack, and Jocelyn was going to let him keep digging that hole just to watch him squirm. It was endearing and human. Like a reward for all of her hard work to break through that tough shell over the past few months. "But they had a good run."

"If you two are done feeling each other up, we've got a problem." Jones Driscoll rounded into the kitchen, a tablet clutched between both hands. The scar running through his left eyebrow dipped lower as he scanned the screen. "Albuquerque's bomb squad is in the middle of going through what they can dig out of the landslide and what's left of your SUV. So far, they're convinced all three bombs were designed and detonated by the same bomber."

And just like that, they were thrust back into reality. Jocelyn severed her physical connection from Baker. "I'm wondering if you know what *problem* means, Jones?"

"They found a body," the combat controller said.

Baker cut his attention to Jocelyn, and her entire body lit up at the hundreds of possibilities of who else had gotten caught up in this mess. "There wasn't anyone else at the scene. We searched the entire compound."

Jones handed off the tablet. "Then you missed someone."

Jocelyn scanned through the report, horrified as a positive ID matched the burnt remains photographed at the scene. "Marc De Leon. I don't understand. He was the bomber. Why would he go back into the house?"

"He didn't. The coroner is examining the remains as we speak." Jones swiped the screen to bring their attention to a close-up of the body. "According to her, Marc De Leon was dead at least four hours before the bomb detonated."

Baker slumped against the counter. "Then who the hell is trying to kill us?"

IT WASN'T POSSIBLE. He'd been face-to-face with De Leon. He'd talked with the son of a bitch.

But there was no arguing with forensics. Baker had scoured through sixteen bombing reports a dozen times. Didn't change a damn thing. The man he'd wanted for his sister's murder was already dead.

He swiped steam from the mirror. No amount of hot water and soap had cleaned the gritty feel of ash and dirt on his skin, but it'd somehow managed to calm him enough to start thinking clearly.

What the hell had he been thinking to sign up for this job? To believe he could make a difference in people's lives? That he could protect the very town that'd welcome him as one of their own? He didn't have any prior experience. He'd never been through the police academy or basic training. Hell, he'd had to teach himself how to hold and fire a weapon from the internet, a secret that would die with him. He'd taken the chief of police position mere weeks after Sangre por Sangre had burned everything he'd loved to the ground, and the world had been so black and white. All he'd had was a promise. To protect Alpine Valley when no one else was stepping up to the plate.

But now... He wasn't the man for this job. And revenge wasn't enough anymore. Cartel raids, two-faced deputies, dead bodies, bombs going off everywhere he stepped—it combined into an undeniable sense of failure. He hadn't been able to stop any of it. And now the only light he'd found at the end of the tunnel had been snuffed out. He'd stepped into the middle of a war that had no end. Day after day, Sangre por Sangre and organizations like it were gaining power all across New Mexico—this place he loved more than his childhood home.

Who was he to stand up against a monster like that?

Memories infiltrated the hollowness pressing in on him from every angle. Linley smiling over her shoulder as she took her first ride around the horse ring. He'd never seen her smile like that. Never seen her so damn happy. He'd known then they'd never be able to walk away from the dream they'd built together. That they'd each found what they'd been looking for. In each other, and here, in Alpine Valley.

But it wasn't enough. Not anymore.

Baker made quick work of drying off and changing into a fresh set of sweats one of Jocelyn's teammates had lent him. The T-shirt was a bit too big, though, to the point that he looked like a toddler dressing up in his daddy's clothes. So he tugged it off, mindful of the aches and pains in his torso as he reentered Jocelyn's bedroom.

The space wasn't much bigger than a hotel room, and the dim lighting within it failed to compete with a massive bay windows that looked straight over the tail end of Alpine Valley. The sun had crept into the western half of the sky. The landslide was hidden at this angle, saving him a small amount of torment, but sooner or later, he'd have to face his failure.

Fire and Rescue, the bomb squad and his deputies were going through the rubble. Part of him wanted to be there with them, getting his hands dirty, searching for anyone who hadn't been able to evacuate. But the other part understood the sooner they found the bomber, the sooner this nightmare would end.

"It's not your fault." Jocelyn's voice slipped from the shadows and surrounded him as though she'd physically secured him against her. Warm, soft, accepting. "What happened up on that cliff. Neither of us could've stopped it."

Baker let his gaze settle on the scrap of land that had once held his entire future. "You and I both know we can tell ourselves we aren't at fault. Doesn't make it true."

"That goes both ways, Baker." She took up position beside him, the backside of her hand brushing against his. "We lie to ourselves just as easily."

She had a point.

"I don't know where to go from here." The longer he stared through the window, the less his eyes picked up the small differences of his property. Until he lost sight of the house altogether. "I was so sure I could protect this town, that I could stop the cartel from doing to someone else what they did to me, but I'm just one man. I've got two deputies heading for retirement, one six feet under from collaborating with the cartel, no police station, no dispatcher and a quarter of Alpine Valley under mud, rock and metal."

His laugh wasn't meant to cut through the tension cresting along his shoulders. It was a manifestation of the ridiculousness of that statement. He was supposed to be running a bed and breakfast with his sister, corralling horses, leading tour groups and making the stack of recipes he'd grown up on. And now he'd actually partnered with the very people he blamed for adding fuel to the cartel flames.

Baker half turned toward her. "This is where you tell me to look at the positives and list them out. Because that's the only way I see a way out of this."

"I don't think I can do that." Her voice seemed to scratch up her throat. "Truth is, the longer I'm with you, the more I realize my positivity has been nothing but toxic. For my team, for the people down there relying on us, for Maverick, even. I told myself if I could just focus on the good things going on in my life, they would be enough to drown out the bad, but partnering with you… I don't want to pretend anymore. But at the same time, you're right. There isn't anybody here who would talk to me about my husband, about what it felt like to lose him."

"You haven't told any of them." He wasn't sure where the thought had come from, but he knew it to be truth the moment he voiced it.

"No," she said. "But I'm sure Ivy knows. She runs extensive background checks on all the operatives. It's her job to ensure the safety of the team. It makes sense she would know about the threats each of us carry."

"Grief isn't a threat, Jocelyn." The irony of that statement wasn't lost on him. Because he'd buried his, too. He'd taken everything he remembered about his sister and replaced it with a dark hole that vacuumed up any unwanted emotion so they couldn't hurt him.

"Isn't it?" She faced him, and Baker suddenly found himself missing that wide smile he caught her with every time they'd come across each other in town. "Losing our loved ones altered our entire beings. There are studies that prove traumatic events such as ours physically change our genes and can be passed down through our prodigy. It lives within us, clawing to get free at any chance our guard is down. It waits for just the right moment to sabotage us, and I can't afford for that to happen in the middle of an assignment."

"So you keep it to yourself. Pretend it doesn't bother you." Just as he'd done all this time. Though it was becoming clearer every day he stayed away from the barn that he and his sister had built with their own hands that Linley deserved better. She deserved to be remembered. The good and the bad. No matter how much it hurt. Because living as an entirely different person obviously hadn't worked out the way either of them had hoped. "What if tonight, we don't pretend anymore?"

"What do you mean?" Her hesitation filtered into the inches between them, thick enough for him to reach out and touch.

"I read Maverick's dog tags." Baker skimmed his thumb along her jaw, picking up the slightest change across her skin through touch alone. It was all he needed for his brain to fill in the gaps. As though she'd become part of him. "I know he was your husband's bomb-sniffing dog up until he died. DHS most likely wanted to retire him after your husband's death, maybe even send him to a shelter, but you brought him back home."

Jocelyn didn't answer for a series of calculated breaths. "When Miles was admitted to the hospital for the last time, it was because he collapsed in the middle of an assignment. The cancer had gotten into his bones, and there was no treatment—nothing—that would reverse the damage. Maverick was the one who got him to safety, then lay by Miles's bed until his final moments." She swallowed hard. "He wouldn't obey the commands of any other operatives. It got to the point Maverick became aggressive if anyone came close to my husband's body. Even handlers he'd worked beside in the field, but most especially the nurses. He hated them."

Her laugh slipped free and settled the anxiety building in his chest. "The hospital wanted Animal Control brought in so they could remove the body without getting bitten, but Mile's superior asked them to hold off as long as possible. Looking back, I think Maverick was waiting. For me."

Her voice warbled, but the dim lighting kept Baker from seeing her tears. "He waited there without food, without water or sleep. Protecting the one person who loved him most in the world, and I will always be grateful for that. It's hard to imagine he has any of those same feelings for me, but after Miles died and we were learning to live without him in our lives, I got so sick. To the point I couldn't get out of bed most mornings. I wasn't eating or sleeping or able to live up to my duties. Maverick was the one who pulled me out of the darkness and gave me the courage to take an opportunity we could both benefit from."

"One that brought you to Socorro," Baker said.

"Yeah." She craned her head to one side, presumably watching the German shepherd sleep in his too-small dog bed set up in one corner of the room. "He helped me get back on my feet. Though we both knew we couldn't go back to the way things were. I'd never be able to leave him behind if I got called up, and he couldn't go back to DHS, even with a handler he knew. We both had to figure out a way to move on. Without Miles. And for all the trouble he gives me, I know he loves me, too."

Baker angled his hands onto her hips and dragged her close as a feeling of empathy and desire and attachment burst through him. He notched Jocelyn's chin higher with the side of his index finger and pressed his mouth to hers. "Does this mean I'm competing for your affections with a German shepherd? Because I feel now is the time to tell you I'm not really a dog person."

Chapter Eleven

Today she would live in the moment. Unless it was unpleasant. In which case she'd eat a cookie. Jocelyn stretched her toes to the end of the bed, coming face-to-face with the man tucked beneath the sheets beside her.

Sensations she hadn't allowed herself to feel since her husband's death quaked through her as memories of her and Baker's night surfaced. It'd been perfect. He'd been perfect. Respectful, careful and passionate all at once. They'd held each other long past cresting pleasure and fallen asleep secure in the moment.

She'd done it. Taken that first step toward moving on. For the first time since receiving the news Miles had passed, she felt…liberated. The weight of guilt and shame and judgment had lost its hold sometime between when Baker had kissed her and now. She'd almost forgotten how to breathe without it.

Early morning sunlight streaked across the sky, and while she normally liked to lie in bed to take it in, she couldn't tear herself away from the harsh beauty of the man beside her. The bruising around his temple was starting to turn lighter shades of green and yellow. The tension had bled from his expression. No longer the high-strung chief of police, she was getting a full view of the man beneath the mantle. Just Baker.

Jocelyn traced her thumb along his lower lip, eager to feel his mouth on hers once more. But she'd let him sleep. That seemed to be the only place he felt safe after everything he'd survived. His skin warmed under her touch, as it had last night, and she couldn't help but lose herself in this moment. One where they had permission to be still— content, even. Where the world didn't demand or push or threaten. She couldn't remember the last time she'd just let herself...be. Always afraid the bad thoughts and feelings would find her if she slowed down enough to let them in.

It'd taken a while to figure out that keeping her hands busy and her mind engaged distracted her from the heaviness she carried. It'd been a lifeline for so long, she couldn't actually remember what it felt like to live in the moment. But this... This was different. This was easy. Comfortable. Watching Baker sleep somehow hijacked her brain into believing she was safe here. With him. Her chest incrementally released the defensiveness always taking the wheel, and for the first time in years, she let herself relax. Because of him. Because of his willingness to take on her grief, to share it with her, to lighten the load.

And she'd done the same for him. Listened to his stories about his sister, of the two of them growing up back east and all the trouble they'd gotten into being so close in age. Only eleven months apart. About how once their mother had passed, their father had remarried and started his life over with a new family. Forgetting what he'd already had.

Maverick's dog tags rang through the room.

"Oh, no. Maverick, stop!" Jocelyn tossed her covers and hit the floor to intercept the shepherd. Too late. The overly loud ping of Maverick's bell pierced through the silence. And she froze.

"I'm up!" Baker shot upright in the bed. Every delicious muscle rippled through his back and chest as he reached for the weapon stashed beneath his pillow, and he took aim. At her.

Jocelyn raised her hands in surrender, her heart in her throat. "We're not dying. It's just Maverick. He needs to go out."

"Maverick?" Seconds split between heavy breathing and the pound of her pulse at the base of her neck. His gun hand and weapon collapsed into his lap. "For crying out loud."

"Sorry. I tried to beat him to it." She twisted the bedroom door deadbolt and let Maverick into the hall. He'd find his way outside through one of the dog doors before heading to breakfast with the other K-9s. Closing the door behind her dog, she padded to Baker's side of the bed. "I wanted you to be able to sleep a bit longer."

He leaned back against the pillows, and she went with him. "Well, that's out of the question now."

She settled her ear over his chest as the sun brightened the sky on the other side of the window. Pulling the comforter over them, Baker tucked her into his side until they breathed as one. She felt her heart rate settle back into comfortable territory, as though every cell in her body had attuned to every cell in his. Funny what surviving two bombings and fighting for each other's lives did for a relationship.

A relationship.

She hadn't really considered the words until now. Was

that what this was? When the investigation ended and they had this new bomber—whoever he was—in custody, would they still have this? Or had last night been a one-time moment of comfort?

Ever since she'd lost Miles, she'd been running from this exact encounter. But now, relearning how to be close to someone, relearning how to trust and love meant it could all be taken away. By illness, by betrayal and the kind of work she did. But her soul craved that connection, and denying it would only make things worse.

Jocelyn committed right then. To make this moment last as long as possible. To not let the past infiltrate the present. No matter how much it hurt to let go. "What happens now, Baker? After all of this is done. What do you see happening between us?"

"Guess I haven't given it much thought," he said. "But I want this to be honest. I like you. More than I thought I could like a mercenary." He took her elbow to his gut with ease, his laugh filling not just the room but the empty places inside of her. The ones she'd denied existed. "Truth is, I'm not sure I could go back to the way things were. You on one side of the divide. Me on the other. We're a team. And I want it to stay that way."

A light that had nothing to do with the sunrise flooded through her. Not forced or created out of a sense of survival. Genuine warmth that could only come from one source. Hope.

"Me, too." But he wanted this to be honest. Something she wasn't sure she could reciprocate. Because the moment she admitted her darkest shame to him, she'd have to face it herself. And she wasn't ready to lose what they had. Not yet.

She ran her fingertips up his forearm, to the measure of warped skin spanning from his elbow to his wrist. She sat up, angling across his lap to get a better look. "What's this?"

"A burn scar." His voice scraped along his throat, barely audible. "Got it the day I found Linley in the barn. Most of the structure was still standing by some miracle, but one of the beams failed when I was inside. I tried to protect myself with my arm. Ended up with this piece of art."

"Marc De Leon had scars like this—burn scars. I remember them from his arrest photo." She memorized the rise and fall of the pattern burned into his arm as pieces of the puzzle they'd taken on flirted at the edge of her mind. Her instincts pushed her out of the bed and had her reaching for her rob draped across the end. She cinched it as carpet caught on the laceration across the bottom of her heel and threatened to slow her down, but this was important.

"Yeah. I catalogued them after the arrest. Scars, fingerprints and tattoos. It's standard protocol so we can register him with the National Crime Information Center, but what does that have to do with anything?" The bed creaked under his weight as he sat up.

Jocelyn shuffled through the file she'd put together on the cartel lieutenant. ATF believed Marc De Leon had been recruited as an adult and risen up Sangre por Sangre's ranks in large part due to his proclivity for brutality and following orders to the letter. But he'd made a mistake. He'd killed an Alpine Valley woman three months ago. Jane Doe. He'd stepped out of line. But what if it hadn't been a mistake? What if it'd been a pattern?

She pulled a photo of Jane Doe free from the file, noting charred skin, curled limbs and missing teeth. An entire legacy of violence and death. Marc De Leon hadn't just killed the woman. He'd made her unrecognizable. To everyone but who he'd wanted the message sent to. "When was Linley killed?"

"Two years ago." Baker slipped free of the bed and reached for the sweats piled on the floor. "Why?"

"Cartels like the misery they cause. They use fear and grief and pain to keep towns like Alpine Valley in line and unwilling to turn on them. That's why they came after your sister. The soldiers who burned down your barn and murdered Linley knew you weren't there that day. They wanted you to see what they'd done." She spread out the photos taken of the scene where Jane Doe had been recovered. A tire had been strung around the victim's neck—just like Linley's—but only after a device packed into a Kevlar vest had destroyed her insides. "They wanted you scared and compliant."

Baker stepped into her, his chest pressed against her arm. The contact was enough to keep her grounded but didn't diminish the buzz of anticipation for him to see what she saw in the details. "I'm going to need you to get to your point a lot faster, Jocelyn."

"You thought Linley's and Jane Doe's murders were connected, that they were the work of the same bomber." She handed him the photo of Jane Doe. "With good reason. The Ghost used the same devices, same amount of explosive packed into Kevlar, same brand of tires strung around their necks after the victims were already dead. But I don't think Jane Doe was the intended target. I think the cartel used her to deliver a message."

"Linley was a message for me." He stared down at the

photo so hard she thought he might tear through it with his mind. "And Jane Doe was left for Ponderosa's Chief Trevino to back off. Right before they killed him."

THE PATTERN WAS becoming clearer by the minute.

All this time he'd been hunting the Ghost—a bomber who'd killed not only his sister but an innocent woman—and the bastard had been right in front of him.

Tremors worked through his hands as Baker rushed to dress into his uniform. This wasn't how this was supposed to end. He'd wanted to confront the son of a bitch, to show him all the pain and destruction he'd caused. To punish him. But Marc De Leon was dead. "I had him. I should've seen it before now. If I hadn't been so focused on justice for Linley, I could've saved Ponderosa's chief from…this."

"Marc De Leon didn't want you to see it, Baker." Jocelyn moved to reach out to him but seemingly thought better of it halfway. Hell, she was pulling away from him. After everything they'd worked through last night, he had to go and ruin it. "He was good at what he did."

"Why would someone else blow up my station to destroy evidence against Marc De Leon and claim to be the Ghost?" The question left his mouth more forcibly than he'd meant, and Baker caught himself losing his tight control on his anger. Just as he had after Linley's death. It wasn't him. It was the vengeful demon inside of him, and right now, there was a very thin line holding it at bay as his failures came into account. "How does that make sense?"

She didn't answer for a series of breaths, to the point that Baker sensed she might turn around and walk right out that door. Pinpricks stabbed at the back of his neck. He was on the brink of falling off that edge of reason.

"Tell me how I'm supposed to stay in this investigation when I can't even send the man I've wanted to arrest for two years to jail. What kind of chief of police does that make me?" The tremors were coming less frequent the longer he focused on her. On the way her right shoulder rose slightly higher than her left when she inhaled. The fact that the hair framing her face had a soft streak of lighter color. Baker memorized everything he could about her to keep himself from losing his mind, but he wasn't strong enough to keep fighting. Maybe he never had been. "Tell me what to do next."

"We know someone else is using Marc De Leon's recipe for the bombs. Socorro is trying to track down the sales of the nitroglycerin, but it's going to take time. There are still a lot of construction and mining operations that use it by the bulk. It would be easy for a few measures to go missing from one of the sites." She paused for a moment. "And I've reached out to a few contacts in ATF. They'll follow up with any reports of missing ordnance. Though if they haven't heard of any to this point, it's likely the bomber covered his tracks." Jocelyn took a step closer to him, breaking into his personal space. "Which means he's far more dangerous than we estimated. If we can't figure out how much nitroglycerin is missing, then we can't predict the next attack."

A shiver raced along his spine at the thought. The Ghost—at least, the man he'd believed to be the cartel's resident bomber—had gone out of his way to ensure Baker had been present at both bombings. First at the station when the son of a bitch had destroyed the evidence linking Marc

De Leon to the death of Jane Doe. Then ambushing them at the lieutenant's compound.

He took a full breath. If Marc De Leon was Sangre por Sangre's Ghost, why would another bomber blow up proof he was guilty of murder and then take De Leon out? Had the cartel wanted to tie up a loose end that might admit to sixteen other incidents connecting back to the cartel? "Has there been any response from Sangre por Sangre for what happened at the compound?"

"Now that you mention it, we haven't seen any movement on their part. Cash would've let us know." Jocelyn grabbed for her cell phone, lighting up the screen. "Kind of hard to miss an explosion that almost buried an entire town. It's all over the news. Surrounding towns are sending in aid and raising funds for the cleanup. Jones has been handling the influx in help so we can focus on finding the bomber, while Cash has been keeping an eye on the cartel. You think they're keeping their distance for a reason?"

"Cartel soldiers are arrested all the time. My deputies and I have put the cuffs on more than our fair share, but the response is always the same. No one talks. Because if you give up the cartel, you won't even make it to your cell." Baker was trying to make sense of the thoughts in his head as fast as he could, but there were still too many moving pieces. The man they'd encountered in the desert had described the pain of watching someone he loved tortured and killed in front of him. Had said Baker had been spared. "No. I'm starting to think this is about something else altogether."

"Like what?" she asked.

"Whoever set that device in the station placed it in the evidence room. I think we were right in figuring it was purposefully detonated to destroy evidence in Marc De Leon's murder case." Baker paced across the room, to the window and back. "But how could the bomber have known we'd go to De Leon's compound? How was he waiting for us unless he knew we'd be there?"

"Easy to draw that conclusion once we realized the first bomb had been a means to destroy evidence in the murder investigation." Jocelyn leaned back against the desk built into the main wall of her room. No family photos staring back from shelves. No personal touches added over the course of her tenure with Socorro. This wasn't a home for her and Maverick. It was just a temporary way station until something else came along. "Could be the bomber has studied your protocols, knew you'd want to take up a case this big yourself rather than assigning it to one of your deputies. Especially if he knows what happened in your past. He went out there to set things up and then waited for us."

Damn, he'd missed this. Someone to bounce ideas off of, to solve puzzles with and test his limits. The feeling of partnership. Like he'd had with Linley. Building and working for something greater than the both of them. Sure, his deputies had his back in any given situation. They were there to do their job, and they did it well, but that didn't make them friends. More like acquaintances who sometimes took turns to bring in doughnuts.

But Jocelyn... She was different. She was more than an acquaintance. More than a friend. She was everything he'd needed over these past couple days—and everything he wanted for his life. Who else was capable of looking him right in the eye and telling him he'd been chasing a ghost? Who else surprised him on more occasion than he could count? She was the kind of woman who genuinely put others' needs before her own, just to give them a sense of peace, and hell, if that wasn't one of the most beautiful things he'd ever witnessed. Not to mention the explosive pleasure she'd ignited in him last night. Jocelyn Carville had ambushed him when he'd least expected it, and he never wanted to give her up.

Baker slowed his pacing. "Or the bomber wasn't there for me at all."

"What do you mean? He strapped a device into your Kevlar and handcuffed you to your steering wheel. The only reason you're still standing here is because you figured out how to disrupt the pager's receiver used to trigger the bomb." Confusion was etched above her eyebrows, and with good reason. "He was going to kill you, Baker. He tried to kill both of us, or have you forgotten there was a bullet in my shoulder less than twenty-four hours ago?"

"Because I was in his way." It was the only thing that made sense. "That's why he shot you. We were nothing but obstacles to what he really wanted."

"The Ghost." Her bottom lip pulled away from the top. "Marc De Leon."

"Everything that's happened since that first explosion at the station has been centered around him." A flash of nervous excitement spiraled through him until Baker couldn't stop the words from forming. This was it. This was how they found the son of a bitch. "Sangre por Sangre soldiers are protected on the inside. Alpine Valley PD had evidence Marc De Leon murdered that woman during the raid, but what if a handful of years in prison wasn't enough for our bomber? What if he wanted the Ghost to suffer a hell of a lot more, without protection and with no chance of some defense attorney giving him an easy way out?"

Because Baker had wanted the exact same thing. For the man who'd murdered his sister and burned his world to the ground to suffer. That drive for revenge had been in his head from the moment he woke every morning and was the very last thought on his mind as he ended the day. Everything he'd done had been to make the bastard feel what Baker had felt upon finding Linley in that barn.

Jocelyn shoved away from the desk with her uninjured hand. "He wanted to add you as a notch in the Ghost's belt to double down on the charges. But why destroy evidence in the murder investigation? Why take away a sure conviction and a chance for Jane Doe to get the justice she deserves?"

The truth hit harder than he was ready for.

"Because the death of a second chief of police by the cartel would bring in the big guns." His blood ran cold at the mere suggestion. "One woman killed by one of their soldiers doesn't get much attention except from the people in Alpine Valley. By now, everyone has forgotten about her and moved on with their lives, but if two officers are murdered at the hands of the cartel?"

Jocelyn's expression fell, and damn it, he couldn't deny how much he hated seeing her without a smile. Forced or otherwise. "The feds would have no other choice than to call in every agency on their payroll, including Socorro."

"We've been thinking this is has been a targeted effort. One man trying to kill another, but we were wrong." Baker scrubbed a hand down his face. "The bomber wants to start a war."

Chapter Twelve

She couldn't be a smart cookie with a crumbly attitude.

Jocelyn hauled herself from the passenger seat of the loaner SUV she'd borrowed from Jones. With her vehicle in a million pieces and her shoulder in a sling, she'd have to rely on the rest of team to get her around for a while. Not a comfortable feeling, but she had too many other things on her mind.

Finding a bomber before he launched a war with the Sangre por Sangre cartel, for one.

She let Maverick out of the back seat as she surveyed the scene.

The landslide had been worse than she'd thought. Rain pelted against her face and soaked into the ground. It made balance harder for the volunteer cleanup crew trying not to slide down the new hill and threatened to land her on her ass. Mud, rock, cement chunks and wood framing had flooded through an entire street of homes. Far too many homes had been lost, and now there was nothing left but their roofs peeking out from areas Fire and Rescue had dug out.

This was a disaster in every sense of the word.

It would take months to excavate, and what happened to those families in the meantime? Jones had reported they'd been evacuated before the slide, but where were they supposed to go now?

"You okay?" Baker rounded the hood of the SUV, setting his hand beneath her slung elbow as support.

"My arm is just a bit sore." An understatement of the highest degree. The wound in her shoulder wasn't just sore. It was on fire. The last of the pain medication she'd received in the medical suite had burned off—most likely with help of last night's heart-racing activities—leaving her in a world of pain she hadn't known physically existed. "I'll be fine."

"You sure? Because you look like you're about to fall over." No hint of humor in his voice, which meant she looked as good as she felt. "Why don't you wait in the car? I can check in with the bomb squad alone."

"I said I'll be fine." Frustration had seeped past her control, and an instant shot of shame and embarrassment knifed through her as Baker removed his hand from her elbow. Jocelyn forced that practiced smile back in place. Everything was fine as long as she was smiling. She could do this. Because waiting in the car while the rest of her team and Baker worked this case wasn't an option.

She navigated up a sharp incline to where the rest of the volunteers and the bomb squad had set up a command center under a canvas pavilion. "Let's just see what they've found."

"Sure." He followed on her heels. Not as close as she'd come to expect. He was keeping his distance, and her skin heated despite the drop in temperature down here in the canyon and shade.

She watched her step as she climbed, but every movement took something out of her she couldn't really afford to give up. Agony was tearing at the edges of the bullet wound. Not to mention the stab wound beneath her Kevlar, but she wouldn't let it get to her. She just had to get through to the other side.

Maverick pressed into her leg as though she was about to collapse. Seemed Baker wasn't the only one doubting her capabilities today.

Jones offered her a hand as she summited the last few feet to man-made flat ground and dragged her upward. "Wasn't expecting you to make it out here today. You good?"

"Fine. How's it going here?" she asked.

"The excavators you recruited from Deer Creek and Ponderosa should be here this afternoon." The combat controller pointed out over the ridge that hadn't been put there naturally. "Right now, the bomb squad is digging to recover any other pieces of the device."

Jocelyn angled her head back to take in the view above. She shaded her face against the onslaught of rain pecking at them. A massive chuck of rock had broken away from the canyon wall, leaving the outline of an oversized bite. Her foot sank deeper into the shifting earth. "How long are they estimating the cleanup will take?"

"A couple months at least," Jones said. "The rains make it more difficult, but we're moving as fast as we can. The Bureau of Land Management sent in a geologist. From what he can tell, the threat of more rock coming down on us has passed, but we've been instructed to keep on alert. Just in case."

Shouts echoed off the canyon wall that'd always stood as

a protection to this town, and the pain inside of her intensified. Jocelyn clamped a hand on her shoulder.

Jones's gaze cut to Baker, then back to her.

"Joce, maybe you should take a break." Baker stepped
into her line of vision. "The pain meds Dr. Piel gave you
are in my pack in the car. I'll get you one."

"No." The muscles in her jaw ached under the pressure of
her back teeth. She bit back a moan and squeezed her eyes
tight, waiting for the pain to pass. It didn't, and she couldn't
stop the tears from pricking at her eyes. One deep breath.
Two. The burn receded slightly, and Jocelyn dared to remove
the pressure of her hand. Straightening, she faced both men.
"I don't...need it."

Maverick *gruffed* beside her. He'd always been able to
tell when she was lying.

"All right, then. Captain Pennymeyer is waiting for us
in the command tent." Jones took the lead, cutting across
the makeshift camp.

The sound of shovels, wheelbarrows and heavy breathing
cut through the patter of rain as residents, Fire and Rescue
and two deputies Jocelyn recognized as Alpine Valley PD
worked to dig out the affected houses.

The combat controller held the flap of the pavilion open
for them, revealing a grouping of cops inside. The Albuquerque bomb squad. The man hunched over the laptop in
the center straightened at their approach. His once muscular
frame had gone soft. Too large on top, not enough stability
in his lower half. The effect said while the officer in charge
ran his department well, he wasn't usually out in the field.

"Chief Halsey. I'm Captain Pennymeyer." The bomb
squad's commanding officer extended his hand past Joc-

elyn to meet Baker's. "We've managed to uncover several materials used in the device detonated at your station to compare with those recovered here."

"Grateful to have you." Baker shook before withdrawing. There was an invisible bond between cops and military units. She'd had that once, on tour, but having a captain of the bomb squad blatantly disregard her presence only added to the pulse in her shoulder. "This is Jocelyn Carville from Socorro Security. She saw the device before it detonated inside the compound."

"Then by all means, Ms. Carville, tell me if we got this right." Pennymeyer maneuvered around the standing desk he'd created toward a long table covered in plastic. Pieces of wire, motherboard and mud-coated plastic had been separated and studiously labeled for study. "Your statement said you saw the device tucked up into the rafters of the home. That right?"

Her mouth dried as she took in all the fractured pieces that'd once made a whole. The intricacy and placement of every one of these materials had nearly destroyed an entire town. "Yes."

"Did you see anything specific?" the captain asked. "Were there any wires leading away from the device? A countdown clock, or maybe you caught the branding on the battery before it went off?"

Her mind went blank as pain clawed down her arm and into her chest. She clung to her sling with her free hand as the world tipped slightly. Scouring the table, she tried to make all these tiny pieces fit into a puzzle her brain was desperate to put together. Had she seen the branding on the battery? Heat flared into her face and neck. "I don't…

I don't know. I only got a glimpse of it before I ran for the patio door."

The captain stepped off to one side, and it was only then that she realized a blueprint of Marc De Leon's compound had been tacked to the flexible wall above the table. "Your statement reports you saw the device tucked into the rafters of the kitchen. Is that correct?"

Her heart rate rocketed into overdrive. She'd already been through all of this. The last reserves of her control bled dry. "If you've read my statement, why are you asking me again?"

Silence enveloped the tent, all eyes on her.

She tried to breathe through the pain, but it wasn't working this time. It crescendoed until it was all she felt. Consuming her inch by inch.

Captain Pennymeyer directed his attention downward to his table of explosive goodies. "We're just trying to get the most accurate information, Ms. Carville. It's been known that victims caught in an event like this tend to remember more a couple days after they've had time to recover."

"I'm not a victim." A barb of annoyance poked at her insides.

"Of course. I didn't mean…" The captain's face flushed, and his oversized upper body seemed to deflate right in front of her. "I apologize. I didn't mean any insult. I understand you've been through something quite traumatic."

Baker inched closer. "Will you give us a minute, Captain?" He lowered his voice. "Let's get some air."

She wanted to argue, but being inside the too-small tent packed with cops was getting to her. Cold air worked into her lungs once outside, but she couldn't distract her body from focusing on the throbbing in her shoulder.

Baker set his hand against her lower back, guiding her roughly ten feet from the men waiting for her confirmation that they'd recovered every piece of the bomb that'd brought down the compound on top of Alpine Valley. He pulled out a bright orange, cylindrical container with a white top from his front pocket. "Here. I had Jones grab your pain meds from the car."

Twisting off the cap with his palm, he dragged one of the pills inside free and offered it to her.

Every nerve in her body went on the defense. She took a physical step back. "I told you I didn't want it."

"You'd rather be in debilitating pain while we're here?" He countered her escape, keeping his voice low enough so as not to be overheard by anyone else. "Not sure you noticed, but if you weren't talking to me right now, I'd think you were dead you're so pale. You're having trouble focusing, and you just bit off the head of the guy running this investigation."

She couldn't take her attention off the pill in his hand.

"Joce, everyone in that tent knows you were shot," he said. "None of them are going to think any less of you for taking the edge off."

She shook her head. She could hardly breathe. "I can't."

"What is this? Some kind of punishment for what happened?" Confusion and a heavy dose of frustration had Baker dropping the pain med back into the container. He screwed the top on. "For not being there when your husband died? Is that it? You've convinced yourself you deserve to suffer? You were shot and stabbed by a piece of debris, for crying out loud. I'd say that's enough penance to last a lifetime."

The pain burned through her, and no amount of distraction was taking it away. Jocelyn headed across the cleanup site, the sound of Maverick's dog tags in her ears. Her shepherd knew she was on the brink of going over the edge. "No. It's not like that."

"Then what is it like?" Baker followed. "Tell me."

She turned on him. There was no hiding it. Not anymore. "I'm a recovering addict."

AN ADDICT.

Baker didn't know what to say to that, what to *think*.

He tightened his grip on the medication bottle, his hand slick with sweat. "I don't…" Clearing his throat, he tried to get his head back into the game. "I don't understand. You were on morphine in the medical unit after what happened up there. You didn't say anything."

Jocelyn released her hold on her shoulder, trying to make it look as though nothing got to her. She had a habit of doing that. Pretending. "Dr. Piel doesn't know my medical history. The nurses at the clinic that first time we were caught in the bombing at the police station had my chart. They knew not to put me on anything stronger than ibuprofen."

"You're going to have to start from the beginning." Baker found himself backing up, adding more than a couple of feet between them. "Because what you're saying right now doesn't make sense."

"What more is there to explain?" Her expression fell into something that could only be categorized as hollowness. As though she'd told this story so many times, she'd disassociated from the emotional toll it took. Though from what she'd just said, not everybody knew. "I lost my husband, Baker. I blamed myself for not being there in his final moments. I was getting messages from his friends, his family, calls from his doctor—all asking me why I wasn't there. Because all he'd wanted in his final moments was for me to be by his side, and I let him down."

Baker tried to swallow past the swelling in his throat, but there was no point. "So when you said you got sick after his death, you meant…"

"The pain hurt so much. I tried everything I could think of to make it stop, but nothing worked. The grief was crushing me, and I didn't know what else to do." The heartache was still pressing in on her. He could see it in her eyes, in the way she practically crumpled in on herself. "One night it got so bad, I thought I might hurt myself, but I found Miles's old pain meds in the bathroom cabinet. I took one." Her voice evened out. "All it took was one."

"You started taking the pills more often." Baker studied the orange pill bottle in his hand right there in the middle of what was left of his town. He'd responded to overdoses of all kinds while working this job. Mothers who'd only wanted to be able to do it all with a touch of ecstasy. Teens who started sniffing coke in the back seat of the bus on the way to school to fit in with their peers. A middle schooler who'd binged two bottles of cough medicine to get drunk. Sangre por Sangre had made it all possible—easier—to drag an ordinary life through the mud. And it turned out, he'd been partnered with an addict all this time. Bringing his gaze back to hers, he pocketed the pills, just in case the sight of them was enough to trigger something compulsive in her. "How did you stop?"

"I didn't. At least not before it got worse." Sweat slipped from her hairline. One push. That was all it'd take, and she'd collapse from the pain. How the hell was she still standing there as though she could take on the world? "The pills ran out. I went to my doctor. He wouldn't help me. Neither would any of the others. The military discharged me under honorable conditions, but I couldn't face the truth—that I was alone. So I did what I thought I had to at the time."

His heart threatened to beat straight out of his chest. Baker licked at dry lips, but it didn't do a damn bit of good. Because he knew what was coming next. "You found something stronger to replace the pills."

"I convinced myself I could handle it." She dropped her chin to her chest, shutting him out. "It was supposed to be a temporary fix, but the longer I used, the more I realized I didn't want to stop. I didn't want to hurt every time I walked through the door or thought about my husband. I don't really remember a whole lot during that time, but it got bad enough no one—not even my friends, my unit or my family—could help."

Jocelyn seemed to let go of something heavy, as though the rain were washing away the weight she'd carried. She stepped toward him. "But I'm in recovery now. I got myself into NA. I have a sponsor I check in with. I've been clean for over a year. It's…hard. Especially when I'm injured in the field, but I don't want to go back to being numb, Baker. I don't. And with you, I finally feel like I can leave that part of me behind. That there's more to my life than my mistakes."

A thousand questions rushed to the surface, but all he

focused on was the hollowness in his chest. There were a limited number of organizations where she could've gotten drugs like the ones she'd talked about, and the entire town of Alpine Valley had slowly been dying because of one of them. "Where did you get the drugs?"

That shadow of enthusiasm and hope—nothing like when he'd first met her—drained from her expression. "Why does that matter?"

"I think you know why it matters, Jocelyn," he said.

Understanding cemented her expression in place. "Seems like you already know the answer you're looking for."

"From a cartel." He couldn't believe this. All this time, he'd trusted her to be on his side of the fight, but she'd kept a major part of her life out of the equation. Lied to him. "I can't tell you how many times I've walked into one of these houses and found a kid barely breathing because of the crap he put in his arm or describe how many babies will have serious complications throughout their lives because their mothers won't look at the people they really are in the mirror. And now you're telling me you're one of them."

Her face ticked at one side, as though he thrown a physical punch. "It's...it's not the same. You know it's not. I changed. I got help so I could start my life over —"

"Has it worked?" he asked. "You paste on that smile and try to find an upside to everything so you don't have to feel your loss. You're so desperate to avoid reality, you've created your own. Christmas parties, cookie bake-offs, movie nights and forced team dinners. You might not be on the drugs anymore, but you're still looking for ways to numb yourself, Jocelyn."

He regretted the words the moment they left his mouth,

but Baker couldn't seem to pull back. The cartel had taken everything he'd ever cared about. The bed and breakfast he built with his own hands, his sister. And now Jocelyn.

"Is that why you started working for Socorro? The reason you came to Alpine Valley?" Baker couldn't stop the words. "To make yourself feel like you were actually fighting the cartel? So you could pretend to be the hero? You outright supported the very people you've been investigating with me. You see that, don't you? You made them stronger while everyone in this town is simply trying to survive."

Tears glittered in her eyes. "And what have you been doing since the cartel killed your sister, Baker? Because I can tell you what you haven't been doing. You haven't been confronting your pain. You might not be going about it the same way I did, but you're just as guilty as I am of trying to escape."

"You might be right," he said. "But I wasn't the one who kept that from my partner."

She didn't have an answer for him.

In truth, he didn't want one. He didn't want any excuses. He didn't want to see reason. Baker pointed an index finger at her. "You know, I thought you were different. I thought we really had something, that it would be worth it to make it work between us, but I can't spend the rest of my life wondering if you're going to relapse or if I'm going to find you dead from an overdose."

He unpocketed the pills and threw them at her feet. The container lid burst free, sprinkling her meds in a two-foot radius. It was childish and petty and didn't do a damn thing to release the tightness in his chest. "Do whatever you want with these. Consider our partnership terminated. I'm done."

"That's it?" Her voice wavered from behind. "After everything we've survived together, after everything we've shared, you're going to condemn me and what we have because of a mistake? I thought you of all people would understand."

He didn't. He didn't understand how someone he'd convinced himself would never betray her beliefs could undermine his trust so quickly. "You were wrong."

Jones Driscoll and Captain Pennymeyer stood at the door flap of the command center, unmoving. Seemed the entire site had turned its attention to him. Waiting for his answer. But he didn't owe them anything. And he didn't owe Jocelyn, either.

Baker kept on walking back toward the command tent. Part of him knew while he hadn't taken up numbing himself the way she had, he'd taken this job to get back at the bastards that'd destroyed his life. He'd lived off of revenge, but he hadn't given up his morals in the process.

"Fine." A low whistle cut through the site, and Maverick's dog tags clashing together reached Baker's senses over the soft tick of rain. "But the next time you're facing down a bomb, don't call me for help."

A car door slammed a moment before the SUV's engine caught.

He crossed back into the command tent, knowing all too well the officers and operatives inside had heard every word. Baker took up position in front of the table with the deconstructed pieces of the bomb that should've killed him—would have if it hadn't been for Jocelyn. His heart dropped in his chest as he caught the tail end of her vehicle through the open tent flap.

"Show's over. We have a bomber to find."

Chapter Thirteen

She would've given up her last cookie for him.

Tears clouded her vision as Jocelyn floored the accelerator. She'd never been so humiliated in her life. Not just by her darkest shame but by having it exposed in the middle of a crime scene, surrounded by her team and other officers she worked with. But that wasn't what hurt the most. A hook cut through her stomach as Baker's words echoed on repeat.

I can't spend the rest of my life wondering if you're going to relapse or if I'm going to find you dead from an overdose.

His concerns were valid. Every day she fought the same demons. Every day she went to bed knowing she'd done her best and tallied another day of survival. Because that was what she was doing. *Surviving.* Constantly on the defense of a threat. But she'd never expected it to come from Baker.

The pain in her shoulder was nothing compared to the agony closing in around her heart. Jocelyn swiped at her face as a pair of headlights inched into the rearview mirror. She'd escaped the town limits, halfway between Alpine Valley and Socorro. Not nearly enough distance to put between her and what'd just happened. Open desert expanded ahead. Ten minutes back to headquarters. Then she could pack and get the hell away from this place.

Maverick whined from the back cargo area. His face centered in the mirror. As much as he preferred to cuddle with a stick rather than her, he picked up on her emotions better than most humans. He was hurting, too.

"I know, but we can't go back." She tightened her grip on the steering wheel. While she hadn't envisioned anything past this investigation, she'd gotten attached to this place. To Baker. He'd unlocked something in her over the past few days. Hope. Trust. Joy. He'd taken her pain and internalized it for himself, leaving her lighter and freer than she'd felt in a long time. He'd listened to her. Convinced her that grief didn't always have to call the shots. That she could be more than an addict. And she loved him for gifting her that relief. Damn it, she loved him.

But he'd made his opinion on her history clear. His personal agenda against the cartel ensured there was nothing she could do or say to change his mind. "There's nothing left for us here."

The headlights behind her got closer. Recognition filled in the paint job along the sides of the vehicle. Alpine Valley PD. Every instinct she owned asked her to slow down and pull over, that she should at least give Baker the chance to apologize, but she'd made her point clear, too. The crossbar lights lit up with red-and-blue strobes. The piercing chirp of the siren triggered her nerves. She tried to make out the face in the driver's seat through the rearview mirror. "Keep trying, but I'm not pulling over."

Jocelyn focused on the road ahead. A couple more miles.

As much as she hated the idea of hiding out at Socorro, it was the one place he couldn't get to her.

The growl of an engine penetrated through the cabin of the SUV a split second before the patrol car tapped her bumper. The jolt ricocheted through the entire vehicle and caused her front tires to skid slightly.

Warning lightninged through her. She hiked herself higher in the driver's seat to get a better view. She didn't pull over, so now he was going to run her off the road? She was going fifty miles an hour. "Are you out of your mind? What the hell are you doing?"

The rear vehicle surged again. The hood aimed for one corner of her SUV. And made contact. The back tires of the SUV fishtailed off to one side. Jocelyn jerked in her seat as she lost control of the steering wheel. Maverick's howl registered a split second before the tires caught on something off the side of the road.

Momentum flipped the SUV.

Her stomach shot into her throat as gravity took hold. The seat belt cut into her injured shoulder just before the crash slammed her head forward. Dirt, glass and metal protested, cutting off Maverick's pain-filled cry.

The SUV rolled again. Then settled upside down.

"Maverick." His name mixed with blood in her mouth. He didn't answer. Jocelyn pressed one hand into the ceiling of the vehicle. Glass cut into her palm, and the seat belt had her pinned. The rearview mirror was gone. She couldn't see him in the cargo area. Visceral helplessness cascaded through her as she clawed for the release. No. No. Maverick wasn't dead. Flashes of that phone call, of the moment when she'd learned she hadn't been there for Miles before his death, were superimposed onto the present. All her husband had wanted in his last moments had been to be with her. And she hadn't been there. But she would be there for Maverick. She couldn't lose him. She couldn't lose the last piece of her husband. "I'm coming, baby."

Her shoulder screamed against the pressure of the seat belt. She jabbed her thumb into the release.

Jocelyn hit the roof of the SUV harder than she expected. The bullet wound took the brunt of her weight as she tried to dig her legs out from under the steering wheel. Pure agony rippled pins and needles down into her hand. If she hadn't lost function of her arm before, she had now. Swallowing the scream working up her throat, Jocelyn rolled onto her back. "Come on, Mav."

A car door slammed, distorting the hard pound of her heart at the back of her head. Followed by footsteps.

Not Baker.

Alpine Valley's chief of police would never put someone's life in danger. Jocelyn reached for her sidearm but came up empty. The impact must've ripped it free of her holster. She reached overhead and patted her hand over the bottom of the driver's seat. It wasn't there. Her training kicked in. Tucking her arm into her chest, she wormed her way between the front two seats. She had an entire arsenal at her disposal in the back with Maverick. She just had to—

The back passenger side door ripped open. Sunlight blinded her a split second before rough hands wrapped around her ankles and pulled her from the SUV.

Her attacker threw her from the vehicle.

Head snapping back, Jocelyn tried to roll with the force. She landed face down, her arm pinned beneath her. Trying to suck in a full breath, she caught sight of a shadow casting above her.

"And here I thought you'd be happy to see me." The voice played at the edges of her mind—the same voice she'd heard right before she'd taken a bullet in Marc De Leon's compound. "I understand. I mean, it's not like we're friends, but I am doing you and that chief of yours a favor."

She blinked against the spider webs clinging to the sides of her vision. Dirt worked into her mouth, down her throat with every inhale, but all she had attention for was the SUV. And the pool of gasoline leaking down the side. Jocelyn stretched one hand out to pull herself forward. One spark. That was all it would take for her to lose everything. "Maverick."

A heavy boot crushed her fingers into the dry earth. "Come on now, Carville. You and I both know this has been a long time coming."

The pool of gasoline was growing bigger beneath the vehicle, and there was no sign of Maverick. She had to go. Now. Jocelyn jerked her body to one side, dislodging his pin on her hand. She grabbed for a rock protruding out of the ground and swung at his shin as hard as she could.

The impact knocked the son of a bitch off his feet.

She ran for the SUV.

A bullet ripped past her ear and lodged into the hood of the vehicle ahead. Then another. The third shot missed her by mere centimeters as she skidded behind the hood. Pressing her back to the front tires, she tried to get her bearings.

"You have nowhere to go, Carville, and you're wasting my time." His footsteps registered again. This time slower. More careful. As though he was trying to hide his approach.

Jocelyn inched to the back of the vehicle, trying to get a line on the bastard's location through the bulletproof windows. Unfortunately, the coating only made things worse. She couldn't see through them from the outside. Her body demanded rest as she pulled as the back driver's side door.

"There you are." A gun barrel cut into her scalp from behind. "On your feet. Slow. You reach for anything, and the next bullet goes in your head."

How had he moved without her noticing? Jocelyn raised her hands in surrender. She cut her attention to the Alpine Valley patrol vehicle parked twenty feet away. A police officer? "Who are you?"

"Let's just say your chief isn't the only one who wants the cartel to pay for what they've done," he said. "What better way than to frame Sangre por Sangre for your murder?"

"Chief Halsey is smarter than that." Movement registered from the inside the SUV, and her heart shot into her throat. Maverick.

"He may be, but what do you think will happen once Socorro discovers you're dead?" the bomber asked. "Do you think your team will listen to him, or will they pull in every available resource at the government's disposal to put Sangre por Sangre down for good?"

Doubt crept through her.

"That's what this has been all about? Dismantling the cartel?" Baker had been right. This entire investigation had been a cloaked frame job from the beginning. Jocelyn followed the motion of the attacker's weapon, taking that initial step toward the patrol vehicle. All this time, they'd been working for the same end goal. "That's what Alpine Valley

PD and Socorro have been trying to accomplish. We're on the same side."

"Yet the cartel somehow still operates without consequences. They raid and kill and take what they want without answering for what they've done." A hardness that sent a chill down her spine added pressure to the gun at her skull. "But with you, I can do what nobody else has been able to."

A low growl pierced her ears. Maverick lunged from the vehicle, fangs bared. He went straight for the bomber's gun hand and ripped the bastard's forearm down.

The attacker's scream was lost to the desert as he tried to regain control of the weapon.

Jocelyn spun. Her fist connected with tissue and bone.

A solid kick landed against Maverick's ribs, and the shepherd backed off with a whine so heart-wrenching it brought up the memory of walking into Miles's hospital room to find Maverick waiting for her.

Air was suctioned out of her chest. She cocked her elbow back for a second strike.

But the bomber was faster. He wrapped his hand around hers and twisted down. Then slammed his forehead into her face.

She hit the ground.

BAKER COULDN'T FORCE himself to focus on the puzzle pieces in front of him. No matter how long he'd stared at them, he couldn't find anything to identify their bomber. The son of a bitch had covered his tracks too well. But worse, he couldn't stop thinking about Jocelyn. About what he'd said to her in those final moments.

"Take a break, Halsey." Jones slammed a hand into Baker's back, and the movement nearly catapulted him forward. "You're going to give yourself an aneurysm. I'll go through everything again. In the meantime, why don't you grab something to eat and catch some sleep. You've been running on fumes for days."

"I'm fine." Baker pinched the bridge of his nose. Truth was, he wasn't fine. He hadn't been for a long time, but having Jocelyn around had helped. Her enthusiasm had been annoying as hell in the beginning. Now he found himself missing it. Her sarcasm had broken through that need to push everyone away. She'd brought out a playful side to him he'd convinced himself had died that day with his sister and given him a sense of adventure. They hadn't just been two people working a case together. They'd been partners. In and out of the field.

And now... Now he felt like he was floating in a thousand different directions without an anchor. Shit. He'd had no right to throw her past in her face like that. She'd lost her husband, the one person she'd counted on being there for her for years. She'd done what she could to survive. Just as he had by making the cartel his personal mission. Two different paths leading to the same place.

He owed her an apology. Hell, he owed her a dozen apologies a day over the next ten years for the way he'd acted. Because despite what he'd said and how he felt about the sickness clawing through Alpine Valley at the cartel's influence, Baker had fallen in love with a mercenary.

"Yeah. You look fine to me." Jones unpocketed a set of keys and tossed them to Baker. "Take my truck. It has a Socorro Security garage pass in the center console. But if anyone asks, you stole it off me. I got you covered."

"Thanks." He let the keys needle into his palm as he headed for the tent's flap but slowed his escape. "What Jocelyn said earlier about her addiction… I don't want this to come back on her—"

"I already knew." Jones turned back to the blueprints, hands leveraged at his hips. A thick scar ran the length of the combat operator's skull and down beneath his T-shirt. "That's the thing about being part of and living with a team as highly trained as ours twenty-four-seven. You tend to pick up on things. There's nothing we can hide from each other. No matter how hard we try." He released a breath. "That's why I know she's been a lot happier since you started coming around. Her hands aren't permanently stuck in a bowl of dough. She's smiling more. Nothing seems forced like it usually does. I just figured she'd tell us when she was ready. Seems she trusts you, though."

"She did." Baker fisted his hands around the keys.

"She still does. You just have to give her a reason." Jones notched his chin higher, accentuating years of disciplined muscle along his neck and shoulders. "But, Chief, if I hear you throw her past in her face like that again, it won't just be some petty bomber coming for you. Understand? You attack one of us, you attack all of us."

Baker didn't have the voice to answer. He nodded instead and slipped out of the tent. Every nerve ending focused on putting one foot in front of the other. The case, the bomber, the impending war with the cartel—none of it mattered right then. There was only Jocelyn.

"Chief!" Heavy breathing preceded his second-in-command hiking up the slight incline to the plateau of mud, rock and cement. The deputy hiked a thumb over his shoulder.

"We just got word of a car fire outside town limits. You can see the smoke from here."

Car fire? Dread pooled at the base of his spine as he caught sight of a thick plume of black smoke directly west. "How long ago?"

"No more than five minutes," the deputy said.

"Anyone injured?" Baker jogged down the slope and hit the unlock button on Jones's keys. Headlights flashed from an oversized black pickup at the end of the street. Ready in case of escape.

"West went to check it out, but his patrol car is missing." The deputy tried to keep up with him.

Disbelief surged high. "He lost his patrol car?"

"No, sir. We believe it was stolen." A hint of embarrassment pecked at the man's neck and face.

Baker's instincts honed in on that cloud of smoke. The base looked as though it was coming from the road cutting between Alpine Valley and Socorro. Which meant... His gut wrenched hard. "Jocelyn."

His entire being shot into battle-ready defense. He raced for Jones's truck. "Get West and round up the Socorro operatives to meet me out there! Now!"

He didn't wait for confirmation. Hauling himself behind the steering wheel, he hit the Engine Start button and threw the truck into gear. Frightened and shocked residents gathered together in groups of two and three as more and more noticed the desert fire. He raced through town as fast as he dared, but the need to get to her as fast as possible had him hugging the accelerator. "I'm coming, Joce. I'm coming."

Trees thinned, exposing the mile-high cliffs on either side of town. Once considered protection, Baker could only look at them now as a threat considering one of them had come crashing down and buried part of his town. But Alpine Valley was resilient. It had to be to survive this long. And though he'd taken up the mantle to protect the people here, he wasn't alone. "Just hang on."

The truck's back tires fishtailed as asphalt gave way to dirt at the border of town. He glanced in the direction of his property, taking in the jagged structure left behind by the bomb and resulting fire, but dragged his attention back to the road. The bed and breakfast, his sister's death, revenge—none of it was strong enough to distract him now. They were in the past. Long gone, and as much as he wanted to hold on to the pain—to get justice for Linley—he had a future to fight for.

Dirt kicked up alongside the truck and pinged off the doors as he picked up speed. The smoke plume had dispersed, and he got his first real look at the fire.

An SUV.

"No. No, no, no." Slamming on the brakes, Baker pulled the truck off the side of the road and threw it into Park. He climbed out of the vehicle, instantly assaulted by the caustic taste and smell of rubber and gasoline. He stuffed his nose and mouth beneath his uniform collar and shaded his eyes before trying to approach, but the heat was too intense. "Jocelyn!"

There wasn't any answer. And he hadn't expected any. If she'd been inside…

Baker lost feeling in his fingers then both arms and that sucking sensation in his chest intensified as the past threatened to pull him in.

The fire grew taller, consuming everything in its path.

The entire roof of the barn was missing. Smoke lodged in his throat. He had to get in there. He had to see for himself. The barn door nearly tore off its hinges as the barest touch. He couldn't see, couldn't breathe. Hay burned beneath his shoes, leaving nothing but ash. The horses. Where were the horses?

A sick smell accosted him as he stumbled toward the stall to the right. His stomach emptied right then and there, unable to take the smell. Baker forced himself away from the paddock into the center of the barn.

And he saw her.

Seated against the barn's support beam. Her hands wedged behind her back. Tied. Baker lost his footing. He face-planted mere feet from her bare feet. The dirt crusted in her toenails said she'd been dragged out here. Most likely from the house. Tears and rage and helplessness had him clawing to touch her to make sure she was real. He reached out—

Course fur warmed in his hand.

Baker blinked against the onslaught of sun beating down on him. The fire's heat beaded sweat along his forehead and neck. Cracked earth bit into his knees as he tried to orient himself in the present. He focused on the K-9 leaning into his hand.

"Maverick." Something like relief flooded through him. Baker scratched behind the shepherd's ears before he pulled the dog closer. "Where is she, buddy?"

A low whine grazed Baker's senses just as he felt a matted section of fur. Wet and warm. Blood.

"Oh, hell. You fought for her, didn't you? You tried to

help." He hugged Maverick closer, as though he could somehow reach Jocelyn. "You did good, boy."

Baker shoved to his feet, fully lodged in the present thanks to Maverick, and hauled the shepherd into his chest. "Don't worry. I've got you. I'm going to get you help. All right? Come on. Let's get you in the truck."

He lifted Maverick into his arms, but a fierce bark racketed Baker's pulse into dangerous territory. The German shepherd tried to wiggle free, his claws digging into Baker's skin. Maverick released another protest—stronger— and Baker set him down. The K-9 ran around the SUV engulfed in flames.

"Maverick, wait!" Baker pumped his legs as hard as his muscles allowed. If something happened to that dog, Jones's warning would mean nothing compared to that of Maverick's handler. He cleared the car fire as the chirp of a patrol vehicle echoed from behind. Backup had arrived from Alpine Valley.

But then who did the vehicles cutting across the horizon belong to?

Baker reached out for Maverick, and the dog took a seat. Dust and heat blocked a clear view, but he made out at least a dozen armored, black vehicles a mile out.

Headed for Alpine Valley.

His heart threatened to beat straight out of his chest.

Sangre por Sangre.

"Halsey, what the hell is going on?" Heavy bootsteps pierced through the adrenaline haze. Jones's voice did nothing to ease the panic settling in. "What do you have?"

Air crushed from his chest. "I think we've got a war on our hands."

Chapter Fourteen

She was a tough cookie. She wouldn't crumble under pressure.

Something splattered into her face. It ran from one cheek down her neck. Jocelyn tried to breathe through the swelling around her nose. Broken. She could still taste the blood at the back of her throat. Listening for signs of movement, she tried to gauge the bomber's location. Another splatter jerked her head back slightly.

"You don't have to pretend to be unconscious anymore." Shuffling scraped across what sounded like a concrete floor. There was a slight echo to it, as though they were in a large room without windows. A piercing shriek hiked her blood pressure higher as the bomber dragged a metal chair closer. "There isn't anything that's going to stop Socorro from finding you dead."

She swallowed the last globs of blood and dirt and risked opening her eyes. To pitch darkness. Pulling at her hands cuffed at her lower back, she gauged her abductor had zip-tied her. Twice. Less chance of breaking through the plastic. Something wet and cold seeped through her cargo pants and spread down her shirt. "Well, that just makes me feel special."

His low laugh wasn't villainous enough to trigger her nervous system, but it didn't fit, either. "You always had a way of making me laugh."

A lantern lit up the entire enclosed space. Cement floor, cement walls, cement ceiling. Another ping of water slipped down her face from the leaking pipe overhead. This place... She'd been here before. There was a slight charred smell sticking in her lungs.

The bomber leaned forward, letting the small source of light catch one side of his face.

Recognition sucker punched her square in the chest. "You."

"Me." There wasn't any pride in that aged expression. No sense of victory in his voice. Just a statement of fact.

"I don't understand." Shaking her head, Jocelyn tried to make every piece of this investigation fit into place in mere seconds. "The reports... They all said you were dead. That there was no way you'd survived that car bomb."

Andrew Trevino. The Ponderosa chief of police—alive and well—settled back in his chair. He'd aged significantly, or the months since his so-called death had been far crueler than she could imagine. Scar tissue shadowed across the backs of his hands. The skin hadn't just aged but smoothed into rivers in some places and valleys in others. Chemical burns. Nitroglycerin?

"Reports can say a lot of things and leave out others depending on who's writing it," he said. "It's all a matter of perspective, don't you think?"

"How?" Jocelyn pressed one hand flat against the wall

at her back. Looking for something—anything—that might help get through the zip ties. Though without the use of one arm she feared she was only drawing out the inevitable. Still, she wasn't going to let her body be used to spark a war between the cartel and her team and Alpine Valley PD. She rushed to resurrect the details of that incident, a bombing of a chief of police's vehicle. Authorities had attributed credit to the Ghost. "You built the bomb and blew up your vehicle, using Marc De Leon's recipe. You faked your own death."

"You military brats are a lot smarter than I expected, especially one assigned logistics." Trevino hauled himself out of the chair. For a man closing in on his late fifties, he was surprisingly agile. No hints of wear and tear. Then again, one needed to be in tip-top shape to take on an entire drug cartel.

"Am I supposed to take that as a compliment?" Jocelyn took advantage of whatever he was doing on the other side of the room. Raising her wrists as one toward what felt like a mass of cement at her lower back, she clenched her jaw against a scream. Her abductor had removed her sling and strong-armed her wounded arm behind her back while she'd been knocked out cold. And now the pain had immobilized her altogether.

"Take it however you want. Doesn't matter to me." He stepped outside of the pool of white light given off by the electric lantern. "Not much does anymore."

He was stalling. To what end? Didn't matter. If she had any chance of avoiding a war, it was because she got herself out of this insane frame job.

Jocelyn rolled her lips between her teeth and bit down

to pull her brain's attention away from her shoulder. Sweat combined with whatever was dripping from the leaking pipe above and soaked into her shirt's collar. "You wanted authorities to believe Sangre por Sangre had ordered Marc De Leon to kill you."

"That was my first mistake." Trevino came back into the weak circle of light, though her senses still weren't adjusting to make out what he'd brought back with him. "Believing one soldier's arrest could make a difference. Believing I could inflict any kind of damage against an organization like that, but it wasn't enough."

A thread of regret laced his words. Similar to the way Baker's voice had changed when he'd trusted her with the loss he'd suffered at the hands of the cartel. Her insides twisted to the point it was hard to take her next breath. "They took someone from you. The woman Alpine PD hasn't been able to identify."

"That's what the cartel does, doesn't it? They take and they take until there's nothing left and nobody willing to stand up and fight against them. They spread their misery and violence into whatever town isn't strong enough to fight back with claims they're offering protection against bastards just like them, but it's all a lie." Trevino dropped his chin to his chest, staring down into whatever item he had in his hands. Still impossible to make out. "My daughter was one of the first to speak out against them when they started selling their poison in the high school. All she wanted to was to make our town safe enough to raise my grandkids while keeping an eye on me. Always said I was no spring chicken."

Dread pooled at the base of Jocelyn's spine. "Marc De Leon was sent to kill her."

"No. He didn't just kill her." The grief and sorrow in his voice was gone, replaced with a hardness she expected of a serial bomber instead of a chief of police desperate to protect the people he cared about. "He tortured her. For hours, right in front of me. He'd beaten me senseless. I couldn't do anything to help her except hear her beg me to save her. And after De Leon had strapped an explosive device packed into a Kevlar vest to her and detonated it, he said he'd come for my grandkids next if I kept coming for them."

Jocelyn pressed her skull into the wall behind her to keep her senses engaged in the moment. Investigators would've known about his daughter's death at the time of the bombing that had supposedly killed the chief. Why hadn't it come up in the past few days? The answer solidified. Because both his and his daughter's deaths had been blamed on the cartel. "So you faked your death."

"Victims die every day at the hands of Sangre por Sangre. The prosecutor's office can't keep up, but the truth is they can't do a damn thing to get justice for my daughter or others like her." Trevino took his seat in front of her.

Baker's sister infiltrated her thoughts, and suddenly Jocelyn was seeing Alpine Valley's chief of police in front of her. Beaten by the years of injustice, desperate to do the right thing, to make the cartel pay. Her heart hurt at the idea, but there were too many similarities between the man in front of her and the one she'd lost her heart to.

The words bubbled up her throat. "But the death of a police chief would get their notice—only Fire and Rescue never recovered your body. So you set about framing the cartel for as many crimes as you could. First with destroying evidence in Marc De Leon's murder case. Then by trying to add Baker Halsey's name to their victim roster."

"I have to admit, I didn't expect Halsey to team up with you, though." The chief's silhouette shifted, losing its caved-in appearance in the limited light. "You've certainly made my job a lot more difficult than I expected. I mean, you two just refuse to die, but then I had another idea. All this time I've been exhausting energy and resources trying to take down Sangre por Sangre alone when there is a high-skilled, highly funded organization equal to the very cartel I want gone."

"Socorro." Her mouth dried despite the building humidity inside the windowless room. "And Marc De Leon? You killed him for what he did to your daughter."

"Son of a bitch got a promotion to lieutenant after that night," he said. "Took me weeks to find him. Thousands of dollars paid in bribes. Nobody wanted to talk. They called him the Ghost. All I had to go off of was pieces of the explosive device in my daughter's chest cavity, but my patience paid off."

Jocelyn strained to angle her wrists against the protrusion from the wall, but her shoulder wouldn't budge. "You found him."

"The bastard didn't even know who I was. Though to be fair, I didn't give him a whole lot of time to recognize me seeing as I was there to kill him." A hint of giddiness contorted the man's voice. And right then she saw the difference between him and Baker. The man she'd fallen in love with wouldn't have let his revenge get this far. "I had everything set up perfectly. Then you and Chief Halsey had to spoil my fun."

Her shoulder ached at the memory of taking that bullet just before the bomb went off. "Right. Because bringing an entire cliffside crashing onto a small town is fun."

"I didn't mean for that to happen," he said. "But I wasn't going to let it distract me from what I was there to do."

"So this is the part where I come in? You leave my body for my team to find. They gather all their federal allies and exact revenge against the cartel on my behalf." The edge of the first zip tie caught on the lip protruding from the wall, and Jocelyn shoved her weight down on her wrists. "Which means you'd have to leave my body somewhere that implicates Sangre por Sangre. Making this the cartel's abandoned headquarters."

Her brain wasn't playing tricks on her. She had been here before.

"I know what you're thinking." Trevino stood, his outline blocking the shape of whatever he held between his hands. Closing the distance between them, he kicked his chair backward to give himself room to crouch in front of her. "They'll never fall for it."

He raised the item in his hands. Forcing the Kevlar vest over her head, the Ponderosa chief effectively pinned her arms to her side and took away her chance of escape. Something vibrated against her chest, and a red light emitted from inside. "Let's just say I've thought of that."

THE CARTEL WAS on the move.

Baker secured Maverick in the back seat of the truck and hauled himself behind the wheel. The engine growled to life at the push of a button, and within seconds, he, Jones and two Alpine PD deputies were charging after the armored caravan.

There was only one place he could think of for them to go this far out in the middle of nowhere. Their failed half-constructed headquarters. It was the perfect epicenter for the oncoming fight. Jocelyn was there. He could *feel* it.

Jones planted one hand against the dashboard from the passenger seat. "Did anyone ever tell you you're a bit intense?"

"A few. Though most of them were under arrest at the time." Baker wasn't in the mood for jokes, but it came easier now that he'd spent the past few days learning from Jocelyn.

"Jocelyn is a fighter. There's nothing she can't handle," Jones said. "You know that now, don't you?"

He did. Because it took a hell of a lot of strength to survive what she had. But being capable of fighting for so long didn't mean she should have to. And she sure as hell shouldn't have to fight alone.

The line of vehicles ahead disappeared off the horizon, and Baker sat straighter in his seat. "Where did they go?"

"The headquarters was built underground." Jones pulled a laptop from the back seat and brought it into his lap. "Last time we were there, the structure was burning at the bottom of a sub-level hole. The cartel planned on burying it to avoid satellite imagery."

"When was that?" Baker's mind raced with every other question, but no number of answers were going to ease the tension in his chest.

"Two weeks ago. Right after Sangre por Sangre's raid on Alpine Valley." Jones hit the keys a few more times. What was he doing? Writing his biography? "Our forward observer, Cash, tore the place apart looking for Elena and her eight-year-old brother. When Jocelyn found them, they barely made it out before the building collapsed."

"It's cartel territory." There was still a piece missing here. If he and Jocelyn were right, the bomber had set about an intricate plan to bring down the cartel by adding a second chief of police's body to the tally. But that hadn't worked. Apart from a few bumps and bruises, Baker was still breathing. Which meant… His skull connected with the headrest. "His plan didn't work. The bomber. He didn't get the response he wanted by coming after me, so he had to raise the stakes."

"The bomber wants to use Jocelyn to pit Socorro and Sangre por Sangre against each other." Jones's fingers hesitated across the keyboard. Dread settled between them in the silence. "In that case, he's going to get what he wants."

Jones turned the screen to show an expanded geographical map. The screen blinked, zooming in on a rough patch of land. Then again. A square lit up around what looked like a car. "A single vehicle parked outside the building twenty minutes ago. An Alpine Valley police cruiser." The combat controller did whatever combat operators did with satellite footage, and another image took over the screen. "This was five minutes ago."

A ring of dark SUVs surrounded the lighter vehicle. Eight of them.

"Well, at least I know where West's patrol car went." Baker checked the rearview mirror. Both deputies were in the car behind them. No sirens. No lights. He caught sight of Maverick raising that caramel-colored gaze to his and floored the accelerator. The uneven terrain threatened to knock them off course, but there wasn't anything that could prevent him from getting to that building.

A chain-link gate materialized not twenty feet in front of them. Baker didn't bother stopping. The metal scratched and thudded over the hood of the car and threw it up into the air before crashing down to one side of the cruiser. The deputies at the back had to swerve to miss it.

"You're going to pay for that," Jones said.

"Submit an invoice to the city clerk's office." The words left as more growl than reason. Baker raced along what felt like the edge of a crater in the middle of the desert. There was a decline up ahead. He didn't bother trying to slow his approach. The cartel was already inside, had possibly already found Jocelyn. The truck's tires skidded down the incline and thrust the hood into the back of one of the black SUVs.

"Come on, man!" Jones's annoyance simply grazed off Baker.

"What? Chicks love scars." He threw the truck into Park, unholstering his side arm. Then he checked the magazine. Half-empty. But, knowing what he did about Socorro operatives, he bet Jones kept extra ammunition on hand. "I'm going to need to borrow some fresh magazines. Watch the dog."

"You realize you're not the one who gives me orders, right?" The combat operative unholstered his own weapon. "And you're an idiot if you think you're walking out of there alive without me."

"Fine. I'll get one of my guys to do it." He shoved free of the truck. "So touchy. Here I thought you might like a baby-sitting job." Baker handed off orders to his deputies—one to watch Maverick, the other to cover the exit.

Staying low and moving fast, they maneuvered as one through the collapsed parking garage to an entrance that hadn't been pummeled with rubble. Shadows clouded his vision the instant they stepped foot inside. It smelled of fire and death and mold the deeper they navigated through what felt like a cement corridor.

"You good?" Jones asked.

Baker waited for the flashbacks, for the paralysis. For the hollowness in his chest to consume him completely. But it never came. There was only this moment. Of getting to Jocelyn. "I'm good."

"Then pick up the pace." Jones took the lead, weapon aimed high. Low voices echoed through the hall, but there were too many directions to pinpoint their location. Pulling up short, the operator handed off a radio. "We're going to have to split up. You take the right. I got the left. Try not to get yourself killed."

"Yeah. Ditto." Baker pinched the radio to his waist and took the corridor to their right. The voices were growing louder, clearer. Slowing his approach, he angled his head around one corner. But there was no one there. He took the turn and followed the hall to the end. Dead end. He pivoted back the way he came. "Shit."

Then he heard her.

Low. The words mixed together and muted as though coming through a wall. But he knew that voice, had relied on it to keep the past in its place. Baker raised his attention to the ceiling, then brushed his palm over the wall. There. An air-conditioning vent. "Gotcha."

He felt his way around the corner and slid his hand over

a door. Pressing his ear to the metal, he made a response on the other side. Baker tested the handle. Locked. Of course—couldn't make it too easy. He backed up a step. Then hauled his foot into the space beside the lock.

The door slammed into the wall behind it, and he charged inside. Weapon raised, he made out two figures in the light of an electric lantern on the floor.

"Baker!" Jocelyn tried to pull away from the wall but couldn't stand. Blood crusted around her mouth and beneath her nose. The son of a bitch had hit her.

"You are a hard one to get rid of, aren't you?" The bomber centered himself between Baker and Jocelyn. All too familiar.

"Trevino." The puzzle fit together now. The lack of a body. The motive to frame and kill Marc De Leon. Ponderosa's chief hadn't died in that car bomb as everyone believed. He'd been exacting his own revenge against the cartel. "It was you."

"Surprise." Trevino raised something in his hand. A small black box, just wide enough for a single button. A detonator. "I'd stick around for the party, but it sounds like my guests are here."

A quick assessment of Jocelyn's Kevlar vest, pulled down over her arms, told Baker exactly what that detonator triggered. She'd been strapped with an explosive—the impact of which could bring down the entire building on top of them. Not to mention kill the woman he loved. "Put it down."

"I don't think you understand, Halsey." Trevino couldn't contain the smile plastered all over his face. "I put it down, and your partner here has a much bigger hole in her chest. You see, if I take my thumb off this button, we all die. So you might want to put down the gun instead."

"You son of a bitch." Baker took a step forward. "I could've helped you."

"Helped me?" The bomber raised the detonator. "No, Chief Halsey. I'm the one who's going to help you. This is what you want, isn't it? To see Sangre por Sangre pay for what they've done? Well, this is how we get it."

"Not like this." Holstering his weapon, Baker charged forward. His shoulder connected with the Trevino's gut and slammed the bastard into the wall behind him. He grabbed for the device.

The chief threw the fist clutching the detonator. Bone, plastic and flesh knocked Baker back, but it wasn't enough to knock him down. Jocelyn struggled to get free of the Kevlar vest in his peripheral vision. One slip of that detonator and he'd lose everything all over again.

Not an option.

Baker elbowed the chief in the face. A sickening crunch filled his ears. The bomber moved to catch the blood spraying from his nose. This was his chance. Baker hooked his arm around the chief's middle and hauled the bastard off his feet. They hit the ground as one. And Baker wrenched the detonator out of the man's grip.

Air eased into his chest as he got control of the explosive, but the adrenaline had yet to fade. Baker rocketed his fist in Trevino's face. The impact knocked the man's head back against the cement. Throwing him into unconsciousness. "That's for breaking her nose."

Staggering to his feet, he faced off with Jocelyn. "You okay?"

"Yeah. I'm okay." She stared up at him, a million things written on her face, but she must've known they didn't have time to hash it now. The cartel was in the building. Their time was up. "I could use some help getting this vest off, though."

Keeping his finger over the detonator's trigger, he crouched in front of her. The vest was heavier than he'd expected. Packed to the brim. But he managed to pull it over her head and make quick work of the zip ties around her wrists.

"I guess I was the one who needed help this time." Jocelyn rubbed at the broken skin on her hands.

"Anytime, Carville." Baker offered her his hand, and for a moment, he didn't think she was going to take it, but she did. Her palm pressed against his as she got to her feet, and that instant contact took the edge off.

Footsteps and flashlights broke through the door. Unfamiliar shouts ricocheted around the room as Baker and Jocelyn raised their hands in surrender. Sangre por Sangre. He blinked against the onslaught of light, fully aware of the device in his hand.

"I think this is the part we get on our knees and hope they don't shoot us," he said.

They both lowered themselves to the floor.

Chapter Fifteen

One of the best things in life was a warm chocolate chip cookie.

And Baker's hand in hers as they faced off with a half dozen armed cartel gunmen.

Trevino lay unconscious behind them. Water soaked into Jocelyn's pants as they waited for Sangre por Sangre to decide what to do next. What were they waiting for? One wrong move. That was all it would take to put her and Baker out of their misery. Seconds pressed in on her lungs. Everything that'd happened over the past few days had led to this. To this one moment. Was this really how it was going to end between them?

She licked dry lips, knowing what might happen if she broke her silence. "Baker—"

"I was wrong before." He squeezed her hand tighter. "About what I said to you back at the camp. I've been so angry since Linley died that I've pushed everyone away for the smallest infractions. Because I was scared. I didn't want to lose anyone else, so I shut down any possibility of letting someone influence the way I feel, including you. I've been so focused on finding a way to bring down the cartel for what they took from me that I blinded myself to the best thing that's ever happened to me. You." He released a ragged breath. "I'm sorry, Jocelyn. For everything. You deserved better from someone claiming to be your partner."

A flashlight beamed straight into her face. *"¡Silencio!"*

Her shoulder burned with the possibility of taking another bullet, but it didn't hurt as much as it had before. Jocelyn moved her opposite hand to block the sensory assault, but there was no amount of distraction that could convince her that the man beside her would be able to ignore her past. Baker was law enforcement. He witnessed the results of addictions like hers on a daily basis, and he had every reason to worry he might find her unconscious and overdosed. Because it was a possibility. This thing she carried inside her wasn't ever going to go away. And as much as she hated it, there was always a chance she'd give up the fight one day. She couldn't do that to him. The warmth given off by his touch urged her to forgive him, to let him into her world, to tell him she wanted to spend the rest of her life proving she was good enough for him. But she couldn't.

Jocelyn pried her hand from his, and she felt more than saw the collapse in his expression. "Let's just get through this."

Movement divided the semicircle of cartel soldiers in half. A single figure materialized at the back. Male, heavily armored from the outline of his Kevlar vest. The flashlights and dim lantern did nothing to highlight his features, but there was something there she recognized. In his walk, in the way he held himself. Former military. Not born or abducted into Sangre por Sangre as most of the others had been. This one had converted to a life of violence, blood-shed and dominance of his own free will.

"Socorro has a lot of nerve showing their face here after what went down on that cliffside," he said.

The voice penetrated through her minuscule amount of confidence. Recognition filled in the shadows of the man's face. "Rojas. It's been a long time. Believe me, I wouldn't be here if it'd been my choice. Don't suppose you'd look past the fact Chief Halsey is holding a detonator that could bring this entire building down on us with the slip of his finger?"

Nervous energy rolled through the grouping of soldiers. A couple backed toward the door, eyes on the ceiling.

"You know this guy?" Baker asked.

Better than anyone. They were going to walk out of here alive, if she played her cards right. "Dominic Rojas, let me introduce you to Chief Baker Halsey, Alpine Valley PD." She nodded at Baker. "Rojas is a high-ranking lieutenant in Sangre por Sangre and a fellow baker. Though I'm not sure I would call what he does baking, really. Cookies aren't supposed to snap like biscuits."

Baker cut his attention to her, as sharp as a blade. "You realize we might die right now, don't you?"

"I knew you were going to go there, Carville." Rojas charged forward, and the lantern caught on his features. Neither Hispanic nor Chinese American, but a combination of the two. It was clear in the shape of his eyes, in the lighter color of his skin. She'd been right before. Former military—the Marines. A damn good one, too. Dominic Rojas had once been a Socorro operative named Carson Lang. And he'd taught her everything she knew about baking.

He shoved his finger into her face, but she wouldn't give

him the satisfaction of knocking her off balance. "That was one time!"

"Yet it was enough for second place compared to my chocolate chip," she said.

Rojas's low laugh that didn't even own a hint of humor vibrated through the room. The lieutenant straightened. "You always were out to prove you have the biggest *cajones*, but this time might be your undoing, Carville. You think you can walk in here, insult my baking and expect I would let you leave alive?"

"That's a valid question." Baker's nerves were getting the better of him.

"To be fair, I think I was dragged in here. By him." Jocelyn tipped her head back. A groan registered from Trevino as he came around. "Recognize him?"

"Isn't he supposed to be dead?" Rojas asked.

"Seems Ponderosa didn't really lose their chief in that car bombing a couple months ago," she said. "The bombings at the station and Marc De Leon's compound? Both devices were built and detonated by him."

"Don't forget the device in my hand." Baker waved with a half smile, but the possibility of war was still very real at this point.

Jocelyn leaned forward slightly. "Oh, right. He strapped me into that vest over there and planned to set it off with this handheld detonator. It's a dead man's switch."

"Why go through all this trouble? Did you insult his baking, too?" Rojas snapped his fingers, and two soldiers lowered their weapons, peeled off from the group and maneuvered around their lieutenant to drag the Ponderosa chief forward. They laid him and the Kevlar vest at Rojas's feet. "Because I'm starting to think he had the right idea."

"Marc De Leon tortured and killed the chief's daughter. Under orders, is that right?" Her heart tried to absorb the heaviness overtaking Baker's body language, but there wasn't anything she could do for him in that respect. Humans were tribal creatures. They craved connections and support and love just like the rest of the animal kingdom. But when that love was gone, they had to grieve on their own. She understood that now.

Rojas didn't answer, which was answer enough in and of itself.

Jocelyn lowered her arm to her side in surrender. "The chief constructed and detonated the bomb that blew up his truck to make it look as though the Ghost had targeted him, too. It gave him time to plan out his revenge. First by killing De Leon. Then by trying to frame your cartel for Chief Halsey's and my deaths."

"Starting a war between us and your employer and anyone else your government sent after us." Registering what she'd just divulged, Rojas backed off a few inches. Then he nudged Trevino's ribs with the toe of his dust-covered boots. "It was a good plan, *amigo*. My bosses have been looking for a reason to take Socorro out for good."

Jocelyn lost the oxygen in her chest. If that was true, Rojas and his men could just finish the job Ponderosa's chief started right here, right now. Effectively eliminating any competition Rojas went up against at the next bake-off and making his loyalties clear. What had started as an undercover assignment in Sangre por Sangre would end with a target on his back from the very people he claimed as his own. Had he been Dominic Rojas long enough that was an actual possibility? Would he even have a choice when faced with blowing his cover?

"Whether that happens or not is up to you," she said.

Her pulse counted off a series of beats. Quicker than a couple minutes ago when she'd been sure they were walking out of here alive. She suddenly found herself missing Baker's hand in hers, wished she hadn't shut down that point of connection in the final seconds they had left together.

Rojas's men waited for the order, each of them all too willing to add two high-priced deaths to their belts. She could feel it in the shift of energy bouncing off the cement walls, a frenzy of battle-ready tension ripping the enthusiasm she'd tried to keep as a shield around her free.

"I'll take that detonator now." Rojas positioned himself in front of Baker, hand extended.

Baker twisted his gaze to her. Waiting.

The device in that Kevlar vest was the only thing guaranteed to get them out of this mess, but she couldn't risk starting a war between Socorro and the cartel. They'd come here to stop it. She nodded, and after a long moment, he handed it off.

"Great. I'll have one of my men bring your police cruiser around. Though you should know tips are not included in today's pardon." Rojos clutched onto the detonator as though his life depended on it. Which it did. All of their lives depended on it. "Oh, and please tell your friend Jones not to shoot me on the way out. I'd hate for our friendly rivalry to turn bloody."

Jones was here? Jocelyn sucked in a breath with the realization Baker had turned to a Socorro operative to come for her. A private smile hitched at one side of her mouth. Seemed he was warming up to the idea of teaming up with mercenaries.

Jocelyn shoved to her feet. "We're not leaving without him." She nodded to Trevino.

"He's not part of the deal, Carville." Rojas folded his hands in front of him, looking for a reason to withdraw his pardon. "He killed one of us. You know as well as I do— we can't let that slide."

And the bomber deserved that fate for what he'd done, but no amount of torture or blood was going to change the past or the pain he'd caused. Ponderosa's chief would see the inside of a jail cell. Not the inside of a flaming tire. "What if I trade for something you want?"

"You don't have anything I want," Rojas said.

That wasn't true. "Not even my chocolate chip cookie dough recipe?"

There was a slight melting of Rojas's expression. Bingo. He shifted his weight between both feet before moving out of their path. "Take him and leave before I change my mind."

Dragging Trevino to his feet with Baker's help, she called into the corridor just beyond the door. "Jones, we're coming out. Hold your fire."

The group of soldiers parted down the middle again, letting her, the bomber and Baker through. Socorro's combat controller met them on the other side, his rifle pressed against his chest, as he took in the situation. Most likely counting how many gunmen he'd have to take out personally if things went sideways. "You good?"

"We're good." Her attention shifted to Baker. Though

she wasn't entirely sure what she'd said was true. At least, not for them.

They moved as a unit to keep up with Rojas's men leading them through the building's remains.

Baker hauled the bomber's arm over his shoulders. "Someday, you're going to have to tell me how the hell we just walked out of there alive."

HEATED DESERT AND blinding sunlight worked to hijack his determination.

Baker pounded his fist against the front door of Socorro's headquarters. The past few days had taken everything he had to stay upright. Witness statements, arresting Trevino under charges, running operations at the cleanup site. And there was still a possibility Sangre por Sangre would change their mind about striking back for the death of one of their lieutenants.

He'd run through those miserable minutes in that basement room a thousand times. There was no explanation for the cartel letting them go. Both he and Jocelyn shouldn't have made it out of there alive. His brain kicked up a new memory as he stood there in the heat. Of Jocelyn in the rearview mirror, pulling Maverick into her lap as they'd driven back to Alpine Valley. She'd set her head back against the headrest and stared out the window, not uttering a single word to him.

She'd disappeared after that. Wouldn't respond to his messages or calls.

The door swung inward, and Baker took a step forward before he lost his nerve. "I love you."

The words he hadn't spoken to anyone—not his father

after his mom had passed, not his sister before she'd died, not even his favorite chocolate glazed doughnut—rushed out beyond his control.

Jones Driscoll stared back at him, one hand ready to slam the door in his face. "Oh, thanks, man, but I just figured our relationship could be more of a casual thing. Not really ready for anything serious."

Baker's confidence collapsed in on itself. Great. Now the first person he'd ever said those three little words to was a smart-ass operator who'd most likely hold it against him for the rest of his life. "Is she here?"

The combat controller leaned his weight into the door-jamb, folding his arms across his massive chest. A roadblock from Baker getting inside. The humor between them was gone. Big brother—whatever that meant for a team like Socorro—was on duty, and Jones wasn't the kind of guy who could be convinced of Baker's sincerity. "She's here, but unless she gives the word, you're not coming in. We protect our own, Halsey. No matter what. There is one thing she wanted me to give you in case you showed up, though."

Anticipation undermined the guilt and shame of what he'd thrown in her face before his whole world had blown up.

Jones dipped to one side and collected an oversized paper bag from near the door. "She said she wrote the heating instructions on each of the containers and that she'll have someone run out another batch next week."

He took the offering, staring down into the perfectly packaged homemade meals. The aroma of marinara and garlic drifted from inside one of the top containers. Lasagna and bread. She'd made what looked like a week's worth of dinners, breakfasts and lunches in the space of a couple days. And despite the way things had ended between them, Jocelyn had come through with making sure he didn't have to live off of microwaved ramen.

"I get it. I screwed up." Baker stared past Jones's shoulder. Not at anything in particular, but he saw the future he'd never thought he deserved. One filled with love instead of revenge, of inside jokes and home-cooked meals, of late nights cuddled on the couch and beneath the bed sheets. He saw him and Jocelyn. Her teaching him how to bake the lemon-cranberry cookies, of them handing out gifts to the rest of the team at Christmas, of movie nights and responding to calls together. Waking to that smile in the morning and kissing her senseless at night.

Of course, it would've been hard. Him dealing with what'd happened to Linley. Her guilt and grief over her husband… But they would've gotten through it. They would've found a way to make it work. Together. As partners.

Baker slipped his hand into his uniform slacks and produced what he'd hoped to hand Jocelyn herself. "Can you give her something for me?"

"What am I? The post office?" Jones asked.

"You're a lot more reliable in my experience." He handed off the collar and new set of tags he'd had made for Maverick. He wasn't much of a dog person, but Jocelyn was worth trying for. "Thanks."

He stepped down off the wide stone steps and headed for his patrol car with the prepackaged meals in hand. There would be other chances to see her. When she was ready. Hell, he'd host an Alpine Valley bake-off if it got her to face him, but for now, he had to accept Jocelyn needed space. From him.

"Baker." His name on her lips paralyzed him from taking another step.

He turned to put her in his sights, and damn, his entire body went into a frenzy. Though this time, he wasn't scared of losing control. This time there was no disconnect. Just Jocelyn.

She stood there covered in patches of flour down her front with a bit of egg sticking to the ends of her hair. White frosting grazed one corner of her mouth. It was obvious she'd been hard at work since they'd walked out of the cartel's headquarters. Had most likely forgone sleep and taking care of herself to process everything they'd been through with hundreds of cookies, and hell, she could probably make a few hundred more and take on the entire cartel given the determination in her expression.

"Why did you do this?" She flipped the collar over her uninjured hand, running her thumb along the strands.

"Maverick's tags didn't have an updated address on them. I figured if he gets lost or separated from you like he did after…" The bag in his hand got heavier every second this distance stayed between them. That was what she did to him. Made everything feel lighter. At first, he'd resented her attempt to bring any kind of lightness into his life, even if it'd been in the shape of a cookie. But now, he couldn't go another minute with this impossible weight. "Anyway, I thought it'd be easier for someone to make sure he got home."

"That's sweet. Thank you." Her voice remained even, but there was no enthusiasm to go with it. Tucking the collar into her cargo pants, she ducked her chin to her chest. Pulling away.

And he couldn't take it anymore. Couldn't let what they had slip through his fingers like he had the past two years. Baker took a step forward. "I love you."

"What?" Her gaze snapped to his, lit up by the sunset striking her head-on. The brown of her eyes turned iridescent, otherworldly and compelling in a way he'd never seen in anyone else before. Because Jocelyn Carville wasn't like anyone else.

"I wanted to say it earlier, when we were coming back from the cartel headquarters, and then I accidentally said it to Jones a few minutes ago." He was getting off track, and his nerves were about to toss him behind the wheel and launch him back to Alpine Valley, but he wasn't going anywhere. Not without her. He was done running. Done not letting himself feel. Done with trying to burn the world and everyone in it. "My point is I love you, Joce."

Her mouth quirked to one side. "Does Jones feel the same way about you? Because I'm not sure how I feel having to compete against someone on my team."

"No. Not even a little bit." The pull they'd shared throughout the investigation took hold, and Baker dared that next step toward her. "Jocelyn, I was nothing but a ghost living in this body before you barged into my station with a plate full of cookies. I'd lost everything I thought I cared about to Sangre por Sangre, and all I wanted was to stop feeling. For people to leave me the hell alone so I could find the bomber responsible for my sister's murder. I took the chief of police job to protect the town I love from the cartel, but after everything that's happened, I realize I was just like him. Trevino. I let myself become consumed to the point

I forgot what it felt like to be happy. Until you gave me a reason to look for silver linings."

Her smile was gone. Instead, a deep sadness had taken hold. Jocelyn swiped at her face, then stared into the setting sun cresting the mountains in the west.

It wasn't enough. What he'd said wasn't enough. The realization constricted his heart, and Baker tried to block the emotional response lodged in his throat, but there was no use. He was going to lose her. He understood that now. "I know I hurt you. The things I said... I wish I could take them back, but I can't. All I can say is I'm sorry, and if you give me the chance, I will spend every day of the rest of my life proving that I believe in you and that I truly love you."

She took a step down, then another. Jocelyn closed the distance between them, sliding her palm over his chest. His heart beat so hard, he swore the damn thing was trying to reach her. Problem was it already belonged to her. Every inch of him was hers. He wasn't sure when it'd happened, but there was no denying it now.

"I need a partner, Baker," she said. "Someone who knows me inside and out, who's willing to talk to me when this demon tries to take over. Because it will. I need someone who doesn't just love and accept the person I am now, but all the different versions of myself. Past and future. Who's willing to work on his own pain while doing the best he can for the people he cares about."

"I want to be that someone." Baker dropped the bag of food at his feet, threading his hands around her waist and pulling her against him. Right where she belonged. "Whatever it takes. Forever."

"Good. Because I love you, too. More than anything."

The smile he'd come to love stretched her mouth wide as Jocelyn leaned in to kiss him.

A tritone sounded a split second before a frenzy of paws, fur and slobber slammed into him. Baker lost his hold on Jocelyn as Maverick tackled him to the ground. The German shepherd licked at his face and neck, settling all one hundred pounds on Baker's chest. Low playful groans accompanied Jocelyn's laugh.

She stood over him, unwilling to help as the dog wrestled him into the dirt. "I forgot to tell you. You'll have to fight Maverick for the other side of the bed."

* * * * *

SWIFTWATER ENEMIES

DANICA WINTERS

To my kiddos,
Keep stoking the fires in your souls.

This book and all those in this series wouldn't have been possible without my strong support team at Mills & Boon. They constantly strive to keep me growing as an author while making each book better than the last.

Chapter One

Everyone was born into something, but it was left to the individual to define whom they became. Leo West was born a cowboy, and no matter how hard he had tried to escape it, he always found himself coming back to the world of whiskey, women and hard living. The only thing he had managed to leave behind was the ranch and the cattle, but he would be lying if he said he didn't regret the loss. However, he couldn't say he missed the scent of cows in the midsummer sun.

The call pulled him from the midday lull and away from busywork as a detective for the Madison County Sheriff's Office. A woman had gone missing after being last seen in the parking lot at a particularly popular swimming hole on the outskirts of Big Sky, Montana. As one of only a few officers in the county, he was on the hook.

Luckily though, he and the other officers were a tight-knit group. Each person did their job to the best of their ability, but also did it with integrity. Well…at least *he* did. A couple of the other guys he couldn't be sure of, as they liked to skirt a little close to the gray edges of the law, but he could say that their loyalty seemed to always be in the right place.

As law enforcement in a small community, it came with its own set of rules and procedures. Instead of writing tickets, they regularly gave their local low-key troublemakers rides home on rough nights and instead targeted the out-of-staters to keep their budget padded—not that he would have publicly admitted their norms.

That wasn't to say they didn't arrest their fair share of locals. There was always something—usually gun-or sex-related—that would lead to him stuffing and cuffing his former neighbor, girlfriend or football buddy on a Saturday night.

Hell, he couldn't even remember the last time he had had a Saturday night off. It seemed like this time of year, he was called out on all kinds of odds-and-ends events, like the one that had just popped up on his computer.

According to dispatch, the woman was twenty-six years old and going through a contentious divorce. She'd been hiking in and around the area of the swimming hole, where her car was later found, abandoned.

It was going to be a long day.

Grabbing his keys, he got into his rig and hit the road. By the time he got to the public river access, groups of people were standing around a white Subaru with outdoorsy stickers in its back window, one of which read "Honk if you ski."

He got out, and before he even had a chance to walk over, a woman rushed toward him. She was talking wildly, which made him reach down and instinctively put his hand on his sidearm. It was amazing how fast a normal situation could go sideways when high-voltage emotions entered the equation.

"Hello, ma'am," he said, putting his hand up and hoping the woman would keep her distance.

As the woman lifted her sunglasses, he recognized her as Jamie Offerman, one of the high school secretaries whom he talked to on the phone on a far too often basis. She was a good woman, but she was always surrounded by drama thanks to her job.

"Jamie, how's it going?" he said, his hand falling from his gun.

"Hey, Leo," she said, smiling and nearly bouncing from one foot to the other in excitement. "We were starting to wonder if you were ever going to arrive. You must have been having one helluva day."

He couldn't tell her that he had been working on pulling together paperwork for a search warrant on a possible house where a guy was peddling drugs to the local students—providing them everything from marijuana to spiked methamphetamine. The dealer's last batch had left one kid in the hospital after barely surviving fentanyl-laced meth. In other words, he had just been having another regular day in the office. "It's been going. Are you the one who made the call to dispatch?"

"Come on," she said, cuffing his shoulder, "you know if I'd been behind this, I would have just called you directly."

"You know I'll always answer your phone calls." He sent her a blistering smile he knew she enjoyed.

She blushed and quickly looked away.

She was twenty years too old for him, but she was a sucker for the uniform and he wasn't above using it to gain favor.

"So, tell me what I'm looking at here," he stated, point-

ing toward the sandy beach where a group of teenagers
were laying out in the early-summer sun, although it wasn't
quite warm enough to warrant the little bikinis the girls
were wearing.

A few of them wrapped themselves in their towels as the
wind kicked up.

"I've been asking everyone around here what happened
while we waited for you to show up. From what I got, that
lady over there called—" she pointed at a woman in her
midthirties who was scowling over one of the bikini-clad
teenage girls who was chatting with a boy "—and she said
her daughter noticed that no one was touching a phone and
gear left on the beach. Nor has anyone been near that car,
over there," she said, pointing at the white Subaru. "The
girl opened up the last video on the phone, trying to figure
out who it belonged to and there's a video of a girl in a hot
pink bikini playing with a dog."

From what he was hearing, this missing woman could
have been picked up or gone for a hike. Any number of
things could have played out. If this went as he assumed,
he'd be out of there in about an hour after the woman walked
back onto the beach from a hike with her dog.

"How long has the woman's stuff been sitting there?"
he asked.

"More than three hours," Jamie said. "At least that's when
the mom and daughter said they got here, but the stuff was
here before."

He appreciated the fact that Jamie had already seemed
to collect all the witness statements; if she wasn't careful,
he would have to start putting her on the county's payroll.

"Can you point me in the direction of the items?"

She motioned with her chin downstream. "They're right over here."

He followed her down the beach and behind a small copse of cottonwoods and willows. On the beige sandy beach was a neat stack of folded clothes. On top were an iPhone, car keys and an Apple watch.

Odd. He stared at the black key fob with the Subaru logo.

He had a few calls about abandoned items each summer, but he couldn't think of a time when he had found someone's keys at the top. Normally, a person would tuck their keys in a pocket or the folds of a towel, but never out and visible. It was like she was asking for someone to steal her car.

He took his phone out and took a few pictures of the stack. Moving to it, he lifted the black tank top from the top; it appeared to be worn but clean. The shorts beneath were the same. No blood or other bodily fluid. They simply looked as if she had stripped down, folded her clothes and intended to return.

"Did anyone see her go in the water?"

Jamie shook her head. "I don't think anyone actually saw her at all, just her stuff. People have been coming and going all day, though. I didn't talk to everyone. Ya know?"

Aside from the woman being unaccounted for, there wasn't much that led him to believe anything had happened to her. For all he knew or could assume, she and her dog had gone into the water and floated down to the next pull-out on the river. Maybe she had met with friends and would be coming back later. Any number of things could have occurred that would have led to this situation.

On the other hand, she very well may have gotten caught in a current and found herself submerged. Drownings happened in this river all the time. People underestimated the water conditions or would get caught in snags. Being as early in the season as it was, the runoff from the mountains was making the water cold enough in some areas that it could have easily been prime conditions for hypothermia.

He clicked on the screen of her phone and the camera opened. It started to autoplay the last video taken, a cute shot of a German shepherd jumping around in the water and then galloping after a stick. The woman was talking to the dog calling him by the name "Malice" as she recorded him returning to her with the stick in his mouth. The video ended.

So, there was proof she had been playing in the river.

His heart sank as the video replayed. This woman, something about this, felt *off.*

Though he hoped he was wrong about the feeling he was getting, and this woman truly was just at the next pullout or something, he had to make the decision. He shook his head. If he called Sheriff Sanderson right now and told him what was happening and preemptively started to get the word out to the search and rescue team, they would be going on a call, and the woman would likely show up, and Sanderson would be irritated. Leo needed to make sure there were no other possibilities as to the woman's location before he called out the big guns and started blowing the yearly budgets for the sheriff's office and the SAR unit.

A woman walked up beside him and tapped him on the shoulder. "Sir?"

Jamie shot him a look like she would have gladly been his bodyguard and push the woman back if he gave her the sign. He gave her a small, almost imperceptible nod.

He tried to push down his immediate annoyance at having been interrupted as he turned back to the other woman. "How can I help you?"

The woman was beautiful, blond, about five-foot-seven and curvy in all the best ways. As she looked up at him, her eyes caught the sun. He couldn't recall seeing eyes the exact same color as the sky before, and he half expected to see clouds float by within them. She was stunning, and that was to say nothing about the red polka-dotted bikini she was wearing.

"So..." She balled her hands at her sides like she was trying to summon the strength and resolve to say whatever it was that was on her mind. "My name is Aspen, I'm on vacation here, but I'm involved in the Minnesota Life Savers group, it's a private SAR unit."

His hackles rose with her intrusion—he could hardly wait for this tourist to start telling him how she could have gone about this call better. "Is that right?" She may have been stunning, but she had already pissed him off twice in a matter of seconds since they had met.

"Yes," she said, chewing on her lip. "I don't want to step on your toes here, or question anything you may be working on, but in circumstances like these, I'm sure you are aware that every minute matters. If she's in the water..."

Boy, did I call that one, he thought.

"If she's in the water and has been gone for three hours..." *Well, the woman was as good as dead. Minutes didn't really matter.*

The tourist waved him off. "I know what you're thinking, but we still have a shot."

It was crazy the number of people who came up to him at moments like these and tried to tell him how to do his job. If she was as professional as she was portraying herself, and in-the-know in his line of work, then she should have known better than to approach him as she had.

"I appreciate your attempt to help me out here, but I've got this handled." He pulled out his phone. "Now, if you wouldn't mind—and I'm sure you are aware, given your line of work—you need to move back from this area."

She opened and closed her mouth as she heard his barely veiled request for her to stay in her lane. Frowning, she handed him her card and then turned and strolled away with the little polka dots on her butt jiggling as she moved.

As soon as she was out of earshot, he jumped the gun and called Sanderson. The tourist was right; there was a slim chance that they could still rescue the missing woman if she was in the water, but it would be close. He and his SAR unit would have to act fast if there was to be any hope of this girl being saved.

Chapter Two

The water scraped against the bank, pulling sediment with its turbulent fingertips. The dirt swirled into the river, making filigrees of mud until they spun together like dancers and disappeared into the crowd.

Aspen Stevens had always found poetry in nature, and it brought comfort and peace in a way no therapist or friend had ever been able. On the water, she found every answer she had ever needed, from when to cut and run in a relationship to when to press hard against the banks and dig until she got what she wanted.

Staring at the muddy eddies, Aspen felt as though it was time. It had been two weeks, and after having watched the headlines in Big Sky, she had found that as of yet, no one had recovered the missing girl or her remains.

She pressed the earbud into her ear and made the call she had known needed to happen, but she had been putting it off for the last few days while she had been training on the Minnesota River with the rest of her unit.

Staring out at the bluffs as she put down the anchor on her boat, she leaned against the raft and tapped the name she had saved into her contact list, Cindy DesChamps—right beside Detective Leo West. The thought of calling him had made her stomach ache ever since their first run-in.

West was a handsome man… Well, if pushed to tell the *truth*, that was an incredible understatement. There was just something about a man in a Sam Browne belt and uniform with the patches creased and a straight gig line that made her entire body clench. And he hadn't made her just clench, he had made her so nervous that she hadn't even acted like her normally confident self—and she had been kicking herself for her mousiness ever since leaving the riverbank.

She wasn't ready to talk to him. Besides, it was easier to just go over his head—it wasn't like she could make things any better between them. She'd already burned that bridge.

Cindy was the director of the Big Sky Search and Rescue team, and as far as Aspen knew, she wasn't going to know this phone call was on the horizon—which meant she very well could be met with a cold shoulder and some ruffled feathers. Yet, she was going to utilize her unit's time and resources to help them; if Cindy cut her off it would not only be bad press, but detrimental in any future attempts to collaborate.

She hated making these phone calls; often departments felt as though her team was invading their territory—especially when they were being paid by private parties or families of victims. As much as she disliked the calls, sometimes upsetting a group of people was just a step in getting her job done and answering a family's questions—they needed answers about the status of loved ones more than egos needed to be assuaged.

Those answers, the ones between life and death and the pain that came from carrying the weight of them, were something she knew entirely too well. Her father's body had never been found. The last time anyone had seen him, he had been ice fishing on Lake Winnie. No one had witnessed him falling through the ice, and no one had even known he had slipped below until he didn't come home that night.

Her mother had been distraught at learning that her husband had disappeared, and Aspen had given up her position as the oldest child and was suddenly thrown into the role of matriarch. Her three younger siblings, Milly and Miles, the twins, and Rebecca, had been too young to really know the full impact of the loss. As they grew older, they had come to understand the costs to the family when Aspen had been the only one taking them to and from basketball and softball practices, and the only one who showed up for games.

Their mother had sunk deeper and deeper into the bottle until her grandparents, two of the biggest saints on the planet, had taken them in and helped to continue to raise them. If it hadn't been for Nana and Pops, she would have probably still been working as a waitress in the diner at Tall Pines Resort after getting married at eighteen to some fisherman who had come in for a beer and left with her on his arm.

As it was, being twenty-nine, a certified diver, single and definitely not looking for a relationship, she had a life that wouldn't have been possible without them. She owned who she was and everything she had achieved to them. Every choice now, every attempt to right the wrongs of her and her parents' pasts was in their honor.

The phone rang as soon as she pressed Cindy's name. Hopefully, this phone call wouldn't cause too many waves and Cindy would see this as her attempt to keep things amicable. This really was a humanitarian call, not an attempt to make anyone feel inept.

The woman answered. "Hello?"

"Hey, Cindy, this is Aspen Stevens from the Minnesota Life Savers."

There was a long exhale on the other end of the line. "Hi." The woman already sounded confused. "How can I help you?"

"I'm reaching out about the recent missing woman in your county. My team and I have been in contact with Genie Manos's family, and they were hoping we could help search for their daughter," she said, her words coming out faster than she would have liked in order to maintain some level of professionalism. "Of course, we would love to work in conjunction with your organization and local law enforcement—as much as law and need require."

"I have no doubts that the Manos family called you in to help locate their missing daughter, Genevieve." There was the sound of ropes being tightened in the background. The woman must be working. "You should know, this family…they are *something*. They are gunning for Genie's estranged husband. I get that money is money and you are working for a profit, but between the water conditions and the family's dynamics, you are probably better off staying in Minnesota."

She held no doubts as to the emotional turmoil the family must have been going through because of the disappearance of their daughter. The Manoses were oil people out of the Texas Panhandle and were deep-pocketed, but she found herself still offended that Cindy would think that she was merely taking this job to get a paycheck.

"I believe you as to the water conditions. I was visiting your state and was actually on the same beach just hours after she went missing. I talked to the officer in charge of the scene."

"Oh," Cindy said, her voice dropping low. "That was *you*. I shouldn't be surprised."

"I've been following the case since I left, as well as the watershed and CFS reports online. Looks like things are moving a little fast over there, but we are hoping to use some new equipment and see what kind of information we can pull to help find our girl."

"Regardless of what the Manoses have undoubtedly reported to you, we have been pulling out all the stops on this assignment, but as it stands right now, we can't even say with complete certainty Ms. Manos is in the water. A lot of questions have yet to be answered in regards to her disappearance."

She had never heard a more polite *Kiss off and let us do our jobs* than the one Cindy had just given her.

Aspen sucked in a long breath, trying to pick and choose just the right words to keep things civil. "Cindy, my team and I would love to work with yours. Maybe you'd like to check out our gear and take us down the river. Who knows? Maybe we can all get something out of this to help our teams. I know we could definitely use more active training scenarios."

There was a pause. "Actually, I do try to get our people on the water as much as possible. It's been a late runoff this season so we are just hitting peak flows, and that means it's going to be some of the harshest water conditions of the year. It's a dangerous time to train, and any day it will be too rough to even get out there until the water recedes and the cubic feet per second, or CFS, is lower."

"We have been paid to work for one week by the Manos family. I'm sure the water will be fine while we are there. During our time in Montana, I would like to help close this case and get answers not only for the family but for your team as well. I know how trying these types of events can be for *everyone* involved."

"Trying doesn't even begin to cut it. The Manos family has been calling us several times a day. They rented a condo in town, and they have been a nearly constant presence at the sheriff's office, according to Detective West and Sheriff Sanderson."

If she was the parent of the missing girl, she couldn't say she would be doing the same thing—if it was her child, she wouldn't have been spending time dealing with law enforcement when she could have been spending that same time searching.

"I'd be more than happy to help control the dynamics with the family while my team is there, if you'd be on board with our search."

"I appreciate that you are trying to help me think I have a choice in your coming out here. Truly," Cindy said with a sigh. "Of course, you are welcome to come out, we want Genie to be found just as much as her family."

"I look forward to working this together, as a team."

Cindy chuckled. "Just so you know, your buddy Leo is a coordinator for the sheriff's office with SAR. From what he told me about you, I'm not sure he may be as welcoming as the rest. Please take him with a grain of salt."

"It will take a lot more than a grain, I'm sure, but I've had more than my fair share of handling men like him."

There were the sounds of ropes again in the background, and Aspen's oar shifted as the river's current pulled at her boat.

"Don't get me wrong," Cindy said, sounding a bit winded. "He is a good man, but he takes time to warm up."

"I'll bring a blanket and canister of salt," Aspen said, trying to laugh, though the knot in her gut tightened.

Everything about this call-out was going to be a struggle, none more so than the fight she was likely to find with the handsome detective.

Chapter Three

Cindy had been vague when she'd called the team out to work the river. Over the last two weeks, Leo and his team had been up and down it, watching the banks and hoping to find Genie's remains. As it stood, all they had were her clothes, her car—which had been clean when they searched—and her parents breathing down their necks.

When he arrived at the SAR building, there was already a variety of vehicles parked outside—one with out-of-state plates. Cindy was leaning against the back of her pickup, tapping away on her phone, but she looked up as he parked on the street.

She gave him a tip of the head as he jogged across the road.

He came to a stop in front of her, adjusting the front of his uniform and his vest. "Don't tell me you let some out-of-stater take my parking spot."

She tilted her head back with a hard laugh. "Oh, man, this is going to go just about as well as I assumed."

"What are you talking about?" he asked, thrusting his thumbs under the edge of his vest.

Like a bell had rung to release the circus animals, the

door to the building opened and his team and a guy he didn't recognize came strolling out. Last, but not least, was a woman. She was blond and strutted out the door like she owned the place. There was something about her that he recognized, but he couldn't quite place her.

"Detective West," Cindy began, "this is the team the Manos family called in to privately conduct a search for their missing daughter."

She had mentioned there was another team coming, but he hadn't expected them to arrive so quickly, or with so many in tow.

The woman walked toward him and extended her hand. "We have met before, Detective. My name is Aspen Stevens."

He stared into her blue eyes, the same color as the summer sky. He jerked his hand back, almost violently.

It couldn't be.

"What are you doing here?"

Cindy cleared her throat. "She is the director of the Minnesota Life Savers group. She and her teammate Chad are here with their special equipment. They are here not only as paid employees of the Manos family, but they are our guests as well. Please remember that when you are speaking to them."

He took the ego check straight to the chin. Admittedly, with such a warm welcome, he had that one coming.

"It's okay," Aspen said, gently putting her hand on Cindy's arm like they were longtime friends.

It shouldn't have, but the simple action put his teeth on edge… That was until Aspen smiled at him. As beautiful and piercing as her eyes were, they were nothing in comparison to the brilliance of her smile. She was more beautiful than any woman he had ever seen, and for a moment he almost forgot that he didn't like her and that she was here to do his job for him—a job that apparently the Manoses thought he was incapable of performing.

He couldn't really blame the family, though. They were going through what would be the hardest and most traumatic period in their life. They may have just lost a daughter.

Leo had been the first one to talk to Genie's parents when they'd arrived in Montana. Her father, John, had a thousand questions, but there was only a handful of information he could legally give the man as there were some major underlying questions Leo and his supervisors had in regard to why the woman had been on the beach that day.

Genie's mother, Kitty, hadn't been satisfied with any of their answers.

Leo didn't look forward to taking on their questions again.

Maybe it was a good thing there was an extra set of hands to help with the search. If he could get this woman's body or location, then the family would have the answers they clearly needed.

"Detective," Aspen said, pulling him out of his whirlpool of thoughts.

He nodded.

"We are here to help you. We do not intend to step in on any ongoing investigation that you may be controlling, but we would like to help bring Genie home."

"You, your team and mine... We all know that the chances this woman is still alive are slim." He exhaled, hating that he had to be the one to speak what they all knew was likely the truth. "I don't wish to be crass or disillusion the family. I've spoken to the father, but he isn't ready to hear me. I would appreciate it if you prepared them for the worst. We don't want them to have unrealistic expectations."

Aspen looked down at the ground. The man who was standing behind her stepped forward like he was coming to her aid. She put up her hand, stopping the man before he could continue his advance. "Detective, we will talk to the family and reiterate your feelings. I agree that if Genie is in the water, that she is deceased."

He nodded. "At this time, I believe she is in the water, but again, this is a matter that is still being looked into."

"Did you call in any partner agencies to help with your search?" the man standing behind Aspen asked.

Cindy's lip quivered in a near snarl as she turned to the man. "We have been running the river. Working the banks and doing what any great team would do. We have people searching the land as well. So far, we haven't found anything that would indicate a need to reach out for additional assistance."

"I heard you only have, like, four deputies in your department," the man continued, looking over at Leo.

His teeth nearly cracked under the pressure as he set his jaw.

Aspen shook her head at the man speaking. "Chad, why don't you go inside, and we will go over this case in a way that makes our hosts more comfortable? Cindy, would you mind giving us a moment?" she asked, motioning toward Leo.

Cindy shot him a look, but he gave her a nod to let her know it was okay for her to escape the hotbed. "If you want to hook up the rafts and get them ready, I'll talk to Sanderson. I'm sure he will give us the thumbs-up to hit the water."

"On it, but I'll wait for Sanderson before I line up the troops." Cindy walked toward the door and waited as Chad made his way inside, Chad going in last and sending him a look that he desperately wanted to punch off his face.

Aspen waited for the door to click shut before she turned to him. "Look, Detective, I'm sorry about that. Chad is a retired marine, and he can get a little...*heated*."

He didn't mind someone who was passionate about their work, but he did hate when someone came in and started stomping on the feet of everyone around them. "I understand that we can't always control the people we work with." He paused. "I hope you know I am having a hard time with you being here."

"Me or *me*?" She pointed at her chest, reminding him of her red polka-dot bikini.

"Your being here makes me wonder how much this family did in getting you out here. Obviously, you called them."

She glanced down at her feet, caught.

"Just like I thought," he continued. "I'm not upset *you* are here, but I'm more than surprised."

She looked back up at him. This time the light played in her eyes and made them seem slightly darker, almost the color of a heat-treated sapphire. "I hope you know I don't have anything against you."

The only thing he wanted to have against him was her.

No. I can't start thinking about her like this, he corrected himself.

"If you did, I'd be happy to prove to you otherwise," he

said. "My team is great and we work our asses off, but that being said we are always open to learning opportunities."

Especially at the hands of a beautiful woman.

"Detective—"

"Call me Leo," he said, correcting her.

"Leo, we can get along and be friends or I can throw you out of my boat." She said his name with a smile. "Don't make me throw you in the river."

Chapter Four

Chad cranked the winch on the trailer tight, locking the teeth in place. The raft was prepped and ready to run the rapids. All Aspen needed now was to make the call to Leo and let him know they were on time and ready to meet.

After she had met with him yesterday, she had spent the night on the couch of her rented house thinking about how he had reacted when he'd first seen her.

What are you doing here? His words rattled against her ribs like a baton against jail bars. *Thump, thump, thump.* Each word hit her and left its mark on her flesh.

She couldn't be hurt by it though; she had known he wouldn't like her coming into his territory and stepping on his toes—he hadn't liked it when they'd first met, either. If anything, he just had an icy exterior, one she would have to take her time to chisel through.

If anything, he looked *tired.* Maybe it was that and just the shock that had produced the undesirable first reaction. She had to give him a pass and put her ego to the side, just as he had.

Her phone pinged with a message from him, like he must

have felt that she was thinking about him. Or had he just been thinking about her?

She moved to answer it, but it started to ring. "Hello?"

"Aspen?" His voice sounded like velvet, rich and textured with his deep baritone.

"How's it going? You ready for this fun?" she said, trying not to sound too excited to be hearing from him.

"I'm calling to let you know that Genie's dad just showed up in my office. He was asking that we bring him along when we hit the water today. I have told him that due to safety and liability concerns, we can't have him on our boats."

She pinched the bridge of her nose and turned away from the raft as Chad opened his mouth, likely to ask her who was calling. She didn't need him trying to corral her right now.

"I'm sure that Genie's father took that news well." She gave an exasperated sigh. "What did he say?"

"It went about as well as a goose in a jet engine."

"Does he know anything about where we will be launching from?" she asked, trying to plan ahead and avoid any potential problems arising with the irate man.

"That is why I'm calling you. He's your client, right?"

She swallowed the lump that was forming in her throat. "He is."

"Then that begs the question as to why he would be contacting me in regard to today's search." Leo sounded annoyed, rightfully so.

"You, of all people, should know that controlling distraught family members is nearly impossible." She couldn't make sense of the embarrassment that was rising within her.

John Manos had acted on his own accord; him calling

Leo and driving spurs into his ass wasn't her fault. She hadn't given him any superfluous information about her activities, and when she had last spoken to him, he and his wife had seemed on board when she had briefed them on the search plan. Yet, going around her now made her look like she was inept. Why couldn't this family just let her do her job unobstructed and without creating more problems?

"Oh, I get it," Leo said, but as much as he proclaimed understanding, his tone didn't convey any empathy for her tenuous position.

"I will go ahead and give Mr. Manos a call," she said, trying to recover some of her professionalism before Leo saw her as just some fly-by-night who was trying to profit on the back of other people's tragedies.

"Thanks," he said. "I'll meet you down at the launch in thirty." He hung up the phone without saying goodbye.

Running her hand over her hair to sweep back any strands that had been blown about thanks to the whirlwind that had just ripped through her life, she placed the call. She climbed into the truck and motioned for Chad to get moving toward the launch.

Chad put the truck in gear and the men in the back seat sat quietly as she pointed at her phone.

Mr. Manos answered on the first ring. "This is unacceptable," he said with a perceptible snarl.

Hello to you, too, she thought.

"What is that, Mr. Manos?" she asked, in an attempt to let him air his grievances in a way she could hear him, deal with them and de-escalate.

"I hired you—"

"This being a SAR-related event, we cannot have you join

us on the boats due to liability issues. Insurance would not cover if something happened to you," she interrupted, not letting him continue down his entitlement tirade.

"I will pay for the damned insurance to go. I'm not being left on the bank. I've had enough waiting."

She could certainly understand his point of view, but that didn't change the fact that he couldn't do as he wished.

"Sir, have you had any whitewater experience?" she asked, leading him.

There was a pause. "I went on a rafting trip when I was a kid."

"Sir, the Big Sky SAR team and I have accumulated decades of experience on swift-moving water. If I thought that you could safely go with us today, I would make the argument that you could ride in our boat. However, this is the first time that my team and I will be navigating these waters, and your accompanying us is not a viable option and may put you and our teammates in danger."

"I don't want to put you in danger, but—"

"I'm sure that Genie wouldn't want you to put yourself in danger, either." There was silence as he stopped arguing. "What would your wife do if something happened on the water? What if she lost both of you?" She drove the nail in her argument home.

There was a long pause.

"How about this…" she said, hoping to offer a solution instead of perpetuating any further problems. "What if we meet up after I get off the water? We can go over any of our findings before any information goes public."

The man sighed. "Just find my little girl."

His voice echoed within her as she slipped her phone

into her go-bag at her feet. This wasn't going to get any easier. No matter the outcome, this family needed to get answers, and she was feeling the pressure to be the one to provide them.

When they arrived at the boat launch, Leo and his team were already there and working on getting their raft ready to hit the rapids. There were three other SAR members with him, and a goldendoodle weaving between them. The dog was about eighty pounds and cute as could be with his apricot coat and teddy bear face. He had a collar on that was emblazoned with SAR in bright yellow lettering, with the accompanying mini patch. As the pup skipped along, he made her smile.

On days like these, sometimes it was the little things that made it slightly less painful.

It also didn't hurt when Leo looked up from where he was working a length of rope on the front aft D-ring to smile at her. The simple action made her heart shift in her chest.

Yes, she needed to get that reaction under control or that could prove to be a liability. They didn't need to make anything more complicated or painful than it already may turn out to be.

Leo stepped out of the boat, turned back and gave his teammates an order she couldn't hear before making his way over to the driver's window of Chad's pickup. Maybe he hadn't been smiling at her at all, maybe he had just been glad to have more hands and she was misplacing her wishes and seeing things that weren't really there.

"Chad," Leo clipped in acknowledgment. He motioned toward the launch. "Let me get my pickup out of the way, and then you can get your boat in the water."

"Sounds good," Chad said with a tip of his head.

Leo slapped the window frame and stepped back, but not before his gaze flickered to her and that sexy smile graced his lips.

He was happy to see her and damn it if she wasn't tied in knots about seeing him. Everything about the job was getting more complicated.

Chapter Five

He wasn't going to take it easy on Aspen. From what Cindy had told him, Aspen had pulled out all the stops in making sure that she had taken this job and gotten herself out onto this river. Now he was going to show her exactly what she had gotten herself into—this wasn't just some wide and lulling Minnesota flatland river; this beast could toss a person in seconds and make them disappear forever—just like he had told the Manos family.

Though Leo liked Aspen, he wasn't going to treat her any differently than he would treat anyone else who didn't want to listen to what he had to say. And he was more than happy to prove that he actually knew what he was talking about and wasn't just all about puffing his chest and being the alpha. He was the leader because he had earned the role.

"Why don't you jump in the SAR boat?" he asked as she got out of the pickup and moved toward her raft.

Another truck pulled up with the other member of her team. She glanced over toward the dude who had just rolled up, and she smiled as the guy gave her a wave. There was a familiarity between the two of them ,which made him wonder if they'd dated. A twinge of jealousy prickled his skin, surprising him.

"I need to talk to my buddy. We have been studying an approach that we want to try—"

"An approach?" he choked out, interrupting her.

"Well, yeah. We've been studying the watershed and the topography of the river and the area surrounding the water. I think we have located a few areas, one about a mile down, where we would like to look a little closer."

"You mean on Badger's Bend?" He motioned vaguely in the direction of where she was speaking.

She pulled out her phone and clicked on the screen.

"Yeah, you're not going to find it called that on your mapping app. In fact, you won't find it called anything at all. Yet, I know exactly where you're talking about."

Her mouth pinched and she looked up at him. "Look, you don't have to be—"

"Yes, I do have to be an ass. Just a little bit. I know what you are thinking, and I appreciate that you did your homework. However, all the maps and the watershed reports in the world aren't going to tell you that there is a large limestone shelf that is exposed in low water. The bend should be running deep and turbulent, according to normal fluid dynamics, but in this case, it is only fast in the inner bend—where it is most shallow."

"So, it's not possible that a body could have gotten held up there?"

"Bingo." He motioned at her. "And why we should take my boat—you have more to learn if you are going to come out here and work this river."

Chad came striding over. Everything about the guy

rubbed him the wrong way, but it could have been the way he walked like he owned the river—it was the same kind of walk that the rich out-of-staters had when they spent three thousand dollars on high-end fly-fishing gear when they didn't know the difference between a Parachute Adams and a Purple Haze fly. It was the stride of someone who couldn't take instruction but would solidly try to argue about how they were always open to learning. The dude was a walking headache.

It was going to be a long day and an excruciating week—or however long it was that they were planning on sticking around.

She walked away from him without giving him a second glance, making him wonder if he had made a major misstep in their burgeoning friendship. He had to be real though, if there was any chance of actually getting to the bottom of what had happened to Genie.

Aspen started to chat quietly with Chad and they kept looking over at him with growing frowns. He definitely wasn't making any friends. The day wasn't over, but he had a feeling that he would have a complete anti-Leo fan club by the end. The idea didn't really sit well with him, but he was here to find the missing woman—nothing more and nothing less.

"Come on, Chewy Lou, let's hit the boat," he said, calling his dog.

The pup beelined to him, wagging his tail and nearly hopping in excitement at the prospect of going on an adventure on the water. He loved his dog, and though he was only a couple of years old, he had already proven to be one of the most intelligent and easily trainable pups he had ever owned. The dog was all love and driven by praise—though the occasional piece of jerky was always welcome.

Chewy came over to him and dropped to his haunches, waiting for his next command. Leo walked over to his pickup with Chewy at his heel, and he grabbed the dog's PFD out. The personal floatation device fit snuggly over Chewy's body, but he didn't seem to mind too much as he always knew that when the PFD came out, fun was about to be had.

"Are you excited, buddy?" he whispered, clipping the last buckle into place and tousling the fur on the pup's head.

Chewy wagged his tail wildly and took his hand in his mouth in what he lovingly referred to as the dog's "mouth hug." It was a habit he was aware he should have broken, but it was so endearing and sweet-natured that he couldn't bring himself to tell the dog "No." Just like everything else his sidekick did, this little action was all about love.

"That's what I thought," he said, scratching behind the dog's ear. "You gonna ride with me or are you going to go with Aspen? She's pretty, huh?" He chuckled, looking at the dog like he was just another person in this little conversation.

Chewy tilted his head, flicking his ear up in his best attempt to show he was the cutest animal on the planet.

"Yeah, she is going to fall for that look. Don't you dare think you are going home with her tonight—at least not without me," he teased. An unwelcome heat moved up into his face.

I can't even joke with the dog about having a night with Aspen... What is wrong with me?

He ran his hand over his face, trying to scrub his thoughts and the embarrassment he was feeling from his features.

Cindy was standing by the boat with fellow SAR teammates Steve and Smash. They looked at him as he and Chewy cruised over. "How's it going? We ready to launch?" he asked, hoping that there was no remaining unruly color in his cheeks that could give even a whisper of his thoughts away.

Cindy nodded. "Everything is in order and the throw bags are ready for use if we need them. I made sure we also have an extra set of radios for their raft. Why don't you take Aspen and I'll captain their boat."

"Great." He loved rolling up and having a team that had everything in place and ready to rock and roll. "You okay running their boat? You can have ours instead, if it makes you more comfortable."

She frowned for a second, likely thinking about taking on the challenge of steering a boat that she wasn't used to down a river that would be questionable thanks to water conditions. Yet, she was a trouper, and a smile broke over her features. "I'm on it. I have Steve going with us. He's always been one of our strongest rowers if I get in a pinch. We are going to have to move a little slow down the first mile or so until I'm used to being on their oars. Sound good?"

He nodded. "Whatever you need. Do you want someone else from our team to ride with you as well, or are you good on your own?"

She shrugged. "From what I've heard, Chad is supposed to be good on the sticks, so we'll be safe on our side."

He appreciated her planning for the worst—he'd found it had saved them from worse things happening when bad things happened, which they always did. They worked in jobs that brought inherent danger and unavoidable pitfalls—making lifesaving and split-second decision-making skills a requirement.

Aspen and Chad dropped their raft into the river, taking the time to make sure everything was tied down and safely stowed for the journey ahead. As they worked, Leo did one more pass over his boat before giving it the all-clear.

"You ready?" he asked, looking over at Aspen, who was clicking on her PFD and checking her paddling knife, which was attached to her chest.

She glanced over at him in surprise, as if she had forgotten that she was there in a role of mutual support instead of running her own operation. "Oh, yeah." She took out her phone and gave it a glance, clicking at it before slipping it into the waterproof bag secured to her vest. "When we get done today, I'm going to take a walk along the edge of the river."

It wasn't a question. "First, you're assuming we can be back in time. It's going to take longer than you think to get down to our take-out point and then back here. And second, you shouldn't be running the riverbanks without more resources. If you do, I need to call in more teammates and have them work with you. The river conditions can change at any minute, and if something happens…"

She waved him off. "No, don't worry about it. I'm just going to be searching the waterline."

He gritted his teeth. "Did you do this on purpose?"

"Do what?" she challenged.

"Completely ignore the one rule Cindy—" he nudged his chin in her direction "—and I required you to agree to for this arrangement to work. What about *mutual support* is so hard to understand?"

The softness in her face disappeared. "I didn't know I had to clear it by you when I decided to take a hike, but it's fine… It was just a tentative plan."

"You have to clear anything you want to do in this state… anything," he said, nearly snarling. "I would like to think that with you working in a similar field to ours, you would be more than aware of how dangerous conditions can become—especially in an area in which you and your team have never trained. Montana is not Minnesota. If you or your *buddy* screws up, and we end up having to send out our teams to rescue you, this will come out of your budget…and your time here will be done."

Chapter Six

The raft was heavier than she would have expected given its size, but there were three of them on her boat, and it had a large frame and gear box. It took longer to hit the step and plane out on the water, skimming the surface at the perfect speed at which to decrease drag and resistance while still giving themselves enough time to scan the bank and look for snags and streamers—anywhere a person could have gotten trapped.

Chad and Cindy's team was running river right while she and Leo's team ran river left, and every ten minutes or so, Cindy would call over to share reports. So far, they hadn't even come up on a downed log—at least so far as she had seen visually or on sonar. However, the dark blue water could hide almost anything under its surface.

She glanced down at her phone as the dog leaned against her legs in the raft—they'd been out for at least an hour, and they had to have been two miles from where Genie had last been seen. The bank was so heavily timbered that she wondered how there weren't more visible logs in the river. Where there weren't cottonwoods and birch, there were cliffs of limestone intermingled with the occasional granite batholith.

The dog licked her hand, and she rolled his hair between her fingers. His vest read "Chewy Lou," and she reached over and scratched behind his ear. His tongue lolled out of his mouth, and he looked at her with what she could read as instant love. She could take this dog home.

It was funny, but she had always thought of dogs as the epitome of their owners—this time, she couldn't have been more wrong. Chewy Lou was friendly and gregarious—the polar opposite of the man whose name was on the dog's tags.

"How old is your dog?" she asked, trying to make conversation in the tense silence as he rowed the boat.

He looked back over his shoulder at them between strokes. "He's two. My ex-wife let me have him in the divorce as long as I let her keep the house. Fair trade, in my opinion."

She would be lying if she didn't admit she was surprised that he would open up and tell her about his divorce so soon after he had chewed out her ass on the bank. Maybe he was feeling bad about how he treated her—at least, a girl could hope. Knowing her luck, and her taste in walking red-flag men, it was more likely that he was just bitter about his divorce and wasn't afraid to let everyone around him have a little taste.

The man sitting next to her on the boat leaned over as soon as Leo turned around. "Hey, my name is Smash. Actually, my name is Richard—don't ask." He sent her a half smile, exposing a chipped front tooth that was so out of place in his round face, it was almost endearing. Something about it reminded her of the little cup in *Beauty and the Beast*.

"Nice to meet you, Smash."

He gave her a dip of the head. "Don't worry about Leo," he whispered, motioning with his chin in the man's direction. "He acts like he is nothing but business, but if you get him talking after work…" He paused, his face squishing like he was reconsidering his statement. "Nah, even then he is still all about work." He laughed.

"That's not a ringing endorsement for him being a laid-back dude," she whispered back, sending him a little wink.

"He just needs a good woman. He has a lot on his shoulders, and he carries it all on his own." Smash leaned back and tapped his chest proudly. "I'm one of the few in this gig who got lucky enough to marry their best friend and the woman of their dreams. She supports me and listens to every bit of nonsense I tell her—when I need them, she gives me answers."

"She sounds like a good woman," she said with a smile. "Does she have a handsome, single brother?"

Smash tilted his head back and gave a long belly laugh, which made Chewy wag his tail like he was also in on the joke. The only real joke was that of her love life. "Dammit if she wasn't an only child. They broke the mold on my lady."

"Sounds just like my luck." She smiled. "Though, I gotta admit that even if she had a good brother, I think I wouldn't like him. I have a thing for guys with egos as big as their belt buckles. It's why I'm still single." She was careful to keep her gaze firmly planted on Chewy's left ear instead of looking over at Leo.

She wasn't sure, but she could have sworn that the boat

had lurched slightly to the left, as if Leo had been listening in and had missed a beat with his oar. "There's a strainer," he said, louder than necessary like he was making a point that it was hard to hear anything thanks to the splash and gurgle of the river.

Near the bank, half-submerged, was a large deadfall timber. Its roots were sticking up and out of the water, still full of the sandy soil and cobbles that had once held it into the ground. The cottonwood's branches were dipping in the water like hands, hiding under the wash of white foam that had accumulated around their grasping fingers—they needed to stay out of those hands.

Instead of steering clear, Leo started to paddle upriver, slowing them down to the point they were nearly sitting still at the edges of the flotsam. "You guys seeing anything on the sonar?"

She glanced over at the screen covered in a myriad of lines and bars that indicated the water depth and any objects beneath the surface. The system was old-school and far from foolproof, but it did its job.

Smash leaned closer to her. "You know how to use this thing? It's probably not as fancy as what you and your team are used to, eh?"

She chuffed a laugh. "I think my dad had this system on his boat when I was growing up."

Smash chuckled, but she could tell there was a little hurt in his tone.

"Not that it's bad, it's just…not what I'm used to is all."

"Anything?" Leo asked again, and as he asked, she glanced up at him and noticed the way his arms were straining as he worked the oars against the current. His biceps were so large that they were stretching the cotton of his blue T-shirt. His left arm sported a large tattoo that she couldn't quite make out.

He shot her a pointed look, like he had caught her gawking and was annoyed.

She mumbled her apology under her breath as she looked back at the screen.

"All I'm seeing is the outline of a downed tree. A few hogs are tucked underneath, feeding on bugs I'm sure," Smash said. "No bodies, but hell we should come back here with our rods and hit it hard when we get the chance. Those buggers must be at least five-pounders."

"What kind of fish do you guys have here?" she asked.

Leo jerked the oar as he glanced up at her.

There was that look again.

No matter what Smash said, she couldn't help her growing feeling that Leo really didn't like her.

"We have trout. Though, we pull the occasional whitefish, sucker and pike." Smash turned away from the screen as Leo pushed them out from the strainer and into the safer water in the main channel of the river.

Leo was truly an impressive boat handler. It took a great deal of strength and knowledge of hydraulics to handle the raft as he had just done. An average paddler couldn't hold and move out of such a prolific current, unscathed.

Truth be told, with so much weight in the boat, she wasn't sure that she had the upper-body strength necessary to perform the same feat.

Smash slapped her on the back like he could tell she was beating herself up. "Don't worry. We will find Genie." He turned to Leo. "There was an outcrop of rocks back there, on the underside of that tree that might act like a turbine and pull anything sinking deep. We looked there on an earlier search, but it may be worth coming back to."

Leo nodded. "You want me to row us back?" He motioned toward the log that was already a few dozen yards from where they were on the river.

It was crazy how fast they were being pulled downstream.

"Nah, it's just somewhere that we may want to take another look." Smash smiled at her.

She could tell that he was trying to throw her a bone, and that he didn't really think the woman's body would be in the deep, churning water, but he wanted to give her some glimmer of hope.

Another strainer appeared on their side of the bank, and they repeated the process, working the sonar—to no avail. Their comms sparked to life. "You guys seeing anything of note?" She was met with Cindy's voice.

Smash picked up the handset. "Negative."

After three hours of their looking and mile upon mile of the rafts skirting along the riverbank, the sun had risen overhead, and beads of sweat started to slide down from beneath her hat. Everyone looked as though they were starting to melt around her. Even Smash had seemed to have lost some of his chipper attitude, especially since he had taken over on the sticks.

Leo sat down next to her. "Sorry there wasn't anything on Badger's Bend."

She felt utterly defeated. As the boat takeout area came into view, her heart sank. She made the Manos family a promise to do her best to find Genie, and yet all she had managed to do today was get a sunburn and realize that she had truly overestimated how much they could accomplish in the limited time they were going to be here.

"I am looking forward to going over all the sonar data. You guys do store it, right?"

He chuckled. "No. Even if we did, there wouldn't be much to look at. You saw everything we've gone over and through today—I wasn't lying when I told the Manos family that we had done our best."

"I never thought you were lying." Aspen had known that it was very possible that they would find nothing on the first day and things would continue like this while they were in Montana. She'd had enough experience to understand that there was a bit of a learning curve in whatever search they were involved in. "I have no doubt that you've put in a lot of time and effort. I just think it is always better to have more people involved."

Leo frowned. "I can agree with you to some extent, but on boats it just doesn't seem to make a difference if there are three people or five. The only difference is the weight."

Of course, he would come at it from that perspective, as the rower. "You don't think you are more effective as a team, though? That you find more?"

He shook his head. "I am not trying to be a thorn in your side, but usually this isn't how we find bodies this far out after a person has gone missing."

"Oh," she said, with the raise of her brow.

He looked tired as he lifted his baseball cap, complete with a set of black embroidered antlers, and wiped away a bead of sweat from his forehead. "Normally, with the water running this fast and hard, we won't find the bodies until low-water season. You know, late summer. Sometimes it's even a year later."

"But you do find them?"

He shrugged. "There are many missing who have never turned up. As I'm sure you know, everything runs to the ocean eventually."

"How do you normally find people, though?"

He looked her square in the eye. "Normally, after this amount of time *we* don't. It's the fishermen and hikers who find remains and call them in."

This really was nothing like being back in Minnesota. Bodies, at least those from persons who were involved in accidents, showed up—unless they were talking about lakes, and then it was hit or miss, but diving was a hell of a lot easier.

Her biggest takeaway was that her chances of providing closure for the Manos family were rapidly decreasing.

As they came around the bend in the river, and their midday takeout area came into view, there was a man and a woman standing on the bank. The man looked to be in his midsixties with his hands over his chest and a scowl on his face. The woman was pacing on the sandy stretch of beach and, though her face was covered by a wide-brimmed straw hat, Aspen could tell she was upset.

Growing nearer, she could finally make out the man's stony features and rounded shoulders—it was John Manos. His voice rang out, heavy and burdened, over the water. "Did you find my daughter?"

Her heart sank. Not for the first time in her life, she was going to have lay the lashes of her words to draw more of a family's pain and blood.

Chapter Seven

Leo felt for the family, he really did, but their being here wasn't going to help matters. As he stepped out of the raft, he could feel the agony resonating off John and Kitty Manos like sound waves. In an effort to protect himself, he put up his guard, though he tried to remain friendly. "Hey, guys. I'm surprised to see you here."

John nodded, watching as they tied up the boat to ensure it wouldn't leave the area without them. There was no way he could handle being stranded with this family. He motioned for Chewy to remain on the boat with the rest of the team until he got this situation under control.

"We weren't about to sit and wait to hear if you had found her," Kitty said, staring at the raft like she was expecting to see Genie.

"Did you find any evidence of her being alive?" John asked, barely letting Kitty finish speaking.

Aspen looked over at him, almost as if she was trying to see if he wanted to field this line of questioning in her stead. It was funny how now, when they were standing in front of the firing squad, she believed in mutual aid, but she'd been fighting teamwork most of the day.

"As we discussed, Mr. and Mrs. Manos, today is more about training your private team on the river." Leo watched as Cindy's boat slowed down on the other side of the river from them and waited. Of course, she was smart enough to see what was happening and avoid the fray.

"So, you didn't even look for my daughter?" Kitty said accusingly, putting her hands on her hips as rage peppered her features.

"Ma'am, I can assure you that we have been expending all of our resources. Today was no different," Leo said, trying to remain calm in the face of hate. "We really are trying to find her, I promise you. We are doing everything in our power."

"It's not enough!" Kitty screamed. The sound echoed off the moving water and filled the small canyon where they were standing.

Her words rained down on him like arrows from the sky, bombarding him until he was afraid that, one more outburst, he'd lose his cool and no longer care.

Aspen stepped out of the boat and moved in front of him as though she were shielding him from the woman's anguish. "Kitty, I agree…it's not enough." She moved toward the woman and wrapped her arms around her, pulling her into an embrace.

Genie's mother began to cry, and he was glad that Aspen was here to help. He'd seen far too many heartbroken parents, and it never got any easier to handle. Aspen didn't seem to be as numb to the pain as he was, and he was grateful for that—and at the same time, he wanted to push her away from the danger. She couldn't become as broken as he felt. He could only help these parents so much, but he could truly help Aspen. There was something so wrong in him letting it happen to her, to watch her soak in another's pain, which she would always carry.

He couldn't protect Genie, but he could protect Aspen. Yet, this life and this assignment was her doing. She had chosen to be here. As much as he wanted to shield her, to do so was intrusive.

Kitty sobbed and her husband came over and put his hand on her shoulder.

"Mr. and Mrs. Manos, I am sorry we didn't make the progress you were hoping for yet," he started, "but we aren't done for the day. For now, we need to make sure you are safe and well cared for. As such, I think the best thing for you both would be for you to head back to your rental—"

"We're not going to the condo," Kitty stated, nearly spitting at him through her tear-stained lips.

"That is fine, Mrs. Manos," he said, trying to remain calm and polite. "If going to your condo isn't something you are interested in, then I must ask you to please go to the press area. It is going to be set up at the Trapper Pullout. Do you know where that is?"

John looked over at him, and he could see the pained expression on his face. The man's eyes were sunken, and there were dark, heavy bags as if he hadn't slept since the day his daughter had gone missing. There were so many things about this situation that tore at him, and he wished he could correct, but he was only a man. He could only do so much.

"Mr. Manos, would you do that for me? I'd appreciate it," he said, trying to graciously lead the parents into making the right decision for not only their safety but also for the team so they could do their jobs to the best of their abilities.

"We're going with you, on your rafts," Kitty told him, pulling out of Aspen's arms and thrusting her arm over her face in an effort to wipe away her offending tears.

Aspen touched the woman's arm. "Kitty, you can't."

"There's plenty of room and you should be through the rapids. I'm not taking no for an answer," Kitty countered.

"Kitty." Aspen said her name like she was talking to a small kitten and not a full-grown woman. "I hate to tell you this, but if you and John don't go to the press staging area as requested, then things will be harder for everyone."

"If you don't take us now, we will just go to the next pull-out and keep showing up until you do. We are not taking no for an answer," Kitty continued to threaten.

Leo pulled in a hard breath. "Mrs. Manos, Aspen was correct. If you do not remove yourself from our investigation area, then we will be forced to call a deputy at the Sheriff's department and have them come and forcibly remove you from the scene."

Kitty glared at him, her hate for him burning so hot that he could feel his skin sizzle.

Doesn't she understand that I don't want to be like this? That I want to make things right for her? Not cause her further harm.

John's dark eyes seemed to grow impossibly darker. "Kitty," he said, squeezing his wife's shoulder, "we don't want to cause trouble. That's not what we need."

"Genie is out there," Kitty said, her tears started to fall again, defying her anger. "Her husband did this to her."

He had heard whispers about their theories of her disappearance before, but Aspen was a softer touch.

"What do you think happened to Genie?" she asked.

"Why don't you tell me as I walk you and John back to your car?"

Oh, this clever woman.

"Genie's husband was abusive," John said, as he started to walk toward the trail that led from the beach and disappeared into the cottonwood stand. "As I'm sure you know, Detective West."

"I have spoken to him, but again, this isn't a criminal case and there isn't any evidence that a crime was committed here. We don't even have a positive location on your daughter."

He didn't want John to hate him as Kitty seemed to. He needed to try to keep on speaking terms with him as they were treading on sensitive ground.

"I have read the charges against Mr. Gull, sir. Yes." He tried to sound impassive and professional, especially given all the things he had come to know about Scott Gull since his wife had gone missing.

"He had been physically abusive toward Genie," Kitty said. "He beat her so badly last month that I made sure she called you guys. It was while John and I were in Mexico on vacation when Genie called us. She was incredibly upset."

"From what she said, she was lucky to get away from Scott. He was furious with her," John added. "We were very worried about her safety."

Aspen glanced over at John. Just because he didn't like Scott or what he had done to Genie, it didn't mean the man was guilty—he hadn't gotten his day in court. It didn't mean he didn't believe the guy didn't have something to do with Genie's disappearance, but without proof he couldn't arrest him or make him tell him anything.

That wasn't to say he didn't have a hunch that Scott had something to do with Genie going missing—he just had to prove it, and in that lay the biggest issues.

It was about a half mile to where they must have parked to hike into this location, and though it wasn't that big of a distance, the two parents struggled with the topography. In several places, they had to make their way down and up the other side of sodden drainage ditch areas, leaving their shoes and socks wet and heavy.

Kitty was gasping for breath as they came through the third drainage ditch, forcing them to stop near a copse of aspens. The green leaves were quaking in the gentle early summer breeze, making it look as though the trees were dancing. The festive nature was in direct opposition to the situation that they found themselves in, but he couldn't help but see the beauty in the simple reality of the world around them.

If Genie had passed away on the river, he hoped her spirit would rest in a place like this, a world of dancing trees as she was finally free from the horrors that might have been inflicted upon her at the hands of her abuser.

Chapter Eight

The mile-long hike had thrown off their schedule, but when Aspen returned to where they had taken out of the water, everyone was sitting around a small pile of food wrappers and water bottles. They were talking, and as they approached, Cindy tilted her head back with a laugh at something Chad had said. The sun hit her face in such a way that she appeared as though she was almost glowing. The effect was beautiful.

If Leo had dated her at some point, or had some kind of crush on his coworker, Aspen could understand. Cindy was cool, funny, strong and beautiful.

"How's it going?" Chad asked, looking away from Cindy with a smile on his face.

"Good," she said, with a tight nod of her head.

Cindy shot a questioning glance at Leo, one Aspen wasn't sure she had been meant to see.

"We delivered Genie's parents to their vehicle," Leo said. "It is likely that we will be seeing them at our final destination this evening."

Chad picked up a couple of bars and held them out for them to take to eat. "You guys will be needing these."

Leo dipped his head in acknowledgment, but there was a tightness to his features that made Aspen wonder if he was just tolerating him—either way, she supposed it didn't really matter just as long as they could work together. Though unlikely, she would have liked if they could all walk away from this day with new friendships; especially one between she and Leo.

He had barely spoken two words on their hike back to their boats, but he had kept their pace so fast that she wasn't sure if he was trying to show off. If that was his intention, it had worked. She had stared at his ass most of the way. Yet, at the same time, she'd had no problem keeping up with him. For that, she was proud.

Suck on that, she thought, looking over at Leo as he took a bite from the snack.

He had green-lensed Costa polarized sunglasses on, but from the angle she was standing at his side, she could make out the gold flecks in his aged-honey-colored eyes. The sun had started to darken his skin, giving him the start of what would no doubt become a rich tan. He lifted the bar to his mouth again, and she found herself staring at his bulging biceps.

Is everything about him, from his ego to his arms, huge? She smirked at the inadvertent naughtiness of her thought.

He probably had hot-man-itis. She and her best friend had come up with the special term for men who were so hot that they didn't really know how to pleasure a woman because all women fell to their knees before them and pandered to the Adonis. If she had to describe her perfect Adonis, damn it if it wouldn't pretty much be this tattooed alpha.

He had to be terrible in bed. *Terrible*, she told herself.

That isn't to say I can't just imagine how good he might be between the sheets. If he is though, he is a damned unicorn.

No woman was lucky enough to get a smart, outdoorsy, hot alpha who could leave her quaking in the sheets.

"You okay over there? Something wrong?" he asked, pulling her from her thoughts as she realized he was staring right at her and had caught her breaking him down.

She blinked, trying to pretend like she had been looking past him and not staring directly at the outdoors tattoo, with a pine tree and a fisherman, on his left arm or thinking about his sexual prowess. He couldn't think that she wanted him, not even for a second.

Chewy wiggled over to her and sat down beside her, giving her a look that told her that the pup could tell what she was thinking and was all in favor. She patted the dog's head. "At least you have my back."

"Oh," Leo said. "What is that supposed to mean?"

She playfully chuffed, pretending to be affronted by his intrusion into her and Chewy's conversation. "Wouldn't you like to know," she teased.

He sent her a wilting smile. "Fine, you and Chewy keep your secrets."

Chad stood up between them. "If you guys are done flirting and screwing off in the woods, I think it's time we got back to work, don't you?"

Her face warmed. They hadn't been *flirting*, just getting along…that was entirely different. She glanced over at Leo, expecting him to say something to the same effect, but instead he was petting his dog, who'd made his way back over to his owner, and looking at the ground.

"Yeah," she said, a mixture of embarrassment and curiosity within her. "Do you want me to go with you?" she asked, looking at Chad.

"Yeah," Leo answered, as he must not have seen who she had been looking at when she had asked.

Chad sent Leo a scalding look. "Yes, Aspen," he replied, saying her name like it held extra syllables. "You should come with *your* team."

Leo stepped around Chad.

If she hadn't been at the epicenter of this strange, indirect love-triangle thing that was happening, it would have been funny to watch the two men pose and growl. However, as things stood, she wasn't here to deal with them acting like love interests. She and Chad had their chance, and there was no way she and Leo could ever be together. For all intents and purposes, their rivalry was completely in vain.

"Chad," she said, "I think I'm going to stick with Leo for now. I want to see how he and his team run the rest of this stretch of the river. That way tomorrow, when we come back, we have a better understanding of what we can expect." She looked to Leo who had an overly pronounced grin on his face.

It made her want to slug him in the shoulder and knock it off, though she also found it sexy as hell. She could get used to his smile.

Chad turned and stormed off toward his team's boat where Steve was waiting. Sighing, Leo turned and followed suit, going to his raft, which was tied up farther down the beach.

Cindy stood up from where she had been sitting on the log, apparently watching everything unfold between the three of them. "If you want to see something really fun," she said, looking at her, "we could make these two ride in the other boat together and we could go without them." Cindy snorted a laugh.

The idea was funny, but Aspen couldn't imagine that it would end well for anyone involved. "We don't want to have to start a search for any other bodies today."

Cindy nodded. "You have me there."

She turned to walk away, but before she could follow the rest of the boaters, Aspen called after her. "Is he always like this?"

"Like what? Grumpy?" Cindy asked with a quirk of her brow. "Or territorial?"

After her conversation with Smash, she had no doubt that Leo was both of those things. "I guess I'm asking if he is always this—" she paused as she searched for the right word *"—possessive."*

Cindy smiled, the action moving into her eyes. "He is a lot of things, but that is one thing I haven't seen him act like before." She winked. "Looks like you are heading into unchartered waters with that cowboy."

Cindy turned and moved to her boat, leaving Aspen standing on the beach with the Clif Bar still in her hand. Standing there confused and at a loss when it came to how to continue their search tomorrow—beyond doing what they were already doing—she suddenly wondered why exactly she had been so fervent in her desire to come here. This search had been in good hands and under control by a team that clearly knew what it was doing. It had been terribly egotistical of her to think she and Chad and the rest of their team could do better.

Yet, the day wasn't over.

There was still time to prove that she had made the right choice in deciding to take on this search.

She had to prove to Leo that they were not just more weight on the boats.

They hadn't begun to pull out all the stops when it came to her teams' resources, and though she hadn't initially planned to break out different equipment today, she had an idea. Making her way over to her raft, she pointed toward the black UAV box that was packed tightly under Chad's seat. "Can you hand me that?" she asked him, pulling his attention away from his phone.

"What?" he asked, not paying attention to her.

It was funny how quickly a man's focus could shift when someone else wasn't threatening to move in on what another man saw as his.

"Can you hand me the drone, please?" she repeated, sounding more annoyed than the situation actually dictated, but she couldn't control her feelings, which leaked into her tone.

He stuffed his phone away and reached under his seat and drew out the box. "I'm glad you are finally going to do something instead of just letting that guy lead you around by the nose."

She twitched with anger. "Excuse me?" She looked over at Cindy, who was reeling in the anchor and thankfully hadn't seemed to have heard what Chad had just said. "I'm not *letting him lead me by the nose*," she stated. "I am doing what I need to do to make this all go smoothly." She took the drone box.

"Sure, you keep telling yourself that. I've seen how you've been with him and his crew all day—giggling and crap."

Oh, this is all too much.

"Look, Chad," she said, uttering his name like it was another kind of four-letter word, "just because I'm having a relatively nice day with another team doesn't mean you need to get all snippy. I'm not leaving Life Savers."

"You know I can't do this thing without you, but that's not what I was talking about," Chad countered as she moved to walk away.

She stopped and moved in closely, making sure that only Chad could hear her. "Then what is it *exactly* that you care about?"

He looked slightly surprised that she would have the audacity to question what he had clearly meant to be a statement she would ignore. "I care about you. If you gave me a chance, I'd make you happy, but what I meant—"

"You don't care about me, Chad. You just want what you can't have. And if you can't have it, you don't want anyone else to have it. You are acting like a goddamn kid, and I don't want any part of it. I'm here to do my job and you need to focus on doing yours." She turned away. "Don't talk to me again until I ask you a question."

Chapter Nine

As they drifted downriver, Leo slowly moved the oars, making sure that they safely navigated their way through the little outcrop of rocks that was pushing through the surface of the water. He was surprised to see anything protruding this time of year. The runoff from the high-mountain snows hadn't really started to hit the main channel of the river. But thanks to the warm temps, they would start any day now. It was crazy how much the water conditions could change in just a matter of a few hours.

As it was, the water was starting to get slightly more silt-filled, and the dark blues of the early part of the day had begun to turn to a murky blue-brown color. Soon, the rivers would be rushing against the banks, carving out the walls and blowing through anything that stood in their way, leaving only a muddy swath when the waters would finally recede in the late-summer months.

He'd seen entirely new river channels created in these kinds of months, and the paths he thought he knew would disappear like they had never really existed as anything more than a figment of his imagination.

The drone buzzed overhead, its blades sounding like

someone had kicked a hornet's nest. It was funny, but when it came to the Manos family, they kinda had.

At the bow, Chewy lifted his nose into the air. He dropped to his haunches, alerting to something.

Leo stopped rowing and looked over his shoulder at Aspen, who was staring at a little screen attached to the controls of the UAV. "You spot anything?"

She didn't glance up. "Not yet, but it is crazy what I am able to see when it comes to the water depths. You guys don't know how lucky you are to have water that you can almost see through."

This was nothing. There were areas in the Rocky Mountains where a person and their dog could sit in a kayak and see the log-littered bottom of a high-mountain lake. From the top, it would appear as if the downed timbers were only a few feet from the surface, when in actuality they could have been dozens of feet below. It was an incredible optical illusion that came only with the cleanest and coldest of waters.

"You would think it would be easier to find people."

She jerked her head up and gave him a pointed look, as though she was gauging to see whether he had made that statement as a jab.

He went back to his rowing. "It's okay," he offered. "When I first got on SAR, I thought that I could come out here and find missing people right away. I thought I was tough as nails, but this job has a terrible way of humbling even those of us who thought we could do no wrong."

"You thought you could do no wrong?" she asked, an inquisitive softness to her voice.

"When you are twenty-two and rolling around with a

badge on your hip, it does some pretty crazy stuff to your sense of self. I was tough, and I knew I was tough."

"You *were* tough?" she teased. "What happened?"

Smash turned around from where he was sitting on the bow with Chewy. "Your dog is acting funny," he said, pointing at the dog's tense body.

Chewy whined and stared off in the direction of the woods to their right.

"I think we should stop and check out whatever Chewy is pulling from the air here," Leo said, working the right oar as he rowed them nearer to the bank. "Smash, you need to let Cindy and the team know."

"On it," Smash said, and he quickly radioed to let them know what was happening and why.

As Leo got close to shore, Smash jumped out of the front of the boat and grabbed the line and tied it around a nearby bush. It wasn't the best or sturdiest location to tie-down, but the water wasn't moving too quickly and he tried not to worry.

The buzz of the drone moved away as Aspen directed the robot overhead deeper into the wooded area. Leo pulled out his phone and dropped a pin at their location, so they could write a full report about the activities later.

After taking off his and Chewy's PFDs, he clicked the leash onto his dog's collar and lifted him out of the raft, careful not to catch one of the dog's nails. As he hit the ground, the pup wiggled, shaking off the nerves. He let out a wide, anxiety-releasing yawn, complete with a little whine at the end.

"Don't worry, buddy, we're going to go for a walk. You

can *search*," he said, using the work word, and Chewy's ears perked up in understanding. "That's right, buddy."

He reached out to Aspen as she slipped off her PFD; she handed the drone's controls to Smash and then quickly stepped out and took them back. "Thank you," she said, looking back down at the screen.

Her hand had been warm, and something made him wish he was still holding it, but he shook off the thought as asinine. Clearly, he just needed to get out more. It had been a while since he had been on a date. Actually, come to think of it, his last date had been with his ex-wife. Just because he was starving for human touch didn't mean he could seek it out during working hours. He had other things to focus on.

"You stay here, Aspen. See if you can find anything overhead," he said, not looking away from the dog.

"Got it," she said.

"Smash," Leo continued, "you stay with the raft."

He gave him a clipped nod.

As Chewy got done with his business marking every tree within his leash's length, Leo walked with him into the brush. "You ready, Chew?" he asked, motioning for the dog to sit. Chewy looked up at him with knowing eyes, tail wagging and his entire body in twitches and tremors as he waited for the command. He extended the length of the dog's leash. "Let's search!"

Chewy tore off down the trail, his nose pressed to the ground as he weaved and bobbed, working the scent.

It was incredible to watch the dog work; it was almost as if with each movement he could read the dog's mind. A few hundred yards into the search, Chewy stopped and lifted his nose into the air as if he had come upon a spot where the trail had suddenly disappeared. After more than a few hours, fresh scents rapidly dissipated and could become harder for the dog to distinguish—especially if there was any kind of inclement weather like heavy winds or rain. This morning it had been foggy in the river bottoms before they had come out to search.

Chewy's pause made him wonder how old the scent trail was that they were following—or if it was a scent trail of a person or animal and not of something else. Chewy had been trained to alert to narcotics, rotting flesh or—in this specific case, thanks to their hours of working the area— Genie. That wasn't to say he wouldn't give false alerts. Dogs were good, but also notoriously fallible.

Chewy jerked to the left, going off trail and into a break in the dogwood bushes that littered the area. The red-barked bushes pulled at Leo's clothing, wanting their pound of flesh in payment for his trespass. Thankfully, as he began to gain altitude, they relented and he found himself in a pine forest. Aspen's drone was still buzzing overhead.

He hadn't thought to ask her how far she could go before he would be out of range, but if she needed to adjust, he was sure that she could accommodate. He didn't need to micromanage her, or this situation any more than required.

Chewy started to pull hard at the leash, moving right and straight up a mountain face. His nails scraped on the rocks as he pulled himself and Leo in the direction of whatever they were following.

As he started to move up the hill, Leo realized how tired his body had become. He'd already had a full morning of rowing and then the hike with Genie's parents, now this.

He was in shape, but he was putting on the miles and had no doubt that he would pay for it tomorrow.

After ten minutes of moving back and forth and switch-backing up the rocky game trails of the mountain, Chewy came to a stop. He sat down, ears perked and body tense—alerting.

At first, Leo couldn't see what the pup was alerting to. Everything around them seemed to belong there. On his left, down the mountain, was a littering of rocks and a few hardy bushes and bunchgrasses that clung to the hillside with their concrete resolve, but little more. Scattered around were the tall, looming ponderosa pines intermingled with some lodgepoles now that they were slightly higher.

A few arrowleaf balsamroots were in bloom, their yellow faces pointing toward the heat of the afternoon sun. The drone was holding steady overhead, and he realized that he had grown so accustomed to the sound that now he barely even noticed it when he wasn't directly thinking about the thing.

Chewy whined, annoyed that Leo was the weakest link in whatever had brought them out on this search.

He walked up to stand beside Chewy, who remained sitting but glanced up at him and then back out to his left. As he stood beside the dog, he was so insistent that Leo could feel him vibrating.

Then, at the base of a ponderosa and right side of the tree, he spotted a shallow hole. Inside, just barely visible was the top of a furry head.

"Dude, if you dragged me off the boat and all the way up this hill for a dead skunk or something, I will make sure you don't get any treats for a week," he said, looking down at Chewy.

The dog wagged his tail.

"Stay," he said with the raise of his hand as he stepped off the trail to investigate.

As he moved closer to inspect the furry thing, the ground slipped beneath him, sending dirt and pebbles down the hillside. This animal, whatever it was, had chosen this spot well to hole up. It wasn't readily accessible by any sort of predators that came its way. If it was still alive and capable of defending itself, he needed to be ready.

He put his hand on his gun, not drawing in the event the hillside continued to crumble beneath him. He didn't need to fall while having a hot round—his team didn't need to have to come to his rescue today.

"Hey," he said, trying to sound soothing as he neared the tree in hopes the animal in the hole would give him some sign of life. "Hey, little guy."

A triangular, erect ear popped up. Slowly, a dog raised its head and looked up at him. It was a German shepherd, but its eyes were sunken with dehydration and the fur on his neck was starting to slough. He didn't look good.

"Oh," he said, his heart breaking as he looked at the dog who was barely holding on to life. "I got you, buddy," he said. He looked up at the sky and motioned at the drone and Aspen. Hopefully, it would be enough for her to realize that he had found an animal.

Growing closer to the pup, he took his time in approaching the animal until he was right beside the hole. The dog sniffed him, but almost as if he knew that Leo was there to help, the animal dropped its weak head back down on its paws.

He reached out and gently ran his hand down the animal's fur. He turned the animal's collar; there on its tag was the name "Malice." Genie's dog.

So where was his owner? If he was out here by this river, Genie had to be out here, too.

First things first, he had to take care of the animal.

Terrified for the future of this pup, he took his time until he had the dog in his arms. He carefully picked his footing until he was back on the trail. Chewy gave the dog a sniff, but Malice didn't respond.

"Good boy, Chewy. Good boy," he said. "You may have just saved this guy's life." Now hopefully they'd have the same luck when it came to Genie.

Chapter Ten

It didn't take long for air support to agree to take the dog to the emergency veterinary clinic. To be honest, Aspen hadn't been sure that this unit would have the resources to allocate this level of care to an animal, but she was relieved. They were constantly surprising her, which made her continue to feel like a heel.

The rest of the team sat on the bank of the river. It hadn't been their intention to camp here tonight, but thanks to the delays and then their finding Genie's dog, it didn't seem prudent to keep moving downriver, as it would likely be dark before they would hit their takeout point. She couldn't say she was disappointed. She'd always wanted to camp in Montana, even if this wasn't exactly what she had intended when she had fantasized about this place.

In her mind's eye, she had been sitting around a fire with a handsome man. They would be having philosophical conversations about the stars and the meaning of life. Instead, she was here with a bunch of other people, listening to them talk about what to have for dinner.

As they waited for the helo to come pick up Malice, she sat down on the ground and held the dog's head in her lap.

She had tried to get the animal to drink a bit of water from her bottle, but so far, he had refused. She ran her hand down the animal's fur, over his skin-covered ribs that were riddled with ticks. Tufts of hair came out with each stroke, but she didn't care about the bugs or the hair. The only thing that mattered was giving the animal comfort in its greatest time of need.

"You will be out of here soon, Malice," she cooed. "We've got you. You're in good hands," she said, looking over at Leo, who was building a fire ring out of stones on the riverbank.

Chewy was lying at her feet, carefully watching over his newly found companion.

Steve, Smash, Cindy and Chad were out in the woods, gathering firewood for the night and putting together a large wooden and tarp structure in the event it rained and they needed cover. It was fifty-fifty, according to the National Weather Service, and from what Steve had said, in Montana that was as good as the weather predictions got when it came to the backcountry. While it could be raining in one area, it could be sunny and dry just a few yards away thanks to the high peaks that surrounded them.

She pulled a tick from the dog's fur, making sure she'd gotten its head, and dropped its engorged body onto a large thimbleberry leaf she had picked. The tick's legs wiggled, but no matter how much it turtled on its back, it wasn't going to go anywhere. She hated ticks.

It was hard to even imagine what this dog had been through in the last two weeks. It was crazy to think that no one had stumbled upon him sooner. This poor animal had to have been eating anything it could find to survive, which accounted for the bugs. No doubt, it had been trying to scavenge from winter-kill animals and anything else it could get its teeth into.

People, nor domesticated dogs, weren't equipped to be out in the wilds of Montana alone. It was a wonder that another, larger predator like a wolf or bear hadn't come across him and taken advantage of his weakened state. It made her worry for Genie. If this dog had barely made it, there wasn't much of a chance for the woman. That was, if the woman was out here at all.

So many things could have happened to have led to the dog being here—maybe he'd been swept away trying to get Genie out of the hands of a kidnapper, or maybe they'd been hiking along the bank. However, everything was supposition.

She ran her hand down the dog's legs, looking for any obvious breakage, but didn't find anything other than his being emaciated. He should have been named Lucky.

Leo clicked a large rock into place around the fire ring and stood up to appreciate his hard work. He gave a little nod, like he approved. The small action made her smile. She liked a manly man, the kind who could go from stacking rocks to making love in the blink of an eye.

Not that they were making love…or that she was thinking about him naked and her riding him like the stallion he was. *Gah.*

After seeing him row all day, then hike the mountain, she had a solid idea of the body and muscles that were barely hidden by his clothes. If she could live in a fantasy world where she could do whatever she wanted without fear of reprisal or concerns about the future, she would *so* lick every curve of every part of his body. She would love to satisfy him and have him watch as she did.

She hadn't realized she was staring until she noticed he was smiling at her and staring right back. "You okay?" he asked.

"Sorry," she said, trying to cover up the fact that she had been doing dirty things to him in her mind. "I guess I was just zoning out. It's been a long day."

He nodded then walked over and sat down beside her. Malice's ear perked, but he didn't move as Leo started to run his hand down the dog's fur. If nothing else, at least the dog knew he was loved if this was going to be his end.

"I understand," he said, sending her a sad smile. Chewy laid down against Leo's legs and closed his eyes.

"I hate this," she said, motioning toward Malice.

"Oh, me, too," he said, running his hand down the dog's side and then giving Chewy a long scratch. "But there is nothing I won't do to make sure Malice lives."

Just like that, her heart swelled two sizes. A man who put animals first…yes, please.

"Do you know when the helo is supposed to get here?"

He looked down at his watch and checked the time. "My best guess is in the next twenty minutes. It takes them a little bit to get going."

"Is this normal? Your team coming in to help an animal?"

He sent her that sexy smile that she had come to enjoy. "Our SAR team isn't like the rest of the nation. We have a great group of folks with huge hearts. I can't begin to tell you the number of rescues we've been on where we have gone above and beyond. A few months ago, one of our other member's dog went missing during a search and we all searched for him."

"Did you find the dog?"

"Yes, and the dog had found our vic as well. Was sitting on her until we could locate them both. Dog barked to be found."

She looked down at the German shepherd in her lap, wondering how long he had been out here and barking to be found. "Do you think that Genie is going to be around here somewhere, too?"

"If her remains were out here, from the behavior I've seen from other animals in situations like these, I'm surprised that he would leave her." He sighed. "Then again, if she has been dead for two weeks, he might have gotten pushed out by other, larger predators who wanted a free meal."

Nature was brutal.

"However," he continued, "I think that his being out here in the woods downstream from the place they were last seen means that they were in the river. There's little chance he would be in this location from just hiking. He is too far away from our launch, and there are too many cliffs and natural barriers between there and here."

"You think we should get a ground crew in?" she asked, careful to make sure that she respected his wishes about them working in tandem.

He quirked a brow as he looked at her, like he had heard her attempt to make things right between them and their teams. "I think that would be the best next step. However, we need teams still working the water."

Her stomach knotted. "Which team are you going to be working with?"

There was a pregnant pause, as he must have realized that what she was really asking was if she was going to be working with him or with someone else. There was a light in his eyes as he glanced from the dog to her. "That is yet to be decided. I have to talk to my team, get a plan figured out."

Was he being vague on purpose, just to drive her wild with desire? Was he teasing her? Or had she totally misread the entire situation with him and she was the only one feeling the draw?

His handset crackled to life, and Cindy's voice peppered the space between them. "West, are you there? Over."

He grabbed the handset and pressed the button. "Yes. What's happening? Over."

"We have located some potential evidence."

Evidence? The word surprised her. There hadn't been any talk of a real crime, but maybe Cindy meant there was evidence of Genie's location. Heck, it could have even been evidence that Genie had been out here, in the woods, alive.

She started to ask a question, but held back as Leo pressed the button. "Let's meet up and discuss in person. Over."

"Roger. We will start making our way back. Out." Cindy's voice faded from the air, leaving behind lingering questions.

Chapter Eleven

As Cindy hit the edge of the camp, she nodded in the direction from which she had come. "I made Chad and the rest of the team stay with the gun."

"The what?" Leo asked, shocked. Of all the things he thought Cindy would tell him they found, that had been about the last thing on the list of possibilities. "What kind of gun?"

She took out her phone. "I made sure that no one touched it. Doesn't look like it's been out there very long." She pulled up a picture and handed her phone over.

There, wedged between two river rocks, was a Glock. It had dried flotsam caked on its grip.

"Did you get the serial number?" he asked.

"Yeah, I was hoping that you could run it through the database when you get back. Find out who the owner is." Cindy skipped to the next picture where it was focused in on the numbers etched into the gun's slide.

"This is a great find." He hit the buttons on her phone and forwarded all the images to his device and the guys at the office. However, it was unlikely they would actually get them until they got back into better cell phone reception. "And you pinned its location?"

She gave him an *are you stupid?* look. "Really?"

He glanced back at Chewy, Malice and Aspen. Of course, he had known Cindy would do her job right, but something about Aspen being so close to him with Cindy around made him nervous. He didn't know why. It was dumb, letting his emotions run the show like this.

"Sorry," he said. "Good job on not reporting this over the air."

Cindy gave him a brief nod. "I figured the last thing we needed was for rubberneckers who might be listening to hear what we found. We don't need anyone leaking information to the press. If they do, we will have a total goat and pony show on our hands—not that we don't already," she said, whispering the last part as she glanced swiftly toward Aspen.

He leaned in. "She's not as bad as I thought. She's been a pretty good sport, but I think we just needed to figure out the hierarchy and who was really in charge."

Cindy stared at his face like she was trying to figure out exactly what he was thinking when it came to Aspen, something more than he was saying. He swiftly looked away. He didn't need her sensing that there was anything more than what there was between him and Aspen. Cindy wasn't huge on gossip, but if she thought there was something going on between them and let it slip, it would burn through the department like wildfire and he would be mercilessly teased.

There was chopping noise of helicopter blades in the distance, and he turned to see a helo coming around the river bend. He moved toward the water, so the pilot could easily see him and his team, and he motioned upriver toward the large swath of open riverbank where they could land—though he was sure they didn't need his help in navigating.

The helo moved slowly, as if the pilot was assessing the area before the aircraft touched down where he had motioned. The skids move gently to the ground, like the pilot had done this landing a million times before. He would never get over how a helo could float. In another life, he would have loved to have been a pilot like his friend and fellow search and rescue volunteer, Casper Keller.

Chewy padded over to him, needing his reassurance thanks to the noise and activity that was filling the air.

"It's okay, buddy," he said, rubbing the dog's ear in hopes to calm his nerves. "You help me take care of Aspen. She needs us right now. Okay, buddy?"

As if the dog totally understood his words, he moved back toward her and sat beside the starved pup. He loved that his dog, just like him, was always wanting to be the protector.

He followed Chewy over and stuck out his hand. Aspen lowered Malice's head from her lap and took his offered hand before standing up. Malice looked up at them, not moving his head. He was getting worse by the minute.

Squatting, he gently moved his arms under the dog and lifted him up. "It's okay, Malice, I've got you. You're a good boy," he said softly as he tried to keep the dog calm. "You're going to get help, buddy."

Aspen reached over and petted the dog in his arms. "You're in good hands, baby."

Her words made something inside him shift as they walked toward the helo.

Chewy walked beside them, escorting his friend. Inside

the helo was a waiting veterinarian. The body of the place was set up like an emergency triage area. He was impressed and made sure to send Casper a thumbs-up in appreciation of his preparation and readiness to help the dog.

He placed Malice on the blue pads the vet had set out. "Did you observe any wounds to the dog's body?" the vet asked as she ran her hand down the animal.

Leo shook his head.

"I think he may be in liver failure," Aspen said. "His gums are pale, and I've picked at least fifty ticks off his body."

The vet nodded, lifting up the dog's lip and taking a look at the nearly white gums. "He is definitely anemic. We will make sure to get him a blood transfusion when we get back to the clinic. Until then, I'm going to make sure we give him some fluids."

Casper pulled off his headset as he looked back at them. "Did you guys want a ride out?"

Leo glanced over at Aspen questioningly. She shook her head. "We are so close to possibly finding Genie. I want to stay with Malice, but I wouldn't be able to live with myself if I left now and the rest of the team located her."

He nodded. "I need to go pick up the gun and search the area for any further evidence with my team. I'm the lead detective on this, so I can definitely understand your reticence in not wanting to leave the scene." He turned to Casper. "We do appreciate the offer, however."

Casper gave him a tip of the head in acknowledgment.

The vet started the clippers and shaved the forearm of the dog.

"Let me know how things go with Malice, please," Aspen

said, holding her hands together as if she wanted to reach out and pet the dog, but holding back out of respect for the vet's work.

The vet didn't look up. "Will do."

They stepped back from the helo, and as quickly as the aircraft had touched down, it was airborne and headed back the way they had come. As the sound of their blades dissipated, he turned back to their little makeshift camp.

"You didn't have to stay out in the woods. You could have come back out in the morning," Aspen said.

Was she saying this because she didn't want to spend the night with him? Or was she just trying to be nice? He wasn't sure he wanted to ask, as he didn't really want to know the answer.

Hell, it wasn't like Aspen had given him any indication that she would be nervous around him. She was friendly enough, but he wouldn't call her overly flirty.

Chewy walked over to Aspen and sat down against her leg, looking up at her like she was the most beautiful woman he had ever seen. Damn if that dog didn't give his thoughts away. Thankfully, she didn't seem aware of his struggle as she patted Chewy.

"You guys wanting to head back up the mountain?" Cindy called to them.

"You ready to hit it?" Aspen asked him, a small smile on her lips.

"I have a feeling it's going to be a long night," he said, looking up at the clouds that had started to fill the sky.

"I'm not afraid of a little rain," she said, scratching Chewy. "I'm not sweet enough to have to worry about melting."

"Wasn't it the Wicked Witch of the West who melted in the rain?" he teased.

"Real funny, jackass." Aspen stuck out her tongue. "Though, admittedly, that is probably a closer representation of who I am." She laughed.

He couldn't disagree more, but he did like to hear the sound of her laughter. "Do you have everything you need to be out here in the wet?"

"Don't you think you should have asked that before we said no to our free ride out?"

He tipped his head. "Fair point."

"I promise, Leo, I'm more than capable of taking care of myself out here."

"I know you are capable." That was true, but a sickening lump formed in his stomach. He wasn't sure what it was that was causing this strange reaction, but as he looked at her, he wanted to protect her by telling her to wait here and stay behind. Maybe it was thanks to everything they had gone through already today.

He opened his mouth to tell her to wait, but then he remembered that she had already made her position clear. She wasn't the kind who would allow him to give her orders, or to miss out on a search.

There was no protecting this woman. She stood on her own feet, and he could only be there for her by trying to remain at her side. Here was hoping he could help when she found herself in harm's way.

Chapter Twelve

It was dark by the time they made it to the location where Cindy had found the gun. When they arrived, the rest of the team was sitting around and waiting. Aspen was surprised they weren't out working a pattern, but at the same time they had to be as tired as she was. Normally, during searches, they were only allowed to work so many hours before they were required to lay up; however, nothing about this search had gone according to their plan and she doubted it would turn around now.

The Glock was wedged between two large rocks as they had seen in the picture. It hadn't started to rust, but there was enough residue on its slide and grip to make her think it had been there for a while.

"Do you think this gun has anything to do with our investigation?" Aspen asked the question that had been plaguing her since she had first seen Cindy's picture.

Leo pulled out his phone and took a series of pictures of the gun with different lighting. Finally, after he appeared to get everything he needed, he took a paper bag from his backpack and delicately picked up the gun, making sure not to touch it with his bare hand.

"Do you need to clear the gun?" Aspen asked.

Leo looked over at her. "Normally, I would, but in this case I don't want to disturb what little evidence may be left on the weapon." He closed the top of the bag and carefully set it on the top of the contents in his backpack before zipping it closed.

She could understand why he didn't want to make sure the gun wasn't loaded, but it made her uncomfortable knowing that he had a potentially loaded gun resting in his bag. The good news was that the trigger wasn't readily accessible.

"Make sure you are hiking out behind everyone," she said, trying to sound like she wasn't overly concerned.

"I'll make sure I don't accidently shoot anyone," he said, sending her what she was sure was supposed to be a comforting smile.

She gave him an appreciative nod. "I'm going to go take a look down the bank. You want to go with me?"

He pulled on his backpack and affixed a headlamp to his hat. Chewy moved to his side. She loved how the dog was his constant shadow, their bond almost as endearing as Leo's smile.

Chad stood up. "I'll tag along."

Her face twitched. "Um."

Smash, who had been sitting quietly with Cindy and Steve, followed Chad's lead. "Yeah, I think it would be good if we all worked as a team." He motioned around them to the encroaching darkness. "Actually, don't you think we should probably head toward our camp?"

Annoyance filled her, but she tried to self-correct by asking herself why she was feeling this way—the answer was simple. She wanted to spend some alone time with Leo.

That is stupid.

She didn't need alone time with anyone. What she needed was to find Genie, and Smash was right. They needed to get back to camp for the night. Everyone needed a break. To keep searching when everyone was on their last legs wasn't just a poor idea, but it was a good way to get people hurt.

"Did you guys follow the riverbank down to this point?" Leo asked.

Smash shook his head. "We worked down from where you found the pup. Everything go okay with the dog, by the way?"

"We got him loaded up and headed out." He pulled his phone back out of his pocket and moved to check his messages.

"Do you have service again?"

"Yeah, thankfully. Casper said Malice is perking up, but they haven't made it to the vet's clinic yet." He scrolled. "Oh, and it looks like one of my guys ran the gun's serial number through the database already."

"And?"

He looked up with wide eyes and, thanks to the light from her headlamp, his face was filled with strange, angular shadows. "You won't believe it."

"Believe what?" Chad asked.

Leo's face darkened, but it had nothing to do with the lighting. She wasn't sure if it was him or Chewy, but she was almost certain she had heard a low growl.

Leo sighed, sounding somewhat resigned. "It appears that the gun was registered to one Scott Gull."

"Holy…" Chad said excitedly.

"This investigation just changed gears," Leo said. "However, I want to make it clear that just because Genie's ex-husband is a piece of work as a human and his gun has been found in proximity to the dog, this is all circumstantial."

Aspen rolled her eyes. Sometimes she hated how law enforcement worked. She was a huge proponent of Occam's Razor—the simplest explanation was normally the right one.

"Seriously," he said, looking over at her.

"We have a missing domestic abuse survivor and her soon-to-be ex-husband's gun… This isn't rocket science," Aspen argued.

"I agree that everything is pointing in this guy's direction, but we still haven't found Genie. It's possible, however unlikely, that Genie is still alive."

She wanted to argue, but she had to hope the woman was somewhere out here just like her dog. "Do you think she would have been the one to have the gun? Maybe she had taken it out in the woods with her?"

"We won't know anything until we find her." His face scrunched. "I had thought of that, though. However, I was told that the last time she was seen she was wearing a hot pink bikini and she left her clothes on the bank. So that doesn't leave many locations for her to be packing."

Aspen's gut ached. *Scott killed her. He did it.*

"If she didn't bring this gun out here, then how do you think a gun registered to her ex would have ended up here?" Cindy asked.

Leo shrugged. "That is a hell of a good question." He turned, clearly not wanting to talk about all the facets of what was likely a criminal investigation.

It didn't seem to take as long to get back to camp as it had to get to the gun's location. However, when she set down her pack, Aspen couldn't deny she was bone tired. Though she would be sleeping on the ground tonight, she had no doubt that she would be sleeping hard.

Smash and Steve got the fire going, while she grabbed her sleeping bag from the raft. She carried it over to the makeshift shelter and placed it on the ground. The ache in her gut hadn't lessened since they had found out about Scott's gun, but the entire way back to camp she had tried to tell herself that the coming days would bring all the answers they needed.

At least, she hoped so.

Leo was petting Chewy, watching as Steve and Smash worked. She walked over to him and put her hand on his shoulder. "Did you let Genie's parents know about the dog?"

He tensed under her touch, like he hadn't expected her, but as he turned and looked up at her, his body relaxed. "No. Did you?"

She shook her head. "I'm not going to give them any information without clearing it by you, first. I don't want to give them any more fodder to be upset with you or your team."

He smiled. "You have no idea how much I appreciate that."

"Yeah," she said. "I am sorry that I bulled into this situation." She wanted to tell him how humbled she felt after today, especially after seeing how hard he and his team worked. Then again, she couldn't admit that she had made a mistake in coming here.

The fire was crackling in front of them, but it hadn't been

going long enough to let off a great deal of heat, so they had to move closer to it and each other to feel any warmth. She didn't mind being so close to him. In fact, he was putting off far more warmth than the budding flames.

"How far are we from the nearest access point?" she asked, trying to think about anything other than how badly she wanted to have her knee rub against his, in fact just to touch him in any way possible.

He pulled out his phone and clicked on an offline map. "So, we are here," he said, leaning in and pressing his knee against hers.

He could have been showing her a picture of the moon for all that she was paying attention. All she could think about as he spoke and moved the map around was how his knee was moving against hers. He was tall; she hadn't realized how much bigger he was than her. Even his hands were huge. His fingernails and skin were well-kept. She liked a man who took care of himself; it meant that he paid attention to details.

"Basically," he continued, his words finally piercing through her admiration of him, "if someone parked here, the easiest route to the water would still be a three-mile hike through some tough terrain. It's the only real nonaquatic access point."

"Do you think that if that gun was Scott's and he had anything to do with Genie's disappearance, that he would have walked in from that point?" she asked, loving the way he was touching her.

Leo looked out at the fire and slipped his phone back in his pocket and then gave the dog a pet.

Leo dropped his hand to her knee. "I don't know what

to think about this Scott situation, but you can bet that I will be talking to him as soon as we make it back to town."

"I bet," she said.

"I'm sure that Scott will tell me something stupid, the gun was stolen, he made an out-of-the-trunk sale and sold the gun or—and what I think is most likely if he and Genie really were having a contentious divorce—he will tell me that she took it when she left and he hasn't seen it since."

She wasn't sure whether or not she should reach out and put her hand on his, even though all she wanted to do was lace her fingers between his.

"Though his juvenile record is inadmissible and supposedly sealed, I happen to know that Scott Gull was kicked out of Job Corps when he was a kid. Do you know what kind of a screwup you have to be to get kicked out of a delinquency camp like that?"

She couldn't say she really knew what the Job Corps was. Scott was a peach… This was known and at this point, it didn't surprise her to hear that he had a checkered past long before he was a legal adult.

He squeezed her knee gently and then let his hand fall away from her. Had that been his signal that he had wanted her to give him some sort of reciprocal touch? Had that been his pitch and she had failed to swing?

Dating and flirtation should really come with some sort of manual.

"I…uh…" she stammered, looking down at his hand as he moved to pet Chewy. She needed to get out of this confusing situation and into the safety of her sleeping bag, where she could think about how she really wanted to proceed with this man. If he was hitting on her and she had missed it, what was that saying about her? And what did she really want from him? Until now, she had thought him completely unattainable and, moreover, uninterested.

"I'm getting warm," she lied, motioning toward the fire. "And it's been a long day. I am thinking I'm going to go lay down for a bit."

"Do you mind if I follow you that way?"

Her cheeks warmed, and she thumbed through the number of ways she wanted to answer that question. *Yes, but only if we zip our bags together and you make love to me all night.* Or, *do you really think you sleeping next to me is a good idea?*

Instead, she went with the simple, "We all have to sleep somewhere."

He stared at her, like he had wanted her to say something else. "Don't worry, I'll have Chewy sleep between us."

"Oh?"

"Yeah, he is a bit of the jealous kind. He won't allow for any of your shenanigans." He gave a little laugh as he stood up and waited for her to stand.

"I'm not worried about *my* shenanigans," she said, shooting him a look as she stood up. He started to walk toward the wooden and tarp shelter they had built.

Her gaze moved to his ass, perfectly lit up by the orange licking light of the fire.

"Your virtue is safe with me," he said, glancing over his shoulder at her.

The rest of the team didn't really seem to notice him as he walked away, and she waited a minute before she moved to follow him. Chad had his back to them, and the rest of the team was wrapped up in a variety of conversations about friends and family back at home.

She slipped into the darkness, thinking about her virtue. That was something she wasn't worried about, or what little remained of it. What she was worried about was not being able to deny herself the pleasure she so desperately needed at Leo's hands.

Chapter Thirteen

This was quickly promising to become one of the longest and most torturous nights of his life. He wasn't sure who he had pissed off in a former life to have set himself up for this special kind of hell, but he knew he would be stuck staring up at the cloud-filled sky all night and thinking about his sins.

Though he knew he should have run, or at the very least stayed at the fireside until Aspen had gone to bed, he'd invited himself and Chewy to sleep next to her.

About twenty minutes ago, a couple of flasks had appeared from someone's bag, and now the rest of the team was sitting by the warming fire sipping from the flasks and telling stories. Their voices echoed off the soothing patter and cascade of the moving river and bounced off the hillsides around them. From where they lay, the rest of the team wasn't visible as they were seated behind a smattering of brush and a few tall pines.

If we're careful, no one would know we are doing anything...

Aside from his nearby bedmate, this night was becoming something he would have wished for—friends, fire and the water. Yet, maybe it was made better with the knowledge that she was close to him as well.

He listened to see if he could make out the sounds of her sleeping, but she couldn't be heard over the noises of the night and Chewy's low, rumbling snores. Unable to control himself any longer, he rolled over. He carefully adjusted his backpack under his head.

He could have sworn he saw her eyes snap shut, but he wasn't sure if that was or wasn't wishful thinking.

Though he was more than aware of the possible risks in making a move, he couldn't see how they could be worse than the benefits. Especially in this moment, while he was watching the shadows of the firelight as it filtered through the underbrush and played with her hair, teasing him as they touched her while he was forced to only observe.

He tried to negotiate with himself. If he moved again and her eyelashes fluttered, then he would whisper something, but if she didn't have a flutter then he would roll over and forget any feelings or desires he was hoping to explore. Yet, that was entirely too abstract. What if he missed such a fleeting movement? Or what if she was just in REM sleep? There was too much to misread. He had to think of something else.

He swore he could almost feel the seconds ticking by as he struggled within himself.

His mind moved to all the things he should have been concentrating on instead of the woman beside him. Hell, he had a full-blown investigation to get into as soon as he got off this river and back to his regular life. This was only a blip in his world, and he had to keep what he was feeling in perspective.

Aspen wasn't the first beautiful woman he had worked with on the job and probably wouldn't be the last—he had never really found himself struggling before. What was it about her that made him want her so much?

Maybe it was the way she had seemed to go against him from the very first time he had laid eyes on her. There was no question that she was single-minded, focused and pigheaded. Damned if he didn't seem to like those traits in a woman. She was also incredibly smart, driven, and when she smiled…every time he could have sworn his heart nearly stopped.

Then again, this could all just be about lust. Arguably though, lust could be considered as one hell of a building block in many a successful relationship. He'd had more than a few in the past himself. His marriage, for example, had come from the fire of the loins—on the other side of that token though, he couldn't argue how poorly it had turned out.

He closed his eyes.

"You know," she whispered, making his eyes spring open, "if you are going to go to sleep the least you could do is say good-night."

He sent her a wide, wild smile. "Is that what you really want? For me to say good-night? I could name any other number of ways to send you off into your dreams."

She giggled, and the sound was so sweet and almost innocent that he couldn't help but wonder how little experience she could have had.

"Do you have someone waiting back home? Or with you?" he asked, forced to finally ask the question that had been weighing on him since they met.

"No. You?" She pulled her sleeping bag down from her mouth and held it with both hands around her neck as she looked up at him.

She looked so damned beautiful.

"No, but I'm open to the idea," he said, smiling at her.

"Oh?" She brushed a wayward strand of hair from her face. "What about you and I? Would you want someone here or something long-distance?"

He wanted to say yes, that he would take her any way he could get her, but he was experienced enough to know exactly how poorly something like that would go. Even when he had been living in the same house as his wife, he couldn't make it work. There was zero chance if he lived thousands of miles away. Or maybe in the information age that wasn't entirely true. It wasn't like they would have to have check-in phone calls. Now, they had video chatting and quick flights.

She shook her head. "Never mind, don't answer that."

"But—"

"No, seriously," she said, reaching out of her sleeping bag and touching the side of his face with her warm fingertips. "I'm getting ahead of myself."

"If you need to know that I'm the kind of guy who wants a real relationship before you kiss me, I can understand that." He reached up and took hold of her hand and her fingers curled around his. He brought them down to his mouth and gently kissed her skin.

She took in a breath, gasping as he rubbed the stubble on his chin against the softness of her fingers.

"I don't need promises of forever to kiss you," she whispered, her voice low and sprinkled with desire.

He moved closer to her, taking her lips with his. She

tasted like cherries and lip gloss, and it was a heady flavor. He let go of her fingers and pushed his hand into her loose hair and pulled her deeper into their kiss. She moaned into his mouth, and he swallowed the sound like he was a starving man.

Her tongue flicked against his and she pulled his lower lip into her mouth and sucked, making him think of all the places he would like for his mouth to travel on her body. She released him and pulled back just enough that they still touched but she could speak. "If we're going to do this, we should go somewhere maybe a little bit more private so we can take our time."

He was glad that at least one of them was thinking with a clear mind. "Yeah," he said, the word coming out as a grumble.

"Give me a few minutes in case someone at the fire notices me, then I'll meet you thirty paces directly west. I don't want anyone to get the wrong idea. Okay?" she asked, motioning in the direction with her chin.

He nodded.

She gave him another quick kiss, one filled with the promise of what was to come, and his entire body surged with want. She slipped out of her sleeping bag, and he watched her as she moved into the forest. Her pants cupped her ass in all the right ways, accentuating her muscular and round curves. The fabric pulled against her thighs and his mouth started to water.

It is happening.

I'm going to pull down those pants and kiss every inch of exposed flesh until she fills my mouth.

He started to count the seconds, each passing like a lifetime and proving that time wasn't a constant. Time was the thief of joy, stealing precious moments from the best times of life and stuffing those stolen seconds into anxious lags. It had never occurred to him, or maybe he'd never given it much thought until he was stuck in this moment of waiting quicksand, but time was truly his enemy—in every facet of his life.

Unable to stand it any longer, he pulled free of his sleeping bag and, leaving his backpack, he quietly worked his way into the woods. He glanced over his shoulder at the team around the campfire, but no one seemed to be focused on anything other than the conversations they were having in the raw, primordial light.

He and Chewy kept walking in the direction of where she had pointed, but he grew nervous the deeper he moved into the woods. She had definitely given him these directions, but it seemed so much farther than what he had expected. Had she been screwing with him? Waiting to see if he would really follow her into the woods to sleep with her? What if this was some kind of game she was playing?

There was the sound of a woman clearing her throat ahead, making him forget any thoughts he had of her leading him astray.

He tried not to pick up speed as he moved toward her sound. Now was the time he wanted the seconds to slow down and drip by, allowing him to languish in the moments of nervous hope and anticipation.

There was the thin light of the cloud-shrouded moon from above and as she stepped out from behind a pine, her naked body looked as though it was wrapped in a silver glow. If she'd had a halo, he would have thought her truly an angel.

She looked too beautiful, too perfect to be real. This had to be some fever dream—no man, and especially not him, could be so lucky.

"Aspen?" He spoke her name like it was a secret.

She floated toward him so serenely that he wasn't sure that her feet were even touching the ground. "Leo…" she cooed, moving into his embrace.

Her skin was cool and he wrapped her in his arms, pulling her against him to shield her from the bite of the night. His body gave his lust for her away, his sex pressing hard against his pants. He tried to hide his nervousness in wanting to pleasure her by devouring her mouth with his kiss and showing her how he planned on making her forget anything but his touch and this night.

She groaned into his mouth and her hand slipped down, rubbing him over his pants gently at first and then tracing the end of him through the fabric.

He kissed down her neck and gently rubbed her nipple with his thumb, feeling it grow hard, he released it and moved to the other. As he moved his fingers over her, she trembled.

Moving his kiss higher, he trailed back up to her lips. His tongue worked against her, and she grabbed his hair. From the way her legs quaked, he could tell she was struggling to remain standing, so he took hold of her, wrapping her in his arms as he feasted on her.

"What in the actual hell?" A man's voice broke through the symphony of sounds and sensations.

She pushed Leo back from her. "What are you doing out here, Chad?"

"I could ask the same of you two, but I think I have my

answer." Chad glowered at them. "You have to know you're being stupid."

Aspen wiped at her lips, trying to innocuously dry her kiss-dampened skin.

Leo stood up. "Who in the hell do you think you are to talk to her like that?" He moved toward Chad, his hands balled into tight fists. Aspen put her hand on his chest, shaking her head to stop.

"Don't," she said, straightening her shirt. "He isn't worth it."

"You don't even know her," Chad said angrily.

"Shut up, Chad, and just leave us alone," Aspen said.

"Listen, Aspen, we're here to work, not for you two to bang in the woods," Chad countered. "This is so unprofessional on both of your parts. If I was your boss, I would fire both of you here and now. As it stands, don't think that both of your bosses won't be hearing about this."

"Shut up, Chad," Aspen repeated. "You have no right to say anything to anyone."

"What we do is our business," Leo added. "We aren't on work hours right now—"

"The hell you aren't," Chad argued.

"You are just pissed off that he isn't *you*," Aspen said, running her hands over her hair, making sure it was in place.

Chad guffawed. "I know you think you are the woman of every man's dreams, but I see you for who and what you are. When we get back to Minnesota, there will be hell to pay. And, if I have my way, you won't have a job and I won't ever have to see your face again."

"Do I have to wait that long? Why don't you just get the

hell out of here right now? We don't need you, Chad." Aspen pointed toward the boats.

"Screw you, you b—"

Before Chad could finish his expletive, Leo's fist struck him squarely in the jaw and the sound was hollow and slapping. Chad moved to send him an overhand left, but his movement was slow and Leo jabbed him low in the abdomen, hard. Chad folded and as he moved downward, he hit him again with a hook to the side of his head near his temple, knocking Chad down to the ground.

Leo moved over him, ready to continue his attack.

"No, stop!" Aspen called. "What in the hell are you doing?"

Leo looked up. He could feel the rage peppering his features. As he looked into her eyes he expected to find vindication, yet in them, all he found was fear.

Chapter Fourteen

It had been a quiet morning as everyone had gone about their business and they hit the river. They didn't find any evidence of Genie. In the three hours it took for them to float down to the takeout where their trucks waited, thanks to the shuttles, Aspen had maybe said three words, none more than a single syllable.

This entire trip had been a mistake. Sure, the team had managed to stumble upon the dog and the gun, but they were no closer to providing the family with any measure of closure.

After pulling the raft out of the water and getting everything stowed for the drive back to town, she sat in the truck and waited.

Leo had been trying to talk to her all morning, but after last night, he was the last person she wanted to talk to.

She had been so mad at Chad for interrupting her and Leo's time in the woods, but in the light of the morning, she realized that he was right. She and Leo had made a *huge* mistake. They had been cavorting during what some could argue as work hours. Though she wasn't in law enforcement, she had heard tell of many officers who had lost their job for something just like what had happened last night.

The press area was going to be a pain in her ass today, especially with Chad looking as he was. He had a split lip, and his right eye was puffy. During the entire float out, he hadn't spoken to her, but on a positive note, she hadn't heard him speak to anyone else, either—not even last night.

After the two men had fought, or more accurately—Leo had kicked the snot out of him—Chad had gotten up from the ground and she had helped him to his sleeping bag. He'd promised he was fine last night, but didn't want her sleeping anywhere near him. He had been only too happy to sleep out in the early-morning rain, by the fire, even though everyone else and even Chewy had slept under the tarped shelter.

That probably hadn't helped his mood.

Chad walked over and got into the passenger side of the pickup and clicked his seat belt into place. He wouldn't even look at her as she started the vehicle, indicating she was ready to leave.

No one else seemed to get the message.

The air between her and Chad almost vibrated with tension, so much so that she finally felt as if she had to say something.

"Hey," she said, turning to him and forcing herself to look at his swollen face. "I am sorry about last night."

He grunted.

She chewed on her bottom lip. "Seriously, I didn't mean for anything to happen between Leo and I—in fact, nothing else *will* happen between us." She motioned to his face. "I hope you know he was just defending me…" She trailed off.

"You don't have to talk to me. It's not going to make anything better or make me feel differently." He pushed his arms over his chest, like a petulant teen.

His response pissed her off. Though she hadn't expected him to really open up and resolve things, she had at least expected him not to continue to act like a jerk.

If anything, he should have been apologizing to her—he was the one who had resorted to calling her names and escalating the situation. Just because his ego was hurt didn't mean that she was to blame. If he had just kept his nose out of her business, none of this would have happened.

Leo walked out from behind his raft and looked over at them in the truck, his hopeful expression quickly darkening. Instead of turning away and letting sleeping dogs lie, he started to walk in their direction. Cindy reached out and grabbed him though, spinning him around. No doubt, she was probably giving him the what for and telling him what a stupid idea it was for him to approach their ticking time bomb over here.

"I don't even know why you are attracted to him," Chad said, like he had noticed her watching the scene unfold in front of them.

Chewy moved around Leo's legs and stood between his master and their truck, as if even the dog knew he needed to block his advance.

"Even his mutt is a pain in the ass."

She turned on Chad. "I can understand why you are mad at Leo, but that dog didn't do anything to you. In fact, he and that *mutt* are the reason we found anything."

Leo nodded to Cindy as he turned his back on them and returned to his raft. He stepped up onto the steel trailer and, reaching into the boat, pulled out his backpack. He opened up the top, fishing around for a long moment.

Chewy walked over and hopped into the back of the pickup and his waiting kennel, obviously wanting to go home. His kennel was built into the back of the truck, and there was a water bowl attached to the side.

Leo threw his bag on the ground in anger, and she could tell he was releasing a tirade of colorful language. He definitely had a temper, and not that she was justifying it by any means, but last night he had lost his cool out of the need to protect her. Emotions had been raw and, if forced to admit the truth, she had wanted to punch Chad in the face, too.

Come to think of it, why did she have to be embarrassed about her sex drive? That she had made an adult decision with a fellow consenting adult while tucked away in the woods? The only thing in question here, as to the ethics of the situation, was the question as to whether or not they were on the clock while making their adult decisions.

Walking into the mess had not been a smart move on either side, but if Chad was not going to try to take the high road and instead chose to throw her under the bus for her unprofessional behavior...well, she would have to make a point of explaining how things had escalated to him taking a punch.

Looking at Chad, who had scrunched into his seat and was flipping through his phone, she wished that at the very least she had a video of him getting dropped.

She let out a sigh. She was being silly.

Leo was walking around the raft now. He was putting his hands up in the air as he moved, talking to Cindy. Smash jumped into Leo's raft and Steve started walking toward the takeout like they were looking for something that might have been misplaced.

After a second, Cindy said something to Leo and walked over to Aspen's window. She lowered the glass and she found that her heart was thrashing in her chest, though she wasn't entirely sure what it was that was making her afraid.

"What's up?" Aspen asked, jerking her chin in Leo's direction.

Cindy ran her hand over the back of her neck and shifted her weight from foot to foot. "So, unfortunately, the gun we located appears to have gone missing. Have either of you seen it? Leo said it was in the paper evidence bag and tucked away in his pack last night. He hasn't been back in his bag since then." Cindy's gaze locked on her.

Aspen's stomach dropped. The only item that could possibly provide them with any answers was *gone.* "How did that happen?"

Cindy shrugged. "That's what we are trying to figure out. First, we are going through everything in hopes it was just misplaced. Before we head out, Leo's asking everyone to do a scan of the area and to go through all their gear."

"No problem." Aspen moved to open the door, panicked.

"Thanks, Leo is in a full panic. If it isn't located, we are going to have some major problems. We've already disrupted the chain of custody by having it misplaced. If this case goes to court, an attorney is going to have a field day." Cindy sighed. "I'm going to go through my bag."

Aspen held the door handle as she waited for Cindy to walk far enough away that she couldn't hear her speak with Chad. She turned to face him. "Chad, did you have anything to do with this?"

"Screw you," he said in a growl.

"First, don't you dare talk to me like that, I'm your boss. And, second, that's not an answer."

Chad chucked his phone onto the dashboard of the truck and threw open the door. "I don't have to sit here and listen to this crap." He got out and slammed the door closed.

She had known Chad for three years and she had never seen him act like this before, but just because he was choosing to be a jerk didn't mean that he had any role in making the gun disappear—in doing such a thing, he was not only interfering with the investigation, but he was also possibly making himself complicit in a crime. He couldn't have been that angry with her, or that stupid.

She stepped out of the pickup and walked over to Leo. He was mumbling under his breath as he was lifting the huge white Yeti cooler out of its built-in rack in the raft. Her stomach ached and was still somewhere around her feet. "Leo?" she asked, her voice soft and nonescalatory in hopes that she wouldn't make anything worse for him.

"What?" he asked, then he looked up at her. "Oh, Aspen."

He sat the cooler on the side of the boat and looked down at the raft's floor. His face dropped in disappointment.

"Anything?" she asked, though his face told her the answer.

"Dirt and a couple of mushy dog treats. Want to see?" He dropped the cooler back into its place with a thump on the hard plastic of the NRS raft. "Damn it."

"Where was the last time you saw the evidence bag with the gun inside?"

"When I was with *you* and I placed it in there." He nearly spat the last word, telling her everything she needed to know about how he was feeling about everything that had transpired between them.

It was strange how her feelings toward things had taken a turn for the better while his feelings had appeared to have taken a turn for the worse. That was about right. Nothing in her life ever seemed to go as she had hoped or expected.

"Leo…" she began.

"Would you just look in your bag?" He gave her a frazzled look as he jumped down out of the raft. "Where is it?"

She sighed as she walked over to her pickup and pulled it out of the storage box in the back. He took it from her and set it down on the ground, unclipping the top.

"I can tell you already that it's not in there," she said, waving off the fact that he was about to start going through her things.

"I wouldn't think it would be," he said, glancing up at her, "but I want to cover all our bases." His gaze flashed to Chad who was now leaning against a tree and playing on his phone.

Leo grumbled something under his breath as he unzipped her bag. Inside, on the very top of her gear, was a rolled paper bag. Leo grabbed the evidence bag and turned to her.

"What the hell?" he asked.

A wave of nausea passed over her. "Oh, my God… I swear… I didn't…"

"Aspen." Leo sounded so hurt. "Why?"

Chapter Fifteen

Leo couldn't imagine that Aspen would have taken the gun or hidden it away in her gear, but then again, given everything that had been going sideways between them, he wasn't sure that she wouldn't. She had made it clear from the beginning she had wanted to take this search on, and she had pushed hard against wanting him and his team to be a part of it until he had forced her to work with them. It made sense that she would want to be the one to report the findings to the Manos family, but she didn't need the actual gun—unless she knew something he didn't…or if they were hiding something.

She had been the one to start things between them last night. Had she been playing him all along?

He stared out at the road as he made his way back to town, the raft in tow. He had planned on going to the press conference, but with everything that had happened, he didn't feel like showing his face. If they wanted to be the big dogs in this search, they could have it.

What he couldn't wrap his head around was why. All she'd had to do was talk to him and he could have given her access to the gun or let her take the credit for its discovery.

It just didn't fit that she would have taken it and put it in her things. *If* she had, then she likely wouldn't have been so forthcoming in letting him look through her bag. She really hadn't seemed to care when he'd opened her things, and she'd even sounded sincere when he'd discovered the weapon.

He ran his hand over his face, letting out a long, tired sigh.

Last night, he'd barely slept after he'd struck Chad. That had been a mistake as well. Sure, he had definitely had every right to knock the guy on his ass given what he was saying to Aspen and how he had been treating them, but he could have handled the situation in other ways.

It hadn't done him any favors with Aspen. Hell, none of what had happened would do him or his department any good. If his captain heard about everything that had just gone down in the last twenty-four hours, he was going to be out on his ass.

His team had been eerily quiet ever since the incident with the gun. It was clear that no one really knew what to say to make things better or to make sense of what had happened. When they finally pulled into the search and rescue warehouse, they made quick work of parking the trailer and unpacking their gear from his truck. Aside from the required comms, no one spoke.

He hated this. It was like they could all tell that he was going to have one hell of a long day.

They weren't wrong.

He did a quick check on Chewy and gave him a couple cups of dog food while he wiped down the boat and the team hit the road.

Alone, he locked up the warehouse and made his way to the evidence lockers. Logging in the gun, he wrote out the location in which the gun had been found and the condition, but when it came to further description, he found himself struggling. It was easy enough to simply omit the details of the gun going missing for a few hours, only the other people he'd been with would have known what had happened.

If he put down that he'd made an error in the chain of custody, he was basically writing his resignation letter. The only way he would come out of this still standing would be if the gun didn't have a role in any criminal activity—or if they found Genie alive.

He shook his head as if he was trying to shake the possibility from his mind. He knew better. Her dog had barely been alive when they'd found him. There's no way a thin, bikini-clad woman would have made it.

If they could just find her body or find out what really happened to Genie…everything would go back to normal and he wouldn't be in this crazy vacuum of what-ifs, hows and whys.

As much as he wanted to leave out the real events of the last twenty-four hours, he made sure to include the gun had gone missing while in his custody and later found in another one of the supporting team's bags. He didn't include Aspen's name. He may be upset with her, but if he was going to go down for this, legally and professionally, she didn't need to go down with him.

JOHN AND KITTY were waiting at the press tent when Aspen arrived. Kitty's eyes were swollen and bloodshot, and she wondered if the two had managed to get any sleep since the last time the team had seen them on the river.

"You need to make this quick. I have a plane to catch," Chad said as she stepped out of her truck.

"Don't let me stop you, Chad. If you want, I'll even pay for your Uber to the airport," she said, having had enough of him and his attitude. Whatever he was going to do, well, he could go and do it. She would deal with things as they came.

She clicked the truck door shut and before she even turned around, John was standing beside her.

"Did you find anything?" he asked, his words coming out so fast that she almost couldn't understand him.

"That's what we are here to talk to you about," she said, holding him off until she had everyone together. "Who all is here?" she asked.

John shrugged. "We haven't been here that long, but I think there are two television reporters and someone from the paper."

That was a pretty impressive turn out for a small town that didn't even have its own independent newspaper. The only one who was missing was Leo. She hadn't expected him to show up. Cindy had mentioned that they were going to take care of their gear, but that had been hours ago. They had to have been done by now, so him not being here felt almost like a slap in the face.

Kitty followed them as they made their way into the tent. Her heart was beating fast in her chest as she scanned the faces of the people standing around her. Everyone was serious and austere.

This wasn't her first press conference, and it wouldn't be her last, but she always hated these things. It was one of those events in which there was no saying the right thing, and no matter what words she chose, they would be twisted and made to sound like whatever the journalist needed in order to support their desired agenda. In other words, depending on the social atmosphere, she could either be the hero or the villain, but little had to do with her actual deeds.

"Hello, everyone, thank you for coming today," she began, moving behind a podium the news stations had set up, complete with their logo-bearing microphones. "My name is Aspen Stevens and I'm the lead member of the Minnesota Life Savers group. We are a private group that has been retained by Genie Manos's family to help in locating the missing woman."

She was interrupted by the sound of a loud truck roaring into the parking area and skidding to a stop on the gravel.

Her heart skipped a beat as her mind moved to Leo. Hopefully he had come to her rescue and she wouldn't have to stand up here to face this group of critics alone.

A man walked in. He had dark unkempt hair, which fell into his gray eyes. The black-and-white flannel shirt he was wearing had dirt on the cuffs, and there was a smattering of paint across the front. His white pants were covered with different colors of paint, and the knees were almost black where he must have constantly knelt on the ground while he worked. At first, she didn't recognize him, but as he flipped his hair back and put a hat backward over his hair she finally placed him—Scott Gull.

Oh, no.

There was stirring the pot and then there was throwing gasoline into it and lighting an inferno. His being here was definitely the latter.

"Excuse me for a moment," she said, "if you would. Please speak to the parents of Genie, John and Kitty Manos," she continued, directing the reporters toward the two who would really give them the most fodder for their stories.

She walked toward Scott, who looked at her like she had a wart in the middle of her forehead. Grabbing him by the arm, she pulled him out of the tent and back out into the open air. He smelled like paint, body odor and cigarettes.

"Whadya want?" Scott asked, pulling his arm out of her grip.

"What are you doing here, Scott?" she asked.

"What business of that is yours, Aspen?" He motioned his chin in the direction of the podium where she had just introduced herself. "I have every right to be here and be a part of finding my wife."

"Are you kidding me?" she countered, staring at a long hair that was sticking nearly sideways out from his hat. "I just spoke with the detective who is working this case, and he said that you haven't showed any interest in coming out here to find Genie. Now, when there is press involved, you decide to show up? I don't think so. You need to leave."

As she spoke, she couldn't help but glance in Chad's direction. Little had she known that she would have a trail of figurative bodies in her wake today.

"You ain't got no right to tell me where I can be. This is a public event. And I gotta know what's goin' on with Genie."

"What's going on is that she has been missing for over two weeks and you are suspect number one."

The man gave a mirthful chuckle. "If I'm the best suspect that detective's got, then he's doin' a piss-poor job. I ain't got nothin' to do with her goin' missin'."

"Oh, I'm sure you are innocent." She scanned him up and down, raising her lip in a near snarl. "I have heard all about what you did to your *beloved wife*."

He spat on the ground. "You think you got all the answers, don't ya?"

She wanted to tell him that they had found his gun, that he was going to go down for Genie's death. Yet, without the body she was more than aware it often was incredibly hard to prove a crime had been committed.

Her only hope in nailing this guy for having a role in Genie's disappearance was to get him the hell out of there before she said something she would regret. She'd already had enough of that in the last day and she didn't need anything else hanging on her conscience.

"If you don't leave right now, I'm going to call the police and have you removed."

He threw his head back in a laugh. "Go ahead and call 'em. You may think I'm some dumb redneck, but I know I got the right to be here."

He wasn't wrong, on either count.

She ran her hand over her face; there had been so much drama in her life, and she didn't need any more crap if it wasn't absolutely necessary. "You and I both know that if you walk back in there and Genie's parents see you, there will be fireworks. Do you really think you getting in a fight with them on camera is a smart idea? If you are trying to appear innocent in all of this, or at least like a somewhat caring husband, it would be in your best interest to go."

Just as she finished talking, a truck appeared around the bend at the end of the road—Leo's truck. Her stomach clenched.

Ten minutes ago, she had been hoping for him to come to her rescue, but now that he was here, she wasn't sure whether or not his appearance would make things better or so much worse.

Chapter Sixteen

Scott Gull was a piece of crap. Every time Leo had ever been forced to be around the guy it had taken every bit of his willpower not to arrest him. When he spotted him standing next to Aspen, his blood began to boil. He had no right to be at the press conference. Actually, if he stopped walking on this Earth that would have been just fine, too.

He parked his truck and made his way over to them. Chewy whined from his kennel, but he could stay put for now.

"Mr. Gull," he said, giving him an acknowledging tip of the head. He glanced over at the late-model, lifted F-150. Originally, the truck had probably been white, but now it was mostly rust and powdery cream. "What are you doing here?"

"Why do y'all keep askin' me that like I don't gotta reason? My wife is missin'. I wanna know what y'all are doin' to get her back to me."

Aspen shot Leo a look, one that told him that she was as weary of this man as he was. John's voice sounded from the tent. Leo put his hand on the guy's arm. "Let's take a little walk toward your truck." They must have finally seen Genie's husband or heard him out here.

The guy shrugged off his hand, the motion aggressive. "Don't you dare lay hands on me."

"Why?" Aspen countered. "You don't like it when someone touches you without your consent?"

"What the hell did you just say to me?" Scott growled, moving to take a step toward Aspen. His arm moved upward like he was considering taking a swing.

"You don't like mouthy women, do you?" she pressed.

Before the guy could take another step, Leo got in his space. "Scott, before you do something stupid, I think it best if you head back to your truck. I have some things I want to discuss with you about your wife's case."

Scott looked at him with hate in his eyes. If Leo hadn't seen that look a thousand times before, he may have almost gotten a hurt feeling. As it was, those kinds of looks generally meant he was doing something right.

Maybe that was part of the reason he couldn't be in a relationship. He was a broken man—what most people considered normal emotions and reactions weren't his. Here he was just hammering that feeling about himself home.

"Let's go," he ordered, pointing at the man's truck.

This time, Scott didn't put up a fight, which was good. Maybe he could tell that Leo was losing his war with his patience.

As Scott ambled off, Leo turned to Aspen. "You just had to kick the hornet's nest, didn't you?"

She tilted her head, as she squinted her eyes with anger. "Seems like there are a lot of those hornet's nests just laying around."

"Fighting with purpose is one thing, fighting for fighting's sake is another. You been around this game as long as I have, you wise up—you learn what's worth the battle."

She opened her mouth to speak, but instead she clamped her lips shut as she must have let the backhanded compliment and admonition sink it.

"Please go sit with Genie's family and talk them down from the ledge," he said, motioning toward the press tent. "Don't let the reporters run away with the story. I will be back as soon as I'm done dealing with him." He jabbed his thumb toward Scott.

"You know he has something to do with Genie's disappearance. After meeting him, I have no doubt. I can feel it in my gut."

Leo raised his hand. "We will see."

Scott was putting a dip of Copenhagen in his lip as Leo approached. "I know y'all don't like me. I don't expect you to like me…especially if y'all have been listenin' to her old man and old lady."

"Oh, is that right?" Leo asked. "What makes you say that?"

"That old lady is crazier than a rat. Used to treat Genie like she was nothin' and nobody. Now, I see her on the news actin' like she was God's gift to her daughter…that they were the perfect family."

"Is that what Genie told you?" Leo put his arms on the hood of the truck, the chalky paint sticking to his skin.

"Genie would talk all about her mom, how she'd get drunk and not come home some nights. When she would come home, she'd get in big fights with her boyfriend. You know John ain't really Genie's dad. He's just some guy Kitty picked up along the way to pay the tab."

Leo tried to hide his shock at the new information. "When you and I spoke last time, you didn't mention any of this to me. Why are you suddenly so chatty?"

"Last time we talked, they hadn't opened their big mouths. I didn't have no problems bein' in the same town as 'em, but now that they are tellin' everyone I'm the bad guy… That I was beatin' on Genie." He spat on the ground. "Well, I had to come and say my piece."

Of course, Scott is going to profess his innocence. Is no one ever guilty?

"Look, you and I both know that you are currently charged with Partner Family Member Assault, a PFMA, and that you are awaiting trial. In the meantime, she slapped you with a temporary restraining order. A person doesn't get the charge just thrown at them unless there was some reason for us to arrest you." Leo tried his damnedest to sound like he was being understanding and not amping up for another verbal battle with the guy.

"You're right… I'm goin' to trial. I ain't been convicted yet." Scott spit again. "You ever wonder how that fight got called in…or by who?"

Leo twitched. Normally, the first thing he ever did on any of his investigations was listen to the 911 call. Yet, in the case of the PFMA, he hadn't. It hadn't seemed applicable to Genie going missing. "Who made the call, Scott?"

He jabbed his chin in the direction of the tent. "That old witch."

Holy crap.

He would have to look deeper into this claim. As much

as he wanted to buy into what the guy was saying, there were always a variety of sides to every story.

"Did you get along with Genie's family before this all happened?"

Scott scoffed. "I got along better with 'em than she did. The only time Kitty ever called her was when she wanted a few bucks and didn't want John to know."

"You have any proof of that?"

"I dunno. I don't think that Genie ever gave in to her mom, but if she did she may notta told me. She knew my feelings on handouts."

"Which were?"

"You give a man a fish and he'll eat for a day, but if you teach him…" Scott said, puffing up his chest like he was a philosopher.

In that, he found plenty of reason for Genie to keep secrets from her husband. It was common that when a person was forced to choose between family and a spouse, they would side with the spouse, but sometimes—especially in cases in which the families were abusive or toxic—things would go the other way. There was always that draw, that desire for the child to get love and affection from the parent who would burn them with cigarettes five minutes later.

The more he learned about Genie, the more his heart hurt for her plight. No matter where this poor woman was, she seemed to have surrounded herself with the worst kind of people. Genie was in a cycle that she never had a chance to break from.

"Do you think it's possible that Genie's parents would have done anything to harm their daughter in any way?" Scott asked.

Scott kicked the front tire of his pickup. "She needs a little air. This damned thing has a slow leak."

"I have a tire that's like that, too," he said. "It's from all the salt on the roads. Eats away at the rims."

Scott huffed. "Don't I know. I drive this beast too hard. She ain't never gettin' a break—hell or high water. Ya know?"

"Oh, don't I. I've been putting in a lot of hours. Even more since this all started," he said, trying to lead the man back to the question he was trying to avoid. "You know, even if those folks are around, I won't tell you that you can't be here. All I want is civility. I don't want to take anything away from our search efforts by having to babysit you three."

Scott dipped his head. "I hear ya. I mighta come in a little hot, but you gotta know—"

"I know all about how it feels to have your name ran through the mud. I'm a cop, remember?" He gave a chuckle.

Scott looked up at him. "I ain't said it, but I hope y'all know that I do appreciate all that y'all are doin' to find my Genie."

"You're welcome," Leo said, some of his dislike for the man dissolving.

While Scott definitely wasn't without fault, and he wasn't what he'd consider a perfect member of society, he was a man who had loved his wife. Though there was a very thin line between love and hate, he hadn't gotten the impression either time he'd chatted with him that Scott had hated her or wished her harm. He'd been angry at the situation, but not at the woman.

"Scott, why would Kitty make a call about a domestic disturbance involving you and Genie? Were you hitting her, being rough at all?" He tried to be careful in how he worded his question. He didn't want to lose ground with his primary suspect in Genie's disappearance, especially now that he finally had him opening up.

"I never laid a hand on my Genie," Scott said, putting his hand to his chest like he was preaching the truth. "We got into some pretty heated fights, I ain't gonna lie, but I never once touched a hair on her head outta anger."

"Did you ever make her feel intimidated?"

Scott looked back down at his tire. "I know how the law works, Detective West."

"What do you mean, Scott?"

"I know that even if I got to yellin' at her and we were goin' around and she felt like I was tryin' to scare her, that in this state, I'm as good as any old wife beater."

"So, you did raise your voice and scare her?"

"She got a recording of me on her phone," Scott said, his voice barely above a whisper. "She sent it to her mom."

Now things were starting to click. "And Mrs. Manos used it to have you arrested?"

"Yeah, but Genie didn't even want to press charges. She was gone when you guys arrived, and they just cuffed and stuffed me. I didn't stand a chance."

"If you were arrested, Scott, then it means that Genie did choose to press charges."

Scott gave a slight, guilty nod. "I know. I can't say I'm prouda how all the things went down. Like I said, we weren't doin' real good. I think Kitty convinced her that if she did press charges that things would be easier in court if we did decide to split." He gave Leo a pleading look. "I told her I didn't wanna get a divorce, but she had other ideas."

"Genie or Kitty?"

"Hell, now you know they were in it together," Scott said with a hard shrug. "I can't say I understand women any better than I did when I was a kid. They are, and will always be, a goddamned mystery."

Not for the first time while they'd been talking, Leo's thoughts turned to Aspen. In this sentiment, Scott was right—women were a mystery, none more than the woman whose flavor he could still recall and wanted to taste again. However, he held no doubt that between kissing Aspen again and finding the answers to Genie's whereabouts, he held better odds in solving her disappearance.

Chapter Seventeen

Aspen was only too glad to get out of the tent and away from the Manos family after the press conference. Though she had made sure to keep the information she shared to a minimum, only saying that they had found the dog and he was currently alive and in the hands of a capable local veterinarian, she had been forced to face a wave of hard questions.

The journalists dug hard about the animal, asking all about where and how it had been found. She gave them vague details. She and the search teams didn't need anyone digging around the area that she was hoping to get back to again in order to give another search.

John and Kitty had been surprisingly quiet during her press update. They had been wholly occupied by Scott and Leo outside. Kitty kept trying to stand up, and she had seen John jerk her back to her seat at least three times. While she didn't agree with a man telling a woman what to do or how to do it, she appreciated that his actions were helping to prevent a battle in front of the news cameras.

As she walked outside, she drew in a long breath and gave a cleansing exhale.

Leo was standing over on the bridge in the distance, staring out at the water with his back to her. It was a few hundred yards from the tent and about a half mile downstream from where they had been taken out, and she was sure that Leo was scanning the riverbanks for any signs of Genie. She checked the small parking area for Scott, but it looked as though he and his truck were gone.

Thank goodness.

Maybe their luck had finally turned. From the get-go, it had seemed as though nothing had wanted to go her way.

Well, except last night.

Even that had ended poorly, though.

Chad was still sitting in their truck, and he appeared to be taking a nap. Now that the conference was over, she should probably make things right between them, but the idea sounded about as appealing as putting her head in a crocodile's mouth. She had just swum through a pool of them and seeing another one could wait.

She walked toward the bridge, her feet crunching on the gravel. It was funny how here it was so dry after the early-morning rains. This state's climate was strange. A person really couldn't know with any amount of certainty what the future would bring—in weather or in life.

"Hey, Leo," she said, looking over the edge of the bridge toward the river running below. Since they had taken out this morning, it looked as though the river had come up a couple of inches.

"Hey," he said, not turning to face her. "How did things go in there?"

"Fine. I took your advice and tried to keep the reporters at bay."

He nodded in approval. "Good for you. Those things can

be a blood bath sometimes. I'm impressed you came out with all your fingers and toes."

"Don't get too excited. We don't know what they will write about."

"How were the Manoses?" he asked, finally looking away from the river and toward her.

"They definitely weren't happy to see the ex." She glanced around, still half expecting to find him lurking in the area. "What happened there?"

His face pinched slightly, but she couldn't make heads or tails of his expression.

"I found out that I'm going to need to look a little deeper into some things."

"Like what?" she asked, not sure whether they were on the right foot enough that he would open up to her.

"Let's just say that everything may not be as it appears with Mom and Dad in there," he said, and as he motioned in their direction, it was as if they had known and they came walking out.

Kitty was talking to Susan Delacorte, one of the reporters Aspen recognized from the meeting they'd just had. The woman was nodding, taking notes about the situation on her phone as Kitty spoke. She could only imagine what the woman was telling her.

"All I talked about was the dog. I didn't let anyone know about the gun."

Finally, Leo smiled. "That's great. I don't want that information hitting the main pipeline."

She opened her mouth to say something about finding it in her bag, but decided against it. There was no sense in even talking about something that couldn't be undone…just like what had happened in the woods. If it was up to her, they could just go ahead and pretend that he hadn't seen her naked and nothing had happened.

"So..." he said, his gaze moving to her pickup. "What is Chad going to do?"

She cringed. "He wants to go back to Minnesota. I think he's planning on catching the first flight out of here."

Leo mumbled something under his breath that sounded like, "Not a moment too soon," but she wasn't entirely sure.

Leo cleared his throat. "Are you going to try to stop him?"

"I can't think of a way to make him stay or to make things go back to the way they were."

"You mean him fawning over you?" Leo asked, a sharpness in his tone.

"What is that supposed to mean?" she asked, trying hard not to be offended and yet failing.

Why would he say something like that?

"All I meant was that..." Leo paused like he was trying to find the right words. "I guess all I meant was that I'm sorry."

She forgot about being offended as he took her by surprise with his apology. Out of all the things she had thought he would say, that was at the bottom of the list. "What are you sorry for?" *Kicking the crap out of Chad or about putting both of our careers at risk?* "You know, you're not the one who walked out from behind that tree naked."

She exhaled again, hoping it would have the same calming effect as when she had left the tent, but she still felt just as tied in knots as she had before.

He sent her a wide grin. "I'm sorry things went sideways,

but I'll never be sorry about seeing you step out from the forest. That is about every man's fantasy."

She tried to check her giggle, but it slipped from her lips. "I don't know about *every man's*."

"Any man who's worth his salt," Leo said, his eyes taking on a brightness.

"Regardless," she said, trying to steer things back on course and out of the emotional chaos that they had become, "I won't take things there again. I'm sorry, too."

"No need to apologize to me for something like that," he said, sending her a smile that threatened her shaky resolve. "You know I'm just wondering whether or not we can both agree Chad had the punch coming?" he asked, looking half proud.

"I think you could have handled that a little differently, but I would be lying if I said that I didn't find it the slightest bit sexy." As the last word left her, her cheeks warmed. "Damn it. Sorry. No more. That's it. I won't flirt with you again. That was just a leftover."

He laughed. "Put that in the *seeing you naked* category... it's not something you need to regret or apologize for."

"Regardless, we have both learned all too well in the last few hours what we want to do and what we *should do* are very different things."

He moved like he wanted to argue, but stopped himself. "I'll respect your boundaries." He scratched harshly at the side of his face where she noticed he must have shaved after they had parted ways this morning.

"By the way," she said, "I appreciate you coming down to help with the press conference. I don't know what I would have done in this situation, had you not been here to intercede."

He waved her off. "I wasn't going to, but I could tell that you were looking forward to this thing about as much as a root canal."

"Was it that obvious?" she said, with a feeble smile.

"It's the same way I feel about what I need to do now." He looked off in the direction of the tent and John and Kitty. "As you are involved and hired by this family, you are welcome to tag along, but I need to speak to them before they leave." He started to walk, but motioned for her to follow.

"What do you need to talk to them about?" She didn't want to go back over to that tent, but just like he hadn't made her face this day alone, she wasn't about to let him go alone now, either. Sometimes it helped to have someone in your corner, even if they said nothing at all.

"I just need to ask them a few questions." He waved toward John. "Mr. Manos?" he called, waiting until the last reporter went to their car.

Genie's father turned toward them and frowned, and said something she couldn't hear to Kitty as they approached.

"Mrs. Manos," Leo said, giving the woman a slight nod in acknowledgment. "I hope you both found some level of comfort in our finding Malice."

Kitty sniffed, sounding irritated.

"We are very glad about the dog." John took hold of Kitty's hand like he was trying to keep her in check.

"I gave them your phone numbers, if you want to take the dog home when he is recovered. Have you spoken to them today?"

John shook his head. "They called, but we aren't in any

position to be responsible for a dog. As much as we appreciate you finding him, he is Genie's."

Their answer surprised Aspen. If she had been in their position, she could have understood their reticence in taking on more responsibilities at the present moment, but this animal was important to Genie. If they held hopes of finding her alive, she would have thought they would want to take the dog in and keep him in hopes Genie would come back home.

"What in the hell was Scott doing here?" Kitty said angrily. "He has no business being around here."

Leo's features flickered with darkness, but the look was quickly replaced by his characteristic alpha stoicism. "Ma'am, while I can understand that you are not getting along with him, he is Genie's legal husband."

"They were getting a divorce. She had started to get the paperwork drawn up."

"Getting paperwork together and being divorced are very different things," he said, but as he spoke she could tell he was struggling to keep his frustration from sneaking into his inflections. "As her husband, he is the only one who can actually make any choices when it comes to Genie and her welfare."

"But I'm her mother," Kitty said. "And John…" She motioned toward her husband.

"About your relationship," he said, pivoting. "Are you two married?"

John looked offended. "Of course we are married. What relevance does that have on any of this?"

"I'm just accumulating information, sir." Leo put his

hands up to his shirt and pressed his thumbs under what must have been a bulletproof vest beneath.

How had she not noticed he was wearing one?

Aspen tried not to stare at the way the vest curved around his body and pressed against his shirt. It wasn't flattering to his body, but there was something incredibly sexy about a man in a Kevlar vest.

She had never worn one.

Focus. I promised I wouldn't flirt.

Then again, I didn't make any promises about staring.

Or wanting.

"How long have you and John been married?" he asked, pulling her from her thoughts.

"We've been married five years. Almost six," Kitty said, sounding self-righteous.

Her tone drew Aspen's attention back to the task that was actually at hand, and not the task she wished was in her hand instead.

"So, John, you weren't really around when Genie was a kid?" Leo continued his line of questions, inquiries she hadn't thought to ask them before.

"Unfortunately, I wasn't," John said, sounding genuinely remorseful.

"So Scott told you all about what a terrible mother I was? Is that what you are getting at?" Kitty growled. "That's about right. He never could take responsibility for *his* actions. Everything bad that ever happened between them was *my fault.*"

"Why would you say that, Mrs. Manos?" Leo asked.

"I didn't say nothing. I was a damned good mom to Genie. I worked my fingers to the bone making sure she had food and clothing." She was gripping John's hands so hard that her nails were digging into the poor man's skin. "Genie wasn't the easiest kid and we definitely had some hard days, but for Scott to go around spitting lies—"

"Ma'am, I haven't said that Scott told me anything about your parenting or your relationship with your daughter. However, your reaction to my questions has me concerned. I feel as if there are some things that maybe you haven't been telling me, or the other detectives on my team, about Genie."

Kitty's mouth dropped open. "How *dare* you."

John stepped forward. "Genie and Kitty were like every mother and daughter. They had good times and bad. Lately, things had been better. Genie needed us, and we were there for her."

"I have no doubt about your helping Genie," Leo countered. "What I am wondering is if you and your wife knew things about Genie that you haven't yet disclosed?"

"Like what? We've told you everything you've needed to know," Kitty growled.

Aspen could tell that Leo had struck a nerve. "That I've *needed to know*?" he repeated. "Mr. and Mrs. Manos, did Genie have a drug problem?"

Kitty jerked toward him, but Leo didn't budge. Aspen took a step back and out of the woman's charge. "My daughter's life doesn't need to be investigated. All you need to worry about is finding her." She turned to Aspen, and her eyes were tight slits that made her appear nearly snakelike. "If anyone's behaviors and choices need to be looked into deeper, it is yours. We heard whispers about what happened at your camp last night. From the sounds of things, Aspen, we may well have made a mistake in hiring your group. As of this moment, you are fired."

Chapter Eighteen

Aspen's color faded from her cheeks as Leo moved closer to her in case her knees gave out and he had to catch her before she fell.

"I…" Aspen stammered, obviously taken by surprise. "*We… My team* has barely gotten started out here." She swallowed, hard.

"You have no right to take your anger out on Aspen and Chad," Leo said, trying to defend her. She was right. They had barely started and if they went back now he would be on his own…and she would be gone from his life forever.

"I'm not firing Chad," Kitty countered. "I'm only firing *her*. She clearly isn't capable. We heard she wasn't even on her boat yesterday. How are they supposed to work as a team if they don't even act like one?"

A sense of relief filled him. As angry as Kitty was, at least she didn't seem to know anything about their moment in the woods. If she had, he would be facing all kinds of inquiries at work. This mother was out for blood, and she was going to take out anyone who got in her way—friend or foe.

"If you fire me," Aspen said, sounding as though she had regained some amount of her resolve, "then Chad and our equipment will be leaving with me. Our fees for this week will still need to be paid."

John put his hand on Kitty's arm. "Look, we are already elbows deep in this. You're upset and we can talk about that when we get back to our condo, but for right now let's just let these good people get back to their job. They are our best chance of getting our Genie back."

He felt the pressure of their hate. Even though they had relatively little information or answers, he could tell that this case could easily become one that would haunt him for the rest of his career—whether or not Genie was located. If she wasn't, there would be all kinds of lawsuits from this family.

From here on out, he would have to tread carefully. Though they needed him, they weren't on the same side, especially given the fact that they were willing to turn on the people they themselves had hired after they thought his team wasn't doing their due diligence. No level of professional performance would assuage the terror and pain this family was feeling.

His heart went out to them. He felt for them, he really did, but he wished they could all be on the same page and working as a cohesive team instead of Kitty marking anyone who hadn't found her daughter as an enemy.

"Mrs. Manos," Leo said, lowering his voice and trying to sound as calm and soothing as possible, "Scott did tell me that you had a video that Genie sent to you. Apparently, it was a video of her and Scott fighting. You used it in order to help Genie press charges against Scott. Do you still have that video?"

"You better goddamn believe it," Kitty snarled.

"Would you mind sharing that video with me?"

"Don't you already have it? I used it to press the charges. Isn't it somewhere in your system or something?" Kitty flipped her hand around like his request was ridiculous and a nuisance.

It was strange, and he wasn't sure if he'd heard her quite right, but he could have sworn she had just said *she* pressed the charges. Regardless, he had bigger fish to fry.

"Ma'am, those charges were not in this county. As such, they are not easily available to my team," he said, though it wasn't entirely true. It was easy enough to make a call to Gallatin County where the fight had taken place and gain access to the video and PFMA report.

"It would help both of our teams if you would provide us with that video and any others that Genie may have shared with you, at least those that could pertain to this case and her husband," Aspen said, backing him up. "If something unfortunate has happened to your daughter, it could help us to understand what took place and perhaps make it easier for us to locate her…" She paused like she had almost slipped and said remains, but he was glad she stopped.

Kitty was enraged enough as it was. He didn't want to have the discussion about the possibility and likelihood of Genie being dead.

John nodded. "We will go through our information tonight after we talk to our lawyer."

Oh…damn. He had known that was coming; he just didn't know the attorney was going to roll into this so fast.

"I think that it understandable," he said, wishing he could tell them his thoughts about working on the same team; but no matter how he tried, they would never be able to see past their pain. "I just want to remind you, this is not currently a criminal investigation of any kind. However, in the future if we locate her remains, we may need to treat this case as such. Due to this, there are going to be elements of this case that we cannot disclose until we have completed our work."

"Just like I thought. You *are* hiding things from me," Kitty countered, stabbing her hand in his direction and looking toward John like he was the one on trial. "I told you, John. I freaking told you that these guys are only about themselves. They don't care about our Genie. They only care about covering their own butts. They are all in this together. They are covering something up."

"Ma'am," Leo said, trying to calm her, "I can assure you that we are not hiding anything that you need to know to find your daughter. We will tell you what we can, but we must be careful with any information that we disseminate. It could be detrimental to our case and our locating your daughter."

Kitty snarled at him. "Don't pretend you care about my daughter. All you care about is your stupid good ole boys club. I bet you're friends with Scott. I bet he is paying you off. I bet this is just some small-town conspiracy you have going on…and my daughter is the victim."

Aspen sucked in a breath like she was going to speak and once again try to come to his rescue, but he gently touched her arm with the back of his fingers to stop her. She didn't need to get in any deeper with her clients.

"Ma'am, you are clearly getting out of control here. I'm sorry that you feel as you do toward my team and myself. However, once again, I can assure you that we are doing everything in our power to find and bring your daughter back home."

"I'll show you out of control," Kitty said, raising her hand as she moved to strike.

John threw his arms around her body and pulled her back. "We will be in touch."

They watched as John led Kitty toward their high-end SUV. He pushed her into the passenger seat. Kitty dropped her head into her hands, and her back began to shake with sobs.

His heart shattered as he watched the mother dissolve before him.

These were the moments that had made him into the hardened man, the man who couldn't sleep out of the fear that nightmares would flood his mind—nightmares filled with moments of watching mothers mourn.

THEY WATCHED AS John started the car and took off, leaving a cloud of dust in his wake. Aspen didn't know how Leo had managed to maintain his composure. She was enraged, and most of Kitty's tirade hadn't been directed at her. If anything, she had been nothing more than collateral damage.

"Thank you, Leo," she said.

"For what?" he asked, taking out his phone and looking at it.

"For saving my job," she said, surprised that he even had to ask. "If it wasn't for you, I'd be on the next plane back with Chad."

Leo threw his head back slightly as he sighed. "Oh, yeah... *Chad.*"

Her gut ached.

"Let's rip off the Band-Aid," he said, stuffing his phone in his pocket.

As they walked by Leo's pickup, he poked his head into the truck where Chewy was kenneled. The dog wagged his tail, but didn't even bother to get up as they peeked in on him.

"At least one of us is having a good day," he said with a chuckle.

She didn't know how to respond. Her instinct was to try to make things better and fix the situation, but there was no fixing or making things better. There was only moving forward through the muck and hoping to eventually make it out to the other side—the side that held some much-needed answers.

Chad had the window down and was looking smug as they approached the pickup.

"Hey, man," Leo said, approaching the vehicle. "How's it going?"

Chad chuckled. "You know I hate to say I enjoyed that, but I thoroughly enjoyed watching that lady own your ass. I had five bucks on her throwing hands."

"I wasn't sure she wasn't. It was a good thing that John was there to keep her under some manner of control."

Chad nodded. "No kidding. It's one thing for me to kick your ass, and it's another for you to get your butt handed to you by a fiftysomething mom."

"Oh, you kicked my butt? Is that how we are spinning this story?" Leo asked, an edge of playfulness in his tone.

"The way I see it. You guys need me." Chad placed his phone on the console. "*You* need me, Aspen."

"Chad," she said, "I need to know that you can be trusted to keep quiet about what you saw last night. If not, everyone involved in this search could be in deep trouble. As you may have heard, they have hired lawyers. It's only a matter of time until we are all dragged into court."

"Then we definitely need to find Genie," Chad said, not really answering. "I hate court dates, and there is no way I'm traveling back to this state just to sit in front of a judge."

"I agree. But again, Chad, can we trust you?" she pressed.

"If I get put on the witness stand, I'm not going to cover or lie for you. However," Chad said looking between them, "as long as you two knock it off and keep it in your pants, we can leave what happened in the woods out there."

"Ass kickings included?" Leo asked, motioning his chin toward Chad's eye.

"I still stand by the fact that I kicked your ass," Chad said, chuckling. "And hey, for what it's worth, I was kind of acting like a jerk. I really shouldn't drink…and hey, I'm sorry about the thing with the gun."

"So that's what's really behind this? You moved that gun?" Aspen asked, trying not to sound too accusatorial.

"I didn't mean to. I just wanted to take a look at it and I thought I put it back in the right spot, but I was in a hurry after I ran into you guys out in the woods," Chad said, a flash of anger in his eyes.

"Well, then, it looks like we all made our share of mistakes last night," Leo said. "I appreciate you owning up to what happened—answers a lot of questions."

"Yeah," Chad said with a slight nod. "Let's just leave it all out there."

She tried not to take Leo's comment to heart and instead remain objective. *They* had made a misstep in falling into each other's arms and Chad had been well… *Chad.* She still thought he was a jerk, but at least he was a jerk who saw that by digging in the mud, they were all going to get dirty.

Chapter Nineteen

After running Chewy back to his house, Leo sat in the main conference room at the search and rescue warehouse. The room was normally set aside for debriefings, planning upcoming training sessions and, when time allowed, working out the details of missions. He'd spent so much time in this room that in many ways it felt like home. This was one of the few places on the planet where everything was secure and where he could trust all those around him. In every other facet of his life, it felt like people were pandering or posing, whatever it took to get what they wanted from him.

Here, in this place, he was allowed the freedom to make the decisions he thought best that would bring them success in bringing people home. Generally there were no politics or favors to navigate, only life and death. He'd take that kind of authenticity every day.

Maybe that was why he felt so out of place in this room today, or it could have been the fact that he was once again face-to-face with the one woman he couldn't stop thinking about.

Aspen was hovering over the PFMA report that he'd pulled from Gallatin County while they waited for both the county and Kitty to send their copies of the videos. While he assumed they would be exactly the same footage, with the way things were going in this case, it wouldn't hurt for him to take a look and make sure. In fact, moving forward he would be looking more deeply into everything involving this case.

"Aspen, are you working for Life Savers full-time?" he asked, curious about how she had found herself in this back-country town in the belly of Montana.

She looked up from the report. "I am."

"Do you own the organization?"

She shook her head. "I am just the coordinator. The group has been around for forty years and it is still held by the family who started it, though they don't take a very active role in its management anymore. The younger generation doesn't hold a great deal of interest."

"That's interesting. I would think that adventurers and rescuers would raise future generations of the same."

The corners of her mouth quirked up. "So, you think that people are born into their roles and personalities?"

"I think free will always plays a factor, but take me for example. My parents were always out in the woods of Montana. I couldn't have been happy cooped up in a cubicle every day of my life."

"Don't you though, you know, working as a detective?" she asked, sounding genuinely curious.

"I spend far more time than I would like, but I do enjoy my job." He picked up a wayward pen on the table and turned it in his fingers. "Though, I have to admit I miss my work on patrol. We were always doing something, even when we weren't busy we were busy."

"You're not busy as a detective?"

"Oh, that's not it at all," he said, taken slightly aback. "I'm busier than I've ever been. I feel like there's never enough time in the day. And most of the time, just like this case with the Manoses, I feel like I'm letting people down."

Her features softened as she glanced over at him. "You're not letting them down."

"You know that I am. Sure, I may not be able to control things, but you and I are the ones who have the most pivotal roles." He paused, suddenly wondering if he shouldn't have said what was on his mind. If she didn't feel guilty, then he shouldn't give her that weight to bear.

"Just because we haven't found her, it doesn't mean that we won't."

Chad and Cindy walked into the meeting area.

"Hey, guys," Aspen said, turning to them. "I'm glad to see you made it."

Cindy had a wide smile. "Actually, I've had my hands full this morning. While you guys were working on the press and getting things handled on your end, I went to check on Malice."

"He still doing okay?" Leo asked.

Cindy pulled out her phone. "Actually, we missed some things when we first looked over that poor pup."

"Did he have gun residue on his paws?" Leo asked, trying to make things light.

Cindy let out a wry laugh. "Real funny," she said, putting her phone on the table in front of him. "Did you know that the dog was microchipped?"

He pulled her phone closer and looked at a picture taken a year or so before of the German shepherd, who was lying on the floor. He looked to be heavier and in better body condition. "What am I looking at here, Cindy?"

Cindy's smile grew impossibly wider. "Well, I found out that the dog actually doesn't belong to Genie. The registered owner is Jamie Offerman."

"Are you sure?" he asked.

Cindy zoomed out on the picture. Standing beside the dog was Jamie, the high school secretary he had originally spoken to when Genie had disappeared.

Jamie hadn't mentioned anything about the dog being legally hers; or that she had even known Genie. Even if Genie had adopted the dog from the local shelter, there was no way that Jamie wouldn't have known the dog when she had seen it. Or had she never seen the dog and Genie? If he remembered correctly, Genie had been reported missing before Jamie had even arrived at the beach and a woman in her thirties had called in the suspicious activity. She had only acted as the mouthpiece.

He talked to Jamie often. She had always been more than forthcoming with information when it involved one of the students at the local high school. If she had any sort of connection to Genie and the missing dog, she would have said something to him. At least, he believed she would have.

Yet, it seemed as he dug further into each of his questions in reference to this disappearance, he kept finding that instead of getting answers, he only found himself drowning in more questions.

There were so many facets to this case, each bringing a new perspective. It was almost overwhelming.

"Where did you get this picture of Jamie with the dog?" he asked, looking up at Cindy and Chad.

"Social media. That pic was from last summer." Cindy looked over at Chad. "He messaged her."

Leo wasn't sure that he liked that they were acting like the detectives on the case, but he appreciated that they were showing gumption and getting answers. "And? Did Jamie respond?"

Chad smiled. "She did. I liked the picture, and we got to talking about her and the dog. She said she didn't have it anymore—got lost. She put out flyers around town, but never got anywhere with the search."

"This town isn't that big. If she put word out on social media that a dog was missing, the animal would have been back the same day," Leo said. "I've seen it a million times on there. She's lying to you." His stomach sank.

"That's what I thought, too," Chad said. "It's why we came to talk to you, right away."

"Thanks," he said, still not trusting that Chad had anything but his own best interests in mind. "Did you talk to Jamie about anything else?"

"She hinted at the fact that she hasn't been out on a date in a long time. I think if you need me to I could pry more information from her."

Aspen sent him a look like she thought it wasn't the worst idea that Chad had ever had, but Leo wasn't sure he was on board with the idea. He didn't like things to be out of his control when it came to investigations, and they were already on unsteady ground.

"I will keep that offer in mind. We will see if we need to take things in that direction. As it stands, I'm going to need to give her a call and ask her some questions regarding the dog and her role in everything."

Chad frowned. "Don't you think that if you do, you'll be tipping your hand too soon?"

He gritted his teeth. Of course, Chad thought he knew more about his job than he did. As much as he wanted to bite, he resisted the urge. They were on civil terms, and it was best to keep things that way.

"I'll let you know if I learn anything of value." He turned to Aspen. "In the meantime, you and I can run over to the high school where Jamie works—she should be in the office today. Gallatin County should have the reports and videos to us in the next hour or so, as long as they aren't too busy. Is there anything else you'd like for us to do, Cindy?" Leo asked.

"Sounds like you have everything under control," she said.

He flipped the pen in his fingers and then set it down on the table like he was marking her spot. "You guys need to look over the water flows. I'm thinking we need to go down the river again."

Cindy gave him a brief nod. "Do you mind helping, Chad?"

He nodded, but there was something in the way he moved toward Cindy that raised a flag with him. There was a familiarity between them that hadn't been there before. He'd like to have assumed it was because of their time on the boat that had bonded them, but something told him there was more to their friendship.

If Chad started to date Cindy, he would laugh his ass off.

Then again, maybe that was part of the reason he had been so suddenly understanding and apologetic about their fight.

It didn't take long for him and Aspen to make their way

over to the local high school, home of the Eagles. The place was adorned with blue and gold, and the parking lot was littered with spent soda cans and discarded homework. There were a few cars in the parking lot, and until now he had forgotten that school had gotten out for the summer holiday last week.

Hopefully Jamie was still working or it would be a little tougher to track her down.

Parking near the front entrance, in what was normally the loop reserved for the buses, he and Aspen got out and made their way up to the front double doors. The entrance was locked, so he pressed the little silver button attached to the intercom by the door.

"Hello?" he asked, hoping there was someone other than a janitor there to answer him.

"Yes?" a woman answered.

"We are here looking for Jamie Offerman. She is a friend of mine. Is she working today or is she off for the holidays?" he asked.

"Leo? You should have told me you were coming," the woman said excitedly. "I'm in the office wrapping things up. Come on in."

The door buzzed as it opened.

"Jamie can come on a little strong," he said quietly to Aspen as they made their way inside. Their footfalls echoed on the hard tile floor as they made their way toward the main office at the heart of the building.

"What does that mean?" she asked.

"You'll see," he said, winking at her.

Jamie was standing outside the door of the glass-walled office and was waving wildly as he and Aspen approached.

He wasn't sure, but he could have sworn that Jamie's smile flickered when she spotted Aspen, but she quickly looked away from her and stared directly at him.

"Jamie." He said her name jovially. "Nice to see you again."

Her smile widened, and a little color rose in her cheeks. She looked like she had been spending time out in the sun and her skin was far more tanned than when he'd seen her a few weeks ago.

"Leo," she said, coming up to him and giving him a little hug and a quick, almost territorial kiss to his cheek. "I'm so glad to see you. I hate when school gets out. I don't get to talk to you as much." Finally, she let go of him and deigned to finally speak to Aspen. "Hi."

Leo turned to Aspen and sent her a guilty, I-told-you-so smile. "Jamie, this is my friend Aspen from Minnesota who works with the Life Savers group. She's helping us look for Genie. You might have seen her the day Genie went missing."

"Oh, yeah." The ice in Jamie's demeanor melted, and she stuck her hand out to Aspen. "Hey, it's nice to meet you—officially. Chad told me a lot about your organization."

"He did? That's great. I'm proud of the work we do." Aspen gave her hand a quick shake and Jamie turned away. "Sounds like you are busy around here, too."

"Oh, yeah, I've had my work cut out for me ever since the kids were let out of school for the break. I'm playing catch up on all the work and duties that get overlooked when I have kids streaming in and out of my office." Jamie chattered away as she led them into her area. "Though, I have to admit I miss all the sounds of the kids. When they are here, I get to listen in on all the coming and goings. It's awful quiet when they aren't here."

Her office was littered with stacks of papers, and the walls were adorned with awards and accolades the school had received over the years. He'd been in this office a number of times, but he'd never really noticed the framed certificates before. It was nice to see the principal and staff were getting recognized for the work they did for the community and the children and families who resided here.

He had gone to this school when he'd been a kid, but it had changed so much in the last twenty years that it was nearly unrecognizable. The only things that hadn't really changed was the constant scent of adolescents and the heavy mask of industrial cleaners they used to try to disinfect the petri dish that was a school.

He missed the days of fall football and the sounds of the crowds in the stands, cheering as he ran the ball. Aspen would have been one hell of a cheerleader, the little skirt riding up as she jumped on the track. Then again, she was far too serious to be the kind to bounce around and do flips. If he had to guess, she was probably more of a basketball player. She was tall enough and in shape, the kind of body that came with years of exercise.

Jamie was still talking, but it took him a moment to realize that she was asking him a question.

"Excuse me?" he asked, trying to act like he had just managed to miss what she'd said instead of being caught completely ignoring her.

"I was just asking what brought you to me today," Jamie said, touching him gently on the arm. "Do you need a drink?

To sit down? I bet you're exhausted after all the things I've heard you've been doing lately."

"Actually, I'm here to ask you about a dog."

Jamie tilted her head. "What dog?"

"We located a German shepherd recently," he said, not adding any unnecessary details. "It was found that the dog was registered to you when he was scanned for a microchip."

Jamie grasped her hands in front of her body as she sighed.

"By chance," he continued, as he tried to make heads or tails of her body language, "did you have a German shepherd who got lost? Or maybe you gave him up for adoption?"

She shook her head. "Malice wasn't my dog."

"So, you do know what dog I'm talking about?" he asked.

She nodded, finally looking up. "Yes, I bought him for my daughter. She needed a pet to help her with her mental health."

That explained why the dog may have been registered under her name, but it still didn't give him the answers he so desperately needed. "I didn't know you had children, Jamie."

"Yes, two. I have Edith and Mary. Mary is twenty-three and she lives in San Diego with her longtime boyfriend, and Edith just turned nineteen. She graduated from here last year and…well, she is taking a gap year and staying with friends for the time being. The dog was hers."

"Did Edith give the dog up for adoption?" he asked.

"The last I knew, she still had the dog, but I guess she must have dumped him—or gave him to a friend." She shook her head, but quickly turned away and hid her face. "Where did you find him?"

"We found him by the river. He wasn't in good condition. He is with the veterinarian now, recovering."

"I would be happy to cover the costs. Do you have the vet's number? I'll call them right away."

Aspen gave him a look of surprise. "Mrs. Offerman, we believe this dog may have been the dog that Genie had with her when she disappeared."

Jamie's mouth dropped open with shock. "What? No."

"Do you know how your dog, or your daughter's dog, would have fallen into Genie's custody?" Leo asked. "Did Genie and Edith know one another?"

Jamie ran her hand over her face, pinching the bridge of her nose. "I don't know if they were friends, exactly. I do know they have been in the past, but lately they've been having some run-ins. She and Genie got into a pretty big tussle out on my front lawn. I pulled them apart and Edith turned on me. That was the last day I saw Edith or Malice— that was the day my daughter wrote me off as her mother."

Chapter Twenty

Though they had some direction to dig deeper when it came to the dog, Aspen wasn't entirely sure that this was the way they needed to push their search. At least, not for her and Chad. It was interesting and there was certainly a great deal of drama at every turn, and everyone had their stories, but she couldn't help feeling like they were falling further and further behind in their search for Genie.

The truck came to a stop at the light as they headed back toward the warehouse.

"Leo," she said, "I know you probably want to do more work on the case, running down leads and everything. I understand that, but I feel like I need to get back out to the river and get my boots dirty."

Leo looked down at the clock on the dashboard. "I hear you," he said, "but if we went out right now, we'd be spending another night out in the woods, and I think we both know how that turned out last time." He sent her an endearing smile.

She wanted to tell him that their night out hadn't been so bad, that was if it had just remained their little secret. Yet, he was right. She wasn't sure that she wanted to be put in a similar situation, surrounded by people at the very least, again.

On the other hand, she had spent quite a bit of time alone with him today, and she hadn't been overtaken by lust or want and done anything that went against the agreement they had made with one another.

He reached over and pushed a button on the radio, switching the station to hard rock. Godsmack was playing, and he started to dip his head in beat with the music. "I've seen these guys three times in concert. Sully is the man."

She had never been huge on hard rock, but good music was good music and Godsmack had never disappointed.

"Is Chewy a fan, too?" she giggled.

"Any dog of mine has to love the finer things in life," he said, sending her a brilliant smile that made her think of his face when she had stepped out from behind the tree last night. That look, that *smile*…it could make her forget her own name.

He was so incredibly handsome.

"Finer things, eh?" she teased, motioning toward the fast-food wrapper that was wadded up and tossed on the floorboard near her feet.

"You can't bag on the double Quarter Pounder with cheese. Like they said in *Pulp Fiction*, they 'are the cornerstone of any nutritious breakfast.'"

There was that smile again, the one that made her body tighten and ache.

"If you are going to pull one-liners from that movie about burgers, I'm shocked you didn't give me the name of it in French."

"Oh, you mean because they use the metric system? They call it the Royale with cheese."

She laughed, sticking out her tongue at him. "Oh, you know-it-all."

"Don't hate, now," he said, laughing. "You had to have guessed I'm a Tarantino fan."

"What?" She feigned shock that this total type A with a proven hero complex would like action flicks with high danger and even higher body counts. "I really thought you'd be more of a ballet fan."

He gave her a look like he was trying to decide if she was serious or just playing with him, and the way he questioned it made her like him a little more. She liked that he was paying attention, and that he looked deeper into what people were saying...and more at how they said it. So much could be gleaned from body language—far more honesty was in a person's actions.

She had needed to find this...*softness* in him. He was such a cowboy, strong and austere, that he was hard to read sometimes. More, he had almost seemed to have perfected the art of masking his emotions. For him to open up and laugh with her meant something. Even Smash had told her that he was the kind who was all business all the time.

It made her smile to think that even after they had made a mistake together, that there was still something there— even if it was a spark that they couldn't capture and use to reignite the flames.

TRUTH BE TOLD, he had really been enjoying having a buddy with him in his mobile office, otherwise known as his pickup, and it surprised him. He spent so many hours alone in this damned thing that had it been anyone but Aspen, he wasn't sure that he would have liked the company. He liked having his own private space where he could work and take lunch, a place away from what felt like a rotating door in his office.

No matter what he was doing, it always felt like he couldn't finish one task without being barraged by a hundred others. Even if he worked all day every day, he wasn't idealistic enough to think he would even make a dent in the workload in the detectives' department.

Aspen was humming as he glanced over at her, and her blond hair was flashing almost gold in the sun. For the first time since he'd met her, she truly seemed happy. Well, except for the brief moment together last night. Damn, she had been ready. And oh…the way she had tasted.

He had to shift in his seat in order to hide what his thoughts were doing to him.

Leo's phone rang and he was grateful as he answered. "Hello?"

The call came on over Bluetooth, connecting to the radio. "Hey, Detective West," a man said. The ID came up as Madison County—it was the 911 dispatch. "We just received a report about a piece of clothing that matches the description of those that your missing girl was wearing. Do you want to take the call or would you rather we sent it out to one of your deputies?"

Leo pulled over to the side of the road. "What was found? Who found it?"

There was the clicking of keys as the man must have been typing. "A fisherman reported finding a pair of hot pink bikini bottoms, size small."

"A fisherman? Did you catch his name?" he asked, thinking about his recent development with Jamie and Edith.

"Some guy named Jordan Vedere."

The name didn't ring a bell. So either the guy was a tourist, which were all-too common during the ski season and then the fly-fishing season, which coincided with bug hatches, or he wasn't a frequent flyer with the department. Either way, he was glad it wasn't someone who they had been looking into regarding their case. He was getting tired of being taken by surprise.

"Would you like me to put it out on the board?" the man asked.

"I got it. Thanks, dispatch." Leo tapped his fingers on the wheel. "Would you please send me the pin for the coordinates where the item was located?"

"You got it." There was a pause and the clicking of keys. "I sent it straight to your phone. Do you need anything else from me?"

"Nah, but thank you, dispatch."

"Good luck. Stay safe." The dispatcher hung up.

He clicked on his phone and stared at the GPS coordinates. He knew the place, but it hadn't been somewhere he'd worked in a few years, so he couldn't recall exactly how to get to the area. He moved the map around, looking for an area where they could park and then hike.

"Do you recognize where the bottoms were found?" Aspen asked.

"Looks like they were a couple miles down from where we took out." He zoomed in on the coordinates. "From the map, it appears as though there is an inlet right after the pin." Leo turned the truck around and started to drive in the direction of the river. He called Cindy as he drove.

"Hello?" Cindy answered.

"We're not going to be back to the warehouse," he said. "We just got a call from dispatch, and it sounds like a guy possibly just located half of Genie's swimsuit."

"Half?" Cindy asked.

"Yeah." He tried not to sound too excited about this newest potential break in their case.

"But no body?" she asked.

"So far, doesn't sound like it. Only thing I know is that it was just the bottoms of her swimsuit near a river inlet not far from where we had been searching."

"Interesting," Cindy said. "Do you need me down there? What about the rest of the team? Want me to make some calls?"

SAR members didn't normally help with evidence recovery; the gun had been an outlier due to the location and his being there, so her offer was more of a platitude than a real option. Nonetheless, he appreciated it. He really did have a great team.

"Thanks, but I want you guys to get the next mission together. I'm thinking we run the river from the point we left off."

"I think that's cool," Cindy said, sounding hesitant, "however, the water has come up four inches today and the CFS is running hot."

The cubic feet per second—CFS—was a factor that would dictate if they could even get on the water or if their getting back out there would have to wait until the river stopped surging once again.

"Crap," he said. "Well, you make the determination whether or not we can hit it again."

"Will do. I'll get more information about what the temps are supposed to be tomorrow morning." Cindy paused for a brief second. "If you want to try it, we may be able to go out, but it's going to have to be as soon as the sun rises and it's cool. We'd have to be off well in advance of noon. We don't want to get put into a hairy situation."

The flows had already been running pretty fast. When this happened, the strainers became even more dangerous and difficult to navigate. Often, trees would be ripped out of the banks and pulled downstream, making impassible blockades in the river that just waited for unwary boaters.

If a team got stuck in one of those dam-like structures, the boats would get torn up and capsize. Once that happened, which could take just a matter of seconds, the people on board would get sucked under by the fast-moving water, or swept against and hooked up on broken limbs and branches. Once, when the water subsided and the CFS went back to normal, he had been called out for a body that had been located hanging three feet off the top of the water.

The person who had found the remains had assumed the person had tried to hang themselves. When he arrived, the man was wearing only a T-shirt, which was pulled up high over his head, his bloated body keeping him in place as the water pounded against his fish-nibbled legs.

At first glance, thanks to the odd placement of the sun-bleached shirt, it did look like the man had somehow strangled himself. However, further investigation had revealed that the man had been involved in a boating accident early in the summer—he had gone under and never resurfaced.

Likely, close to the time he sank, he'd gotten wrapped up in the downfall and he'd never come back out.

For being out in the elements as long as he had, his body had actually been in pretty good condition; it had been an unusually cold spring and summer.

"You okay?" Aspen asked, motioning toward Cindy's name on the truck's screen.

He gave her a curt nod. "All right, Cindy, you plan on things for tomorrow. Let's just keep our fingers crossed that the river doesn't blow out while we get things together." He hung up and looked over at Aspen. If the river was out, then Kitty Manos was going to go absolutely bonkers on them— none more so than Aspen.

If they didn't get some kind of answers soon, Aspen would most definitely be going home.

Chapter Twenty-One

The guy who had called in the bikini was sitting on the bank of the river, eating a sandwich that looked like it came from the local diner. As they approached the guy didn't seem to notice them, and as Leo neared, he spotted the little earbuds stuffed in the guy's ears.

He'd never understand why someone would want to come out to the middle of nature and then block out the sounds. He found the sounds of the birds calling and the water rushing incredibly calming and peaceful, though he was rarely alone out here anymore. All his time was spent at work, training or working with SAR.

If anything, he envied the guy that he even got the chance to check out from the realities of life—even if he squandered it in a way.

The guy jumped as they approached from behind and Leo tapped him on the shoulder.

If they had been a bear or other predatory animal, the guy would have been as good as dead. He took a little bit of guilty pleasure in the realization, though he knew he shouldn't have.

"How's it going?" he asked.

"Hey." The man pulled his earbuds out and put them away in a little white case, then looked up at him. "You a game warden?" he asked, looking at Leo for some kind of identifying markers and then to Aspen.

She was wearing a thin jacket with the Life Savers logo embroidered on the chest.

"No," Leo said. "I'm Detective West from the Madison County Sheriff's Office. We received a call that someone out here had found an item of interest. Are you Jordan Vedere?"

Jordan stood up and brushed the sandwich crumbs off his waders—waders that looked nearly brand-new and that Leo knew cost at least five hundred bucks at the local fly shop. "Yeah, that's me." He didn't stick out his hand, instead he stuck his thumbs into the straps of his waders and puffed his chest out.

"Catch any today?" he asked, trying to make nice.

Jordan nodded and stepped over toward where his clean-handled Winston sat haphazardly on the rocks. The sight of the very expensive, brand-new rod sitting so unloved and uncared for made Leo cringe.

The man grabbed ahold of a seven-inch rainbow trout, which had started to dry out and stiffen in the sun. "Got this hog." He smiled proudly.

There was no way Vedere was from around here. No one around here kept their catch. It was all catch and release because it was part of being a good sportsman and conservationist, and most people couldn't stand the muddy and fishy flavor—not that this fish looked remotely edible. By the time he got it home and out of the sun, it would likely smell to high heaven.

Ah, tourists.

"Nice job," Aspen said, but Leo could hear the tone in her voice, which told him that she was holding back a judgmental laugh.

He was glad that she saw Jordan for who he really was—someone who didn't understand the beauty of the experience and cared more about the pomp and accessories than the actual sport.

Regardless, he was glad the guy had been out here. Well, *maybe*...that was, if the bikini was actually tied to their case.

"So, can you show us to the area in which you found the item?" he asked.

"Yeah, no problem," Jordan said. His boots slipped on the wet rocks as they made their way farther down river, near the inlet.

There, near the edge of the water, was a hot pink woman's bikini bottom. It looked as though it was wrapped around a large stick.

"There you go." Jordan pointed in the direction. "You guys mind if I get back to fishing? I've been waiting for you for a bit. Need to get more on the bank, ya know?" He sounded genuinely excited.

"Did you disturb the suit at all?" Leo asked, before allowing the man to leave.

Jordan shook his head.

"Perfect. I have your information from dispatch. If I have any questions, would it be all right if I call?"

"Yeah, whatever you need is fine."

"Good luck," Aspen said, but there was a huge smile on her face.

The guy might catch another fish, but he wasn't going

to catch anything of value so far away from a good food source. Regardless, he was allowed his fun.

"Thank you for calling in your find," Leo said.

The man waved, turning away from them and carefully picking his way down the riverbank until he wound around the bend and out of view.

"You think those are hers?" Aspen turned to him and asked.

"I'd say the odds are pretty good." He took out his phone and snapped a few pictures of the item as they approached.

At first glance, he'd thought the bikini bottom was merely wrapped on the stick, but now as he looked closer it appeared as though the stick had ripped into the fabric and was caught. The branch was still covered in bark, but some of it had been ripped away where it looked like the fabric had rubbed hard against it...probably due to the weight of the person who had been wearing them compounded by the inertia of the water.

"Oh," Aspen said.

"You know what this likely means...finding this here and presenting like this?" He paused. "Our girl was in the river and at some point, she was probably caught on a downed tree and pushed by the current. She must be out here in the river or on a riverbank somewhere if she broke loose from that tree—but now, between the dog's location and this, I think it is safe to assume she is dead."

Aspen ran her hands over her face like she wasn't exactly surprised by the news but was disappointed. "Kitty and John aren't going to take this news well."

He shook his head. "No, no they aren't."

They stood staring at the pink bikini bottom. Leo moved

around it, snapping a few more pictures of the item in situ. He squatted, taking a few more pictures close up, making sure to get the tag on the suit, the spot where the limb pierced the fabric and the way the fabric seemed stretched and marred by the bark and pressure. He was positive that Genie had been wearing these when they had caught on a limb. With the increase in the CFS, maybe it had created enough pressure to pull her body free of her piece of clothing. He'd seen this kind of thing before and it never led to a happy ending.

Without a doubt, they were working on body recovery as there was no longer any residual hope of a rescue. He was saddened, but at the same time he was glad they were getting some answers for the family. Their daughter could likely be presumed dead. As such, they could move forward with all the legal work that came with his finding.

He would have to call Scott.

This entire situation was a tough one, but it was hardly the first time he had witnessed a family at odds during an investigation. More times than not, families wanted to point fingers and blame everyone around them when it came to the death of someone they loved—especially when that person was young.

For all involved, he hoped that if they found Genie's body it would come to light that this was nothing more than a tragic accident. If not, Scott and his in-laws would probably sink deeper into their war with each other and with him and the folks he worked with.

He would have to call the family later, but first he wanted to get his ducks in a row. He took a series of notes about the bottoms and his collection methods before he stuffed his phone into his pocket and, putting down his backpack, he reached inside and took out his evidence collection kit. He slipped on a pair of nitrile gloves and removed a plastic bag that would be large enough to fit the section of the broken branch as well as the bottoms. If he had to guess, his tech would likely be able to pull more trace evidence to support his belief that these had been worn by Genie. It wouldn't even surprise him if they found skin cells buried under the rough bark.

"Do you want to run this over to the crime lab and then we can come back and continue our search?" Aspen asked.

He sighed. It was an option, but now that they were gaining ground and he felt like he was approaching real answers, he didn't want to leave. "Let's work the area until dark. We'll search the bank for the next mile or so downstream. I think that this should be the point where we work from, as this is a good indicator that she was here. Let's treat this as her last known location."

She nodded. "Great idea." She smiled, her perfect teeth shining in the sun and pulling his thoughts from their somewhat macabre discovery and reminding him of how beautiful she was.

This was going to be a great day, he could feel it—the energy in the air was palpable and he wasn't sure if it was because of the thrill of gaining ground on their case or if it was that smile and the fact that he was working with the most beautiful woman he'd ever known. If pressed to answer, he would have had to admit it was likely a combination of both.

It would be a hell of a thing to be able to have her at his side all the time. They made a pretty great team. She was good at this line of work and she seemed to love it as much, if not more, than he did.

He gently put the evidence he'd collected into his backpack and then slipped it onto his back, and it reminded him of the misallocated gun. His stomach knotted. He hated what Chad had done.

Regardless, that wasn't happening again. It was critical that these bottoms never leave his personal gear. Though, he had doubted it was Aspen who had taken or moved the gun. Thinking about his faux pas and the gun gave him a headache.

He sighed.

"We will find her," Aspen said.

He nodded. "I hope so."

"Do you think this was an accidental drowning?" she asked, sounding genuinely curious.

"I want to say yes, but finding that gun registered to Scott is throwing me. I can't imagine why she would have been swimming with a gun. And if it hadn't been on her, there were no reports of her being there with another person… so how did it get out there by Malice? Ya know?" His face scrunched.

"I've been thinking about that, too." She nibbled on her lip like she was deep in thought. "I'm hoping we find her with a fanny pack on or a chest harness, or something."

He nodded. "That would be nice, but in the video she was only wearing the bikini. Though, that doesn't mean anything. She could have put something on after she played in the water with the dog." He started to pick his way down the riverbank, looking for anything else that might have been tied to their search.

"That's my hope." She moved a few feet to his right, searching the area not directly in his line of sight and expanding their coverage.

"Okay," he said, "let's say we are right and she was the one who had possession of the weapon. Why would it not still be tucked away on her person? Why would it have been found by the dog?"

"That is the part I can't make sense of."

They walked in silence as he pored over all the different possibilities and explanations, but nothing he came up with made logical sense. They just didn't have enough information.

They made their way down the bank, working the area until the sun started to slip behind the tops of the mountain. "Let's head back," he finally said, somewhat disappointed that they hadn't found more.

Aspen nodded and even though he could tell she was physically tired, she looked as beautiful as ever thanks to her ruddy cheeks and sweaty brow. "I needed this."

They turned and started to work an area tucked farther away from the river in an effort to cover extra ground.

"What do you mean by that?" he asked.

She looked over at him and smiled. "I just meant it feels good to be putting my boots to the ground a little more. I like working the water, and I think this will help if we get the chance to hit the water again tomorrow. But you've been great in helping me to learn the terrain."

He was taken slightly aback by her compliment. "Where did that come from?" he asked.

"You know," she teased, "most people say thank you when they get a compliment."

He chuckled. "Yes… I mean *thank you*."

She moved a little bit closer to him until the backs of their hands brushed against each other. The action made electrical sparks race up his arms and his heart sputter.

She had promised that she wasn't going to flirt with him or allow things to go the way they had last night, but as she touched him he found himself wishing that she would.

"You are seeming to like Montana," he said, trying not to delve down the path of questioning why she was touching him and if it was on purpose or inadvertent.

She couldn't have been doing it on accident, though. They both were experts when it came to searches like this, and her being so close to him definitely broke the rules. Which meant she had to *want* to touch him.

He wasn't sure if he should make a move and slip his hand into hers. If he did, he also wasn't sure how she would respond. This, being around her and wanting her more, was driving him wild.

Maybe if they just had real, down and dirty sex, then maybe he could go back to focusing on their mission and not the fact that he wanted to rip her clothes off and pull her down on top of him. Yes, he could really go for that right now…on the riverbank as the water slipped by.

They were alone. The only other person out here was the fisherman, but he had to be at least a mile upstream…*if* he was even still out here. It was starting to get dark, which meant it was hard to see his knots or the flies on the water, so he had probably packed it in and was headed back to his car by now.

Really, except for the agreement they'd made to leave

their relationship as just a friendship there was nothing else to stop them from taking things further.

Plus this time, there was no ethical conundrum as to whether or not they were on the clock. They had completed their search and were just heading back.

He gave a small laugh as he realized he was trying to talk himself into sex when really there was no need—he knew what he wanted. The only real question was whether or not she wanted him or if she was playing with his body and his heart.

He had to find out, but how?

As they moved up a hill, she was breathing hard. He let her walk slightly ahead of him so she could set the pace and, slightly selfishly, so he could stare at her ass. It was nearly in his face as she dug the toes of her boots into the hillside and climbed.

He loved the way her pants pulled against her muscular behind. She definitely hiked a lot back at home in Minnesota.

Minnesota. He'd never really hated a state before, and yet he found himself hating it like it was a person who had kicked his dog.

Cresting the top of the hill, he paused, not ready to give up or rush this private time together. He turned toward the river below, looking down on the bank where they had walked earlier.

As the sun set around them, the sky turned colors, the pink, purple and orange fingers reaching out overhead. The sunset reflected off the water, mirroring the grandeur of the snowy peaks of the mountains and the sky.

Aspen stepped beside him, slipping her hand in his without saying a word.

It was perfect—her hand in his, the sky, the river, the heat of her body pressing against his. He could have lived in this moment forever.

Chapter Twenty-Two

Aspen leaned against him on the overlook as they stared out at the sunset. She hadn't expected this moment, but she was grateful she had been given this chance to stand with him and share what was hands down the most breathtaking moment she'd ever experienced in nature.

It had to be a sign.

Leo ran his thumb over the back of her hand, and she gripped his tighter, hugging him in the only way she could think of to gently show him that she still wanted to be with him—even if she had said otherwise.

"Aspen." He whispered her name as though he was afraid that the sound of his voice would take something away from the moment.

"Mmm-hmm?"

"I hope you know how much I still want you," he said, turning to look at her.

His directness surprised her. She looked up into his brown eyes and found that they were reflecting the rainbow of colors cast by the setting sun. It felt as if she was looking into the eyes of some otherworldly god.

He was so incredibly handsome that her mouth watered

and, for the first time, she wondered if she was pretty enough to be with him. Leo was the kind of man who could have anyone he wanted, and yet…here he was, choosing her.

She was the luckiest woman in the world.

She pulled his hand around her back and let go of his fingers. Reaching up, she ran her fingers through his damp hair. "You're sweaty," she said, her voice soft and supplicating.

"Mmm-hmm," he said, staring down at her lips.He pulled her hard against his body. "Do you have any idea how beautiful you are?" he asked, finally looking up from her lips and their eyes locked.

She smiled.

"From the first time I saw you—"

"You mean when you hated me?" she interrupted playfully.

"I didn't hate you. I've never hated you."

"You didn't seem to like me when Cindy introduced us."

"I wasn't happy about the circumstances, but I didn't dislike you. Besides, that wasn't the first time we met." He smiled and the light intensified in his eyes. "The first time I met you was when you were wearing that polka-dot bikini on the beach."

She giggled and glanced away, embarrassed. "Not how I would have liked to have met you, if I'd been given a choice—either time."

"I have no complaints." He smiled. "The only thing better than that bikini was seeing you last night…in the moonlight. *Damn.*" He exhaled. "I can't tell you what that did to my heart."

Speaking of hearts, hers sputtered in her chest. Part of

her was questioning what they were doing and if it was the smartest thing, but the overwhelming majority of her didn't care. All she wanted was him and this moment.

He kissed her forehead as if it was a question. There was only one answer.

She moved to him, taking his lips with hers...owning him with her mouth as he had once owned her with his.

He took her face in his hands, his fingers gripping her and pulling her harder against his mouth like he was as hungry for her as she was for him.

She unzipped her coat and let it drop to the ground in a flurry of motions, all while refusing to break their heated kiss.

His tongue swept against hers, making her ache for more...for all of him. She needed to feel him inside her.

He let go of her hair and pulled her shirt over her head, followed swiftly by her sports bra.

I should have planned that better, she thought.

However, he didn't seem to mind as he kissed the hollow at the bottom of her throat and moved his way down. His hair smelled of sweat and fresh air and she pushed her face deeper into it as he popped her nipple into his mouth, forcing her to hold on to him out of fear the sensations would bring her to her knees.

He flicked his tongue against her as she closed her eyes, and he unzipped his pants and worked himself loose. He let go of her with his mouth and lifted her and moved her legs to wrap around his waist. He moved toward a birch, its papery white bark pressed against the middle of her back. He kissed her hard as he entered her.

She gasped with the beautiful ecstasy of feeling him

inside. He was so big, and she stretched around him. He moved slowly at first, letting her body welcome him fully. She could feel her wetness on her thighs as he moved more quickly. Every thrust drove her closer and closer to the edge.

Hard enough to help, but soft enough not to hurt him, she bit the top of his shoulder. The action made him drive gloriously harder into her, faster, and she had to let go of him as she leaned her head back with a moan.

"Leo." She breathed his name, and it felt nearly as erotic coming off her tongue as he did inside her.

He paused, looking at her. He kissed her softly, slowing his stroke. She grabbed ahold of the tree and arched her back, working her body in rhythm with his until she could feel him grow harder—to the point of no return.

She didn't want to let him release, not yet.

"Leo," she said his name as if begging. "Lay down."

He wrapped her in his arms, moving deeper into her as he moved them down to the ground. As they moved, he groaned, and she could tell that he was fighting his body.

If they had only these few stolen moments together, she wanted to ride them out.

The ground was covered with a mat of soft grasses and early summer flowers. She plucked a yellow and brown arrowleaf and, taking a moment so he could slow down, she pushed up his shirt and traced the flower down the line of muscles at the center of his chest.

She had known he was muscular, she had seen him rowing, but seeing him through his shirt and seeing his muscles exposed and awash with the colors of the sunset on his skin…there was no question in her mind that he was her Adonis.

She dropped the flower on the ground beside him and stared at the perfection of him and this moment. This was so much better than anything she had ever even imagined. With time, she couldn't even begin to dream about the heights of euphoria they could reach.

As she lowered herself down more, he was so large that it made her ache in a way she had not experienced before. Gentle at first, she moved on him. Driving her hips back and forth. She'd never been on top of a man. This was so new, so fresh. She was at the mercy of her body's wants and as she answered them, she felt her own edge nearing.

It was too soon, though. She had made him wait. Now she was the one who wanted to pause, but as she slowed he took hold of her hips. He moved her on him, keeping the pace she had been going.

"It's okay, baby, let it go. Don't fight it," he said softly, coaching her as he moved her on him. "I want to see you release. This is for you."

The words were enough to push her past any restraint she held and her body melted. Tilting her head back, as she moved to close her eyes she spotted the moon. With it, she howled.

Chapter Twenty-Three

He would live this morning a thousand times thanks to his memories. After running the bikini bottoms to the crime lab and making it back to his house and Chewy, they had made love three more times until they had both passed out in the morning, fully aware that their need for carnal lust would cost them in sleep—and neither of them had batted an eye.

When nature had finally called him from bed, he'd been forced to gently extract his numb arm from under her body. He had held her all night, afraid to give up a single moment of having her so close.

He pumped the blood back into his hand as he stood at the coffee maker and waited for it to brew. As he stood there, flashes of everything that had happened between them last night filtered through his mind, and even as exhausted as his body was, he felt himself wanting more.

Aspen was perfect in every way, from the curve of her hips to the round tip of her nose. She was incredibly sexy, and he was grateful she had given him the chance to finish what they had started. That was definitely what it was—the end.

He pulled two cups from his cupboard and looked out

the window at Chewy. He was running around the yard and sniffing wildly in his search for a wayward squirrel. Chewy hated the damned things and he didn't blame him; nothing blew a person's cover when moving through the woods faster than one of those little bastards.

Chewy tore off in the opposite direction and out of sight. He turned away from the window and set about grabbing a loaf of bread and a carton of eggs. He didn't have much in the way of food in his house, but he would make it work.

There were the sounds of soft footsteps moving toward him and he started to smile. "You should be resting," he said, turning to face her.

Instead of finding Aspen standing in the doorway as he expected, there was a teenage girl. Blood dripped down her face and covered her white T-shirt. "Detective West?" She said his name, but her voice was faint.

"Who are you? Are you okay? How did you get in here?"

She opened her mouth to speak as she pointed toward the back door where he had just let Chewy out. "I… I'm sorry."

The girl dropped to the floor in a heap. He ran to her as the blood flowed freely from her head, but he wasn't sure if it was from a wound or from her hitting the hardwood floor. She lay on her side, the left side of her face on the ground, and her eyes were closed.

He put his fingers against her neck, finding a slow and sluggish pulse. "Aspen!" he yelled. "Call 911!"

"What?" Aspen sounded groggy.

"We need an ambulance! A girl broke in. She's hurt."

Aspen ran out of the bedroom, already dialing. She was talking to the dispatcher, telling them to run a trace for his address.

The girl's lip was split, and it looked as though her tooth was chipped. Her eye was bloodshot and her cheek was black and blue, the bruise so dark that it bordered on black. If he had to guess, she was between seventeen and twenty-three, but in the swollen state her face was in it was hard to tell for sure.

Under normal circumstances, the girl was likely pretty. Now, however, her dark brown hair was matted with blood and stuck out at weird angles around her head. She was wearing leggings and as he assessed her, he noticed that the backs of her arms were bruised and battered. Without seeing her legs or torso, he couldn't be 100 percent sure, but she looked as though she'd had the living daylights knocked out of her before dropping before him.

A few minutes later, the doorbell rang and he rushed to let in the two men with EMS. It only took five minutes for the first responder to arrive, but it felt like an hour. He hadn't moved from the girl's side even though she hadn't responded since going down. Aspen was still on the phone with dispatch, but she hung up as the team went to work taking vitals.

"Do you know who this woman is, Detective West?" one of the EMS responders asked. He recognized the man from the office, but he didn't work patrol enough to know his or the other EMS worker's name though the guy knew his.

Leo shook his head. "No clue."

"Any idea what happened to her?" the other EMS worker asked. He pointed out toward the street that ran behind Leo's house. "Was she hit by a car?" The man put his hands on her belly, palpating the area like he was checking for any internal injuries.

"I didn't hear anything, and we didn't see a car that belonged to the girl outside. She literally just walked into my kitchen. She said my name and that she was sorry and passed out. There was nothing more," Leo said, trying to remain calm and collected. "If you look at her arms though, she does appear to have defensive injuries. However, without further assessment, I'd hate to say that with any degree of certainty."

The guy took her limp arm in his hand and moved it gently as he inspected the injury. "I don't know if anything is broken, but we will have the doctors give her a look."

Within what felt like seconds, they had her loaded on the gurney and they had started an IV to provide a fluid bolus. The young woman remained unconscious as they did their work and readied her for transport.

He followed them out the front door and to the waiting ambulance.

"We will admit her under Jane Doe until she wakes up and tells us her name or she is identified," the first EMS worker said. "I'll let the hospital staff know that they can share information with you. Were you going to press charges against this woman?"

The common practice in this kind of case was to wait until after the hospital care was over to arrest a person as then the county wouldn't be financially responsible for the perpetrator. However, in the case of especially heinous or egregious crimes, they would arrest them bedside. In this case, the girl had merely broken an entry—and apologized.

"I'll decide when and if she wakes up. For now, just write your report as normal," he ordered.

The EMS workers gave him a nod. He watched as they

took off down the road and toward the hospital, red and blues flashing. Several of his neighbors were standing outside their houses, curious about the drama that had unfolded at his place. He was sure he would be getting calls from his HOA president and every nosy neighbor under the guise of checking to see if he was okay, as soon as he went inside.

His phone was buzzing on the counter as he walked back into the kitchen. Aspen was sitting on a bar stool, Chewy at her side—she must have let him back inside at some point. "Do you want me to start cleaning up the blood?" she asked, motioning toward the pool on the floor by the back door and entrance to the kitchen.

He waved her off. "No, you don't need to worry about it. Thanks, though."

"Did you know her?" she asked, getting up and walking over toward the coffee maker.

He shook his head.

"She was here to see you. Do a lot of people know where you live? I would think that kind of information would be something you'd want to keep under your hat. Unless…" She paused, looking over at the blood on the floor. "Are you sure you didn't have a relationship with her or something? Something you didn't want to tell them or me?"

"Hell no." He nearly choked. "I wouldn't hide an ex from you or anyone else. I know we haven't known each other long, but I'm not the kind of guy who is about to lie to or betray someone I care about."

"I didn't mean it like that," she said, trying to correct her misstep. "I just know how it can be…and she *knew you*."

He walked over to her, put his hand on her shoulder and gently rubbed circles with his thumb to help calm her. "I wish I could identify her, but the thing is that there are a lot of people in this community who know me. I'm recognizable. That doesn't mean I can even name them."

"I know how it all works—you're a public figure of sorts." She grew more relaxed under his touch, but not nearly as much as he'd like.

After such a great night, it sucked that this was what they were dealing with. He had to remind himself that their stolen moments were just that—*stolen*. Reality and the needs of their worlds had barged back into their lives in a big way.

Chewy got up and wandered over toward the blood, sniffing it.

"No, Chewy. Leave it," he ordered the dog.

He didn't want to deal with biohazard cleanup, but then he rarely got to do the things he wanted when he wanted… which was why he needed to hold on to the thoughts of last night all that much tighter.

Grabbing the roll of paper towels and kitchen cleaner spray, he walked to the pool of blood on the floor. Aspen moved to help him, but he waved her to a stop. "Just drink your coffee," he said, motioning toward her cup. "I've got this. You don't need to worry about it." He turned to the dog. "If it wasn't for this guy, I wouldn't want to do this, either."

"Chewy, come here," she called.

The dog pranced over to her and sat back down at her side. He looked up at her and there was a look of love in his eyes. He loved that his dog loved her, but it would only make it that much harder when Aspen had to leave.

He started to wipe up the blood.

It would have been nice if there was a way he could explain to Chewy not to get too attached, and that this wouldn't last long and things would be going back to just being the two of them.

As he looked at the blood on his hands, it felt like it could have as easily been his. His sticky lifeblood could have spilled as a result of the death by the thousand cuts that came with relationships—or, in this case, a *situationship*.

Chapter Twenty-Four

After checking to make sure the Jane Doe had gotten to the hospital and was safely tucked away, and after calling his team to let them know what had happened, she and Leo made their way down to the river to resume their search. The CFS was running hot and, thanks to their delay in getting out this morning, they would have to wait until they got down to the water to assess what their options were. But Aspen was afraid they wouldn't be able to get out there on rafts today, or in the near future.

Which meant as soon as she told John and Kitty, they would likely be sending her home. Her situation with them was, at best, tenuous and this inability to perform the duties that she'd been hired to do would undoubtedly mean they would send her and Chad packing.

She couldn't say that she would blame them, but she would also do her damnedest to make the argument that they needed to keep her on to help with the search—especially given their new findings.

Facing them will be a losing battle.

She watched out the truck window as she and Leo pulled up to the boat launch. Luckily, they were the first ones there so she didn't have to see Chad or anyone else's face pucker that she had failed to come back to their hotel last night and was now rolling in with Leo this morning.

With everything that had happened though, they could go to hell.

She followed Chewy and Leo out of the truck and toward the raging river. What had been questionable was now impossible. The water was running fast and ripping at the bank and in a matter of hours since they had last been out here, turned from a dark blue to chocolate milk brown.

Picking up a large stick, she threw it out in the water and watched as it raced past them as they moved down the bank. They weren't moving slowly, which meant that even if they could get out on the water, the current was moving too fast and too hard for them to adequately or safely search.

She was definitely toast.

"I'd ask what you think," Leo said, his face pinched into a tight scowl, "but I bet you are thinking exactly what I am."

"That my ass is fired?"

His scowl deepened. "They can fire you all they want, but you are here as mutual support, which means that you are here with us, and at our invitation. While they can choose to no longer pay you, you can stay for the rest of your allotted time—time that's already been approved by the sheriff and SAR."

Though she was sure that he had meant his words to make her feel better, they also made her feel as though she had been stabbed in the gut. *They could stay the week—* that was all.

What had transpired between them last night hadn't changed the reality that they and their time together were finite. Though she was a realist and hadn't truly expected anything to come of their naked time, she'd be lying if she said she hadn't been hoping that he would at least make a feeble attempt at getting her to stay.

She tried to swallow back the pain. She was being unreasonable at best and a hypocrite at worst. She had been the one steering the ship of their relationship, and he was only doing as she had instructed.

Besides, she was here for Genie first—everything else needed to remain in second place.

"I appreciate the offer," she said. "I would like to stay until we find Genie, if possible."

He motioned toward the river. "Yeah, it's totally blown out. There's no way we are going to find her if she's in the soup now."

There was a creak and *whoosh*. On the opposite bank, a huge green pine listed and tipped. The creaking grew louder as the falling tree splashed into the water. Its roots were still attached to the sandy bank, but as the river swallowed the behemoth the sand crumbled from the roots and cascaded into the swirling water. The chocolate milk turned into near mud, flowing hard and pounding against the tree.

Danger didn't even sound like a powerful enough word to describe how out of bounds the water was proving to be—hell, it was *deadly*.

She'd had such high hopes after finding the bikini bottom yesterday. Yet, now it felt as if that would be the closest they would ever come to finding the missing woman.

With the speed of the water, her remains could have been to the ocean by now.

Leo whistled for Chewy, who was sniffing around the base of a bush. "Come on, buddy."

The dog ran over and he clicked him onto a retractable leash.

Her phone pinged. *Chad.*

From his text, they were back at the boat launch. She would have to tell him the bad news—even though she was sure that he was smart enough to realize what was happening, or what wouldn't be happening.

The entire team was there when they walked back.

Cindy's face was tight, and she had her arms crossed over her chest.

"So," Leo said, not bothering with the niceties while they were dealing with the impotence that nature had wrought.

"So…" Cindy repeated. "How is the girl doing?"

"Still no ID and she's not awake," Leo said. "Sounds like she has a brain bleed, and they had to do a shunt to relieve the pressure. No one has called looking for her, yet."

"Are you okay?" Smash asked, giving him a glance. "She didn't hurt you, did she?"

He shook his head. "I don't think that was her intention."

Smash gave him a brief nod. "Well, damn. You guys had one hell of a day already."

"It's been one hell of a week."

"Did your team manage to pull any further information from the evidence you located last night? Or from the gun?" Chad asked, but thankfully there didn't seem to be any weirdness in his tone.

Cindy offered him a small smile.

Yep, they were definitely sleeping together. Aspen smiled. She should have been bothered by the fact that Chad had been a hypocrite. He had seemed to be so enamored of her and then could so quickly move his attentions to another woman, but she was happy for him. He could be a jerk, but that didn't mean that he didn't deserve to be with someone who cared about him. Plus this would make it easier for all of them.

At least until they had to leave.

She sighed. Thinking about their situation didn't make her own any easier. Maybe they had come to the same understanding. Oddly, considering how awful Chad had been to them, she felt for his and Cindy's impending loss.

"I'm thinking that we work in pairs," Leo suggested, pulling up a map of the area on his phone. "Let's each take five-mile stretches. This way we can cover fifteen miles of riverbank. Let's check in every hour, assuming you don't find something before." He gave a feeble smile.

Cindy nodded in agreement. "Steve and Smash, you guys take this section. Chad and I will work the next five-mile point."

"We'll use the drone," Chad said, sounding excited.

Cindy nodded her approval. "Leo, you and Aspen take the last stretch. Sound good?"

She nodded. "I think we should all plan to meet again after we get done, and we can go over everything we have."

Leo nodded and he started to reach for her, but checked himself and instead played it off like he was readjusting Chewy's leash. It pulled at her to know that he was struggling in wanting her like she wanted him.

As they separated, she and Leo got into his truck and made their way ten miles downriver. The point where they were supposed to start their search wasn't far from an old logging road, but they had been driving for thirty minutes already and they were still a quarter of a mile from where they would need to begin. It made sense that it would be so remote, but it still surprised her how inaccessible everything seemed to be in this state.

As soon as a person stepped out of the little town of Big Sky, it was like they were taking a step back in time. She had thought they had been in the middle of nowhere when they had found Malice, but that location was nothing in comparison to where they would be going.

"If we don't find Genie," Leo said as they bumped down the rutty dirt road, "I don't want you to take it too hard. This isn't the kind of country that lends itself to finding victims. We actually had a known drowning five years ago. The daughter got caught up in the rapids and the dad moved to save her. She ended up making it out, but he didn't. They saw him go under, but he *never* came back up."

"Never?"

He shook his head. "Last year, a hiker found a skull not far from where we thought we might find him. We sent it for DNA, but it turned out that the skull was an antiquity and was Native American." He paused. "I guess what I'm saying is that people go missing and haven't been found on this stretch of river for hundreds of years. We are just repeating cycles that have existed long before and will exist long after us."

She nodded. "I will still feel like I failed."

"I feel like I fail every day. In my line of work, a lot of the time all I can hope for is to solve crimes—but even if I do, that doesn't mean I bring justice. In that, there is a huge division. It's up to the county attorney to prosecute. I see crimes that are so egregious and yet, they are swept under the rug—sometimes for leverage in other cases or charges, and sometimes I never find out why."

"You're not a failure," she said, reaching over and taking his hand with hers and giving it a squeeze.

"And neither are you. We are just always going to be moving against the current of the world."

She couldn't help wondering if they were also going to get as lost as the woman they were looking to find.

He pulled the truck to the side of the road, careful to leave room for another car to get by if one came by them on the one-lane road. So far, they hadn't seen another vehicle. This kind of isolation was something that she could get used to, if nothing else but to be a reprieve from the stresses of their lives.

Maybe that's what this place had been for Genie, too. They had been looking so hard for her, but the one thing she hadn't really considered was the fact that perhaps her disappearance wasn't unintentional—maybe Genie had been going through so much between the divorce, work and family, that she'd chosen this place to end things for herself. That would explain the presence of the gun—even if it had been in a strange location.

She moved to the back of the pickup and pulled out her backpack, followed by Leo and Chewy who readied for their search.

Aspen opened her bag then took three bottles of water from the twenty-four unit case. As she was about to drop them inside, she spotted a little black square of Gorilla Tape on the inside of the backpack, near the bottom, that she hadn't noticed before. She set the bottles on the truck's open tailgate and opened her bag wide.

Leo moved beside her, grabbing the bottles.

She pulled at the edge of the wayward tape. Its edges were firmly adhered to the canvas bag, and she had to work to get it free. Removing the tape, she flipped it over. She gasped as she looked at the AirTag. Someone had been tracking her.

"You put that in your bag?" he asked.

She shook her head.

"What?" he asked, taking the tape and offending item from her hand and looking down at it. "Isn't this a GPS tracker?"

"Yeah, but it's not mine."

"And it's not anyone else's from your team?"

She shook her head. "We don't track each other without their knowledge and permission."

Her thoughts moved to Chad and how he'd admitted he'd been in her bag, but she didn't think he would have done something like this. There was no reason for him to; he knew where she was and there was nothing work-related that she had ever hidden from him.

"The only people I can think who would want to track me is the Manos family. No one else but my team, them and your team knows I'm here or what I'm working on." She paused as a possibility came to mind. "No one from your team would do this, would they?"

"Hell no," he said, shaking his head vehemently. "We don't do that kind of crap. If we did, we'd find our butts in court in no time. Montana is a little behind the times, but it wouldn't be hard to sell it to an attorney and a judge that placing a GPS monitor would actually constitute stalking."

He paused, tapping his chin. "Though, to prove stalking, it has to happen more than once. Also, we would have to prove that people were conducting themselves in way that is threatening."

She felt the color drain from her face. "Do you think someone wants me dead?"

"I don't think anything points in that direction. I think someone just wants to know where you are at all times." He rapped his fingers on the tailgate. "If I had to guess, I'd say Chad."

Some of the blood returned to her body. Though she didn't like the idea of someone tracking her, no one had tried to kill her—at least, not yet. The thought made her stomach clench. "Nah. He has his own thing going on with Cindy."

"What? No way," he said, sounding absolutely shocked.

"Haven't you seen them together?" She motioned in the direction from which they'd come. "I bet money that they spent last night together, too. Why else wouldn't they say something about me riding around with you and Chad having to work with Cindy? Forty-eight hours ago he would have been all over my ass about it."

Leo chuckled. "That's funny. I guess I'm glad he found something—or, rather *someone*—to do with his time."

"Oh, my God, you did not just say that," she said, with a laugh.

He sent her a smirk that almost made her forget about what was really happening. He reached over and put his arm around her and pulled her into him as he gave her a soft kiss to the head. "Looking at everything, I think we should throw the tracker in the river. Let it float for a ways. Whoever turns up out of formation downriver...well, we will have our answer." He picked up the device and pushed it onto the piece of tape.

She couldn't think of anyone else who would have had access to her bag.

"You've never left it in the back of your truck?"

She zipped up her backpack and put it on, snapping the straps around her waist and adjusting it so it sat well on her shoulders as he did the same with his. Her thoughts moved to her time here. There were definitely times, especially when they had been in and out of the warehouse and in meetings that her backpack had sat in the truck unattended. This was a small town, and she hadn't been concerned about the backpack being stolen or tampered with.

"Yeah, I did." She really had been a fool.

As they started to hike, her thoughts went to all the people she had encountered since being here. Her thoughts moved to the reporters. At home, there were some who would do anything to get the scoop on a juicy story. Then there was Scott. If he really did have anything to do with this, then it would have been to his benefit to follow their every move.

Whomever it was, there had to be something to gain—or something major to lose.

As they got down to the river, Chewy picked up a large branch that was floating on the edge of the water.

"Look, we even have an assistant," Leo said, taking the stick from the dog.

It had a few teeth marks in the wood, but it would be perfect for their task.

"Good boy," she said, giving Chewy a scratch behind the ear.

Leo dabbed the stick with the bottom of his shirt, drying it the best he could. Then he wrapped the tracker in the tape to keep it dry and wrapped a piece of tape around the stick. He held it up with the large swath of black tape at its center. "You want to do the honors?" he asked.

"It would be my pleasure." She took the stick from him. "You hold on to Chew."

He clipped the leash on the dog and snapped it onto a carbineer on his backpack. "He's not going anywhere. Launch it." He smiled.

She drew her arm as far back as she could and threw the stick and its offending cargo as hard as she could with a grunt. Every ounce of anger and fear she had been feeling seemed to leave her hand with it. A laugh escaped her lips as the stick hit the water with a splash. It was strange, but with its release she felt free.

Chapter Twenty-Five

After about a quarter of a mile, Leo couldn't see the stick any longer. It bothered him more than he wanted to let her know that someone would be tracking her—it wasn't a big step to someone wishing or doing her harm. His hackles raised at the thought. If anyone dared to touch her, he would crush them.

What little riverbanks had been exposed yesterday were now inundated by runoff, forcing them to move into the brushy undergrowth and making it harder than ever to see. The grasses were so high that they hid the downed trees and branches, which grabbed at their ankles and tripped them up. Though he had known things were going to be tougher due to the conditions, he hadn't thought about the added difficulties of the summer growth and hidden pitfalls. They would be lucky to make it five miles in these conditions, not to mention the fact that they would also have to work their way back.

"Had I known that this was how things were going to go, I would have brought our other drone from Minnesota," she said, sounding somewhat winded from the brutal push through the gripping branches and heavy undergrowth.

"We have a drone back at my office. When we come back, I'll bring it out," he said, trying not to sound as tired as he was already starting to feel.

Though they had been going for over ninety minutes, they had barely covered a mile of the river as they had to keep pushing out of the underbrush in order to check the water. At this speed, he wasn't sure whether or not they would make it to their waypoint and back to the pickup before dark.

"I'm sorry for underestimating you," Aspen said, pausing ahead of him and Chewy and turning back.

"What do you mean?" He stopped beside her and looked out at the river. The water was roiling, reminding him of how glad he was that they had decided not to risk going out in those conditions.

"I mean that this search is probably one of the toughest I've ever been involved with. I didn't understand how hard it would be. I mean… I understood that there would be a variety of conditions, but I didn't realize the changes in elevations and…this…" She motioned to the briars and underbrush that surrounded them. "I really thought we'd have more time on the water."

He smiled, vindicated that he had been right in his initial indignation and annoyance with her team inserting themselves into his search. "If it helps, I'm glad you decided to stick your nose in," he teased.

"Oh…" she said with a laugh. "Is that what you think I did—stick my nose in?"

"Absolutely, and you know you did. You out-of-staters come in and think you are so much smarter than us backwoods folk," he said, rolling his eyes in contempt.

The action made her laugh. "Did you seriously just roll your eyes at me? What are you…ten?"

He loved when she teased him. Very few did. She leaned over and gave him a playful kiss on the cheek. "You are a pretty great man. I know why most people would be intimidated by you, but when you do silly things like that I get to see the real you. The you few others get to witness." She paused, letting out a long breath. "I hope you find a woman who is worthy of you. You need someone so special."

Did that mean what he thought it did? Was that her way of gently saying that while she could tease and kiss him, that they were never going to last?

If she had wanted to hurt him, a knife straight to the chest would have been more humane.

Then again, he had known what he'd signed up for; he couldn't be upset.

"So do you," he said, trying to muster the strength to say what was right, instead of breaking down and telling her to stay here with him and never go back to her real life.

She moved to him and he took her in his arms. Their kiss was long and deep and filled with all the things he wanted to say to her, but knew he couldn't. She wasn't destined to be his, no matter how badly he wanted her to be.

He wished he could hold her like this forever. Their place was this river, and it was the perfect metaphor for all that he felt. His feelings had started off clear and calm, but over the last few days they had torn through his barriers and flooded the banks of his heart.

Chewy whined and pulled at his leash like nature called. Not really looking or paying attention, he unclipped the dog's leash from his backpack.

He put his arm back around Aspen and pushed his nose into her hair, taking in her scent. She smelled of floral shampoo, fresh air, sweat and cottonwoods. Even her scent called to him. She nuzzled her face into his neck and her lips brushed against his throat. The softness of her lips on him made him moan and she giggled.

"Hmm?" he asked, lost in the feel of her kiss.

"That felt weird," she said, touching his throat with her fingertips.

"What?"

"Your moan on my mouth," she said with a suggestive smile.

It reminded him of last night's adventure in the trees. What he wouldn't give to have her legs wrapped around him now. He would relive that memory for many years to come.

She pulled from his embrace. "We better keep moving," she said, but there was a rosiness to her cheeks that made him wonder if she was fighting her body as much as he was fighting his.

She was right in moving forward, though. They had both learned the hard way what would happen if they fooled around on work time—and he had a feeling that he wasn't done paying for his misstep a few days ago.

He took a moment to collect himself and then moved slowly behind her. The riverbank was steep to his left, but the brush lightened up as they moved forward and gave way to an aspen stump.

There was a bend in the river, and it forced the water to move so fast and hard that it was difficult to hear anything over the rush of the rapids. Some of the bank had washed out, leaving it cliff-like. Ahead, according to the maps, it straightened out and slowed, and in another half mile or so the river itself dropped a few feet. In the late summer, it created a small waterfall but this time of the year it appeared as only a deep swirling mass of water and currents.

His heart raced as they watched the torrential movement of the river.

They were never going to find Genie. Not with this.

Aspen paused. "Do you see Chewy anywhere?" she asked.

He looked around, whistling for the dog, but Chewy wasn't anywhere to be seen. He called his name, but again the dog failed to respond.

"He must have gotten ahead of us. Maybe he can't hear us."

"The last time we let him lead, we found Malice," Aspen said, a spark of hope in her voice.

"Chewy!" he called again, picking up his pace.

There were the manic sounds of barking ahead of them. The sound was panicked.

"Chewy!" he yelled.

The barking changed pitch, becoming higher and more frenzied, almost bordering on pain. He sprinted in the direction of Chewy's sounds. They didn't stop, but every few barks there was silence and then the fervor of barking would increase.

The sounds terrified him. Aspen was behind him as he ran as fast as he could through the thickening underbrush as they entered another thick and heavy willowed area.

He cussed as he rushed through the tearing limbs, one wild rose catching him on the cheek and ripping at his flesh.

He didn't care. The branches could have his flesh so long as he got to Chewy in time to help him.

Chewy was smart enough not to go in water. He'd eyed it warily as they had been hiking together. Something else had to be hurting or scaring him. Sometimes old-timers put traps out in the woods and near the water for beaver and different animals. If his dog had gotten caught, he'd find the trapper and do whatever had happened to his dog to the person.

"I'm coming, Chew!" he yelled.

The barking grew faster and more panicked, but he was close. So close.

"Chewy!" he called, trying to pinpoint the sounds of the pup's barks.

The dog yipped, the sound coming from his left...near the river.

He charged toward the bank, breaking through the thicket. The ground under his feet crumbled, and he grabbed at the bush near him that had been hiding the drop. The bush tore away from the soil as the world caved in below him, sending him down. Chewy's barks were the only sound he heard over the rush of the water and the echo of his shout of surprise.

The water sucked him down, the bush still in his hand, now untethered by the earth. He gasped as he fell into the frigid water and the muddy river filled his mouth. He sputtered, trying to remain calm as the world around him became flashes of light and dark, brown and sky.

A woman screamed.

Chewy howled, the sound coming from downriver.

Water. So much water.

This had to have been how Genie felt.

They would only find his backpack.

Chewy.

There was the flash of movement on the bank and he saw Chewy's wet head bobbing over the surface of the water, coming toward him.

"No," he ordered. "Go back. Get help!"

Chewy ignored him, moving toward him in the fast current.

"Go back!" he screamed. A wave crashed over his head, pushing him down and under the water.

Something grabbed and pulled at his feet, reminding him of all the movies he'd seen with the ghosts of the underworld pulling at the living and forcing them to enter the realm of the dead.

The world was nothing but mud. Darkness. Fear. The roaring of the water in his ears. He couldn't breathe.

He struggled to swim, throwing his arms out in the direction he hoped was up. The currents turned him, flipping him over and spinning him like a tumbleweed as he tried to swim. His hand hit a rock.

His lungs burned. He needed air. He needed to breathe.

He tried to throw his feet down to launch himself off the rock his hand had hit, but it was already gone, making him unsure if down was really down.

It was all so disorienting.

The darkness in his mind started to creep in at the corners of his vision.

Air. He needed air.

Fight. I have to fight.

The darkness moved in. He was losing this battle—just as he was sure Genie had lost hers.

This was it. With a single misstep and the urge to save his dog, he belonged to the raging river and the unrelenting grip of death.

Chapter Twenty-Six

Aspen screamed as she watched Leo being swept downriver. Every nightmare, every terrible thing she had witnessed… nothing compared to the horror of this moment.

"Leo!" she screamed. "Leo!"

She ran as fast as she could, but the underbrush held her back and Leo grew smaller in the distance. He disappeared under the water as Chewy swam out toward him. He didn't resurface.

A scream of anguish pierced the air, sounding so primal and pain-ridden that she barely recognized it as her own.

Leo was gone.

Chewy was swimming in circles, but soon he was pulled downriver and around the bend and out of view.

Hot, stinging tears ran down her face as she struggled to move faster. The world felt like glue, sticking to her and holding her down while all she wanted to do was run and save them.

The tears moved faster as she struggled down the bank, careful to stay back and away from the invisible crumbling undercuts.

He was good in the water. Leo could get out.

However, he was still wearing his backpack. Water-logged, the thing had to add a hundred pounds or more, and that was to say nothing of its likelihood to get snagged on something.

She tried to breathe and remain in control of the fears and possibilities that were running rampant through her mind.

Leo would make it through this. He had to make it through this. She had finally found a man who she could be herself with, unreservedly. The world couldn't steal him from her now. He couldn't die. She couldn't live without him.

HER SCREAMS RANG in his ears as Leo's head broke above the surface of the water, and he pulled a sharp, welcome breath into his burning lungs. He could do this. He could make it. He had to think.

His body slammed against something hard, and the pressure of the water pulled him back under. He grabbed at what he'd hit, his fingers tearing at the bark of a downed tree. He tried to press his fingertips between the jigsaw texture, but the chunks of bark ripped away as the water rammed against him and pushed him deeper under the strainer.

He grasped wildly, hoping to find any handhold that he could use to self-rescue.

His hand touched something cold, slimy. He moved fast, taking hold of whatever it was in hopes it would hold him. The water crushed him, but he pulled himself downward and broke free of the current created by the log.

For a strange moment, the world stopped moving and the water stilled around him. It was eerie and he opened his eyes. The dirty water stung his eyes, but as he looked down at what had saved him, he saw a human arm. He nearly gasped as he let go of the rotting flesh. The body moved as he released it, and for a flash of a second, he recognized Genie's sunken eyes and lifeless face.

He slammed his eyes shut.

His backpack started to sink, pulling him downward in the pocket of still water. He struggled, trying to free himself from the straps, but failing. Reaching into his front pocket he pulled out the knife he always carried. He sawed at the polyester straps that tethered him.

The knife was sharp, but his lungs were bursting in his chest as they yearned for him to open his mouth and gasp for another freeing breath of air. This was taking too long. He was going to die. He was going to die right here next to the remains of the woman he'd been sent to find.

Maybe they'd find them together in some haunting poetic beauty. Rescuer and victim, one and the same.

They'd probably use this event as some lesson to tell kids to keep them away from the water and to rescuers in order to teach them the terrors that awaited. If they were like he'd been, they'd think themselves smarter and more capable. How painful this lesson was, this lesson of humility.

Nature would and *did* always win.

He reached into his bag and took out a loop of rope, trying to work as fast as he could. As he slipped free of his backpack, he grabbed hold of Genie's wrist and slipped the rope around her. He closed his knife and pushed it back into his pocket. Moving around her body, he felt a thick chain clamped tightly around her neck. He followed the chain back, finding it wrapped around a branch of the tree overhead.

This river never wanted to set her free.

Making sure he had hold of the rope tied to Genie, he pushed upward off the bottom of the river and emerged from the top of the rushing water, stealing a burning breath. He searched for the bank. He swam as hard as he could, moving with the water instead of fighting the currents and the weight of his bag.

He slipped toward the bank, the rope still in his hand.

Ahead of him downriver was John Manos. Chewy stood next to him, prancing and barking.

The man held out a long stick, the one covered in tape. "Grab it! Grab the stick!" John yelled.

Leo stuck out his hand, his head bobbing under the water as he moved for the stick. It struck his palm, and he took hold with all the strength he had left in his body. The water grabbed at him as the man pulled him free.

John grabbed him under the armpits as he got closer, and he pulled him up onto the bank. His feet were still in the water as Chewy came bounding toward him, licking his face.

He was alive. Chewy was okay.

"Mr. Manos…" he said, taking in gasping breaths. "Thank…thank you." He lifted his shaking hand and gave the man the rope before the answers to so many questions could slip away.

Chapter Twenty-Seven

It took a few hours for everyone from his team to arrive, including Steve, who was going to be their primary diver on the SAR team today as he'd had the most experience in swift water. Aspen had been an emotional wreck ever since she had caught up to him. From where he had gone in, to where he had been pulled out had been over two miles. For Genie, it had been more than twenty from the beach where she had gone missing.

As soon as he'd caught his breath and did a once over on the wet Chewy, he texted his fellow officers at the sheriff's office, making sure they brought everyone. Then he'd let the SAR team know, via text, what had happened, that he was safe, and he had believed he had located Genie's body.

His hands had finally stopped shaking after an hour of sitting on the bank. Gently following the rope, he, Chewy and John worked their way upriver to the point where the rope was perpendicular to them, indicating the body's location.

At first, John had continuously asked him if he was okay and if he needed anything, but after Leo seemed nearly catatonic as he stared out at the water with the taut rope in his hands, John finally stopped asking and they waited in silence.

He had been careful not to say anything. He couldn't, not until Genie's remains were out of the water and she had been positively identified.

For all he knew, when he'd been under water his mind may have been playing tricks on him. He had been low on air, and the worst thing he could possibly imagine was to tell John that he'd located his daughter and that she was deceased, only to later learn it had been nothing more than some sick hypoxic mirage.

Everyone was quiet and little had been said besides the prerequisite hellos. Steve and his dive team were busy setting out their gear and readying for the dive. These weren't the conditions they typically dived in, but given the situation and the distance from shore, they had agreed to help in the recovery of the body.

Leo wasn't sure how he felt putting his team into the water in which he had just gotten himself out of, but at least they were better prepared and they would work under a strict set of parameters and with safety lines. No one would go into that water without a team helping them from shore and acting as spotters.

Kitty and Cindy were walking together from where everyone had parked their cars about a mile away. Chad had brought the drone and was getting it ready to capture the footage of the teams at work as well as the body recovery. He appreciated the help.

Aspen fidgeted, her hands balling into fists as she looked over at John. Finally, like she couldn't withstand it any longer she turned to him. "Why were you tracking me?"

Kitty walked up beside her husband. "I told him to do it," she said, sounding petulant. "And look how it turned out. If we hadn't been, your *boyfriend* wouldn't have been pulled from the water. If anything, both he and you owe us your thanks."

Leo nodded. "Tracking someone without their knowledge is, at best, questionable and, at worst, we could argue that what you were doing was a crime."

Kitty opened her mouth to argue, but John took her hand and gave it a sharp squeeze.

"Given the situation, and how it has all turned out, in this case…" Leo paused. "I do owe you my deepest gratitude."

"What did you find in that water?" John asked. "Are you finally going to tell me the truth…don't you think you owe me—"

"Us," Kitty said, correcting him.

"Yes, *us,*" John continued, "an explanation? More, the truth?"

He pursed his lips. "As I've told you from the very beginning, we have to be careful in what we release due to legal reasons. I absolutely appreciate your action in helping me, John. Without you I'm not sure I'd be standing here right now."

"That's not an answer," Kitty countered.

Aspen shot her a look. "Kitty, please… All we are asking is that you be patient for a few more minutes."

Leo nodded, giving Chewy a scratch behind the ear. "What I can safely say is that I believe I found a body while I was submerged in the water." *A body he wouldn't have found without his pup.*

"You don't think we know that?" Kitty argued, pointing at the dive team. "Is it Genie?"

Leo held his hands in front of his body as he delivered the tragic news. "I'm sorry, but I think that there is a good possibility that it is."

Kitty dropped to her knees, a strange wail escaping her as sobs racked her body. Aspen kneeled and wrapped the woman in her arms, whispering to the heartbroken mother. He hoped she could bring her some comfort.

John stared at him, the color completely gone from his face.

"I'm not saying that it is. We will need one of you to provide a positive identification," Leo said, putting his hand on John's shoulder. "However, that can wait. What I would recommend, given the circumstances and the possible state of the body, is that you let us retrieve the decedent and let us move her to the crime lab where they will clean her up. I think it could be very hard to see her come out of the water. I don't want to put you through that."

John looked from the dive team to the water. Leo said nothing as Kitty's sobs filled the disquiet between them. After a long moment, John squatted beside his wife. "Baby, let's go back to the condo and let them do their work." He glanced up at Leo and gave him a grateful nod. "I'm sure they will call us as soon as they have any definitive information. Isn't that right?"

Leo nodded.

Kitty looked up, and there were tears pouring down her face. "Please…call us as soon as you can. Either way."

"I will let you know as soon as I can." He thought of

Scott Gull. Legally, he'd be the first person he'd have to notify of the death.

Aspen helped Kitty to stand. Leo and Aspen watched together as the couple walked down the trail and headed back toward their car. When they slipped behind a far set of trees and disappeared into the forest, Aspen finally turned to Leo and threw her arms around him.

"I'm so glad you're okay," she said, but there was terror flecking her words. She reached down and patted Chewy's head. "What about you, you little stinker?"

"We're fine. Just a little shaken up." He gave her a kiss to the top of her head, no longer caring who saw them.

"Are you hurt at all?" she asked, leaning back and looking him over like they hadn't just spent the last few minutes together.

"I'll be fine, like I said. I just got rattled." He closed his eyes, and he could feel his body swirling out of control in the water again. He would never forget that feeling, and he was certain it was a sensation that would fill his nightmares for many nights to come.

That was to say nothing of the woman's face in the muddy water—she'd only been inches from him—and the feel of her skin slipping in his hands...

"You're not okay," Aspen said, hugging him tighter.

He couldn't tell her that she was right, but he wasn't in a place or position to let others see how badly he was struggling with the events of the day. Later, he would debrief and could sit down and process what had occurred, but for now he needed to get through this and the rest of the day.

"I can't tell you how much you mean to me," he said,

whispering the words gently into her hair for only her to hear. "I needed your touch."

She pressed her head against his chest as though she was listening to his heart, and he found the action so sweet and pure. "Our hearts and our souls are in sync," she said, looking up at him with a gentle smile. "I'm not going any-where…when you're ready to talk."

"I know that, Aspen, and I'm so grateful," he said, lifting her hand and giving it a sweet kiss. "Let's get through this."

"As long as we're together, everything will be okay," she said, meaning to reassure him but then also reminding him that this could be the end of their time together. If these were Genie's remains, she had no reason to stay.

It wasn't fair, but for a split second he wanted to believe he'd been wrong about the face he'd preliminarily identified.

He squeezed her hand as they started to walk toward the divers. The future could wait.

Steve wore a wet suit and had a single tank, and was getting his mask wet and ready.

Smash was getting the throw bag ready in case he needed it, but was also readying a safety rope for Steve to hold. "You need to be careful out there," he said to him. "I want you to make sure you don't get wrapped up."

Steve gave him a thumbs-up as he waded into the water. "Four hard tugs mean I'm ready for you to start pulling."

Smash returned the gesture as Steve took to the water. There was a steep drop-off and Steve disappeared into the water. The rope moved as he watched.

Leo's stomach churned with anxiety for the man who was now searching the area where he had come so close to dying. Steve would be fine. He wasn't tumbling and he wasn't searching for air. Though the water was fast, he was wearing weights and prepared for the conditions.

Leo tried to remain calm. Thankfully, Aspen stepped to his side. Just her presence made him feel more at ease. It was odd how in very little time so many things had passed between them, so many feelings and shared moments—moments that had changed them and brought them closer together. In a matter of days, she had become his everything.

Everyone was silent as they stared at the water eddying behind the massive log in the water. When he'd first found himself pressed against it, he'd known it was large, but looking at it from above he now realized it had likely been one of the old-growth trees. It struck him how this behemoth had lived hundreds of years and had fallen victim to the fickle changes of the river and the pounding of its waves. Then, in its death, it had gripped Genie and had tried to steal him. It wasn't normal to anthropomorphize a tree, but what if this tree had a soul like a person. In its anger and rage, it had wanted to find comfort in death by not having to go it alone.

There were four tugs on the rope and Smash and the team started to pull. Steve appeared first, his mask poking out of the water.

In his arms was the discolored, muddy and battered remains of Genie. Her dark hair covered her face. As she came out of the water, he spotted the golden chain around her neck and there was a deep laceration where it had been holding her when he'd located her body.

He motioned for Chewy to lay down and stay put on the bank before he stepped forward to help. He and Smash grasped the woman under her arms and hips as they tried to gently move her to the bank without causing any further damage to the body. Her skin was slipping as they moved her onto the black body bag they had set out on the shore in preparation.

Aspen and the rest of the team helped Steve. He was fine, but he was quiet as he took off his mask and tank. There was a long moment of silence as they all gazed upon the woman. She deserved to be honored in this small way.

Looking out at the water, he silently thanked the river for letting them bring some comfort to the family and to their team by giving her up.

Her face and body were puffy, but there was no doubt it was Genie. She was consistent with having been in the water for a number of weeks. Her hair was swirled and matted in places, and dirt and flotsam caked her naked body.

She was bruised all over, and near her thigh there was a large gash where she had likely hit against rocks during her tumble down the river. For a moment, he wondered if under his still drying clothes he was even remotely as covered in bruises as her.

Hell, this could have been him.

Aspen turned away from the body for a moment, making him wonder if she had been thinking along the same lines. He moved toward her. "It's okay," he whispered, touching her gently on the arm.

She looked over at him, unspent tears in her eyes.

"I know," he said, not wanting to make things worse. "I'm okay. *We're* okay."

She touched his hand and gave him a nod as she tilted her chin to the sky and closed her eyes. It wasn't the time or the place, or he would have pulled her into his arms and just held her until she was ready to face this, but she knew as well as he did that they had a job to do. These were the moments when they weren't allowed to be human. They had to push through, but at least they were doing this as one and facing it as a team.

He stayed with Aspen, refusing to move until she finally took a long breath and looked to him, silently assuring him that she was all right.

"You ready?" he asked, making sure she wasn't going too fast.

She nodded.

The other members of his team were waiting for him, as was the coroner. "When you're ready, let's take a look."

The coroner squatted beside Genie's body and pulled back her hair. The right side of her face was bruised. He moved slightly and, taking out a pair of tweezers from his kit, he pulled at the skin.

The coroner looked up at him. "There appears to be peri-mortem trauma." The man paused, moving the tweezers around. "It's perfectly round, and I'd have to say that is consistent with a gunshot wound." He stepped to the other side of the woman's head, adjusted around her hair, and paused. "Yes, the margins here are shattered," he said, pointing toward the area in the hair. "Here is what looks like an exit wound."

This was no longer a drowning.

The man moved downward, examining the body. "Smash," he said, pointing at him, "can you roll her gently on her side?"

Smash squatted and pulled the body toward himself, exposing her back.

After a moment of poking and moving, he had Smash roll

her in the other direction, then he finally looked up at Leo. "There's another area of trauma on her back." He motioned to her right side, just above the kidney area.

"Trauma?" Leo asked.

"Yes," the man said with a sigh as he started to move the bag around Genie. "I believe your victim was shot in the back." He started to zip the bag. "Her death was not an accident. I think we can assume that this was a homicide."

Chapter Twenty-Eight

John and Kitty had taken the news as poorly as Aspen had expected. While they'd known that their daughter was missing and that the body had likely been hers, it didn't make it any easier when she had called them yesterday. It had been a long night of documentation and writing reports, but she had never left Leo's side—even when they had gone together with the coroner to take the body to the crime lab.

It would take some time for the medical examiner to report their findings, but there was no longer a question as to the cause or manner of death—Genie was murdered.

Leo was in his office at the sheriff's department, on the phone. She was standing with Steve looking at pictures they had taken of the body when Leo finally opened his door and motioned for her to come back inside.

"Yes?" she asked, walking into the small office devoid of any windows or outside light. The effect of the flickering industrial lights overhead made her tense.

"I just got off the phone with the mother of the girl who initially reported Genie missing. I didn't really pull any new information, but if need be I'm going to run down there and talk to her again in person. She said she had some photos she had taken on the beach that day, and maybe there was something else we could manage to pull." He ran his hand over the back of his neck. "She will be sending them my way."

"What about the video?" she asked. "You know, the one that Kitty used against Scott? Did you look it over?"

"Yeah, but just quickly. You want to watch it again with me?" He clicked on the video on his computer screen and it started to play.

Genie was screaming at the top of her lungs, calling Scott every name in the book. The video was out of focus, like Genie was holding her phone in her hand as they fought. The images flashed between black and moving faces and body parts.

There was the sound of a hard slap, but it was impossible to tell who had hit whom.

"You need to leave, Scott!" Genie yelled. "I don't want you. I've never wanted you." She called him a series of expletives, but her words were slurred.

"This is my house. I pay the bills. If anyone needs to leave it's you. You're high."

"I'm acting high?"

There was the sound of someone being punched in the gut, followed by a groan, but again she wasn't sure whose.

The video flashed to the beige carpet of the floor. There, she could make out a pair of women's purple running shoes and the tip of a cowboy boot. The feet moved, turning to the right as the video turned to the left and stopped.

Aspen huffed. "You're right. There really isn't anything, is there?"

He shook his head, running his hand over the back of his

neck. "There was only enough to make it clear they were having a fight."

"And this was enough evidence for the other county to charge him with a PFMA?" she asked, somewhat surprised.

"They hadn't taken it to court yet, but yes. If a person feels at all threatened, they can call the police and it is enough for them to press charges. It would be up to the judge to decide further recourse, but there was enough here for a temporary restraining order to be placed against Scott."

"From what I saw, couldn't he have used this in his favor as well? To get a restraining order against her?"

"That would be tit for tat," he said, shrugging. "The result would be the same."

"Do you think it was her hitting him?" she asked.

He nodded. "It's definitely a possibility, but most people don't think of physical abuse happening from a woman toward a man."

"But it's not unusual?"

"A woman abusing a man? No." He sighed. "It is, however, uncommon for a man to call the police and report it."

"Do you think that may have been what was happening in that video? And maybe that was why Genie wasn't the one to turn it over to the police? Her mother was the driving force." Aspen stared at the play button on the computer screen like it would hold answers.

She couldn't wrap her head around what was going on.

"Even if Genie was the one who was abusive, it still doesn't explain how she ended up at the bottom of the river," he said. "But I think you might be onto something. Scott isn't the kind of guy who would open up and tell people his wife had been hitting him. I think it would be smart if we went to talk to him."

SCOTT ANSWERED THE door on the first knock, must having heard them pull up outside. "Hey, Detective," he said, shaking Leo's hand and then waving him inside.

Aspen led the way.

As Leo followed, he noted the beige carpet of the living room that perfectly matched the carpet in the video they had watched in his office. The place was clean enough, but not so clean to make him think Scott had scrubbed it down before they'd shown up. Scott was barefoot, but there was a pair of purple running shoes and brown cowboy boots perched beside the front door that matched those from the video.

"I appreciate you making yourself available for us on such short notice," Leo said.

"Yeah," Scott said, leading them toward the couch and motioning for them to take a seat. "I'm glad y'all found Genie. Thank you. And yeah, thanks for lettin' me know."

"Have you heard from her parents at all?" Leo asked, sitting down on the leather couch beside Aspen.

Scott shook his head. "I'm sure they think I got somethin' to do with it, but I'm tellin' y'all there's no way."

The guy was fidgeting as he sat down in his recliner. He was pinching the fabric of his jeans and twisting it in his fingers as he talked to them, clearly nervous.

"Scott, *did* you have anything to do with your wife's death?" Leo asked.

Scott threw his hands up in the air. "Absolutely not," he

said, shaking his head. "I loved her. I did. She was the reason I came up here from 'bama."

From his body language and the tone of his voice, Leo wanted to believe him. Yet, some people had devious gifts when it came to the art of deceit.

"Did you and your wife ever have physical confrontations?" he asked.

Scott dropped his hands back down to his pants and started pinching the fabric again. "Yeah."

"Can you explain this video of you and Genie fighting?" Leo lifted up his phone and started to play the video he and Aspen had just watched at his office.

As it came to a stop, Scott sat in silence.

"Scott?" Aspen asked softly. "Did you slap your wife?"

"I tried to tell the cops who arrested me that she was the one who went to throwin' hands," he said, finally looking up.

"Did you hit her?" Leo asked, needing a clear answer.

"I'd be lyin' if I said I didn't get pissed off at her, but as mad as she made me... I never once touched her in anger." Scott looked him in the eyes. "I loved her, and my momma raised me a gentleman."

"What were you guys fighting about?" Aspen asked.

Scott shifted in his chair and his gaze moved to the hallway, but he didn't answer.

"Is there something you haven't been telling me, Scott?" Leo pressed. "If there is anything that is going to turn up on or in Genie's body that I need to know about, please tell me now. I don't want to have to come back here with information I learn after the fact that could potentially be damning for you or anyone else."

Scott wrung his hands.

"Scott, Kitty alluded to the fact that Genie had a drug problem," Leo said.

Scott jerked and shifted his gaze to them. "Why would she tell you?"

Aspen glanced over at him like she had heard the admission, too.

"So, you're not denying the fact that Genie was using drugs?" he asked, leading Scott to give him the answers that they all needed.

"Genie had gotten in a bad way," Scott said, looking torn. He stood up from his chair and started to pace around his small living room. He picked up a misplaced handmade quilt and started to fold it, like he needed something to do with his hands. "She and her best friend, Edith, were peddling meth. When I found out…that was the fight. I kicked her out." Scott placed the blanket on the back of his chair and walked toward his television, which was sitting on an old, rusting trunk.

Leo took out his phone. Opening up social media, he typed in the woman's name. There, at the top of the list, was the individual who'd barged into his kitchen, bloody and battered. He tried to control his excitement.

"Is this the person Genie had been using and selling drugs with?" he asked, holding up his phone in hopes Scott would positively identify her.

Scott nodded.

"When did you last see Edith?" he asked, thinking about the blood that had been smeared over the floor in his house.

Scott cleared his throat. "Last time was the day I got in

the fight with Genie. She ran out when Genie started to hit. I don't think she wanted to catch a stray fist."

Or she didn't want to go to court to act as a witness— or worse, as an inmate getting arraigned on drug charges.

"Scott, were you or are you involved in buying or selling drugs?"

"Are you kiddin' me?" Scott countered, slapping his hands down on the blanket. "Drugs are what caused all this. If I'd been good with 'em, she'd probably still be alive and sittin' right where you are now."

Leo stood up and brushed off the knees of his pants before standing. "Scott, I want you to know how much we appreciate your time and help in this matter. We will be in contact with you as soon as we know anything else."

Scott relaxed and gave him a slight dip of the chin. "I just wanna find out what happened to my girl...whoever did this needs to pay."

Leo shook his hand in appreciation. "If you think of anything else, don't be afraid to give me a call."

As soon as they were in Leo's truck, Aspen turned to him. "I believe him. I don't think he hurt her."

Leo nodded. "Me, either, but I think we may have just figured out someone who would."

They made their way to the hospital, where Edith was still a patient. She was still listed as Jane Doe, but as he walked up to the third floor and her room, he was met by Jamie. She was standing outside her daughter's room, leaning against the metal door frame.

When she saw him, her face fell. "Leo," Jamie said, her voice faltering. "I'm so sorry."

He tried to control all the feelings that welled within him

as he was vacillating between anger at the situation and the secrets that Genie's family had tried to hide, and relief in the fact that they were finally making progress.

"Hi, Ms. Offerman," he said, but as he spoke she twitched like his using her formal name was a form of flagellation. "How did you find out about your daughter being here?"

"I have a friend here, it's a small town—you know." Jamie ran her hands over her face. "I tried to call Edith after you stopped by. I wanted to make sure that she was okay, but she didn't answer. No one knew anything about her and I panicked."

"Is she awake?" Aspen asked, moving to peer into the room.

"I don't want you going in there," Jamie said, trying to move between Aspen and the doorway.

Jamie reached back and moved to close the door, but before she did, Edith's voice pierced the air. "Come in."

Jamie turned toward her daughter. "You don't have to talk to these people. Don't tell them anything until we have a lawyer."

Leo pushed past Jamie and walked into Edith's room. "Hi, Edith, I'm glad to see you again," he said, walking over to her bedside and touching the waffled blanket over her toes.

Edith twitched slightly. "I'm sorry for barging into your house. I didn't know what else to do."

"How did you end up at my house, Edith? Do you remember?"

Edith started to cry, tears cascading down her bruised cheeks. "I followed you home… I'm so sorry."

Aspen walked over beside him and put her hand on his

back. "Edith, no matter what happened, if you tell us the truth, we can help you move past it."

"I didn't mean to kill her." Edith choked out the words. "Everything just went wrong..." she said between sobs. "The guy we bought the drugs from...when he heard what happened..."

"You need to leave!" Jamie said, moving between Leo and her daughter. She put her hands on his chest and started to push.

"Jamie," he said, trying to remain cool and collected with his friend during this difficult time. He put his hand on hers but stood his ground. "Jamie."

She looked up at him and she started to cry. "She's my baby girl. She didn't mean to hurt anyone."

He squeezed her hands. "Jamie, your daughter shot and killed her friend."

Jamie sank to her knees, reminding him of the moment he had told Kitty her daughter was dead. He was filled with anguish for both mothers.

Aspen squatted next to Jamie. "Your daughter screwed up. You and your family are going to have some hard days, but at least she is alive."

The words tore at him. Here his friend was struggling, but at the same time it was her daughter who had pulled the trigger.

"Edith, I'm going to need a full statement when you can," he said, turning back to her. "We will make sure that good things can come from this, not just bad. For now, recover and I want you to work on getting and staying clean."

Chapter Twenty-Nine

A month later, Edith was sitting in jail awaiting trial for Genie's murder. From what Aspen had been told, it sounded like she would get at least fifteen years in the women's prison in Billings. According to Edith's statements, she had been doing meth with Genie on the beach early in the morning. Things between them had gotten heated as Genie owed their dealer money. Genie had pointed the gun at her, but Edith had wrestled it away.

She had shot Genie in the back as she had tried to run into the water. She'd gone down, and Edith had panicked. Not wanting to have Genie turn her in to the police, she had shot her in the head. The dog had tried to jump in after her, but like Genie's body, had gotten swept up in the currents. After they'd disappeared, Edith had set up Genie's clothing to make it look as though she'd fallen in—in hopes her body would never be recovered—and tossed the gun into the water. When she showed up at Leo's house a couple weeks later, it was obvious she had been struggling after the attack and that drugs had clearly won. Thankfully, she had admitted everything and it had nullified any fears about the broken chain of custody.

Neither Genie nor Edith was innocent. Life had taken them down a dark path. In the end, it had cost them both their lives in very different ways.

While her heart broke for all the people who had been affected, Aspen was relieved to have found the answers they had been searching for. At least...most of the answers she had been trying to find. There was still one major question that haunted her—what she and Leo were going to do.

Since she had gone back to Minnesota, things were *fine*. They had been doing the long-distance thing, calling and video chatting as much as their lives would allow, but it hadn't been the same as when she had been in Montana.

Everything about the state called to her. She loved the open mountain air and the remoteness of the riverbanks—and the birch trees.

Her cell phone rang; it was Leo. "Hello?"

"Hi, babe," he said, but there was something off in his voice.

"What's up?" she asked, excited at hearing from him but worried at the strain in his tone.

"I'm having a bit of a problem," he said.

Her heart sank. This was it. She was sure of it. They were breaking up. "What's going on? Are you okay?"

"Actually—" there was a long pause and there was a tap on her front door "—I am lost."

She stood up and walked out from her office. Standing on the other side of the glass was Leo. He was holding a handful of ropes, each piece tied in a shape that made it look like flower.

She dropped her phone and ran to the door, throwing it open. "Oh, my God, Leo!" Chewy was at his side, prancing as he waited for her to greet him. "And you brought my boy!" She squatted and gave the dog a quick pet before throwing her arms around Leo.

"Oh, you're crushing me," he teased, laughter marking his words.

"What are you doing here?" she exclaimed, not letting him go and pressing her face against the rope flowers and his chest.

"I got lost," he said, laughing.

She let go of him as she looked up at his face. "Lost? I don't think so, you are standing here."

He sent her a melting smile as he knelt down in front of her on her doorstep. "I just meant, I'm lost without you. I need you, Aspen. You are all I think about. You're the woman I want to be at my side for the rest of my life. Together we make each other better, and I never want to spend another moment apart."

She clasped her hands over her mouth as he reached down to Chewy's collar where he'd attached a little box. He opened it and retrieved a little velvet case.

"I know it's not a big diamond ring," he said, opening the box. Inside was a solid gold band inlaid with channel diamonds. "I can get you something else if you don't like this, but I wanted something that you could always wear—when we are working in the river or when we have our hands in the mud. I want you to know that I'm always with you. Aspen, will you marry me?"

She bounced from foot to foot as she nodded with excitement. "Yes, Leo… I'll marry you."

He moved to take the ring out of the box, but paused. "Wait, one more question…" He smiled.

She stopped moving. "What?"

"Will you also adopt Chewy as your dog? It's critical… make or break."

She giggled as she put her hand in his and helped him to stand. "If you think I'd want you if you didn't have a dog, you'd be ridiculous. I like him almost more than I love you," she teased, laughing as she pressed her lips against his.

"Never mind then, you can't marry me," he joked, moving the ring box away.

She grabbed his wrist. "I don't think so. I think the ring is perfect, and you already made your offer. No renegotiating," she said with a smile. "Yes, my Leo… I will adopt Chewy."

He reached into the box and took out the ring. "And, just to be clear, will you marry me?"

"You know I will. I've wanted to almost since the moment I met you."

He slipped the ring on her finger. "Any conditions?"

She nodded. "Two."

He pulled her into his arms, kissing her forehead as he held her. "And they are?"

"One, we have to get married at the top of a mountain after I move to Montana and join your search and rescue unit."

"Easy. Done." He ran his hand over her cheek and gazed into her eyes. "And what is the second?"

She smiled wildly and her heart threatened to burst in her chest. "You have to love me forever as I will love you."

"This is the easiest negotiation I've ever taken part in," he said, leaning down and kissing her lips. "I can promise you…you have my entire heart and it will be yours until the end of time."

* * * * *

COMING SOON!

We really hope you enjoyed reading this book.
If you're looking for more romance
be sure to head to the shops when
new books are available on

Thursday 14th March

To see which titles are coming soon, please visit
millsandboon.co.uk/nextmonth

MILLS & BOON

afterglow BOOKS

Introducing our newest series, Afterglow.

From showing up to glowing up, Afterglow characters are on the path to leading their best lives and finding romance along the way – with a dash of sizzling spice!

Follow characters from all walks of life as they chase their dreams and find that true love is only the beginning...

OUT NOW

millsandboon.co.uk

LET'S TALK

Romance

For exclusive extracts, competitions
and special offers, find us online:

- 📘 MillsandBoon
- 𝕏 @MillsandBoon
- 📷 @MillsandBoonUK
- ♪ @MillsandBoonUK

Get in touch on 01413 063 232